TAMING *the* HEART

ELLIOTT ROSE

kensingtonbooks.com

KENSINGTON BOOKS are published by:

Kensington Publishing Corp.
900 Third Avenue
New York, NY 10022

kensingtonbooks.com

All Kensington titles, imprints, and distributed lines are available at special quantity discounts for bulk purchases for sales promotions, premiums, fundraising, educational, or institutional use.

Special book excerpts or customized printings can also be created to fit specific needs. For details, write or phone the office of the Kensington sales manager: Kensington Publishing Corp., 900 Third Avenue, New York, NY 10022, attn: Sales Department; phone 1-800-221-2647.

The K with book logo Reg US Pat. & TM Off.

First Kensington Trade Paperback Printing: August 2025

ISBN 978-1-4967-6063-0 (trade paperback)

10 9 8 7 6 5 4 3 2 1

Printed in United States of America

Electronic edition: ISBN 978-1-4967-5897-2

Interior art by Cosmic Imprint Publishing
Author photograph by Elliott Rose

The authorized representative in the EU for product safety and compliance
is eucomply OU, Parnu mnt 139b-14, Apt 123
Tallinn, Berlin 11317, hello@eucompliancepartner.com

For the readers ready to ditch the horse
and ride a 'stache instead

Introduction

Hello dear reader,

Welcome to Crimson Ridge...
For those of you who wish to go in to this book blind, please keep in mind this taboo romance is a work of fiction.
This is an interconnected-standalone, Forced Proximity, cowboy romance, with a happily ever after.

Please be aware that if you have triggers or content you prefer to avoid, this story may contain topics or subject matter that you might want to consider before proceeding.

Content Notes

Please scan the code below:

My website has a full list of Triggers, Content notes, including a chapter by chapter break down if required.
ELLIOTTROSEAUTHOR.COM

Please note, you can email ELLIOTTROSE.PA@GMAIL.COM For more information or clarification.

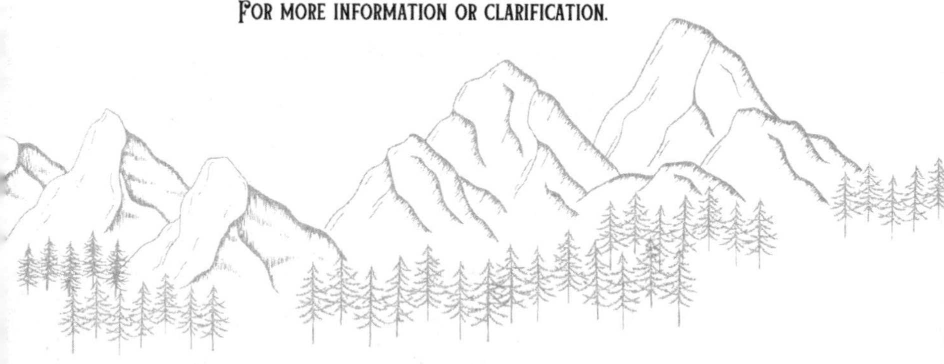

The Playlist

There Was This Girl . Riley Green
King of the Rodeo . Kings of Leon
After Midnight . Chappell Roan
Gold Dust Woman . Fleetwood Mac
Horses & Hellcats . Shaboozey
Wild Ones . Jessie Murph, Jelly Roll
Eat Your Young . Hozier
Beautiful Crazy . Luke Combs
You Should Probably Leave . Chris Stapleton
Wildflowers and Wild Horses . Laney Wilson
Runnin' . David Dallas
Wrong Ones . Post Malone, Time McGraw
Last Night . Morgan Wallen
Ain't No Love In Oklahoma . Luke Combs
RIIVERDANCE . Beyoncé
Pretty Little Poison . Warren Zeiders
Kiss You All Over . Exile
She Likes It . Russell Dickerson, Jake Scott
Cowgirls . Morgan Wallen, ERNEST
Devil in a Dress . Teddy Swims
Diet Pepsi . Addison Rae
High Road . Koe Wetzel, Jessie Murph
When the Levee Breaks . Led Zeppelin
Wild One . Troy Cartwright
Miles On It . Marshmello, Kane Brown
Torn . Riley Green
Sugar Sweet . Benson Boone
Steal Her From Me . Shaboozey
illicit affairs . Taylor Swift
Relapse . Warren Zeiders
Stop Draggin' My Heart Around . Stevie Nicks
Cowboy Cry . CeCe
ocean eyes . Billie Eilish
Dog Days Are Over . Florence + The Machine
Never Tear Us Apart . INXS
Single Again . Josh Ross
Worst Way . Riley Green
2 hands . Tate McRae

CHAPTER 1

Beau

"Come here, you cocksucking little slut."

My head whips up from mindlessly scrolling on my phone, jerking on reflex at the sound of the female voice yelling from opposite me on the sidewalk.

Goddamn. I'm in my biggest hoodie, even though it's seventy-eight out, with my cap pulled as low as possible. The last thing I need is some crazed fan thinking they know anything about me or my life to launch a tirade of obscenities in my face.

I'm in the process of moving back to Crimson Ridge to get *away* from the city psychos. Not having them running at me yelling weird shit in public just to try and get me reacting a certain way on camera.

My hackles raise, and my teeth clench to match the way my fist wraps around my phone. I cast a furtive glance around to see what the hell is taking Tessa so long.

"*Aghhh*. Fuck you. Don't you dare."

The voice gets louder, and a series of thudding noises helps me pinpoint where the source of the commotion is originating from.

I'm standing with my ass resting on the hood of my truck. It would be an easy escape to hop in the driver's side and lock the door, which I'm about two seconds from doing when a waterfall of crap spills down the steps of the art gallery storefront a few paces directly in front of me.

"You motherfucking, cheap whore, piece of shit."

A whirlwind of long black hair, black jeans, and black boots to match comes into sight, clattering down the flight of stairs while chasing after an explosion of belongings. Whoever this is has their hands full with a to-go coffee in one, a cell phone in the other, as the contents of their handbag—which seems large enough to comfortably contain a small dog—are busy forming a tsunami of personal items down the flight of steps.

The bottom of the world's largest purse has busted apart, leaving everything inside to imitate a tumbling bag of marbles pouring down the staircase, with her shit busy flying in all directions.

Shoving my phone in my back pocket, I take a couple of steps forward. The least I can do is stop this lady's stuff from rolling straight out into the street.

"This is what you do to me? After everything? Little bitch." She's bent double, trying to trap notebooks and pens and highlighters from skittering down the steps using only her feet. While the useless bag with no ass hangs limply at her side.

I have to bite my tongue not to laugh. She hasn't even noticed I'm here gathering up as many bits and pieces as I can in an effort to help.

Another quick glance up and down the sidewalk confirms that Crimson Ridge is just as sleepy and unpopulated as ever, so at least there's no one lurking or watching this all unfold.

Surely, even if someone passed by, they wouldn't recognize me with my hat pulled low. Or, at the very least, they'd have to get right up close before they made a connection as to why I look vaguely familiar.

Still crouched down, I start gathering up shit like her water bottle, more pens—Jesus, how many pens does one woman need—fluttering receipts that threaten to disappear into the gutter. I quietly tuck as much as I can under one arm.

Darting a glance up, I see that she's set the coffee down and is busy scooping up items off the stairs, hidden behind a curtain of shiny, dark hair.

I can't see her face. What I can see, however, is a fantastic ass. Curvy thighs and figure-hugging charcoal denim that makes sexy-as-hell creases just below her waist. A simple black tank skims the high waistband, and holy shit, that's when I realize my eyes have drifted up. The side profile of an incredible pair of breasts hidden beneath silky fabric leaves my mouth dry and the back of my neck heating instantly.

Fuck.

This is not the time or the place to get busted gaping like a horny teenager at a pretty girl on the main street of Crimson Ridge.

Dropping my eyes, I do a final sweep of the sidewalk, and it seems like I've mindlessly gathered up just about everything while down on my haunches. I clear my throat in order to grab her attention, since she's still muttering obscenities at her handbag beneath her breath and doesn't seem to have noticed that I'm right here.

I'm preparing to thrust everything into her arms and beat a hasty retreat to hop in my truck, when she seems to finally notice my boots where I'm standing before her. One hand whips up, flicking her loose waves out of the way, and fucking hell... honeyed, dark eyes meet mine.

There's a flash to them. A spark catches me entirely off guard.

"Oh, Jesus. You saw all of that? What a clusterfuck." She stands up and dusts her palms on the front of her jeans in the process. There's no double take, no lingering curiosity. This girl just matter-of-factly tucks her hair behind one ear and huffs out a frustrated breath.

"You ok?" I suddenly remember how to form words.

"Me? I'm fine. This bag, however, is going to be sacrificed on a ritual bonfire at the soonest possible opportunity." She nudges at it with the pointed toe of her black cowboy boot. They're cute and suit the all-black look she's got going on, but aren't overly girly either. It certainly looks like the couple of inches of heel she's sporting could stomp on hearts without a second thought.

"Here." One syllable is about all I can offer. Why am I suddenly tongue-tied?

She meets my eyes again, then drops her gaze down to where I'm still clutching a bundle of items rescued from the exploding handbag situation.

As I hold out my fist, her eyes widen, drawing my gaze to see what she's reacting to. Immediately, my gut clenches because my first instinct is to consider that maybe she's recognized me after all...

"Oh, well, aren't you a real gentleman cowboy."

My brows scrunch together, a little confused, trying to figure out her meaning.

Clutched in my palm is a small drawstring bag. It's gold, velvety fabric, and something juts from the top where the strings haven't been pulled tight. A purple silicone curve peeks out.

"Huh?" Confusion must be etched all over my face. As she arches one eyebrow at me, followed by that pretty mouth of hers tipping into a wicked smirk, my slow-ass fucking brain catches up with the play.

I'm standing on the sidewalk, waving this girl's vibrator around like a hot dog vendor at a ballpark.

Her *wearable* vibrator.

The tips of my ears start to singe. What the fuck am I supposed to do? Tuck it neatly back inside the pouch before handing it over like it's a goddamn credit card to settle the tab while out for dinner?

"Do they not have toys to play with in this little part of the mountains?" Bright flecks of amber glow in amongst the rich ochre of her eyes, which in turn match the deeper, sun-bronzed brown of her skin.

"Cat got your tongue, hot stuff? You know, it's got ten different speeds and customizable settings. It also does this awesome pattern if you set the mode just right where it really makes your eyes roll back."

Her head cocks to one side, almost as if she's daring me to touch it, or not touch it. I don't fucking know. What I do know is that there is a place beyond the tenth level of hell awaiting me if I get snapped in a compromising position like this.

"Shame really." Mystery girl makes the decision for me, reaching out to pluck the bag and its contents from my hand. "As much as I'd love to give you a Ted talk about finding a woman's clit before I've even had a drop of caffeine, alas, I've got places to be."

With no more than a shrug and a wink, she tucks the toy away and pulls the side strings to seal up the bag. Not a hint of embarrassment or shame or annoyance at this situation. We could be standing here discussing horse feed for how casual this girl is. She's entirely unbothered, and I'm rendered speechless. Officially incapable of forming a coherent string of words in her presence.

No hysterical behavior to contend with. No toddler-like tantrums, threats, stomping around, or insisting on calling a publicist on speed dial at the first sign of a minor inconvenience. At the prospect of a *public* scene that doesn't fit the carefully crafted persona.

It's... refreshing. Like settling down in the cool grass, finding relief in the shade after a long afternoon spent in the saddle beneath the baking sun.

"Wow. Really melted your brain there, didn't I, cowboy?"

I clear my throat. "I don't need the Ted talk."

A devastating curl touches her lips as she looks me up and down.

"Sure about that?"

"You betcha." My skin prickles, and the words come out sounding a whole lot like a grown man growling, even to my own ears.

Mystery girl looks mighty pleased with herself for continuing to get under my skin. Meanwhile, I'm still clutching half her crap, minus the wearable fucking vibrator I'm not gonna be able to stop wondering about now.

Why does she have it in her purse?

Does she use it often?

What does it look like nestled inside her soft pussy?

Christ. Stop. This is not a drill, I need to exit through the emergency doors right this instant.

"Well, since you're standing there stumped by a vibrator, can you at the very least do a gal a solid and point me in the direction of where I might find myself something to shove all this crap in? Better yet, could you be a country gentleman and duck into the gallery upstairs and see if they've maybe got a cardboard box or something?"

She clamps the velvet bag between her teeth, freeing up both hands and proceeds to relieve me of all the things I'm still holding onto. As she steps closer, her scent drips into my awareness, hitting my senses like a dropper from a vial. It doesn't just gently breeze in, no, the fragrance of wild orange and honeysuckle demands my attention and floods my veins. Just like everything about this girl, it's not a performance. It's purely magnetic and sexy, and holy fucking shit, I absolutely cannot be looking at this girl with that bag tucked between her plush lips and its sinfully hot package inside, thinking these thoughts.

Even if I wanted to, I can't.

Even though I *want* to.

Clearing my throat like it's full of rust, I readjust my cap, squeezing the brim. "Wait there."

Turning on my heel, I duck and look around on reflex. Town is still deserted. There are a couple of older ladies on the opposite side of the street, but they're busy chatting amongst themselves as they walk. From the other direction, a vehicle draws closer, and I dip my chin. Better to be on the safe side.

My grip wrenches open the back door to my truck, and I fist the duffel sitting on the floor. Upending it without so much as a second look, I let my own things tumble out, then proceed to head back to the far-too-beautiful girl who I am absolutely not looking at in any way.

I'm helping a stranger. This is just me doing a good deed.

Not like I'm desperate to ask her name or find out if she works in town or something insane like that.

"Lovely." Her eyes roll as I shove the faded canvas into her hands. "Do I get to keep your sweaty gym socks, too?"

"Best I could do. Left my spare designer purse back at the ranch."

She's crouched down now, shoving everything in the bag. As I stand there grumbling and trying not to stare at the patch of skin on her spine between the waistband of her jeans and the hem of her top, she hits me with a quirked little smile, plush lips twitching, and my asshole cock gets far too interested in this scene.

A pretty girl with fire in her eyes kneeling in front of me.

I have to cough into my fist and think about the last time I had my nuts nearly crushed during a gnarly ride.

"I'm not gonna find a dirty jockstrap you've stuffed in here as a memento, am I?" Her nose scrunches as she efficiently shoves everything in and zips up my duffel. I guess *her* duffel now.

"No. Maybe just a cock ring, if you're lucky." The retort is out of me before I can do anything to stop it. Fuck it, I want this girl to know I'm not boring, I'm not usually so tongue-tied, and I certainly don't want her thinking I'm a stuffy old country bumpkin.

"Well, if the wearable fits..." Laughing a little, she stands up then slings the strap over her shoulder. With one hand now reacquainted with her coffee, the other shoves her phone into a back pocket, and then she sticks out her palm.

This is the moment, right here, when I could take her hand and shake it and feel how soft her touch might be in contrast to that sharp tongue.

It's tempting, hovering right there. Urging me on and recklessly goading me into doing the thing I shouldn't do—the thing I can't do considering my life and my circumstances—to ask for her name, her phone number.

Her eyes hold mine, flickering for just a second as if a force is tugging her gaze; she's fighting it as we stand in the middle of the sidewalk with only an arm's length between us.

Just as I lift my hand, reaching out to take her extended palm, just as I see the split second when her gaze falls to my mouth, another arm snakes through the crook of my elbow.

My fingers curl into a clenched fist, dropping back to my side like a stone.

"Hi, babe. Sorry I took so long."

I watch as my mystery girl's eyes bounce rapid-fire taking in the woman glued to my side, flicking down to where her arm threads through, interlinking with mine, before landing with a thud on the spectacular diamond adorning her left ring finger.

Before I can say a word, she plasters on a polite veneer. "Right. Well... thanks for the help. You guys have a good one." Her smile flashes with a tightness to it, a glance that avoids my eyes, and she whips around on her heel.

All I see is a last flutter of her dark mane and smooth brown skin as she rounds the corner and disappears out of sight with my bag slung over her shoulder.

"Jesus, Tessa. Did you fucking have to?" I wrench my arm away. "*Babe*? Really?"

"Oh, excuse me, Beau Heartford, for doing my job."

My goddamn sister flutters her eyelashes at me, thinly disguising an eye roll. The extensions I pay for, along with her fabulous salary for being the best damn manager I could have ever hoped for.

Doesn't change the fact that she's my baby sister and gets on my every last nerve.

"You don't have to do that every time, you know." I hiss, well aware there's a black cloud forming over my head.

"Oh, shit..." Tessa's blue-gray eyes, the ones that match my own, widen. "Were you into her? I can go get her number if you want?"

"No. It's fine. Leave it be." Shaking my head, I hurl myself into the driver's seat of my truck. My sister has been running interference for me for just about my entire pro career. Keeping the buckle bunnies and overzealous fans away with her well-oiled routine of flashing that damn rock on her finger and clinging to my arm like an octopus.

"You sure?" She slides into the passenger side, studying the side of my face like she always does.

My teeth grind, and I white-knuckle the steering wheel. Nope. That girl is too young. A PR nightmare waiting to happen. I'm not interested in looking for anything but some peace by finally moving out here, and if that means being on my own, then so be it.

"You done all the shit you need to do?"

"Jeez. Let's make a stop to get you a coffee or something on our way outta town, because I sure ain't paid enough to put up with your grumpy ass."

Tessa's phone rings, and as she takes the call, I can feel her give the side of my head a glare before cheerily greeting her husband on the other end of the line.

As I pull out into the quiet main street lined with lush trees and flanked by all the quaint goddamn store frontages that make up Crimson Ridge, my head pounds.

Fuck the circumstances I've found myself in. Fuck the world and their opinions and their incessant need to demand I be someone I'm not.

I'm going to put all that just happened clear out of my mind.

I have to.

I'm not going to cheat on my *wife*.

CHAPTER 2

ONE MONTH LATER

Sage

"Did you land safely? Did your bag arrive? If you meet a nice cowgirl or cowboy, please promise you'll bring them home to meet me. Don't make me fly out to Montana just to get a scrap of information about your love life."

"Mom… Christ… take a breath."

"Well?"

I readjust the wide duffel strap on my shoulder and make my way through the small crowd milling around the baggage claim area. It takes all the effort I can muster not to grin at the ratio of Stetsons on display.

It's like I've stepped off the plane and entered into an alternate reality, one where everyone walks around wearing their best hats, boots, and belt buckles.

Though I'm certainly not complaining at the way all these pairs of jeans are hugging asses like it's their only job.

God bless the mountains and the array of denim-clad, perfect, perky rear ends.

"Sage Ashwini Maloney, are you even listening to me?"

"Oooh. Did you just *middle name* me? Fine. No, we spiraled into a fiery heap on the runway. Sadly my bag has been charred amongst the wreckage, but on the upside, a cute cowgirl in faded cut-offs saved me. Would you believe we're currently on the back of her horse clip-clopping off into the sunset together."

"Good lord. What did I do wrong in a past life?"

"Remember, I'm the gift that keeps on giving." As I continue to taunt my saint of a mother, I spot my luggage coming around the far bend. Making some smiling apologies, I squeeze past a group of lads who certainly look like they're in this part of the country for a weekend of *pretending* to be cowboys.

One of them has forgotten to cut the price off his plaid shirt, the swing tag clearly hanging down the back of his collar.

"Excuse me." I tuck my phone against my shoulder and gesture at the slowly approaching siren-red suitcase.

"Here, let me, pretty lady." One of the dude-ranch tourists closest to the carousel reaches out to grab the handle and sweeps the case off the conveyor with the kind of flourish you'd expect from someone landing the catch of the day.

Do not wear your mood on your face.

I mouth a silent thank you, and quickly whisk myself away from their eau-du-frat-boy.

"Who was that?" Mom pries, as she loves to do, and I can hear my younger sisters giggling. Their pop music blasts and chopping sounds add to the background commotion as they help out with their usual after school chores and make dinner alongside Mom.

"He had a better manicure and more regularly moisturized hands than I do, is who that was. No, thank you." Pausing once I get to a quiet spot on the edge of the baggage claim hall, I pull my phone away from my ear and check the time. "Look, I'm going to have to wrap this interrogation up. I'll text you when I get to Crimson Ridge, yeah?"

"At least Layla is there to keep an eye on you." She sighs at me.

"I'm pretty sure there's only one place her eyes are occupied these days. Besides, I'm not gonna be doing anything but working my ass off this summer. Remember, I've got three different client projects all going on."

"And we're mighty proud of you. Maloney's will take over the world." My dad's deep voice calls from somewhere in the distance.

"Thanks, Dad."

"Is your boss picking you up?" His voice comes closer, Irish accent always sounding thicker over the phone somehow. My mom's laugh is slightly muffled when she scolds him in that sweet way she does when he insists on stealing a taste of something as it's still cooking. My parents are sickeningly in love, and deserve every single moment of their happily ever after.

It's probably no surprise my standards are so skyscraper high, soaring amongst the clouds—set to have my heart turning to ice from living at such an altitude. In my experience, nothing and no one has ever come close to the kind of relationship they have, and I simply refuse to settle for anything less than the person who lets me shine the brightest while being myself.

So, rather than dull my spark, or shrink to fit someone else's expectations, I have plenty of fun and keep my heart safely locked away. A foolproof plan. The kind that I probably should talk about more in therapy, rather than sidestepping all the time.

"Highly unlikely. Mrs. Diaz, the ranch manager, is meeting me. When we spoke on the phone for my interview, she said the owner is retired, hates social media, and enjoys working his ranch, *alone*. I'm fairly certain I'm never going to see the guy. Pretty much guaranteed he isn't going to be over the moon at the prospect of dealing with a twenty-something-year-old hired to run the ranch PR, either. He's probably going to be allergic to cell phones and shooting me glares from his rocking chair on the porch at every opportunity."

A buzz comes through as a text arrives, and I pull the phone away from my ear to take a quick glance.

UNKNOWN

Sage, it's Tessa Diaz.

I'm so sorry to do this to you when you've only just arrived. Something has come up, and I can't be there to meet you at the airport.

Look for your name on a board when you get to the meet and greet area.

MY DARLING MOTHER is chatting away in the background, having three different conversations between me and wrangling my sisters. "Fleur—no—that's far too much salt... Sage, you'll be fine, love... Pia, baby, wait, you need to make sure the oil is hot enough... make sure to mention—"

"Mom, *IloveyoubutIgottagobye*." Pulling the phone away from my ear, I talk loudly into the speaker and hit the end-call button.

With a long, blown-out breath, I regather myself amongst the bustle of luggage trolleys and electronic chimes, followed by droning arrival announcements over the loudspeaker.

This is the opportunity of my dreams—not only have I landed multiple clients for my freelance marketing business straight away, but this gig with the ranch I've secured includes bed and board as part of the deal. A full package to see me through the summer I'll be working there.

Mrs. Diaz—Tessa—insisted that it would be the best solution to base myself at the ranch rather than attempting to find temporary accommodation in Crimson Ridge. Shit, do I owe my bestie, Layla, the biggest hug ever for her connections. As soon as they heard I'd come recommended by *Stôrmand Lane*—a friend of her man, Colt, and local rodeo celebrity—what was supposed to be an interview instantly pivoted to become a straightforward conversation confirming my rates and when I could begin. Naturally, I jumped to sign and agreed to start at the earliest opportunity.

Tessa didn't hesitate to confirm my contract on the spot, without even needing to talk face-to-face.

So, here I am, back on Montana soil, preparing to settle into life among the mountains for the next few months. At least, until fall flutters her first golden leaves to the ground that is. By then, I'll be on my way to the next project calling my name.

Not only will I be able to experience first-hand what it's like to be on the ranch, I'll be staying there as if I'm a future guest. Getting a sense of how the place will feel once the business eventually welcomes booking into the cabins on-site. In addition to that, Tessa was so determined to have me on board that I'm going to be able to work with my other clients I've got lined up at the same time.

All of which suits me perfectly, because the last time I was in Crimson Ridge, I managed to leave town not only with a list of prospective business opportunities, but a lingering crush on a complete stranger. The kind of fuckery that never happens to me. Ever.

I'm not the girl who can't stop thinking about a five-minute interaction on the sidewalk. More to the point, I certainly do *not* need to spend this summer distracted by thoughts of whether I'll run into a certain gorgeous cowboy again on the sleepy main street.

In no universe do I need to be stuck thinking about the kind of man who gives you bedroom eyes one minute, only to discover he's got a wife with a big fuck off wedding ring that could poke an eye out if she so much as wiggled a manicured finger, the next.

As much as I enjoy a whole lot of fun, I'm in no way interested in being a homewrecker. Single, uncomplicated, and down for no-strings-attached fooling around: that's the only bio I'm interested in swiping right on. Other than building a stellar reputation as the hottest new boutique marketing agency of the year, the kind of sizzling hot summer I intend on having up here in these mountains is one where the adventures come complete with a pair of cowboy boots. The kind that aren't already parked under someone else's bed.

Life is too fleeting, too precious, not to enjoy every moment with both hands in the air and head tossed back, screaming your favorite lyrics at the top of your lungs.

A man or woman with baggage? Nope. Do not pass go. Do not collect two hundred dollars.

Quickly typing a reply to acknowledge Tessa, I re-shoulder my bag, grab the handle of my luggage, and make my way toward the doors leading into the public arrival area. From what I remember last time, there won't exactly be a grandstand crowd waiting on the other side.

This is a part of the country where the skies are vast, and the environment is breathtaking. Nothing moves quickly out here. While it's a whole different scenario to city living, I'm more fond of Crimson Ridge after a few visits to see my bestie than I'd dare admit to her.

Knowing Layla, if she catches wind of the soft spot I've developed for this sleepy place and the unending assortment of cute cows at every turn, she'll have me lassoed to the back of a horse and force me to settle down permanently. She'll do it all within a blink of those emerald eyes she wields so effortlessly, too.

As the frosted glass doors swish open ahead of me and warm summer air hits my cheeks, my eyes scan the cluster of tiny white boards with names scrawled on them.

Miss Maloney.

Mine peeks back at me over the top of the heads of the few others waiting on passengers, and I flick my eyes to follow the arm holding my name aloft.

An arm that extends, muscled, tanned, and deliciously veined beneath a white t-shirt.

Holy shit.

My mouth gapes, and the words tumble out with no hope of stopping them.

"Cock Ring? Is that you?"

CHAPTER 3

Sage

"Oh my god. *Cock Ring*? It is you."

Tilting my head to one side, I take in the sight of the cowboy I'd left standing on the sidewalk on my last visit.

He's just as goddamn handsome—if anything, more so with his stupidly golden tan from obviously being outdoors so much, paired perfectly with unruly dark hair curling out from beneath his cap. To make matters worse, that mustache is also just as dreamy as when I first laid eyes on him.

Pity. The best ones are always fucking taken, aren't they?

What he's doing here, and why he's clutching a placard with my name on it leaves me slowing to an almost stand-still.

"*Christ*. Keep your voice down, would you?" His face is unreadable, but judging by the way his jaw just slammed shut, and he's hissing at me through gritted teeth, I'm not sure this is a welcome reunion.

In fact, this man looks like he wants to shove me back through the doors I just emerged from.

"Do you work for Tessa—I mean, Mrs. Diaz, too?"

This guy is tall, towering over my short stature, as he gobbles up the distance between us and grabs hold of my luggage handle without asking. His strides outmatch mine as he yanks it to wheel along behind him.

"Apparently," he snaps, without looking my way.

Well, hottie cowboy sure as hell is losing his luster now that I'm getting a chance to see his cold shoulder up close. This is miles away from the flirty conversation we exchanged while the guy helped gather my things and juggled my wearable, looking adorably flustered the whole time.

Yet again, I have to remind myself that none of that even matters because this dude is locked down, living in wedded bliss, hitched to his forever Mrs. Mustache.

Lucky bitch.

"You're Miss Maloney... Sage *Maloney*?" He doesn't look back, but dips his chin and talks so low out of the corner of his mouth I feel like we're in some sort of weird whispering game. What is his problem? Immediately my hackles start to prick up because it wouldn't be the first time someone has been a judgmental asshole about a woman who has her own business, or doesn't believe a *young* female to be capable enough.

"Problem? Is there something wrong with that?" I arch an eyebrow. This is really going to put the final nail in the coffin of any perceived attractiveness of this man if he doesn't explain himself.

He tugs on the brim of his cap forcefully, pulling it lower over his brow, then glances side to side.

"No... of course not... it's got nothing to do with you—or your name." The man looks as if he'd gladly climb the walls in search of an escape hatch hidden in the roof of this airport.

"Then what?"

"It's—I just—I wasn't expecting *you*."

"Ok, well, cool your jets... I wasn't expecting *you* either, cowboy. I was preparing myself for Daddy Dentures and pureed TV dinners."

That finally catches his attention, and he gives me a completely bemused look. One that makes me feel mighty pleased on the inside, because, yes, I intend on being as completely confounding as possible to get under this guy's skin if this is how all our interactions are going to go down.

"Holy shit. It's him—I mean, it's you." A voice cannons our way from across the expanse of polished concrete flooring, and for the briefest second, there's a flicker I see in the blue-gray of his eyes. His expression tightens, the line of his brow furrows deeper, and then he turns with a forced smile toward the direction of the eager voice.

"Beau Heartford? Man, my dad is fully gonna kick himself that he ain't here right now." The golden-haired cowboy, who looks to be all of eighteen, stands rooted to the spot with hearts in his eyes and a breathlessness in his voice.

Cocking my head to one side, I look the man before me up and down, trying to figure out if there's something I'm missing here.

"Do you mind?" He gestures at his phone clutched in one fist.

"Not at all." Mystery cowboy—*Cock Ring*—keeps that forced smile tightly pinned to his face and poses for a selfie with the young buck, who flashes a broad grin and thumbs up at the camera.

"My old man watches replays of your championship year all the time. Says there's never been a run to take the buckle like it."

"Appreciate it. You want me to sign something for him?"

"Hell yes… I mean, thank you, sir." He whips his trucker cap out of the back pocket of his jeans, and then looks crestfallen for a second.

With a sigh, I unzip the side pocket of my duffel and pull out a marker. "Here."

"You're a lifesaver, ma'am." Blondie looks like he's about to cry, or melt, or who knows, maybe piss himself with excitement, as he hands over the hat and the pen.

Who the fuck is this guy?

As the mystery man sent to collect me scribbles on the hat, I feel eyes dart in my direction, then linger.

"Is Mandy not traveling with you?" The young cat asks, but I can feel the way he's side-eyeing my presence ever so subtly, or maybe not subtly, because it's clear he's wondering who I am and how I fit in the picture.

The air thickens instantly. If there was ever a moment to pull out your sashimi knife and slice away at the immediate tension, this would be it.

"Mandy's currently touring for the latest album, but I'll be sure to let her know you asked after her." Cowboy looks ready to stuff the hat down blondie's throat. "How about you give your email to my assistant here, and she'll organize tickets for you and your family to the next rodeo champs."

"Oh, man, for real?" All of a sudden, I've got a bouncing puppy in front of me, and this time, I'm almost certain he's going to pee all over my boots. All side-eyeing from a second ago has been forgotten in the face of receiving free shit.

Assistant? Jesus. Whatever, I'm not going to argue the point. But things aren't looking particularly healthy in the feminine-empowerment department either if this is going to be a regular occurrence. I'm certainly not here to scratch around pandering to men who think the workplace pair of tits is only good for fetching coffee and running errands.

Fighting back the scowl that wants to come out to play, I bat my eyelashes and pull out my planner.

After taking down the guy's details, we're on the move, this time with far greater urgency. *Beau Heartford,* the cowboy apparently worthy of being called by both his first and last name, takes off like there's a rocket under his ass. An ass that I am most certainly not looking at hugged by those wranglers. My luggage clatters behind him like a red flag waving in the wind as he hardly breaks stride between the terminal and the parking lot.

By the time we reach his enormous white truck, I've got an armory of questions locked, loaded, and ready to fire his way. Except, the cold shoulder treatment continues. After a brusque and efficient process of climbing into his large, gleaming-new vehicle and buckling up, we set off for Crimson Ridge.

He's gripping the steering wheel so tight, I decide to zip my lips and not waste my breath. This guy has clearly got a problem with me, and I really don't fucking care to understand why.

Hopefully we won't have to work together much this summer. A fine ass doesn't compensate for having the personality of a urine cake. His wife must be something else if she puts up with this kind of bullshit. I bet she's gladly away doing whatever it is that she does *touring*.

My thumbs are literally itching to search his name and start snooping on who these people are. Unfortunately for my curiosity, I can't exactly do that while entombed in stony silence the longer we're in this vehicle.

After about ten minutes of deafening quiet and passing mountain scenery, he grunts.

"What did you do to my gym bag?"

I glance down at the duffel tucked at my feet. "Oh, that? I made it more fashionable."

"It's got weird shit stuck all over the place."

"It's bedazzled. Cute, huh? Do you want the bag back, by the way? Since this is a weird little moment of fate bringing our worlds back together again."

"There are *pink* rhinestones on it."

"And?"

I'm stonewalled once more. Apparently, Beau Heartford isn't a man who appreciates a little bit of glamor being added to his boring old sports bag. His loss, really.

Puffing out my cheeks, I watch the familiar looming sight of mountains and the red ridge projecting into the skyline, kissed by late summer sunlight. *Crimson Ridge* graces us with a pretty bronze glow worthy of a San Tropez tan.

"So... Mandy?" I decide to approach the elephant in the room. Recalling the sight of the woman latched onto his arm, flashing her diamond in my face, she was certainly very pretty. A sweet little country-Barbie-doll package to match her dashing, dark-haired cowboy-Ken.

His knuckles blanch as he grips the steering wheel tighter.

Christ, the urge to roll my eyes is almost overwhelming, except I really do need to keep this contract. So, for the sake of my new boss, I will put up with this man's hot and cold behavior.

"Your wife?" I press.

This time, he exhales a long breath through his nose and holds up his ring finger, spinning the metal band around with a thumb. "Yep."

There's something in that single word that I can't quite place. Regret? Anger? It's not the response I was anticipating, and it throws me for a loop. I know absolutely nothing about being married, but the way he fidgets with that band seems as though the damn thing is burning his finger.

I give up on any more attempts to discover who this man is, or why he's the one picking me up from the airport in this scenario. He's like a turtle who has suffered a shock and whipped himself into his shell. I'm knocking on that rugged, roughened exterior, but to no avail. The charming cowboy I met a month ago, with a hint of a crooked smile, has disappeared.

Pushing him to the furthest edges of my mind, I settle back in my seat and focus on the view rushing by. This is just a job. I'll knock it out of the park, scoring myself a stellar client testimonial with a glowing recommendation to build my portfolio while I'm at it. Not to mention I'll do it all with a wink, a smile, and my bad bitch boots.

Crimson Ridge won't know what has hit it.

CHAPTER 4

Sage

The remainder of our trip passes in silence, until the sight of mountains rising above wide-open pasture greets us. We turn onto the long gravel drive leading up to what is presumably *the ranch*. As we pass beneath a wooden framed entranceway, it's impossible not to notice the obvious lack of a nameplate in the location where I would have expected to see one hanging proudly.

"She doesn't have a name yet?" I say under my breath. There's a fluttering sensation in my chest, while my eyes bounce everywhere at once because this place is fucking breathtaking. We've arrived right on golden hour, with the setting sun coating every blade of grass and summer leaf in a shimmering, glittering dusting of twenty-four karats. I wouldn't be surprised to see pixie dust flying in every direction with the way the light sparkles and dances and winks at us while driving past.

It's taking everything in me to remain in my seat with all arms and legs inside the moving vehicle. The urge to hurl myself out of the passenger door, hurdle that fence, sprint to the nearest field, and start taking photos is almost overwhelming. Missing an opportunity to capture a scene like this feels criminal, because holy shit, it looks like a dreamscape out here.

I can already hear the credit cards swiping to book up a week-long adventure beneath expansive skies and the watchful gaze of those striking mountains.

This place is cool as shit. Utterly drool-worthy. In my mind's eye, I've already created half a dozen promotional graphics and banners, and oh my god, I just want to get my laptop fired up so I can begin throwing ideas together. My creative itch demands to be scratched at the earliest possible opportunity.

Then, there's the main house itself.

We draw closer to a cluster of buildings, and I have to bite back an audible whimper. The facade of cedar, stonework, and double-peaked roof gables are all bathed in that warm glow of an impending sunset to swoon over, and I catch sight of a circular outdoor fire pit set up out front of the main living and dining area.

Winding my window down, I hang halfway out, trying to take it all in. Oh, yes, this is going to be a picture-perfect summer, indeed. This ranch is going to be a dream to promote. All I have to do is try and do her justice.

"There aren't any horses or stock here?" My eyes keep scanning over all the details—spotting the barn and other smaller buildings that must be the cabin accommodation, set a little further back from the main house.

"Not yet." We pull up to a stop outside a garage where a similar white truck is already parked.

"Is Tessa around?" I start to gather up my things. "She texted to say she'd brief me once I'd arrived."

"She's not here," he mutters and pulls out his phone before frowning at the screen. Whatever he reads leaves him fidgeting with the brim of his cap before lifting it and dragging a couple of fingers through his hair. Certainly, none of which I'm looking at out of the corner of my eye.

Nope. Not looking at the way his eyes have a slight crease around the corners, giving him that roughened, older, *experienced* look. Not catching a glimpse of a few silver streaks feathered along his temples in amongst the dark brown strands either.

I'm not even ovulating right now, yet my body and brain are in two completely different universes where this man is concerned. What is clear, is that I need to get this shit under control for any number of reasons. Starting and ending with that ring on his finger.

"Ok. Clearly, this is going to call for a re-do." I clear my throat while swiveling in my seat and stick out my hand. "I'm Sage Maloney—founder of Wild Jasmine Studio. I've been hired for the summer to run the ranch PR and marketing. Tessa was supposed to fill me in on everything I needed to know, except without her to navigate this voyage, I'm going to need some help to get a feel for the lay of the land, cowboy. So do you fancy rummaging around in that vocabulary of yours for a few more words than just yes or no?"

His blue-gray eyes contemplate my outstretched palm, then tip up to meet mine. A wave of goosebumps makes an unwanted appearance down my shoulders. Little bitches that they are. There's something about this man that I still can't pin down, but I'm certainly not going to spend time examining what that might be.

His gaze drops back to study my hand with an indecipherable expression, and this is a repeat of exactly how our moment on the sidewalk felt all over again. He stared at my hand that day with something in his eyes that, if it were any other guy or girl, I'd say it was longing.

Except that absolutely cannot be the case here. So I need to shove that notion aside.

"C'mon, cowboy. I'm not gonna bite." I wiggle my fingers. "Let's give the whole introduction thing a little re-run, *hmm*. Clean slate?"

I watch as his throat dips, and he reaches out to take my hand in his own. His palm swallows mine with a powerful grip that wraps me up inside his calloused, hard-worn, and unbelievably warm hold. Tingles sweep up my forearm like fireflies prancing through my veins as he squeezes my hand.

"The name's Beau." This time, he holds my eyes, and I

genuinely wish he wouldn't, because the energy of that day when we first met races back into the space between us. It feels like we've suddenly been transported back in time, and we're no longer in the front seat of his truck. Instead, we've stepped back to the flirty conversation when we were about to exchange names and a handshake. Only, as much as I might have been hopeful at that moment, it never eventuated.

I have to fight back a shiver, realizing I've been lost staring at the depth of blue in his irises. They remind me of a lake in the stillness of dawn. *Peaceful. Reassuring. Calm.*

"Just Beau? Not 'Beau Heartford' as our buddy back at the airport insisted on calling you? Not some fancy triple-barrel name I should apparently be aware of?" He's still holding onto my hand as I tease him, and a flash of gold strikes his cheekbones from that rapidly setting sun.

"It's Beau." He must realize the handshake has been lingering a little too long, and drops my palm.

"Is *Beau* short for something?"

Silence.

"You know... I might just have to make it my mission to figure it out. Peel back those onion layers of yours. Like, discovering what inspired the mustache? Fan of classic eighties aviation movies?"

He gives me nothing to work with, but wets his lips slowly.

"Nice to meet you, Sage." His voice is rich, velvety, and damn, I like the way my name sounds when he says it.

"Great... uhh... likewise." I swallow hard and stick to the safe zone of playful banter. "Wanna fill me in on what I need to know? Since Tessa isn't here and all." I collect my bag from the footwell and climb out of the truck. My palm is still flush with warmth from his touch, and I have to tell the butterflies kicking up in my stomach to go the fuck back to sleep because this is a married man.

Married.

Those winged assholes sigh and pout and try to remind me just how insanely sexy his mustache is up close.

"You'll be staying over here." My luggage is hoisted out of the backseat, and cowboy strides off in the direction of some exceedingly cute, freestanding wooden cabins. They're set amongst groves of spruce trees with a pretty bluish tinge to their clusters of needles.

"Do all the staff stay on site?"

"Tessa will call you in the morning, and she can answer all your questions." He stops at the porch of the cabin closest to the barn and deposits my bag for me. "Keys are in the door. Linen, towels, everything you need is inside."

The guy looks like there are a million other places he'd rather be as he scrubs one hand over the back of his neck.

"Alright, *Beaufort scale*. Thanks for the grand tour." My lips roll together. He thinks he can get rid of me that easily? Not a chance.

His broad shoulders stiffen.

"I figured you'd want to settle in. After traveling and all." With one of those big paws, he gestures at the door to my accommodation.

"Sure, but help me out here. Am I gonna bump into my new boss over breakfast, or what? You'd be doing me a solid, giving me at least a crumb or two to go on."

A muscle flexes in the side of his jaw.

"Have you not eaten?" Grooves form between his brows. He seems genuinely concerned, and I suppose in cowboy-land, they're probably attached to hearty meal times.

"Uh—Yes. I grabbed something earlier before my flight." Why do I feel like I can't get a straight answer out of this guy? "Circling back to my question though, does the owner live here, or is it staff only, or what's the situation?"

"You're looking at him." The man before me mumbles.

Ringing chirps of cicadas and the quiet rustling of leaves fill the air as I digest those four words.

"What?"

"I own this place. Tessa is my business manager." He scuffs the ground with a boot and shoves both hands in his pockets.

"Oh my god. You let us drive all the way out here, and I had no idea. Why didn't you say something?" Christ, it'll officially haunt me forever that I called my new boss *Cock Ring* in the middle of the airport.

"Tessa was supposed to be here to explain all that."

"Ok, well—god, I suppose I want to say thank you for the contract. I mean, this place is incredible." I'm still gaping at him as I gesture a sweeping arm in the direction of his exceedingly beautiful ranch.

"Still got a lot of work to be done," he mutters, looking anywhere but at me. "Anyway, I'll leave you to it."

My fingers tighten around the strap of the bag slung over my shoulder. His bag. God. My new boss' duffel bag that I have indeed prettied up with pink rhinestones.

My hot, married boss who has seen my vibrator.

The skin on my nape prickles. This situation could not get any weirder.

He's already started off in the direction of the barn, wide shoulders rapidly moving away from me, and I have to call after him.

"The ranch... why doesn't it have a name? Now I know you're the boss dog around here and all."

He pauses, shrugs, and squints up at the mountain ridge line.

"That's part of why you're here, isn't it? To help with that sort of shit."

With that, Beau Heartford's long strides carry him off into the setting sun.

"I'll see you at 0800 hours for flight training, then, I'm guessing?" I let my voice ring out, but he doesn't so much as turn back, nor appreciate my joke.

Looks like I'll be very much left to find my own feet around here, after all.

CHAPTER 5

Beau

I'm going to murder my baby sister.

After forty-one years, today is finally the day.

Her phone keeps on ringing as I pace up and down the aisle, kicking up dust between the stalls inside the barn. If I didn't already have gray hairs, this would surely be the moment they'd make their entrance.

"Did you know?" I bark down the line the second it connects.

"Why are you yelling at me?"

"Did. You. Know." I bite out each word, one hand shoved beneath my cap, gripping my hair by the roots.

"Jesus, just give me a minute..." She whispers something, and then I hear her heels clip against echoing linoleum. "Oscar is out of surgery, by the way. Thanks for asking. *Dick*."

Scuffing my heel, I grunt something akin to an apology. "I saw the replay. Lucky that bull went the other way when he hit the dirt."

"You fucking rough stock riders. I swear to God, I don't know how I ended up marrying one."

"What's the damage?"

"Ribs. Femur. Full shoulder reconstruction."

He's going to be out for the rest of the season, that's for certain, but at least my baby sister didn't become a widow tonight.

"Are you doing ok?" Letting my fingers rake through my hair, I stare at the scuffed leather on the toes of my boots. My sister is a tough nut, but finding out your husband was almost trampled in the arena is never the phone call you want to receive.

Not that my own so-called wife ever seemed to care any of the times my night ended up at the hospital, rather than returning to my own bed.

"I'll be fine. Now, can we rewind to the part where you were chewing me out for no apparent reason?"

"The girl."

"She has a name, you know... Sage."

"Yeah, her." I clear my throat. "Did you know it was *her* when you went ahead with the hire?"

"Did I know it was the cute girl you were chatting to that day and got all weird about immediately after? Yes, I did. But before you go nuclear on me, I hired Sage on her merits. She's incredibly talented, and we're lucky to have someone who is not only bright and vibrant and knows her shit, but who just so happens to come highly recommended by your best friend."

That makes me pause. "Storm knows her?"

"He was the one who put us in touch with each other in the first place."

Fuck. This is not what I needed. If my closest friend has given this girl a tick of approval, then I'm going to be damn well stuck with her.

"So, you're going to be nice and welcoming and help her settle in, since I can't be there to do it myself."

My heart feels like it's about ready to bust out the front of my chest with a deafening roar. This sounds exactly like some sort of fresh hell, especially considering my circumstances.

"Do you want me to tell her? I don't mind. It'll save you needing to explain."

"No, it's ok."

"It would probably help a lot if you just let her know right from day one. That way, you won't go beating yourself up when you've been a cute ol' ball of anxiety but come across more like a snarling bear when you don't mean to."

Rubbing the heel of my palm over my sternum—the hand that can still feel exactly how soft Sage's touch was when I clasped her fingers—doesn't do shit to ease the tightness forming there.

Tessa might have still been talking, I don't even know. All I can focus on is the lingering sensation of feeling her skin beneath my own, and a building sense of dread.

"... you said you weren't interested, right? So, what's the problem?"

"I dunno, how about the fact that if Mandy gets a single sniff of me being in any sort of proximity to another woman, I'll be locked into this marriage for even longer, Tessa? I'm so fucking tired—it's been ten years—I'm so close to being out—" It's mostly just gasps and unfinished statements coming out of me now as the wave hits me out of nowhere, and the urge to bend double grips my stomach.

"I know, Beau. I know." Tessa soothes me down the line, the way she has had to do so many times in our adult life. "It's ok, just take a deep breath for me, ok? Focus on my voice."

"I can't keep doing this anymore... you know how toxic... if I get stuck longer..." There's no completing that sentence, because the thought itself is abhorrent. Right now, my fingers are raw and bleeding from climbing almost all the way out of this hole I've been stuck in for far too long, and I can scent fresh air at the surface. However, one slip, one wrong move, I could end up tumbling right back into the darkness.

If I lose my footing, I'd be swallowed back up by the belly of the beast. Possibly never to escape again.

"Beau." My sister's voice echoes in my ear. "I need you to listen. Count with me. That's all you need to do right now. You're gonna inhale through your nose 'til we get to four, yeah?"

One. Two. Three. Four. I do it as slowly as possible, sucking the warm evening air into my starving lungs.

"That's all you have to do."

Blowing out a stream of air, I readjust my cap.

"I should be talking *you* down... you're the one with a husband just out of emergency surgery." My teeth clench.

"Annnnnnnd, out... two, three, four." She ignores me and continues to count through the breathing technique she swears by, but I'm still not one hundred percent sold on. Yet, I do it anyway, for her.

"Thanks," I say, after a few more rounds of counting and trying to ease the cement-like feeling lining my jaw, the boulder sitting on my chest.

"Hang on—stay on the line, Beau—" She covers the mouthpiece with her hand, and in the background, I hear a muffled, rapid-fire conversation with a nurse. "Crap, I gotta go, but you know I'm right here if you need to text me."

"I'll be ok. Just... I got jumped by a fan at the airport, and they started questioning me about Mandy... and..."

"You're gonna be out of it so soon. Beau, you are an outstanding man, and I'm not just saying that because I'm your sister or because you pay me. That woman can go dive into a vat of boiling oil for all I care. You don't have anything to worry about. You are going to be free of her bullshit before you know it, and you've got a gorgeous ranch and future freedom to look forward to."

Hearing her say it out loud at least leaves my lungs feeling like they can expand a little further on my next sucked-in breath.

"You know..." I hear a sparkle in Tessa's voice. "I wouldn't blame you if you did like her. She's smart, accomplished, not to mention gorgeous. But please be thinking like the boss of a new business, and not a grown man developing a crush. There are things we can write into business contracts, but you're gonna need to disclose if something happens..."

"Nothing is going to happen. With *anyone*. I'm still goddamn married."

I know what that little huffing breath she blows out on the

other end of the phone means. Tessa is rolling her eyes silently at me. "Ah, yes, but only for what, another two months? Eight weeks and counting, the last I checked my calendar."

"Get back to your guy. Give my love to Oscar... and tell him he was far too pretty. It was about time he got scuffed up a little and earned himself a little hoof print on his chest."

"Oh my god, you have such a fucked up sense of humor. Go cuddle that asshole horse. He'll probably bite you, and then you really won't have time to spiral about Mandy or her crap."

That makes me chuckle, and I look in the direction of his stall. Repetitive munching sounds come from the creature in question. Teddy really is the biggest piece of shit, but he's grown on me. Even if I'm only stabling him here on behalf of Storm and his girl, Briar.

"Bye, Tessa."

After the line goes dead, I puff out my cheeks and shove my cap back down roughly. There's always plenty of shit needing to be done, but since it's sundown, I set about making sure the one and only horse we've currently got here is taken care of for the night.

Walking over, I lean on the door to look in on him. All glossy black coat and ears that whip back and forth with irritation. The prick stamps a hoof even though I'm the guy who brings him breakfast and treats every goddamn day.

He's a rescue, and ended up here as part of a future equine therapy program we'll eventually set up. In the meantime, he and I are still coming to terms with each other.

Teddy adores Briar, just like Storm does, but that's about where his tolerance for people begins and ends. After a shitty life with previous owners who mistreated him, the guy is ready to give everyone hell.

Can't say I blame him. In fact, most days, I feel like the two of us have more in common than he will ever know.

I suppose I should appreciate this period of quiet, when the barn is almost empty, and we're yet to start acquiring our stable of horses for the ranch. I suppose I should be grateful that we're still a few weeks out from the head of cattle I've got due to arrive.

Things around here are in the phase of impending explosion into life. Like studying the inky black sky through a viewfinder, ready to capture the exact moment a riot of dawn color appears on the horizon. By the time fall rolls around, we'll have stock and a barn occupied with horses all needing to be taken care of.

Yet, I can't enjoy a single moment of that peace right now because my mind is firmly stuck on *her*.

The girl who I've been unable to shake—the beautiful fascination preoccupying the majority of my thoughts—no matter how often I've told myself to get over that encounter and move on. I've lost track of how many trips to Crimson Ridge I've taken, where my attention has been only half on what I was supposed to be doing. When, in fact, I'd been keeping an eye out for a glimpse of glossy midnight hair and smooth brown skin.

How often have I parked up outside that art gallery and waited, just to see if she might reappear?

How many nights have I lain in my lonely bed, fantasizing about the stranger with soulful dark eyes I see whenever I close my own?

A mystery girl who has left me unable to focus on anything but the way her wicked smirk graced the corner of those pretty lips. Not to mention, the memory of her ass in those jeans being the ever-present reason for my dick to get hard.

Christ. Now she's here? On my ranch?

What my sister doesn't need to know, is that I'm *more* than interested in the girl currently making herself at home in cabin number six. She thinks I didn't, or don't want anything to do with her, but that couldn't be further from the truth.

I've been endlessly fixated on a girl with no name. She has an allure about her which kept me captive ever since a single chance encounter. A flash of a moment between us that lasted all of ten minutes, for fuck's sake.

As I'm about to head back to the house, a text arrives. I quickly check to see if it's something from Tessa. But it's not. Rather than my sister, it's the source of misery herself. Or, rather to the point, her moron, ass-kisser of an assistant.

MANDY:

Lawyers are going to be in touch. Mandy has an exciting idea to run past you!

- Z *star-eye emoji*

They can both fuck right off. I don't even bother acknowledging the message. Mandy goddamn Spires has always got *ideas.* None of which are ever of any benefit to anyone except herself. It'll be something inane and childish in an effort to try to secure herself some kind of front-page news. The woman thrives on a diet of clickbait for breakfast, lunch, and dinner.

Another text arrives straight away. The double-edged game those two always like to play, to come at me from all angles.

ZEB:

Hi Beau, if you could make sure to post the following to your Instagram this weekend. I've attached a photo and text caption pre-made for you, along with having flowers delivered to M's tour dressing room on your behalf. Make sure to tag her account in the image so that all her followers can see your post and read about how excited you are for your wife's next stop on the tour!

God, I want to smash my phone. Polluting my screen is a photo taken of the two of us years ago, in some ridiculous staged performance for the cameras, that was meant to look as if we were vacationing together. When the reality was she flew in for the hour-long shoot, then jetted straight back off to some studio executive's villa. Whichever one she'd been holed up in at the time, pretending like it wasn't plainly obvious she was busy fucking her way to the next album deal.

I'm so damn close to being rid of her bullshit. We've got a

contract in place that guarantees my freedom, and signatures on divorce papers will be happening in all but a matter of months.

There's nothing I want more than to never have to hear the name Mandy Spires ever again.

All I gotta do is keep my head down, quietly survive the next couple of months, smile for the cameras, and post to social media to appease the terms of our agreement. To avoid the comparisons that will inevitably come if there were any hints that this marriage ended because of me.

Just like his daddy.

To the outside world, I have to portray the image of the faithful husband until the carefully staged and perfectly curated announcement is made.

Then, I'll be free.

Which means, I absolutely cannot allow myself to even look twice at the gorgeous girl who is going to be here all summer long.

CHAPTER 6

Sage

When I was eight, I decided to cut my own bangs, all because my mom told me I wasn't allowed to get them. So, of course, my stubborn ass decided to prove that I did, in fact, *need* them, or else I might simply expire.

Instead of the cute, stylish, face-framing style of my dreams, I looked like I had sprouted stubby little lopsided devil horns, which stuck out from my forehead at right angles. To compound my humiliation, the second it became humid, they would curl into tiny comical nubs, and make the whole situation infinitely worse. I was stuck having to clip my disastrous experiment back for what felt like an eternity, until my hair finally grew back.

Even that fiery hell of shame pales in comparison to now knowing what I know, thanks to a one a.m. internet sleuthing session.

Not much can make a girl like me feel the sting of embarrassment at twenty-five years young, but knowing who my new boss is, seeing his professional rodeo career spelled out in online search terms, and discovering that he's married to *Mandy Spires* of all people... well, I'm not sure how to describe the cluster fuck of thoughts occupying my brain.

The man who owns this ranch is practically the patron saint of bull riding in this part of the world. A god-like creation, born to carry a cowboy swagger while displaying a fearlessness that is simply heart-stopping.

Is it worse that I told him he didn't know the way to a woman's clit, or that I called him Cock Ring in a busy airport? Or maybe let's just land on the fact he had to scoop my vibrator off the sidewalk.

It's not that I'm embarrassed about who I am, or being a person who happily takes her own pleasure and desires into her own hands. I'm not ashamed of being an outspoken woman. No, I'm simply mortified that all those things somehow ended up coexisting in the same whirlpool of circumstances with the man I have to look in the eye while handing over an invoice for my services.

Beau Heartford is indeed worthy of being first-and-last-named in the same reverential breath. He's good. As in *really* good. A superstar on the back of a bull throughout his pro career. I suppose past tense is appropriate in this instance since he's been retired for a few years now.

My online sleuthing as to why my new boss has starry-eyed fans stopping him for autographs brought up a never-ending series of video clips of him being tossed around on top of a bull. Slow-motion footage featuring chaps and a cowboy hat to leave a gal with a fluttering pulse between her thighs, along with interviews and sponsors' promos seemingly everywhere.

One thing is undeniable… the man was a dream come true as an athlete, between his natural talent and good looks.

And then there's her.

The wife.

I didn't recognize the name at first, but then I saw a few press photos of them together on a red carpet somewhere, and it all slotted quickly into place. She came third runner-up in some god-awful reality TV contest. I remember watching rerun episodes with Layla, lying on the couch together on lazy Sundays while we were still in high school.

Apparently she went on to make it big in the world of country and western music charts, but I can't say I could name a single song of hers. Nowadays, the woman appears to be Nashville's darling homecoming queen, with her perfect blond curls and seemingly endless product endorsements flooding her social media. Not a hair or nail ever seems to be out of place, and her aesthetic is certainly all about being the country music starlet with her rodeo hubby on her arm.

They definitely make the picture-perfect couple, but Beau's response in the truck yesterday when I asked him about his wife doesn't match what I'm seeing on my phone screen.

If there's one thing I know, it's clever marketing and storytelling... my curiosity is officially piqued about these two, even though the nosey little hussy inside me really should take a beat and find something else to fixate on.

As I bask in the early morning dappled sunlight, listening to birds chirping and rocking my favorite playlist of seventies queens through my headphones, I fix myself a coffee at the little kitchenette my cabin comes with. It's seriously cute in here. Even though I can't exactly cook for myself with this limited setup, I've got the essentials. A mini fridge and a coffee maker will ensure I'm more than comfortable for the duration of my *ranch life* summer.

I've just wandered out the back door for the first time, with a steaming mug in hand, when my phone starts ringing with an incoming video call. As I go to swipe the green button, my mouth drops open. Oh dear sweet cherubic cowboy heavens, there's an entire private tub out here looking out toward the mountains, one of those simple freshwater trough designs. It's got my name and a hot date with a glass of wine written all over it.

"Hi Sage—oh god, is everything alright?" On the other end of the call is a face I now recognize immediately as being the woman I saw that day in the high street attached to Beau's arm. The woman who, at the time, I incorrectly presumed to be his wife, and now see her name flashing on my phone. Two and two get put together real quick. This is *Tessa Diaz.*

"I've fallen in love." I sigh wistfully. "You caught me just as I saw the tub outside my cabin, and the swoon-worthy *view*. It's enough to fall head over heels for."

Tessa laughs. "You've sold me. I'll book my vacation immediately."

"This place is seriously a dream. I'm still not quite sure how to say thank you for giving me this opportunity. Can I offer you a non-vital organ, perhaps? Actually, you know what? I can probably make it work if you need something vital. Take your pick."

She smiles broadly, but her eyes look tired.

"Did you settle ok for your first night? Were you comfortable enough?"

I nod and take a sip of my coffee, hoping she cannot see my own bags under my eyes. Proof of exactly how long I had lain awake past midnight trying, and failing, to stop thinking about *Beau Heartford:* insanely hot bull rider and married boss.

The fact that I am so persistently distracted by thoughts of him is probably a sign I need to schedule another appointment with my therapist. We both know my heart is a faulty, fickle, black cat of a creature, with a laundry list of commitment issues. The problem is, I don't think this little obsession has anything to do with my heart and rather, has a whole lot to do with my misbehaving hormones. They've all started jumping up and down, high-kicking like a chorus line while waving cowboy hats in the air. Proclaiming just how *perfect* they've judged the man who owns this ranch to be.

Which is entirely ridiculous, on so many levels. If there was a tick-box checklist of all the ways someone could be off-limits, I'm pretty certain 'married' and 'boss' come in positions one and two, respectively.

"—Beau will be up at the main house. I've asked him to show you around properly tomorrow, but give you a day to yourself first so you can settle in."

Wonderful, not only am I barely listening to the woman who hired me, but I'm replaying the sight of his corded forearms and veined hands flexing as he readjusted his cap.

Snap the fuck out of it, Sage.

"You know, I feel silly that we've actually met before, and I didn't even know." It feels prudent to broach the subject because I don't know how much Beau has explained about our first encounter. After his best efforts not to speak to me yesterday, I'm unsure he would have mentioned it at all. "The last time I was in Crimson Ridge, Mr. Heartford helped me out, and I think you and I exchanged a very quick '*hello*.'" I chew the inside of my cheek.

"Oh, please. It's Beau and Tessa around here. Don't go giving my brother any special treatment. He would much rather be treated like a regular ol' cowboy."

"Your brother?" My coffee is halfway to my lips, and my god, am I glad not to have a mouthful because that shit would have spluttered everywhere.

"Yep, my big brother, and please don't tell him this, but I do actually love him dearly... even if his Virgo is showing ninety-nine percent of the time."

"So, you're his business manager?"

"Well, prior to having the ranch to his name, I was his manager through his rodeo career. It's been a natural transition to this point now that he's not busy trying to get himself trampled by bulls half the year."

"Can I assume you have the patience of a goddess, if you've put up with working alongside an older sibling for that long?" I chuckle. "I don't mean any offense, but lord knows my kid sisters would never. We would probably have strangled each other after one week."

"Comes with the territory." Tessa stifles a yawn. "My husband competes on the pro circuit... actually, that's why I'm not able to be there to work with you as we had planned. Oscar had a bad accident yesterday, and I'll be here with him while he's in recovery for quite a while, then most likely will have to work from home to help him out."

"Oh my god. I had no idea." My stomach flips.

"Please, Sage, don't give me that panicked face, girl." Tessa shakes her head. “This is a routine we are all more than familiar with. It’s not anything you ever wish to happen, but he’s doing ok, and that’s the most important thing.”

“How are you so calm right now?”

“Blame Beau… he put me through far too many hospital trips, specialist appointments, and sleepless nights sitting by his bedside worrying about his ass. It’s like I’ve been mentally preparing for this moment for a long time.”

A shiver runs through me. The grim reality hangs unspoken of what Beau’s career must have been like beyond the glitz and glamor and highlights of eight-second rides ending in glory.

I’m also immediately wondering where his *wife* was in all this. Wouldn’t it have fallen to her to stay by his bedside, rather than his sister?

“Ok, so here’s the run-down for you, Sage. Feel free to text or call me anytime and as often as you need, but I know you’re going to be more than capable to start working your magic without my help. A second vehicle is there, which is yours to use for the duration of the summer, and you can pick up the keys from over at the main house.” Tessa looks down at something, presumably her notebook, as she licks a finger and then flicks through a couple of pages.

“That’s very generous, thank you.”

“Don’t mention it. The fuel card is in the glove compartment, and use the truck to get around as much as you like. In terms of Wi-Fi access, we only have coverage over at the house, not out in the cabins, as you’ve probably already discovered, so set yourself and your laptop up wherever you like. There’s plenty of room. Use the place as if it’s your own. Cooking, meals, whatever you like. The kitchen is fully stocked, and everything is provided for you. It’s only Beau who will be mooching around, and he’s like a wolf who only turns up now and then when he sorts himself out with a hot meal, but prefers to spend most of his day out on the ranch somewhere.”

Those damn butterflies have no business starting to circle

around in my stomach at the mention of his name and hints of his day-to-day routine.

I clear my throat. "Are you sure I won't be in his way? I don't want to impose."

"Not at all. Make yourself entirely at home. The place is yours to use any time of the day or night. It will give you a good feel for the ranch itself and what guests will want to know as part of the promotional material, you know, all the *ranch comforts* side of things."

Tessa is a sweetheart, and gives me a few more pieces of information I might find helpful before she hangs up and leaves me staring at the patchwork of green rolling beyond the picture window of my cabin.

I'm certainly going to make the most of exploring today and getting myself settled in order to be prepared for tomorrow. Eyeing my planner on the bedside table, I realize I'll also need to confirm a time to meet with the new owners of the local cowboy bar, The Loaded Hog, who I'm working with on their full rebrand. Not to mention, tracking down my bestie perched on top of Devil's Peak, tucked away in ranching bliss with her cowboy Colton Wilder.

While Layla might have the world's most picturesque location to call home these days, and dozens of horses to surround herself with while living out her brightest horse-girl dreams, the place is isolated as fuck. No cellphone coverage. Patchy Wi-Fi. Enough snowfall to leave you trapped for long stretches throughout the year.

I'm very comfortable being able to stay in a part of Crimson Ridge in an area where my phone still works, and the internet has a backbone. It'll need enough grit to withstand the rigorous workout I'm going to put it through once I get stuck into activities like website building, photo editing, and designing graphics.

Layla and I might be damn near joined at the hip, but I'd rather take a horse tranquilizer to the face than live on top of a mountain forever more.

After double-checking that my devices are all happily charging,

I dig out my running shoes from my luggage and toss my hair up in a ponytail. There's an endless lush landscape outside my front door just waiting to be explored. Feeling a warm breeze on my skin while inhaling cleansing lungfuls of Crimson Ridge air seems like the perfect recipe for nourishing the soul and starting my days while I'm here.

Jogging on a treadmill can kiss my peachy ass. I've never been more relieved at the prospect of clocking up some miles out in the wilds of Montana instead of being crammed in at the gym next to some sweaty dude who keeps staring at my rack.

Except, there's one slight inconvenience as I leave the cabin.

Straight away, I'm confronted by the sight of Beau Heartford, and the motherfucker is shirtless. He's in those jeans he wears far too well, with his t-shirt tucked into the back of his waistband and cap flipped backward. Is he for real? This feels like a setup. Like I'm a helpless trout being drawn in by a shiny lure floating in the current.

As he goes about hefting giant bags of something from the back of his truck to the barn, all I can see, as I crouch down to triple-check my laces, is an athlete's frame gleaming with perspiration.

Goddamn, the guy is *cut*.

The hormones I had barely managed to rein back in all begin whimpering unanimously when presented with a generous helping of sweaty, hard-working cowboy.

Going for a very, very long run sounds like an outstanding idea. One that needs to take me as far as possible in the opposite direction from all of *that* currently on display.

"Morning, *Captain Beau-gainvillea*." I yell over my shoulder as my feet hit the gravel path, and I start racing away from the far-too-handsome source of tingling and heat flooding my body. There's absolutely no way I'm pausing to see if he acknowledges my presence, because I desperately need to outpace whatever slutty little miscreant has decided to set up camp inside my body.

With pounding steps, I decide my best course of action is to treat my off-limits *married-cowboy-boss* the same way I would a pretty pair of heels. The kind my bank account simply cannot justify the cost of.

Nice to look at.

But ultimately, not for me.

CHAPTER 7

Beau

It's a hell of a walk to get to the best swimming hole on this ranch by foot, as opposed to the ease of driving my truck or whatever amount of time it would take to complete the trip on horseback.

Not that I would know, because the asshole walking at my side isn't interested in allowing anyone to ride him anytime this century.

Teddy's black mane and glossy coat of his long neck bob along beside me as we stroll our way through the shade of lush trees—following one of the trails future guests will use. At least we've gotten to the stage where he'll allow me to put a halter on him without leaving teeth marks embedded in my shoulder. Although, it's still touch and go some days, depending on his mood.

Which is why I'm taking this horse for a long ass walk on a lead rope, as if he's the world's biggest and grumpiest dog, so he can get a feel for the ranch and get used to walking with someone by his side. Hopefully, it's what the guy will do when Storm and Briar's equine therapy sessions start to take shape. For now, we're just approaching things one day at a time where Teddy is concerned.

I haven't gotten any of my other horses in yet, and I'm still waiting on the herd of cattle that are coming soon, so there are extra hours in the day to kill. A luxury of free time when I can give Teddy this type of treat. It's the kind of late hour when there's enough scattered cloud overhead, and I'm in the mood for an activity that will keep me busy long into the evening.

The girl who is now occupying my house, also occupies my mind, and I'm not entirely sure how to get a fucking handle on the way that relentlessly shakes me up.

It shouldn't be like this. I spent a pro career never having my head turned by anything pretty, always remaining focused on doing what I did best—competing and training and showing up for all the media shit required of me. Of course, the tour was overflowing with buckle bunnies who would have loved nothing more than to prove just how well they could take care of a lonely cowboy on the road, regardless of whether there was a wedding ring on my finger or not. But none of that was ever my scene.

Now?

One glance at Sage, a few short minutes with her on the sidewalk that day, has been enough to leave me enticed by all sorts of prospects of what it might mean to get closer. She's got this goddamn magnetic pull on me. Illicit thoughts are just about a full-time endeavor to avoid—trying not to spend the entire day thinking about that smart mouth and fire sparking away behind those brown eyes.

The trickling of water grows louder, and I see Teddy's ears flip around with curiosity, figuring out what the new sound is once we draw nearer. Hot air coats us, crisp and baking, without a puff of wind. Summer evenings on a day like this hold on to that last radiating heat long beyond the moment the sun sets. It'll be sweet fucking relief to dive into the cool, gently flowing pool that eddies at the riverbend.

Teddy doesn't need any encouragement. I give him a longer line to explore on, and set my camera down where it'll stay good and dry. He makes his way down the shingle riverbank, taking the time to have a long drink while I do the same, crouching to scoop a couple of handfuls to my mouth and then splash some water over my face.

"Well, go on then, you big bastard. Have a swim." I chuckle as the horse gives me a sidelong glance and swishes his tail.

Leaving him to make up his mind, I settle my ass down on the bank and strip off my t-shirt. It's fucking roasting, which seems to be the deciding factor in Teddy wading forward. His haunches flicker as the cool rises up to meet him. I can't hide my grin when I see how much he seems to love it.

He might be an asshole, but it's only because he's had a rough life. Seeing him enjoying the water with confidence feels like a win. Even if it took what felt like forever to walk here. Once I've collected my own horses, it'll be much easier to pony him up and lead him along while I can at least ride on horseback.

Teddy turns into a different animal, clearly relishing the feeling of water swirling and drenching his coat, to the point that I end up sitting on the gravel for a long while, simply letting him muck around. He keeps coming up to the shallows and stamping a hoof to splash the water, then goes deeper up to his chest with sass written all over his face, making sure I'm taking notes that this is his new favorite thing to do.

Looks like Storm and Briar are gonna be bringing their cocky boy for a few more river outings this summer.

I pull the lens cap off my camera and make sure the settings are looking right with a few test shots. Then run off a whole series of frames as he goofs around. Briar will be beside herself seeing her guy this content.

Eventually, Teddy decides he's had enough and emerges dripping wet. He proceeds to take himself off, rolling around like a thousand-pound puppy after a bath—all long skinny legs and teeth and whites of his eyes as he wriggles around. Once he's finished with his antics, I hitch him to a tree in the shade.

There's no way in hell I'm passing up the opportunity to plunge beneath that water myself after sitting out here sweating my ass off. Stripping right off, I dump every stitch of clothing and dive in. Hardly surprising Teddy was so content to be in here, the temperature is a sweet goddamn relief to the relentless heat. A summer night that has left my skin coated in a sheen of sweat.

Diving right under, the water bubbles around me, crystal clear and feeling like the kind of soothing calm my brain needs after everything lately. As I pop back up to the surface, I run my hands over my dripping hair and simply stand there, immersed up to my waist, staring at the willows and mountains. A sensation grabs hold of me, that this is how life gets to be. *Finally*.

Away from all the bullshit, free of the life I'd been stuck in for so long.

I drop back to lie in the water, staring at the sky. The only thing that sticks resolutely in my mind is a nagging little seed of an idea. A goddamn dangerous one. It taunts me with the whisper of what it might be like to have someone to share this kind of moment with.

Not someone. *Her*.

Scrunching my eyes closed, I try to block that thought straight away. It's the worst kind of realization that Sage is right here on this very ranch, but I'm supposed to be keeping to myself, seeing out the last days of this divorce. And here I am, already thinking about my new employee in a manner that isn't in any way appropriate.

Christ. There's got to be something broken in my brain.

Water gliding over my heated skin suddenly feels like a tempting hint of an idea. A glimpse of her touch. What would it be like for her delicate fingertips to trace over my body?

There's no avoiding it. It's already been enough of a battle against the tension that keeps pooling low in my stomach. From the moment she arrived, it's been a challenge, a battle with my cock to not continually find myself getting hard. I'm so goddamn endlessly attracted to her, even when I tell myself not to be.

Except that never seems to work. I'm pissed at myself for even thinking about the young woman who works for me. Not only that, I can't remember the last time my dick was so interested in someone that I couldn't keep a lid on that sensation.

When was the last time I felt like I had no control over when and where I decided to jerk off? When was the last time I even felt sexually aroused to that point? Ten years chained to Mandy were never like this, and most of that time, we weren't having sex anyway—a decision cemented after the first couple of years of being married had drifted by, and I suspected she was cheating.

But here I am, cock rapidly hardening and demanding I give in and give myself what my body seems to continually seek out these days. What it has wanted ever since that day she burst into my life, and she was still just the mystery girl I bumped into on the main street.

Letting out a heavy exhale, I cast a quick glance around. Which feels like the dumbest fucking thing, because I'm in the middle of nowhere. The only witnesses to my giant goddamn erection right now are birds and clouds and mountains looming up into the sky.

There isn't any point denying this. And as much as I feel like a randy old perv fisting my dick over a girl so much younger than me —one who works for me—not even being riddled with guilt can stop my hand from wrapping around myself beneath the water as I sink down to my chest.

My throat bobs as I close my grip, and that familiar electric feeling races straight to the base of my shaft. I'm thickening and lengthening on that first contact, and I slide up to press the silver barbell at my tip. A shudder grips me in time with how hard I'm stroking myself. The added sensation of water gliding over the pierced head has my balls tightening in anticipation of release already.

Ironic really, how it ended up working in my favor. Once Mandy eventually found out that I'd had it done, she scrunched her face up and told me it was too weird. Not that I got pierced with her in mind. By that point, we'd already gone a long time without being in the same bed, or even the same location as each other. Either way, I couldn't have been more relieved to know my wife had no interest in any further attempts at sleeping with me anymore. At least it guaranteed I wasn't going to catch anything after she had fallen into bed with god knows who.

Bringing my hand up out of the water, I spit into my wet palm, then grip myself harder. Fuck. It's too easy to give into thoughts of Sage, and as much as I hate that fact considering I'm still married, I can't seem to kick the habit.

She's so supple, right there in front of me. The way her body rubs up against mine, her softness and curves and smooth brown skin all on luscious display. It's always the same... imagining what it would be like to roam my hands all over her naked figure, to hear the little breathy noises she makes when my touch discovers the places she enjoys.

I swallow thickly and keep gliding my hand up and down my length, feeling the heat already primed and building in the base of my spine. Apparently, where this sordid little daydream is concerned, I'm damn near ready to explode at the first twist and squeeze of my fist.

Thumbing my piercing, I get lost in the image of it being her delicate fingertips teasing me instead. She climbs into my lap, bare and tempting, reaching down to knock my hand out of the way. I've got free rein to touch her as she strokes me slow and firm, all while watching me with a sultry little look from behind thick lashes. When I palm and cup her full breasts, she gives me a delicious, wicked noise, and that only spurs her on, working me harder.

God, I'm a fucking terrible person, but I can't stop. My hand moves faster beneath the water, and my heart damn near stutters in my chest as the pressure intensifies. With gritted teeth, I feel the way her body gives beneath my rough touch. She likes her tits being tortured, arching her spine to press into my hands as I pinch her nipples in time with the increased pace of my fist shuttling up and down.

Fuck. Her body moves, and that's when the version of Sage imprinted in my mind chooses to wield her power, undoing me.

She guides my tip against her pussy. White-hot sparks flash straight to a point low in my stomach, landing in my balls as I imagine just how wet and silky she feels.

I hear her moan as my piercing slides through her slick cunt, and that idea, the dream of pressing into her, has me choking out a desperate noise. My dick jerks and swells, the gasp of a ragged curse flying past my lips.

My climax thunders through, exploding at the very bottom of my spine as I feel the added slickness pulse over my hand beneath the water. Running my hold up and over the metal through my tip and back down leaves me light-headed.

Christ. The pleasurable surge of relief is immediately followed by a deep sense of guilt flooding in.

I'm not meant to be out here daydreaming of this girl nearly what... twenty years younger? Did Tessa mention she's in her mid-twenties? Jesus. I'm already past forty, and what the fuck kind of business do I have fantasizing about her in such a carnal goddamn way. What sort of boss am I that it only takes one moment alone with her on my mind, and I'm busy fucking my fist?

Tension sits square in my jaw as I wash away the lingering evidence of my sordid little moment of weakness, and make my way out of the river. This has got to damn well stop. I've got to find some way of taming whatever this obsession is that I've developed since she arrived in my life.

This ranch is my focus. Getting free of the toxic marriage I've been trapped in. That's the goal. That's where my head has gotta be at, not continually giving into thoughts of her.

Fortunately for my guilty conscience, I've got a long trudge back to the ranch to give myself one hell of a cursing out. By the time I've finished getting Teddy stabled for the night, shadows have crawled in to claim the ranch. On leaving the barn, darkness has blanketed everything, revealing only a faint outline of the mountain ridgeline still visible. It lays out a jagged imprint against an inky-bluish sky.

I make my way toward the main house, and as I do so, my steps unwittingly slow. Sage's cabin lights are still on, even though it's long past nightfall and beyond the time when I imagine she would be curled up in bed.

A warm, inviting glow spills across the pathway, forming a beacon illuminating the direction of her front door. The sight teases like a spotlight, reminding me of my filthy thoughts and unwavering fascination with the very person I'd find just beyond that threshold. A taunting finger hooked my way, luring me to follow the pull I feel to knock on her door, which would be about the most irresponsible fucking thing I could do.

In contrast, this big house I've taken on, the grand structure looming before me where I lay my head, is dark, and filled with nothing but sleepless nights spent tossing around in an empty bed.

Clenching my teeth, I stride away from the source of all my chaotic, irresponsible thinking. This life? Being alone? It's exactly the way it is, because that's all I damn well deserve. I made a mistake; I messed up, so here's me getting my life back on track. Ride out the next couple of months, until that door to a regrettable fucking time finally slams shut for good.

Enduring the need to shove aside whatever feelings of desire are intent on creeping up on me. Yeah, that's the very least I deserve.

I gotta keep my hands to myself, and my focus set firmly on this ranch.

CHAPTER 8

Beau

"Reporting to the flight deck for duty."

The raspy voice and inquisitive eyes of the woman I've been avoiding since she first set foot on this damn ranch appear in the kitchen doorway, looking like she's undoubtedly going to tear my soul straight from my chest.

Sage Maloney is so beautiful; it's enough to flip my entire world, and morals, upside down with a single flutter of those thick, dark lashes.

"Help yourself to some breakfast, if you're hungry," I mutter, while gesturing vaguely in the direction of the fridge and pantry. I've got one eye on my phone screen, one fist clenched around my coffee, and a head full of rogue thoughts after seeing her ass in those running shorts yesterday morning.

Apparently, hauling horse feed for hours wasn't enough to erase that sight from my mind.

"I'm good. To be honest, I'm not really a breakfast person, but I'll take you up on the offer of mainlining caffeine and maybe just some fruit, if that's ok?" Sage rummages around, finding things with ease. Of course she does. "So, what's on the agenda for our squadron today?" As she pours herself a coffee, those plush lips curve into a smirk.

"Are you going to be like this all summer?"

"Resolutely." Her smile grows wider.

I run my tongue over the front of my teeth. "I've got orders from Tessa to show you around the ranch today."

That makes her tilt her head to one side. "Aren't you the one in charge, Mr. Heartford?"

My asshole cock twitches, hearing the challenge in her voice.

"Leave me to the horses and the cattle. My sister is much better at everything else, trust me."

"Well, lucky for you, I was the gold star pupil. My report card always read: excels at taking the initiative and displays an aptitude for leadership." Sage sips her coffee, and those dark eyes dance at me in the bright light spilling into the kitchen. "In other words, once I'm set up with my laptop and in my creative zone, you'll barely notice I'm here."

She couldn't be more wrong on that front.

"How are your horse skills?"

Her cheeks puff out. "Passable… my best friend is certifiably horse-besotted and has insisted on me learning to ride at every opportunity. It'll take me a minute to find my rhythm again, but as long as you don't play a dirty trick and put me on the back of a frisky bastard, I'm sure I'll be fine."

Goddamn, what sins have I committed to be stuck with a girl who has this much spark to her? It's a monumental effort to maintain some sort of distance. To keep her at arm's length, and not just give in to the urge to match her round for round, and joke for joke. I'm going to have to tiptoe my way through this entire arrangement, stuck inside my shell, because I'll be absolutely done for if I let myself go there, even for one second.

Sage's feistiness calls to a side of me I haven't been able to let roam for what feels like forever. Certainly, a part of myself that has been locked away behind bars for the entire duration of my miserable fucking marriage.

"Are we riding today?" She lifts her eyebrows while crunching down on an apple. A fleck of juice hits the corner of her lips, and the back of my neck prickles as I drop my eyes immediately in a valiant effort not to stare like a creep when she swipes away the wetness with her tongue.

"Not today. We'll take the truck." I drain the dregs and load my mug into the dishwasher. "We haven't brought in our quarter horses, yet. The only fella who's here so far is a rescue and likes nothing more than to leave his friends with a bruise or two."

"He sounds spunky. I'd love to meet him."

Pushing off the counter, I stuff my phone in my pocket. "You ready to head out? Anything you need to grab from your cabin before we go?"

"Can I bring a fresh supply with me?" She wiggles the mug.

"Sure. There's a thermos in that cupboard over there."

Sage follows my direction to find herself a travel mug before stocking herself with more fruit, a gallon of coffee, and clutches her tablet tight to her chest. "Perfect, now I'm going to be well-fueled for a morning of witty remarks and a keen eye for all the best angles this ranch has to offer."

I scrub a palm over my mouth.

"Lead the way, boss."

"You—You can just call me Beau, you know."

"I do... but this game is much more fun."

With a sigh, I lead us out toward the vehicles. This fucking girl. I really don't know how to handle what she's batting my way without crossing lines that absolutely cannot be crossed.

Do I just need to be a sullen asshole twenty-four-seven?

Or is that just as likely to end up in some sort of employment dispute for being miserable and unreasonable to employees? Jesus. Fuck. This girl is so much younger than me; she's been hired by my company, and I've got no business looking her way if I'm going to successfully escape the hell I've been trapped in for too long.

"Have you heard from your sister? I spoke to her yesterday morning," Sage mumbles through a mouthful of apple while juggling her supplies and opening the passenger door. "Is her husband doing ok?"

"He'll live. Oscar is tough as nails," I grunt and slide into my seat. The scent of her still lingers in the cab after our trip back from the airport, and now that she's buckling in on her side, those fragrant notes wind their way around me once more with much more insistent force, like a cat rubbing up against my ankles.

Fuck. *Fuck.* That is absolutely the wrong thing to say to myself. Do not for one-second start thinking of this girl's pussy.

Not when she's wearing those denim cut-offs I've been trying to avoid looking at. Now, here we are in close quarters once more, and all I can see is an expanse of rich, supple brown skin on her upper thigh.

"We're building toward being up and running by next summer." I start the engine and get us moving. The best goddamn thing I can do right now is concentrate on driving, and talking about the ranch. Yep. Talk about the business 'til I'm blue in the face. Be the professional boss I need to be.

In other words, be boring as shit, and perhaps the gorgeous girl beside me won't spend more time in my vicinity than is absolutely necessary for her job.

I fucking hate the idea immediately.

At least driving us past the barn and in the direction of the furthest reaches of the property gives my brain something to focus on. I don't know why, but there's something about driving that settles my brain into a pattern where I feel like I can process my thoughts. My best thinking happens when I'm behind the wheel. The same goes for getting on the back of a horse and riding into the hills with my camera strap slung over my shoulders.

It's when my boots are still that the noise inside my brain starts to spiral far too easily.

"So you're aiming for the first guests to be pre-booked in time for the next summer season?"

I nod.

"Have you considered a soft launch? Offering some opportunities to travel bloggers, or content creators during the spring?" Sage starts tapping on the screen of her tablet. "You could partner with them in exchange for sharing about their experience... nothing beats a rave review. Then word of mouth starts to do its thing in the future."

"I suppose."

"Will the ranch offer hands-on opportunities? Or is it strictly for experiencing the view and the atmosphere kind of vibe?"

"They can get on the back of a horse... camp... fish... there will also be an equine therapy aspect that folks can participate in if they like."

"And at the end of a day filled with petting horses and gulping down lungfuls of fresh mountain air, they can wander over to watch cowboys kitted out in chaps and hats, roping some teeny-tiny baby cows?"

"If they're into that kind of thing. And they're called calves."

Sage gives me an exaggerated eye roll. "I think you'd be surprised just how many people would gladly volunteer to take their place and be the one getting manhandled by a rugged cowboy." She's busy noting something down on her tablet, but from the corner of my eye, I catch the way her lips twitch. "Truss 'em up with a bit of rope, wrestle them into the dirt, pull their hair. I think they'd say thank you and never want to leave."

"Think I'll stick to rounding up cattle." Please, for the love of all that is holy, don't tempt me to start thinking of whether she likes that kind of thing in bed.

"Pity." She sighs wistfully. "Fishing sounds about as appealing as watching paint dry... apologies if that's your idea of a good time."

"Have you ever tried it?"

Sage chuckles. "My kind of *fishing* involves a tequila body shot, my best push-up bra, and a dancefloor at two a.m."

Christ. I'm near strangling the steering wheel and silently threatening my cock to stay down.

"So, beyond frolicking around playing cowboy for the duration of their stay, what else can visitors expect from their time here?"

"What do you mean?" I grunt, continuing to drive us toward

the river running through the property. She might not be interested in casting a rod, but I still need to show her around.

"Well... what sets you apart from other players in Crimson Ridge? Why *here* rather than Devil's Peak Ranch, for example?"

"Other than not having to trek up a mountain?" My hand rubs over my jaw. "If folks are interested, we've got the river to swim in, hills to explore on foot or by horseback." I focus on listing off things that sound pretty simple in reality, but I guess might be helpful, or appealing. "There's also a workout room back at the house, the kitchen is top of the line and set up for groups to bring in their own chef if they want."

"A workout room? Like a gym set up?"

"Sure. You're welcome to use it, too," I add. Even though I'm offering, I don't know if I'll survive running into her while working out in more of those short-shorts and tank tops, so make a mental note to always triple-check from now on before wandering in there.

Christ, it's like I've never seen a woman before in my life.

Not like I've been damn well married to one for years.

"That's actually a really unique asset. You could definitely work an angle for retreats, athletes, wellness-focused stays..." She trails off as her fingers fly across the screen in her lap. "Especially with your rodeo background. *Mmm*, that gives me an idea." It seems as though she's talking to herself more than anything as she hums and twists her lips in thought.

She works as we keep driving, and I do my goddamn best to continue shoving aside all memories of our first interaction. Even if there was a brief flirtation there—that I was an absolute idiot to even entertain for a second—there's no way I can allow that idea of finding her attractive to bloom into something.

Whatever her age, for me, my mid-twenties is a time that feels like a million lifetimes ago. Years spent with the solitary goal of prize money, winning buckles, and outrunning comparisons to my father. Christ, she's filled with all that vitality of *youth*. I'm her boss. I'm at the tail end of a drawn-out separation, with a vindictive blood-hound of a wife who will stop at nothing to keep me shackled to her. There's no escaping the reality that I am very much still a married man. Even if our lives have been separate for years now, it's not like I ever truly allowed my heart to become involved in the first place.

Mandy Spires loves nothing more than the fame and notoriety that comes with having a world champion for a husband. She's built her entire brand around the false promotion of our marriage, and I was the idiot who was too busy with my own pro career to notice what was happening until it was too late.

She took advantage of the fact I was distracted and zoned in on perfecting every little thing as an athlete. By the time I realized the mistake I'd made in falling for her bullshit, I was neck-deep, firmly locked in a glass prison she'd carefully constructed around our *fairytale* marriage.

If I'd tried to end things, like I originally wanted to, she held all the cards to tank my career in the court of public opinion. Blackmail is too polite a term for the emotional and legal manipulation that woman wields like a stock whip.

"How much land do you have out here?" Sage interrupts my thoughts.

"Around two thousand acres."

She's still typing fast, but manages to glance up at our surroundings.

"This looks like a super cute spot." We draw closer to the willows lining the banks of the swimming hole. "Not in a 'let's bore ourselves to death hunting fishies' kind of way. However, I certainly *will* be adding skinny dipping in that gorgeous-looking water to my summer to-do list though."

She's gotta be fucking with me. This is like the moment when I was holding her vibrator and she gave me that look of daring.

Clearing my throat, I'm hanging on by a thread trying not to imagine that exact picture she's just painted. Not after what happened the last time I was out here on my own. "Want to get out for a closer look?" I put the truck in park.

Sage is already out the door before I've finished speaking.

I simply sit there for a moment, heart pounding inside my chest. This is too tempting, too mouthwatering a prospect. The fact she hasn't shied away from my quiet side is more refreshing than she could ever know. I'm not a complete introvert, but I'm happiest in my own company. Other people drain me, rather than recharge me. For the most part, I simply like a whole lot of peace and alone time.

When it comes to Sage? I don't feel anything but the need to be around her. Fucking hell, if I'm already thinking that way, I've got a bigger problem on my hands than I could ever have bargained for.

"C'mon, even fighter pilots need to hop out of the cockpit for two minutes," she yells from her spot on the bank, looking back at me over one shoulder while shielding her eyes from the sun.

Fuck me. The mid-morning light hitting her brown skin, and loose tendrils of raven, sleek hair frame her face, make Sage look absolutely goddamn luminous.

I swallow down the rock wedged in the back of my throat and slip out of my door. Shoving my hands in my pockets, I scuff at the grass with my boots as I make my way toward her.

"Tell me, Mr. Heartford. Why rodeo? Why bull riding?" She looks out across the water, still shielding her eyes and takes in the rippling, bubbling surface where it flows over the shallow rocks on the far bank.

"My grandparents got me into it." I shrug, and bend down to pick up a smooth pebble from the gravel bank. "I was with them a lot as a kid." No point in mentioning the asshole who should have been my idol, who gave me my first taste of bull riding. He might as well be dead.

"What about Tessa? Did she get into it, too?"

"She did. Was a talented young barrel racer, but Tessa wasn't in it for the competitive edge like I was."

Brushing my thumb over the cool, smooth surface of the rock, I focus on the water instead of the gorgeous girl at my side.

"You like winning, Heartford?"

I hear it. I hear that undeniable challenge again. That invitation to spar and play, and step into an arena that I absolutely have no business going anywhere near.

"I like knowing I've refined something." I clear my throat and readjust my cap. "Riding bulls... I guess that was my thing. What I perfected."

"Sure looks like you did." The way her voice rasps as she says those words has me seriously contemplating throwing myself into the deepest part of that swimming hole. My lower back prickles with sweat and the tension of being so close to her, yet having to remain so far away, lest I tumble straight into the fiery pits of a hell I can't ever escape from.

She's too young, too forbidden. Even if our circumstances were different—even if I didn't have this goddamn noose of a marriage around my neck—nothing can, or should happen with someone I damn well employ.

That's the way it's gotta be.

Stick to the agreement I made. The bargain I struck. See out the remainder of my sentence; then I'll have gotten myself out of this awful fucking situation once and for all.

CHAPTER 9

Sage

It's the worst realization possible that my boss has the mustache of my every teenage dream and fantasy. I have a crush the size of Jupiter, and bitchy little fluttering wings swarming my stomach every time I catch sight of him.

It's the absolute pits.

How the hell did I end up stranded here in futile longing-ville, population one?

I'm notoriously the frozen-hearted, *fun time, not a long time*, gal. I'm your go-to for a spontaneous round of shots at two in the morning, and have a unique gift for sniffing out a karaoke bar where I can wail my lungs out in my best Stevie impression, clutching the microphone singing about *dreams* and a *gold dust woman.*

Now, I fear I'm chronically afflicted by a handsome cowboy, who I absolutely cannot fucking keep thinking about in the way that I have since arriving here. My mind has been in the gutter, and my vibrator has been getting a strenuous workout.

A girl has gotta be resourceful in the face of such trying times.

Thank god we've had a couple of days going about our own business since the man trapped me in his truck and chauffeured me around the ranch. All while damn near drowning me alive in the masculine, woodsy scent of him. He's got this highly intoxicating hint of leather thing going on, too, that I did *not* anticipate finding so appealing.

Beau Heartford smells like hard-working cowboy, and horses, and I'm not at all equipped to handle being in close quarters with him while he grunts at me monosyllabically and fidgets with the brim of his cap. It's endearing, damn him.

I've already caved and searched online for leather-scented candles for when I leave here, because there's every chance I'm going to be worryingly addicted to how good this place and the cowboy who owns it smells.

Now that we've established the finer details I need to know for the work I'll be doing—like how the business is going to operate, what the grand plans are for the coming twelve months—and I've been given the cowboy equivalent of 'show and tell,' I've had a few days with only my laptop for company.

My ovaries might be protesting at the lack of hottie mustache to fawn over, but it's a welcome and necessary detox. Being around Beau is far too much of a temptation, luring me to ignore all the reasons for simply window shopping. Certainly not indulging in any illicit thoughts of *touching*.

Goddamn, do I want to run my nails up that man's back and hear the kind of purr he might let out.

All of that thigh-clenching distraction is exactly why I'm currently strolling through the vacant main street of Crimson Ridge. I'm being an extremely good girl by putting some added distance between us. My rules of looking-only are being put into practice, as I exercise heroic restraint and leave the ranch for a few hours. A wonderful plan I came up with to distract myself by poking my nose into a few of the quaint local businesses, and generally settling into the vibe here in this picture-perfect mountain town.

Consider it a day spent compiling a little market research for my clients and refreshing my memory on what the sleepy row of heritage shop fronts have to offer. I've also been a dutiful daughter and checked in with my mom, confirming I am indeed alive and thriving, which should keep her off my back for a while. Instead of needing to find words to put to my strange circumstances, and dancing around the illicit crush I really need to figure out how to shake, I've been sending her photos of the main street.

Between the woodwork and hanging flower baskets, framed by lush trees casting dappled green sunlight beneath their branches, everything looks to be plucked straight off a movie set. I can't help feeling like there's every chance I'll bump into a grumpy guy, dressed in flannel, slinging coffee and sarcasm at the one and only café in this town.

As I wander into the solitary clothing store, with walls racked and stacked ceiling-high with everything a cowboy could require —including boots, hats, shiny buckles, and a cut of jeans to flatter every derriere—my thoughts are still hovering around the first interaction I had with *him* on the footpath only a few feet from this very spot.

If there's one thing I excel in, it's picking up on the tiniest details of a person. My gut never steers me wrong. I've always been guaranteed to walk into any room and, without a word needing to be uttered, read the play.

My very married boss definitely flirted with me the day we first met, that much I *know* to be true.

And what about it, Sage Maloney? Who cares if he did? What does it matter that he hasn't mentioned his dearly beloved, other than when I asked him directly about her?

Ultimately, I cannot feel any kind of way about Beau Heartford, because no matter if he's attractive or not, why the hell would I want to go near a man with a ring on his finger? I've never felt drawn to a taken man or woman before. It's absolutely not my style. And besides all that, I'm determined to remain single until the moment the *perfect* person comes along for me.

I've got to sweep these cobwebs from my brain and evict the slut who has set up camp inside my skull. She is Trouble with a capital T, likely to cost me this job and future client prospects the way she's carrying on. The version of me who desperately wants to pry into his personal life, and dig around in the baggage that I'm beginning to suspect comes along with the Mrs. attached to his vows.

Which is an absolutely and resolutely terrible idea.

Would there be a worse way to launch your dream consultancy business than to chase after the man paying your wages, while ignoring the wedding band on his finger?

My all too perceptive brain insists on jumping up and down to make sure I remember he seems to only wear it when out in public.

Internally, I eye-roll my own damn self. The guy runs a whole dang ranch, Sage Maloney, get a grip, would you? It's probably a health and safety thing. Not wearing a ring is sensible *rancher* type of thinking, he most likely doesn't wear it around fencing or tools or machinery it could catch on.

Don't go trying to paint a picture where there's no canvas to begin with.

Behind me, a throat clears.

"That one looks like it has your name all over it, ma'am." A gentleman sporting a head of silver hair, and an equally striking polished metal belt buckle, comes over to where I'm standing.

Apparently, it's the perfect timing to interrupt my roaming thoughts. I blink and look down to discover that I am, in fact, clutching a black cowboy hat with a pale leather band around the middle, absentmindedly stroking the felt rim.

"Kinda seems that way, doesn't it?"

"Gonna try it on? Let us get a good look at you?" He points toward the mirror set up by the dressing room for just the kind of peacock preening that is a necessity when choosing the perfect hat.

Setting it on my head, I hear him give a low whistle, and obligingly strike a pose. His gruff chuckle is kinda endearing, definitely not too in my face, just a guy who is in the trade of helping customers walk out that door feeling like a million bucks. He's already cast a spell on me because there's no chance I'm leaving without this particular addition to my wardrobe.

"I think I have to agree with you, cowboy." I flash him a smile, and he gives me a friendly wink in return while re-folding a pair of wranglers.

"A lady with great taste. Nothing quite like the feeling when a hat finds its new home."

"I'd say this one has already laid claim. No going back now, huh?" I brush my fingers over the brim and hear a deep hum in agreement. Looks like I'm already one step closer to being a true Crimson Ridge local. At least for the summer, anyway.

Who needs a cowboy to toss their hat on my head... when I can have my own?

Paging my mountain goddess.

I have an important message for a Layla Birch.

Could she please take a half-time break from riding her cowboy dreamboat to kingdom come and remember to message her best friend back?

LAYLA STARTS TYPING her response immediately.

I'll have you know I've worked my ass off all day. If it just so happens my reward is multiple orgasms. I'd expect you to be the first to congratulate me on a job well done.

Bitch, you don't have to lift a pinky finger, and you'd still be treated to a banquet of toe-curling O's.

True. I'm not sorry either.

How are you settling in?

I can't believe you're here in my town, and I still haven't had a chance to see you.

Sigh. Criminal really, isn't it?

I'm currently designing a website to have prospective guests drooling and creaming their pants on sight.

Is that what you list in your portfolio as one of your package offerings?

"Graphic design so fabulous, it'll make your customers jizz everywhere."

Catchy, huh? I'm thinking of trademarking it.

We talk shit for a while longer, before Layla calls it quits on me for the night.

It's late. Make sure you actually sleep, or you might achieve your final nocturnal gremlin form.

Pop some magnesium and turn that laptop off. I know you won't be able to resist being hunched over your keyboard in the dark.

Also, this is your friendly reminder to eat a meal.

Proper dinner, too. Not snacking while working.

Yes, mom.

Hey... aren't I supposed to be the irrepressibly bossy one?

Always, my Sergeant.

You're still coming for the bonfire on the weekend, right? I will confiscate your devices and drag your ass up here by force if I have to.

Wouldn't miss it. You know I desperately need to squeeze you and steal you away from your cowboy for some girl time.

Bring an overnight bag. You and Beau can drive up together, and I'll drop you back after we've had a chance to work on those ideas for the Devil's Peak branding.

Completely obsessed with that color scheme you sent over, by the way.

Knew you would be. My gifts are rare and coveted across all the realms.

As rare as your humility.

Love you, can't wait to see you.

Bye, bitch.

Go get that D.

Layla leaves me with a middle finger emoji. To which I add a rapid-fire flurry of eggplants and water splashes. Girlfriend can deny it all she likes, but I know those two are busy *getting busy* at every possible opportunity.

One thing I do have to reluctantly admit—as I un-pretzel myself from the contorted position I've sat in for far too many hours back to back—is that I'm in need of something to eat.

With a lengthy stretch and a pause to triple-check all my work has been backed up, I patter my way into the enormous stainless-steel-clad kitchen. It's like an episode of MasterChef vomited in here. All the appliances are sparklingly new, oversized, positively commercial in scale.

This is no homely ranch kitchen. It's a rocket ship, ready to launch and set course for Mars on autopilot.

I'm no slouch in the cooking department. I'm just not a fan. There are a million things I'd prefer to spend my time doing. However, I was practically still in nappies when Mom had me perched beside her on a chair, cubing vegetables and learning to cook perfectly fluffy rice. Blowing out a breath, I survey the expanse of high-end whiteware and pristine surfaces, assessing the best course of conquest.

Thoughts of Mom bring on a sudden wave of gnawing desire for home-cooked comfort food. I'm lucky to be super close with my family; not everyone is so fortunate. Especially with my mom being so young when she had me, we've felt like sisters at times more so than a parent-child dynamic.

For a while there, before my dad came along and delivered the sort of fairytale marriage and love my mother deserves, it was just the two of us against the world. That's why the biggest piece of my heart will always be reserved for the strongest and most inspiring woman I know.

Even if it does leave me feeling like I'll never live up to the example she set me at times.

Before I know it, I've piled ingredients on the enormous kitchen island, with my favorite masala firmly in my sights. It's an easy chicken and potato-filled dish which requires minimal effort on my part.

Until now, I've mostly only slunk in to throw together a quick plate of something here and there, painfully aware of Beau's presence and trying to stay out of his way. Though, the man certainly lives up to his sister's description of what to expect.

He truly does seem to spend every daylight hour outside, appearing like a fleeting mirage on the odd occasion I've heard him come in while I've been working.

Or, more accurately, I've noticed him out of the corner of my eye while keeping my noise-canceling headphones firmly affixed to my head. Somehow, it feels easier to be here in his house, occupying half his dining table, if I'm squirreled away in a bubble of my own making.

I chop and prep and let myself get lost in the familiar rhythm of cooking. Living on your own certainly leaves a girl equipped to step up to the plate in the kitchen as and when required. I'll begrudgingly whip something together, but take out, leftovers, and snacks are my best friends the majority of the time. I'm pretty sure I can't be the only one-woman empire out there who wants nothing more than to get lost in following after the whims and desires of her creative muse, in preference to flapping around in the kitchen.

Don't even get me started on baking. That is something I avoid, like the plague. At least with cooking, you can pinch and dash and eyeball ingredients, somewhat making it up as you go. Baking is a dark art, the kind of sorceress-given gift I do not possess a single ounce of.

The stove top is gas-powered, forceful, and sleek, filling one wall. In the blink of an eye, my diced onion and garlic are sizzling, an aromatic cloud filling my nose as they start to brown. Turning to grab my chopping board piled with roughly cut vegetables, I lean over, and searing pain shoots up my forearm.

Fuck. *Fuck.*

The metal handle is a red-hot poker, a horseshoe plucked straight from the fire pit, a lump of glowing coal. The exposed skin of my arm feels like it's aflame, and I can't help the violent yell that bursts out of me.

The board clatters to the ground, scattering cubes of potato and carrot like confetti. The speed at which I whip my scalded arm back tosses the pan and its sizzling contents everywhere, showering all surfaces in a spray of searing oil while boiling hot metal crashes to the ground.

I cradle the burn against my front like a dove with a tattered wing. Just as I'm trying not to scream with agony at the same time as fumbling to turn the gas off, I feel the rush of a figure appearing at my side.

"What the hell?" Beau barks.

A strong, tanned arm dives across my blurry, pain-smeared vision, cutting the flames.

As I blink away the tears building at the corners of my eyes with how much this fucking hurts, I notice the man towering over me with a furrowed brow has cheeks and a jawline covered in shaving foam. In his free hand, he clutches an electric shaver, and it's too weird of a combination for my screeching brain to take in.

His blue-gray eyes flare as he takes in the sight of me set against the backdrop of the absolute dumpster fire I've turned his kitchen into.

He looks furious with me.

To top it all off, he's half naked.

CHAPTER 10

Beau

"Ok, Heartford. Now's the time."

I pick up the shaver and stare at my reflection bathed under the glow of lights above my bathroom mirror.

My brows scrunch as I look at myself, caught in the middle of whatever this is. Some kind of spontaneous decision to make a change. It's about time I got rid of this mustache once and for all.

Fuck it. The only reason I grew the damn thing in the first place was to rebel against the media image that 'little miss perfect' curated. Mandy constantly tried to control every facet of my life. At first, I grew it to annoy the shit out of her, and lucky for me, it worked better than I could have ever anticipated.

She could never fucking stand it.

Having a mustache became my own mini rebellion. A prominent middle finger to the primping and preening and forever obsession she had of going through life without a hair out of place. If there's one thing I learned immediately after saying *I do* to Mandy Spires, it's that she had a determination to manipulate every aspect of our lives to fit an aesthetic for her brand.

Career, fame, and stardom first. Human decency a distant, and neglected, second.

Little did I know, the woman I walked down the aisle with was going to transform the minute she secured her happily ever after narrative. It was as if I'd been plucked straight out of a cowboy catalog the woman had perused and chosen. A marriage prospect curated, secured, and locked in as part of her *ten steps to stardom* manifesto.

The sucker I was, that I fell for her ploy, hook, line, and sinker.

I'll give her credit. The woman can perform a role to perfection, and she managed to play all the chords of my heartstrings and weaknesses like a goddamn concerto. Besides my rodeo career and competing being my only focus, I was fucking lonely. Being on the road all the time? Watching everyone around me seem to have found their person? Yeah, I yearned to belong, to feel like I was important to at least *someone*, in a way I'd never had after my parent's marriage blew up.

I'd wanted something deep—being a foolish fucking asshole, who at that time still believed in shit like soulmates—and it was as if I had a homing beacon floating over my head.

Sucker available for a far-too-spontaneous wedding, right here.

She convinced me to go all in so rapidly. Like I had been struck down with a fever and walked around in a daze until the moment the affliction lifted. My head spins if I give those memories too much attention nowadays. Fucking hell, just thinking about the way I jumped in, boots and all, eager as fuck to say yes, leaves me queasy. All because I thought the woman I'd been dating, for way too brief of a moment in time, was *the one*.

Tessa did her best. I see that now. My sister wasn't able to make me see things from a different perspective. Certainly not while I was riding the cresting wave of rodeo success and growing fame in the arena. Back then, I was caught up in all the glittering trappings that came with every damn thing I touched turning to gold.

It was too easy to get sucked into the whirlwind, to forget myself, only to fall off the ride and hit my knees with a sickening thud when I met the real Mandy.

The woman who would do anything to climb charts, to scale her own personal mountain of record deals, while stepping on as many necks as necessary—not to mention bouncing on as many dicks as possible—in order to get there.

Well, since I'm nearly at the end, rapidly approaching the final buzzer to signal this torrid ride is finally over, I'm planning on moving forward with my life. I guess part of that means I gotta get rid of this thing occupying real estate on my upper lip. Ironically, the iconic version of *Beau Heartford* that has kept me company throughout the duration of my marriage.

I weigh the razor in my hand and take in my reflection, with shaving foam on my jawline and the line of dark hair I've trimmed and shaped and kept in place for so long sitting right there. Yet, I hover. Almost, but not quite ready to actually do the deed, to go through with it and erase that part of my identity. It feels so fucking strange to consider getting rid of that guy staring back at me in the mirror once and for all.

We've been through a lot, he and I.

Look to the future, right? That's what Tessa keeps reminding me. A new look, a fresh start. It'll help to distance myself from the *old* Beau Heartford if I'm not as readily recognized anymore.

Though it's gonna be fucking weird to be a smooth-lipped, fresh-faced cowboy. Jesus, I don't even think I know how to be that guy. Maybe it'll be good business for the ranch to have a more clean-cut image.

I click the shaver on and the electric blades buzz softly, reverberations bouncing off the tile and glass in the enclosed space.

Just as I lean forward, pressing the skin to stretch taut above my upper lip with my free hand, I hear a crash. A yelp rocks the house. Smashing noises follow and a pained cry comes from the direction of the kitchen.

Racing out of the bathroom, I skid to a halt in the doorway, taking in the sight of Sage clutching her forearm. She's gone ashen, with eyes round like saucers. My gaze drops down, taking in the sight of sizzling oil splattered everywhere, along with whatever she'd been trying to cook.

Christ. Did she cut herself? Burn herself?

"What the hell?" I'm trying to assess if she's hurt bad enough that we need to get out of here and start speeding to get to the nearest emergency doctor when I see the strip of red-raw skin on the underside of the arm that she's favoring.

"What happened?" I herd her toward the large, double-wide sink, gently encouraging her to step away from the mess that I'll clean up later.

"My arm. Flames. Pan." Sage is usually a woman with all the sharp quips loaded into her arsenal, but right now, they're failing her. Under the force of pain that must be coursing everywhere, she's bereft of words, and her face tightens.

"It'll be ok. Sit." I chuck the shaver onto the benchtop, then reach for her waist. Tough shit if she wants to protest or fight me, or whatever challenge it is that Sage Maloney seems to live for throwing my way whenever we're around each other. I hoist her ass onto the counter and immediately guide her burned forearm beneath a stream of cool running water.

"Ahh. *Shitcuntfuckowww*." Those pretty features scrunch into a tight ball, and she hisses through clenched teeth. "Knew I should have stuck to takeout or... or..." Her words falter and die with the effort of continuing that thought.

It's something seeing her disarmed like this. I'm worried about her, of course, but I also find myself noticing just how much I've grown to enjoy her sharp sense of humor.

How much I have, in fact, missed having her close these past few days. When I know I absolutely cannot think that way, at all.

"Keep your arm there." I dip a finger beneath the faucet, checking it is, in fact, the right temperature, and then set about fetching the medical supplies I've got on hand.

"Anticipating a retirement dabbling in amateur surgery, were you?" Sage eyes me warily as I lift the hard-shell case from the cupboard where it's stored.

"I'll bet you'll be real happy I've got this beast of a kit when I tend to that burn." Quickly setting a timer on my phone, I fish out everything I'll need. "Give it fifteen minutes, then we'll see what the damage is." My chin dips in the direction of the water sluicing over her burned skin.

"Ok." She slumps back against the wall and lets her eyelids fall shut as the sound of the faucet fills the night.

"What were you cooking?" I want to keep her talking, to make sure she's ok.

"Doesn't matter." Sage scrunches her nose. It's cute, she's cute, and my eyes keep drifting back to her face, eating up the opportunity to take in her features this closely. In the way I've been so tempted to since that first day, and yet, of course, I haven't been able to.

"You know, you've got a little something..." Sage's dark lashes rest against her cheeks; she's not looking at me but uses her free hand to dab delicately at the corner of her lips. A mouth I should absolutely not be looking at while standing as close as I am to this girl.

"Do I?" Feigning ignorance, I monitor the timer, checking how long she's kept her arm under running water for.

She laughs, a full-bodied, decadent sound that comes from deep in her stomach, and something damn well expands in my chest that she's genuinely laughing. It doesn't feel fake.

Of course, I didn't even think or pause before rushing out upon hearing her in pain. As I stand here, bare-chested, with shaving foam smeared over half my face and a pressing need to deal with my upper lip, I can only imagine what a sight I must be.

"Why do you have clippers? Were you in the middle of a hot date with your undercarriage doing some manscaping down below? I guess it's fortunate for my eyes you didn't race out here with your balls half-shaved and scandalize the neighborhood."

Hearing her wit pop back to the surface leaves me wrestling to hold back a grin.

"Here." I nudge her hand to take a couple of painkillers. Those dark, honeyed eyes pop open, struggling to focus on me a little hazily at first. Once she tosses them in her mouth, I follow that by offering up a glass of water to wash them down with. You know, in an effort to be useful, and not simply linger like a creep staring at her from such close quarters.

"Thanks," she murmurs. "Sorry if I interrupted your little pampering session. Not that I know much about what cowboys usually do as part of a nightly self-care routine. What do you use? An exfoliating scrub? Some retinol cream? Have a ten-step secret to achieve a dewy look and minimized pores you'd like to share with the class?"

Touching my tongue to my teeth, I look over her arm, all while feeling her curious eyes on me. "Think that should be almost long enough under the water. Just a few more minutes should do it. How does it feel?"

"Like I want to hex that pan, put a generational curse upon that stove, and never attempt to cook again in my life."

"The arm, Sage." I shake my head.

She winces. "Very ouchy."

"Any better after being under the water?"

"Yes." She pauses. "Thank you, by the way."

"No need to thank me. It's part of the job."

"Boss, part-time fighter-jet pilot, and medic." She lets out a low whistle. "A man of many hidden talents, you are indeed."

The back of my neck prickles, feeling the compliment Sage just gave me, burrowing beneath my skin. Goddamn, what is it about this girl that makes me feel so drawn to her spark and flare that is so uniquely *her*.

I shrug. "Rodeo teaches you a lot of things... you get used to dealing with all sorts of shit. Figuring it out and handling whatever comes your way on the fly, you know." It's nothing, really. This is part of the life I've always lived, having to deal with injuries and know how to take care of what you can, and turn up at the emergency room at other times.

"So... the clippers?" She presses me again, inquisitive eyes following my every move.

My throat bobs as I rummage through the medical kit for burn salve I'm pretty sure I stocked up on.

"Nothing as interesting as *manscaping*." I raise one eyebrow at her. "Just decided it was time for a change, that's all."

"A change?" Her brow scrunches.

"Yeah. You know... get rid of the mustache you enjoy giving me such hell for. Figured I might as well ditch it. That way, I can have a summer in peace, without the non-stop 'stache jokes."

Sage gasps, and her words blurt out. "Don't you dare shave it off."

She blinks at me rapidly, then buries her face in the glass of water I'd handed over only moments before.

CHAPTER 11

Sage

My cheeks are ablaze, and my arm feels like it has been plunged into hellfire.

Beau gives me a bemused look following my outburst, before leaning over the sink, scooping some water to splash over his face, right here, using the stream of water still running over my arm. He's so close to the place where he set me on the counter, the denim of his jeans scratches my knee, where his hip brushes up against me.

As I try to recover my composure after almost revealing just how enormous my crush is—on both him and his mustache—I'm forced to endure the up-close masterpiece of water droplets clinging to Beau's damp skin as he uses a hand towel to get rid of the last remnants of shaving foam.

While I might be in a world of pain, at least he's an incredibly gorgeous sight to soak up, strutting around half-naked, playing nursemaid. If only all pain relief came in the form of such a soothing balm.

"You—You're not going to finish what you were doing—" I swallow thickly, words feeling lumpy on my tongue. His blue-gray eyes pierce mine from over the top of the towel he scrubs along his stupid, perfect cheekbones.

Goddamn him, I swear there's a faint quirk dancing on the corner of his lips, but the man keeps me guessing as to what might be running through his mind.

"Nah. I'll fix you some dinner."

"Oh." My eyes sweep the chaos I've unleashed all over his fancy new kitchen. "You really, really don't have to, boss. Let me slap some salve on this burn, and then I'll clear up this crap shoot."

"Sage." With one single word, his voice is more commanding than I think I've heard him be with me before. At the sound of my name, uttered in a gravely tone, all my previous attempts at ignoring the way my body seems to come alive in his presence dissolve as fast as spring snow. Yet again, I'm struck by the way Beau is the epitome of calm on the surface, yet there's a vast undercurrent I can detect lurking within him. This man has the depth of an ocean trench, and charisma that simmers within his veins, if only he'd allow that side of him out to play every now and then.

It makes me wonder what might have been the reason for his hardened, cool exterior to become so firmly fixed in place.

"I've trashed your kitchen like a fox let loose in a henhouse, and now disrupted your night of preening and primping." I shift my weight, preparing to hop down off the counter. "God, look at the state of your pretty new cabinets. I feel awful." Looking on in horror, I see the true extent of my destruction. Oil, grease, little lumps of soggy onion. Roughly chopped cubes of vegetables litter the floor as far as the eye can see. It's like garden gnomes went to war in here, and all that is left behind is culinary debris scattered across the battlefield.

"This is a working kitchen. Do you think I had it refitted to be a show home? No. It's meant to get scuffed up, and now you've given it a true baptism."

My grimace is accompanied by a throaty noise. "Let me just fling holy oil with a side of fried garlic around. What a delightful house guest."

"Run that arm under more water." He instructs and, oh so very efficiently, starts to tidy up. Unfortunately, the display of bunching and flexing abs gets hidden away when he emerges from the laundry with cleaning products and alas, has apparently sourced a t-shirt while in there. Though I'm still given the gift of his ass in wranglers, so a girl can at least have her mind taken off the white-hot, blazing track running from wrist to elbow.

"How's the level of *ouchy* now?" He eventually straightens up and disposes of the used paper towels. Dirty cloths and cleaning products get tossed in the bucket he carried in.

Damn. I like this unguarded, at-ease side of Beau too much for my own good. No wonder he got snapped up by his wife. Imagine coming home to someone who will take care of you and not think twice about taking the reins when needed.

"Still up there... but I think those painkillers will be doing something soon." Yeah, doing something for me, just like the sight of dark, scruffy curls, facial hair, and serene blue eyes.

"Do you think you can manage rubbing some of that on yourself?" He picks up a burn salve and then hovers in front of me. "Or, do you need help?"

My throat tightens, the way his voice just dipped into a slightly lower register feels far too much of a temptation. It calls to me, luring me into saying yes in an effort to know what his touch might be like against my bare skin. Allowing Beau Heartford to put his hands on me is absolutely, most definitely a terrible idea.

"I'll manage." Reaching out, I pluck the tube from his hold.

"Good." He coughs into his fist. "Tell me what to do, what you were cooking, and I'll make it for you."

As I slather on the cool, soothing balm, I gape at him. "No. Seriously. Just... I dunno... hit me with a carrot and some dip or something to nibble on while I retreat into my cocoon of shame. I'll be fine."

"Nope, sorry, that's outta the question. Proper food. Them's the rules."

He sets to work without hesitation, chopping onions and garlic, a replica of what I had prepared before, then points the tip of the knife between the coconut milk and untouched raw chicken I'd diced before my disastrous turn of events.

All the while, I'm rendered speechless. Alert. Abort. This is absolutely not my usual mode of operation.

"Alright, Miss Maloney." He taps the point of the blade against the board. "Tell me what you need me to do, chef."

"I SWEAR TO GOD, this is better than I would have ever been able to make. You're a really good cook." Resisting the urge to give this man big ol' moon eyes takes intense effort as I clean my bowl and leave hardly a stray speck of sauce behind.

Beau Heartford just whipped up dinner, like it was absolutely nothing, and then chose to sit with me at the kitchen island so we could eat together. Admittedly, that part has been largely in silence, not because our first meal together is awkward, but because I've been inhaling each mouthful with a feverish appetite.

"Don't mention it. Tastes like there are family secrets hidden in that recipe." He pushes back in his chair and lazily runs fingers through his locks, tousling them into an even more unruly display of sexiness.

"My grandma taught my mom, who then taught me. The recipe was adapted from her home in India to London living when she settled there. Then, we gave it the American spin once we moved out here. But the core ingredients always stay the same."

"Were you close with your grandmother?" Beau leans one arm on the back of the chair beside him. I'm caught a little unprepared for him to want to linger and chat like this, but it's kind of nice after so many nights working on my laptop, with only my focus-playlist and headphones for company.

"Sadly, I never knew her. I'm not sure whether I would have given her gray hairs prematurely or whether she would have found my wild-child ways endearing. I think my parents have mixed opinions on the matter, depending on the day."

"I'd say she would have been extremely proud of you."

The way his eyes crease ever so slightly as he says those words leaves me a little breathless. It's hard to focus on not getting swept up in this man, especially when it's so convenient to forget certain facets of his life—namely his marital status—beyond this ranch exists.

"Maybe," I murmur. Not wanting to dwell on things like families and broken homes and stories long left where they belong. In the past.

"Your folks moved out here when you were young?"

"Mom met my dad—he's been my father since I was five—at the company they both worked for in the UK. They were both recruited by their firm to move out to Silicon Valley, so we upped and shifted to sun and heat. My mom fell in love with the lifestyle, so I guess that's why we stayed. By the time I was in grade school, the twins came along. Sometimes, I think my parents don't know whether to laugh or cry that they've got three entirely Americanized daughters, but here we are."

"Not a lot of open plains to roam down there," he says. "What lured you to the middle of nowhere?"

"That's where my bestie Layla comes in. She's been responsible for my love affair with this part of the country... and my riding education."

"Had some lessons, have you?"

Is he making this flirty? It definitely feels like it. With the lateness of the hour, and the warmth of a delicious meal sitting in my belly, I can't figure out if Beau is allowing a side of him to peek out once more, the one that feels extremely fucking tempting to dance with, or if I'm imagining things.

"A few. Nothing like what I'm sure a few cowboys, or cowgirls, might be able to show me this summer while I'm here."

I swear to all things holy, Beau's mind looks like it has just stalled on the spot. The track scratches behind his eyes, and he scrubs a palm over his mouth.

"For the record, I'm a big fan of *both* methods of riding lessons." I prop one hand beneath my chin and watch on with amusement, waiting for his brain to come back online.

God, he's adorable when flustered.

Christ, I really, *really* need to stop thinking about him as anything other than my boss. Or maybe a friend? But that's all. This is dangerous, us sitting here surrounded by dim lighting, while I'm intentionally bringing us into territory that might potentially cross a line if I'm not careful. Because if there is one thing I'm not going to do, it's openly play temptress with a married man.

I fear, however, that I might be entirely too slow to locate my moral compass where this cowboy is concerned.

Sage. For god's sake. Get your crap together. Ask him about his wife. You really would be the biggest piece of shit if you didn't at least make a feeble attempt to steer the conversation back onto a safe course. One where the focus remains on his marriage—the fact that he's locked down—and you're respecting that.

So, I swallow down the inherent distaste of that idea, and dive headfirst into waters I really wish didn't exist, and I have precisely zero interest in navigating.

"Will Mandy be home from her tour soon?" I ask lightly. My eyes dart to his jaw, then back down to my empty bowl, and I chew on my bottom lip. Am I smiling... politely? The way my face loves nothing more than to betray me at every turn is a constant challenge, always showcasing my true feelings plastered there like a billboard.

"Unlikely," Beau mutters, as he heaves himself off his stool. At first I think it's with the intention of escaping the conversation, the room, my very presence, but then he returns with two beers. One is offered my way, but I shake my head.

"I'll take something a little stronger if you have it," I add.

He disappears into a cupboard, before sticking out a long arm to poke around the corner, wiggling a bottle of whiskey. I make a small noise of agreement.

It's all I can muster. The reason I am, yet again, devoid of words, is that his arm beneath the sleeve of that soft cotton t-shirt comes complete with a corded map of muscles. A display that goddamn, my eyes can't help but trace the length of. Heat glows high on my cheekbones as I immediately notice the equally prominent veins on the back of his firm hand, wrapped around the bottle in a way I'd really enjoy having done to me... only around my throat instead.

My thighs squeeze, and I'm tempted to whack my burn against the wooden surface just to get my rampant horniness back under control.

Beau pours me two fingers, then slides the glass over.

"I guess that'll help with the pain a little, too." His brows knit together while contemplating my arm. "I'm sorry you got hurt so easily. I feel guilty as all hell."

"Don't be. It's not your fault, although this kitchen might require a PhD prior to usage."

He sighs heavily, stabbing thick fingers into his hair. "If that starts getting worse tomorrow, make sure to tell me. I'll take you straight to see a doctor, alright?"

"Ok... Thanks." A hasty gulp of my whiskey is my only recourse in the face of a fluttering pussy. Who would have known I'm a slut for a cowboy with that protective tone to his voice. Surely, I can find myself a replica, a Beau-doppelganger, hiding out somewhere amongst these mountains.

"Back to Mandy..." Setting my glass down, I simply will myself to persist with this conversation, ignoring every protest and complaint swirling through my blood. "She's not going to be back for a while?"

Beau studies his beer with a sudden dullness behind his eyes before puffing out his cheeks. "We're on track for a divorce."

There's a carnival, a multi-color fiesta complete with fireworks, trumpets, and confetti rioting where my stomach should be. However, I cling to my composure on the outside. Only just.

"I'm sorry to hear that." No, I'm not. Fuck yes, bitch, this man isn't quite as off-limits as I believed him to be. Thank you, Universe. Hail every Goddess, and let me say my prayers at the altar of whatever anti-cupid's arrow grants couples their separations.

"It's been a long time coming. I guess, I just haven't really told many people... don't trust others very easily, ya know." His throat works as a sip of beer goes down. "In my world outside of Crimson Ridge, it was too easy for rumors and bullshit to spread like wildfire."

My heart is hammering inside my chest.

"Consider me a high-security vault." With one hand, I mime turning a key over my lips.

"Thanks." A muscle in the side of his jaw pulses.

"Full permission to tell me if I'm being nosey as fuck..."

"You wanna know why? What happened?"

I shrug and sip my drink. Enjoying how pleasurable the burn down the back of my throat feels, in comparison to the steady, dull thud of pain in my arm. "Only if you wanna say, otherwise, forget I asked."

"Beneath her facade, the country starlet, everything was airbrushed and faked to shit. Turns out I married an idea, and the person I hitched my wagon to wasn't who I thought she was. The jealousy and insecurity alone, never mind the other drama, well, it meant things were rotten from the outset."

"Did you give her any reason to be?"

"What?" He splutters.

"To be jealous?" I run my tongue over my bottom lip. "Everyone is so quick to blame *women* for being insecure or bitchy or whatever... but often it's the man who is flirting with other women in their DMs, or liking other girl's photos on social media. But of course, if you happen to have a vagina, you get labeled as being the problem."

He drags his fingers through his hair again. "Hell, no way. Of course not."

"Sure about that? Weren't busy being the rodeo star *Beau Heartford* enjoying attention from all the buckle bunnies sliding into your inbox at two a.m.?" One of my eyebrows lifts as I sip my whiskey.

The man across from me develops a fire in his eyes. Something smolders there, hot and powerful, in a way that captures me from across the expanse of table between us.

"Sage, I can tell you now... I don't even look at my phone half the time. Don't even touch the damn thing if I can help it, let alone reply to shit. Tessa has handled my social media pretty much since day one in my pro career, long before Mandy arrived on the scene. If anything, it was always the other way around. I was spending my nights lying in bed watching videos on stupid fucking stuff like aperture settings... and, well..."

"Little Miss Country Music wasn't?" I venture.

"*Little Miss Country Music* wasn't even in my bed. She was halfway around the country, or the world. Trust me, there were plenty of offers on the daily for her to be in someone else's sheets. Whether she took them up on that offer or not..." Beau lifts a shoulder, eyes fixed on his beer. "I was aware of enough, that ultimately gave me the reason to stop caring entirely, before long."

I swirl my whiskey, musing for a long pause over the words wanting to bubble up. The ones that I shouldn't say, but can't seem to shove back down.

"Life must have been lonely."

The air crackles as if charged with a high-voltage current. "The pro tour was like being part of a family." His voice is roughened, so tempting I can't think straight.

"Doesn't mean you can't still feel alone, even while being in a crowded arena."

Beau swigs back his beer, fixing me with those blue eyes the color of a fall sky.

"Do you get lonely being here, tucked away on this ranch?"

God, I should stop. However, he's not rushing to leave this conversation, nor is he answering. He watches me closely over the lip of his beer bottle, and my skin shimmers, hums, damn well transforms into a million pin-pricked sparks beneath the spotlight of his gaze.

"I find ways to manage." When he finally speaks, it's such a low, gruff admission... holy fuck, I have to beat back the intrusion of images in my mind's eye of what it might look like when Beau takes matters into his own hands.

"I'll clean up." The croak in my voice makes it come out almost as a whisper. There are so many things I want to say, want to speak life into, yet for the sake of my professional career, I bite them all off and swallow them hastily.

Getting to my feet, I gather up both our bowls and just as I finish sliding the dishwasher closed, Beau fills my periphery. His irrepressible heat and masculine scent coils around me and drifts into my lungs.

"Let me look at your arm." Those words are gruff. Laced with something far more dangerous and tempting than simply being alone in this kitchen together late at night. They're filled with a genuineness I'm ill-equipped to handle.

I'm so used to being independent. To being the girl who needs no man, or woman, to make me feel anything. I don't need anyone to help me, or hold me, and I certainly don't need them to make me feel *good*.

Yet, I'm counting my frantic, fluttering heartbeats as he lingers ever so close. He deposits his beer and phone onto the counter and proceeds to reach for my arm.

That's when it happens. That's when Beau Heartford insists on fucking with my already questionable self-control when it comes to this particular cowboy. His roughened fingertips clasp my wrist, and those ocean eyes flicker between my own and the site of my burn—yet I could almost forget that raw patch is there at all.

The only thing I'm capable of feeling is the way his hold is secure and warm. It's a delicious sensation against the sensitive inner curve of my wrist. He's got me trapped beneath a feather-light grip and ever so tenderly turns my hand inside his own in order to closely scrutinize the strip of burnt skin on the underside of my forearm.

With a solemness about him, Beau takes his time to look—to thoroughly and slowly observe—the site of my wound. My stomach has churned into a mess of flapping wings and sparkling hopefulness, considering the fact this *married* man isn't quite so married after all. The fact he's touching me and lingering so near it would take nothing at all for my other hand to slide up the front of his shirt, has my pulse thrumming. It would be so easy to allow my fingers to explore him, if the invitation was there to do so.

Beau doesn't speak, but his eyes appear hooded beneath dim overhead lights, and oh hell, he's so achingly sexy. That gaze I'm studying far too closely for my own health flicks to meet my own, and I find myself swallowing down the dryness in my throat.

Beneath his hold and his stare, I wet my lips, feeling every crackling molecule of air intensify as he zeros in on that movement. Beau follows the glide of my tongue, and his fingers press a fraction harder into my wrist bone, as if he's considering tugging me into him. His torso dips forward in that same moment, and the weight of him leans in closer. Oh, sweet Jesus, he's leaning into me...

The silence and thudding of my pulse in my ears is shredded.

A relentless buzzing startles us, coming from his phone lying face-up on the bench top, barely five inches away.

And as we spring apart, our attention jerks to the photo filling the screen at the same time. The name front and center, right there, lit up and droning for attention.

I see it immediately.

Blond hair, curled and styled to perfection.

A wedding band and sparkling diamond ring, paired with French-tipped nails, settled against his chest.

Beau's unmistakably broad shoulders wrapped around the woman who fills the screen.

His wife.

CHAPTER 12

Sage

If there was ever a way to successfully blast a cold-water hose on myself and douse the embers flaring between me and my *sort-of-unavailable-but-maybe-actually-is-single boss,* seeing Beau's wife appear on his phone screen certainly did so.

I booked myself a one-way ticket out of that clusterfuck. Pronto.

Whatever happened between Beau and I that night in the kitchen after burning myself, well, that spark was stomped out just as quickly as it dared to flicker in the darkness.

I'm busy.

He's busy.

And therefore, we have been remarkably skilled at keeping to ourselves and our respective corners of this ranch.

Besides, I truly am spinning a lot of plates, between the work I'm doing here, the proposal I've been putting together for The Loaded Hog, and my design work for Devil's Peak Ranch. There isn't much time for anything except shoving my headphones on and descending into my creative cave.

Summer adventures, care of Crimson Ridge, and a chance to finally let my hair down, will be long overdue by the time my boots land on the top of Devil's Peak for the bonfire they're hosting this weekend.

As for Beau? He's gone all day, and long into the evening, too, it would seem. After answering the call from his wife that night and stalking off into the darkness, the sight of his retreating shoulders was my last proper glimpse of the man. Since then, it might as well be only myself here on the property. Tessa checks in on me via email daily, so at least I'm able to ping back and forth with her. We collaborate virtually on ideas I've come up with and directions I'm going with their marketing.

It's fine. This is absolutely for the best.

My arm is all but healed, unlike the awful little affliction residing inside my chest.

This morning, even before the sun has dragged its ass above the mountaintop, hugging the horizon, the heat is stifling. Cicadas are thrumming, birds are chirping their shrill melodic tunes high amongst the trees, and it's far too fucking hot to go for a run. But I absolutely need to move my body before I resume my curled-shrimp position in front of my laptop for the remainder of the day.

I decide to wander over to the workout room at the main house in search of shade and a fan while getting my daily dose of endorphins. As per Tessa's instructions, I should really take an opportunity to explore this facet of the ranch accommodation as if I were one of their prospective guests. While head down, scrolling through my phone to find my go-to playlist, my hearing pricks and I slow to a pause only a few feet from the open entrance. A wild assortment of grunting noises come from within, and I scrunch my eyes, because I already know what I'm going to discover if I poke my head to take a glance inside.

It would undoubtedly be the worst idea to look.

I'd be an absolute fool to step closer to that doorway.

Yet, my feet carry me forward, and with a rapid-fire, bouncing gaze, I take in the sight that leaves my hormones all but audibly moaning.

Beau was obviously in the mood to work out this morning too, it would seem, and only one glance is required—only one sinful peek is necessary—to discover just how much time this man still dedicates to being an athlete close to his prime.

He has his back to the door, with headphones settled over his ears, and is mid-workout, pumping iron. He's lifting a pair of dumbbells in fly raises, hefting the weights with a rhythmic pulse out to the side, extending his arms from hip to shoulder height, and lowering down again in rapid succession, and oh my fucking god. The man's back is a glistening sheen, a cascade of defined muscles. Every indent and sculpted ripple from his shoulder blades down to the hint of the curve—that spot giving a glimpse and a tease—where his ass disappears below his low-slung waistband. Seeing him from this angle is mouthwatering in the extreme.

My greedy eyes bounce everywhere, gobbling up the sight of bulging biceps, flexing shoulder blades, those impressive goddamn lines of muscle running straight down his spine. Beau Heartford is every inch a specimen of cowboy who hasn't allowed his retirement to get in the way of intense training. He's in there showing off the sort of focus to make it seem as though he'd fling himself on the back of a bull and lunge back in the rodeo arena at the first invitation.

He looks cut, powerful as a weapon, and holy fuck, I am going to have to brave stepping outside to take myself for a long, long jog. Immediately. Backing up, I blow out an unsteady breath and rapidly make my exit. Screw the summer heat, I'll just have to handle that bitch. Being confined within the four walls of a workout room with him and all his glistening muscular pheromones would be an atrocious idea.

In my current state? I'd be a complete liability.

According to my period tracker, I'm going to be ovulating any minute, and in that case, I probably need to consider how to chain myself to a tree like a werewolf on a full moon.

Unfortunately, no matter how far I jogged earlier today, my footsteps have been unable to carry me beyond the reach of Beau's ever-present appeal.

A text arrives, interrupting my rhythm. I'd been lost in a long stretch of photo editing and gallery creation to showcase the ranch's cabin accommodation.

TESSA DIAZ:

Beau has a couple of guys coming to the ranch to help out with unloading a hay delivery. I won't volunteer you for the task, but it'll be the perfect opportunity to grab some photos and video content while they're hard at work.

You did mention you wanted some more images of the working side of the ranch, so I figured I would let you know in case you need to plan around other clients you've got scheduled in.

I know it's late in the day, but they thought the evening might be best. I heard it's been hot as all hell up there today.

The guys will be working for a couple of hours, I would say, so head over whenever suits you.

Oh, good.

Today, it would seem I've been cursed with an overabundance of Beau Heartford looking like a sweaty cowboy dream.

Squeezing my eyes closed, I tip my head back to the ceiling. Am I seriously being punished for misdemeanors in a previous life? Was I some kind of vicious homewrecker, who is being given a swift kick in the vagina as penance for coveting someone else's beloved?

I tap out a brief reply, letting Tessa know just how *thrilled* I am to venture outdoors in search of the sight of her brother and his glistening muscles hard at work. Then grumble to myself the entire way as I wander toward the barn, with a fairy floss-pink sky and wispy clouds scattered overhead. A truck and large flatbed trailer are immediately visible, parked up on the side closest to the arena for the horses.

Just as promised, when I reach the front of the vehicle, I'm greeted by the sight of not just Beau, but two other cowboys. All three are exactly what I need for promotional material for the ranch, complete with cowboy hats, jeans, and not a single shirt between them.

One, in particular, is entirely responsible for causing heat to pool low in my stomach.

"Sergeant." The familiar sight of Kayce Wilder's golden boy grin beams down at me from where he stands on the trailer in amongst hay bales. He drags the back of one hand over his brow.

"Does everyone feel the need to call me that? Layla really did a number on me in my absence, didn't she?"

"Absolutely. So, you came to your senses and decided Crimson Ridge was the best place to be, after all?" He grins.

His cheeky attitude receives a withering look from me in return.

The guy is my best friend's ex. Also, the son of the man who is *very much* the true love of Layla's life. Sure, it's complicated, but no one in their right mind could deny that Layla and Colton Wilder are a match made in cattle-ranch-heaven for each other.

"Here for the summer, to brighten all your lives as promised, Wilder." I prop my hands on my hips, trying my damndest not to glance over at the place where Beau occupies himself, hefting bales onto a growing stack along the side of the barn.

"Gonna hop up here and give us a hand, or have you come out to boss us around?" Kayce shoots me a toothy smile, all pearly whites set against his bronzed skin and cream color hat.

"Something much worse. I'm here to objectify you." I wave my phone in the air.

The other cowboy working on the flatbed doesn't stop what

he's doing, but chimes in with a smirk to his voice. "Make sure to crop out old man Heartford over there if it's marketing goods you're on the hunt for. No one needs to get an eyeful of his builder's crack and ugly fucking 'stache."

"Sage Maloney... you haven't had the pleasure of meeting Hayes here yet. Watch him. He's chaos."

As Kayce introduces me to the other cowboy who is currently putting on an ab show to die for, I swear I hear a gritty noise coming from the direction of the third man.

"Always a delight to meet a fellow menace. Are you mad enough to be a rodeo superstar, too?" My grin grows wide.

"Broncs for me, just like Wilder." He nods. "Pleasure to meet you, ma'am."

Oh, dear. Another charming cowboy to add to the catalog? What potion do they infuse the water with up here?

"You're working with my brother on the spit and polish of The Loaded Hog." *Chaos* Hayes observes as he straightens up and lifts his hat, ruffling strong fingers through his sandy brown hair. Sun-bleached strands that he shakes out where they hang long and wild around his ears, before fixing his hat back in place again. One glance and it's clear, this looks to be the type of creature capable of devouring his meal whole, with green eyes that sparkle in the setting sun.

Snapping my fingers in his direction, I shake my head and chuckle. "That's right, I forgot that everyone is related in these mountains."

He gives me a lopsided smile that I'm fairly certain has left a trail of broken hearts in its wake. "Folks might love to refer to us as the 'Chaos Twins' around these parts, but ignore my brother if he's a grouchy asshole when you catch up with him at the bar. Fuck face barely knows how to string more than two words together on a good day. He's the kind of destruction you don't hear coming."

"I'm sure I'll wrangle him just fine." With one hand, I shield my eyes against the golden ball currently dipping behind the bronzed ridgeline climbing into the sky. "Carry on boys. This will be a quick and painless procedure, I promise."

Kayce snorts, and fists the twine on the closest bale to his boots. "Sounds like Sergeant Maloney here is about to go for our nuts and make steers out of all of us."

"Only if you use your manners and ask me very politely." Batting my eyelashes, I continue taking photos of them bending and lifting and twisting, and it really is an impressive sight. Objectively, of course. I can appreciate a premium specimen of cowboy. Kayce and Hayes are rodeo bucks through and through, and well, then there's *Beau*.

Whereas the other two are extremely camera-friendly, a pair of golden boys with a playfulness to them, Beau is something else entirely. He's wild and rugged and alluring in his silence. Not to mention, has that stern, older, *let me show you a trick or two* thing going on that leaves my knees a little weak.

Damn, the quiet ones really do get you.

Through the camera lens on my phone, I see exactly how that muscled v disappears below the waistband of his jeans. The ridges along his stomach are even more prominent thanks to the dust and smears of dirt coating his skin, and he's once again coated with a sheen of sweat.

To make it worse, he's got a stone-gray cowboy hat on. When added to the whole package with that sexy-as-hell mustache, I'm fighting a battle not to sigh wistfully out loud.

Couldn't this man be unattached and *not* my boss?

On my phone screen, the video highlights all his best angles, and that ache I thought I'd managed to get rid of after the night in the kitchen rapidly and determinedly blooms back into life.

There is a situation between my thighs I can no longer ignore. I've been oh, so very good today, and this scene right before me is pure torture, the kind that I have no interest in continuing to edge myself with or hang around any longer.

"Great, that's perfect." I do a quick scan of the camera roll and make sure everything is saved where I need it, then prepare to make my hasty exit. "Thanks, guys. Nice to see you, Kayce. Good to meet you, Hayes, might see you at the Hog sometime."

"Old man gonna pay out royalties when our pretty faces are front and center, plastered all over your website?" Kayce teases Beau, who hasn't looked my way this entire time.

"Fuck off, Wilder. You'll probably drive away any prospective business." He heaves a bale and grunts through a firmly locked jaw.

"Hardly. Sarge here seems to think otherwise. Did you get my good side? All my best assets?" Kayce has a shit-eating grin on his face.

"Would do perfectly fine without you two fucking peacocks." Beau scowls.

Hayes simply shakes his head and keeps working, but I see his ghost of a smile.

"I'm sorry, but three rodeo stars with their eight packs out? I'll have this ranch fully booked, with a waitlist queued past state lines, quicker than you can flip your cap backward." I call over my shoulder and wave a peace sign in the air above my head. Yep, I definitely need to extract myself right away. "Wait 'til I make you all famous, boys."

Behind me, I hear their gruff banter carry on, but I don't dare stop. I'm on a direct course to reunite with my cabin, that beautiful outdoor tub, and my trusty bullet vibe.

It takes me next to no time to shed the tank and cut-offs I'm wearing, then slip into my yellow bikini that has seen me through many a summer adventure. Every inch of my skin prickles not just with the rolling heat shimmering off the ground as I exit the rear of my cabin, but with the intensity of my lingering obsession with the man I should not, and cannot for the sake of my job, keep looking at.

Yet, it's all I seem capable of doing.

On repeat, like a sailor intent on tumbling overboard following the allure of a siren calling to them from the deep, I'm drawn to Beau and his quiet intensity... it's a massive fucking problem.

Sweet relief coats my limbs as I slip into the cool, still water. The setting sun is putting on a pastel-painted sky above the blue haze of mountaintops, and the entire scene before me is reminiscent of a daydream. A moment I should, in all practicality, be documenting, recording... someway and somehow taking advantage of. Considering how stunning this vista stretching out before me is right this second, setting up my phone to create content with *marketing* in mind is where my attention should be.

However, I'm not doing any of that. Instead, I'm focused entirely on the slickness between my thighs. My brain is unable to concentrate, rendered a useless lump of gray matter by the swirling ache and throbbing sensation occupying my pussy.

Is this lust of the worst kind? A mortal affliction I've succumbed to? Here lies Sage Maloney—daughter, sister, friend. Cut down in her prime by a perfect mustache, low-slung jeans concealing all manner of cowboy virility, and an adonis belt coated in a dusting of dark hair.

As I dip my vibe beneath the water's surface, I can already feel the sigh of long-anticipated relief flutter through my veins. For someone who owns a wearable, and could easily have myself on edge all day long under the rippling command of the connected app on my phone, I am undeniably a mess. The irony being that all of *this* is the responsibility of my mind and my strange addiction. A longing I have developed for the man less than a hundred yards away hauling hay bales with ease.

Well, shit. One glance at how effortlessly he tossed them around, confirms he could very much manhandle a woman like me without so much as breaking a sweat. Curves and thick thighs and all.

Dragging the vibration over my nipples, I float and watch the sky, losing myself in this hidden moment. It's private back here, but not fully enclosed. There's a wide-open expanse of pasture and grazing land extending up into rolling hills, giving a picturesque scene for my much-needed interlude.

Already, I feel it curl up, wicked and insistent, from my toes.

The appeal of being like this, where anyone could see? It plays perfectly into my exhibitionist side, and I stifle a moan as the awareness lands of just how easy it would be for someone—one particular cowboy—to discover what I'm doing back here.

That pulsing heartbeat in my clit doubles down. Throbbing need builds and demands to be given the attention I've been denying myself until now.

I give in, plunging my hand beneath my bikini bottoms, seeking out my slickness. The evidence of my arousal is there, slippery and coating my swollen clit, ready to be toyed with immediately.

This isn't shameful. It isn't in any way embarrassing that I needed this escape. However, it is a profound and prominent reminder that I'm going to have to be even more careful. I'm far too easily swept up in this man's appeal, and that recognition glows hot and bright in my bloodstream as I work over my clit in small circles.

My body feels delicious, almost weightless, thanks to the water and the pretty scene, while rippling pleasure carves a heated path through every limb.

As I inch ever-closer to the point where the building wave will inevitably crash, I'm trying to imagine someone else in my dirty little fantasy this evening. That girl with the septum piercing that I hooked up with a couple of times over winter? The gamer boy with the gritty, hot voice I exchanged a few naughty videos with long-distance?

Unfortunately, none of them hold my attention for long. My pussy has fixated upon one much-coveted object of my affections and desires, and the second I allow him to sweep to the front of my awareness, those sparks shoot around my body like fireworks.

My body tenses, heat pooling low, my climax already furled up tight, ready to explode.

Oh, god.

That all-consuming wave approaches fast, demanding, and I swear there's a ringing in my ears. The thought that does me in, the final detail that pushes me over the edge, is an imaginary sound of boots scuffing across gravel. As my hand flutters beneath the sodden material of my bikini bottoms and my rock-hard nipples rub inside the thin material of my top, I hitch in a breath.

Dream-Beau appears. He leans one broad shoulder against the wooden exterior of my cabin, and simply *watches.*

He likes what he sees, with hooded eyes flitting over my damp skin, taking in the sight of where my arm disappears into the crystal-clear water.

The corner of his lip tips up, and he drags a thumb over his jaw as he silently urges me to keep going. A challenge to get myself off right here, in the open, all for him.

My mouth hangs open, and my eyes squeeze tight. It's too much, oh so good, yet oh so wrong. As I clench up and tumble over the edge, there's no suppressing it.

I have Beau Heartford on my lips, gasping his name as an offering to the pastel-colored night sky, and his blue-gray eyes affixed in my mind.

CHAPTER 13

Beau

"Devil's Peak Ranch sure looks like a hot piece of ass tonight."

The prettiest girl on the planet leaps out of my truck and rushes to smother her friends in hugs, raining kisses down on both of the girls over by the roaring bonfire. Layla and Briar squeal at the force that is undeniably *Sage*.

I've been to Colton Wilder's property a handful of times now since arriving in Crimson Ridge to settle full-time. It's a stunning place, and I can't help but feel like a weight has lifted every time I set foot up here. Perched all the way at the top of the mountain access road, there's nowhere else to go and only the endless horizon stretching out flanking Devil's Peak herself.

I swear the air in this place has something a little extra special to it.

"About time you dragged your sorry excuse for a mustache out this way, Heartford. Can't have you damaging those soft hands of yours pretending to be a rancher full-time these days."

Stôrmand goddamn-pain-in-my-ass Lane hits me with a wink and curious blue eyes before nodding in the direction of the cooler propping up his boots. "Help yourself."

"Wild one." I narrow my eyes on him, and the spot where his

palm rests on the hip of the sweet brunette standing at his side, talking animatedly with Sage and Layla. "Good to see you two are still keeping it in the family."

Storm shoots a scowl my way that makes me want to crack a smile a mile wide.

"I hope you're taking good care of my boy, Teddy, for me." Briar glances over her shoulder at me and clicks her tongue with a hint of a smile. "Also... I *heard* that."

"Well, good thing *Uncle Storm* here is providing the beers, since I'm still sporting a horse bite you could see from space, thanks to your boy."

"Fuck off." Storm grunts. Pouting at the fact I'm still determined to milk the ins and outs of their relationship for every point I damn well can. "You deserve whatever that horse sends your way." He points the neck of his beer bottle at me.

"Beau." I'm given Briar's chestnut eyes and a scolding look that morphs into a laugh. She's a sweet girl, and has done the impossible where Stôrmand Lane is concerned... taming the wildest creature of them all from our days on the rodeo circuit together. Of the two of them, Briar is also much more liable to join in with my jokes at Storm's expense, especially where their *unique* connection is concerned. While she might initially come across as a timid thing, his girl has a wickedly dry sense of humor hidden away.

"Thanks for bringing my girl home." Layla smiles widely, with her copper curls fluttering a little in the warm summer evening breeze as she side-hugs Sage, then keeps hold of her waist. "If it wasn't for the contract with your ranch, Beau, I don't know if I would have successfully dragged this one back to Montana any time soon."

Sage rolls her eyes. All this immediate chatter of the group is such a contrast to the silence consuming our drive up here when she was busy tapping away on her tablet the whole time and hardly looked my way. "Hey, you know I need to see your bosom and freckles on the regular. Besides, you can hardly talk, what with Mr. Wilder over here whisking you off around the world every five minutes." She circles a wrist in the general direction of the man who is every inch the epitome of this land and this place.

Something I guess I find admirable as fuck about Colton Wilder is the way he's dedicated a lifetime to living and working this land. Being up here, I can't help but feel like it's what I've been missing so far in my own life. Outside of bull riding and pro rodeo, what was I doing with myself? What legacy was I nurturing? Taking on the ranch has been an opportunity to settle my soul in many ways after a life on the road and a career in the spotlight.

"Good to have you back here, Sage." He shakes his head and gives her the *Colt* equivalent of a smile. Which is a barely-there thing, but you can see the affection he holds for someone who is deeply important to his girl, all the same.

A truck draws closer, accompanied by a bellow. "Alright, listen up, assholes. Time to earn your keep so that we can all fucking eat, and preferably do so sometime before midnight." A voice calls out. One of the Devil's Peak Ranch trucks pulls up, complete with a grill strapped on the back tray, and Kayce gives us his typical golden boy grin from his position behind the wheel.

I'm still undecided whether I've forgiven him for parading around half-naked in front of Sage the other day. I mean, ultimately, I think I'm screwed no matter what with that girl, because I could have brought in a team of cowgirls to work with me while unloading the hay, and there's every chance she might have found one of them nice to look at, too.

She's so confident in who she is. I think that might be one of the things I'm most obsessed with. Sage Maloney is a woman who might be young in years—certainly far too fucking young for me to be looking her way, at any rate—yet, is so self-assured, so immensely secure in herself. When I think back to being twenty-something, I was too preoccupied with being on a fast track to rodeo success. There was never a pause to breathe or stop for one single second to figure out who I might be beneath the sponsor's vest and chaps. I was caught up trying to be the embodiment of perfection anytime I hopped on the back of a bull, to the point I shoved aside anything that didn't correlate with being the dream candidate for rodeo stardom.

Too busy trying *not* to be my father.

Turns out I was incredibly fucking capable of being what others needed me to be while forgetting to find out who I was when the crowds went home, and arena lights turned off.

Not only that, but Sage understands herself. She owns her sexuality, wearing it like a luminary glow I find impossible to ignore, and that alone is unbelievably attractive.

Jesus. I'm just endlessly fucking churned up over her, and it's been a battle ever since that night in the kitchen to try and refrain from thinking about her pretty lips, her gorgeous eyes, and Christ, here I go again.

At least my freefall into all too many epically-bad-wrong thoughts about Sage—how dangerously close I got to losing my goddamn mind and crashing my mouth against hers, the night I held her wrist to look at her burn—is interrupted by Kayce hollering at me as he climbs out of the vehicle.

"C'mon, old man Beaumont. Get your sweet cheeks over here and gimme a hand."

Everyone is busy settling themselves into comfortable spots around the fire now that we've filled up on BBQ, and the sundown sky is filled with laughter and chatter.

Some of Kayce's rodeo buddies have arrived, a couple of guys and girls that he trains and travels with. It's funny, really, sitting here at the end of a glittering career, watching the damn shimmer in their eyes as they talk about events and tour stops and upcoming possibilities for the season.

A part of me feels the pull to join them and talk about the one thing that has nourished my lungs for so many years. Then again, I find myself equally as comfortable to sit here, drink my beer, and mind my business.

What do they care what I have to think or say? I'm out of the game now. It's a different arena for their generation of rodeo stars. They know who I am and where to find me if they wanna know shit I might be able to give advice on. Kayce sure as hell loves to pick my brain at every opportunity. I'll give the kid credit, he's managed to turn things around after it looked like he was determined to smash onto jagged rocks surrounded by an angry sea of shitty choices and sinking to the bottom of a bottle.

Glancing around the orange glow cast by firelight, there's one of the horse ranchers and his girl, Lucas and Skylar. Talking quietly alongside them are his son and boyfriend—Brad and Flinn, who also live and work at the property they all run together, Rhodes Ranch.

Scattered around are some groups of other locals, faces I recognize but haven't necessarily had much of a chance to get to know. Since I've spent ninety-nine percent of my time with my head down, avoiding the public, while focusing on getting my ranch ready for stock and horses and eventually having guests booking their accommodation, I haven't exactly had the time or inclination for socializing.

However, it would seem Sage doesn't even live in this town and somehow appears to know every single person joining us to gather around a fire to share a meal and spend an evening shooting the shit.

One thing I'm endlessly grateful for, as I sit with my back propped against a round hay bale and one knee bent to rest my elbow on, is that this crowd couldn't be less interested in *Beau Heartford*. Of course, I still catch the occasional knowing smile or double take when I shake hands, but these people are Colt and Storm's buddies, and by extension, they're fucking good at appreciating I would quite gladly be left in peace. I'll comfortably spend the entire night seated here, nursing a drink, listening to the conversation ebb and flow like a tide around me.

I'm not much for talking. I like to be on the fringes, watching on. It doesn't mean I don't have anything to say, I'm just usually content to simply *be*.

A life in the spotlight of the pro tour, the cameras, the interviews... I'm fucking done, and relieved as hell to leave all that in my dust without a glance back in the rear-view mirror.

Years slip by real fast when you're training and competing. Suddenly, I was staring down retirement and nearly a decade with a person who I didn't even know, a stranger I had to pretend to be happy spending my life with. It wasn't until I had the ranch secured that I knew I could finally push for a divorce and that next step to get the legal headache resolved.

We might have been tied to each other through paperwork for that long, but we've lived separate lives for most of that time. If I wasn't on the road, she was, and that's just the way I got used to doing things.

What did I have any business bitching about, when I was the idiot who got married in the first place? My job was to put up and shut up until I'd called time on my career. All I had to do beyond that was ride out the ensuing few years, getting my plans in order for the ranch. Figuring out what life might look like once we'd negotiated an end date and point when divorce papers would finally get signed.

Except, in the here and now, one thing that is impossible to ignore in this scenario is how *coupley* it is. Storm has Briar seated in his lap, and judging by the way his mouth is attached to her neck, he's probably been whispering filthy shit to her the entire time. The guy loves nothing more than to make his girl squirm, especially in public. I know more than I want to about the games those two like to play.

Colt has Layla tugged against his chest, settled on the ground together. Lucas and Skylar are much the same, with her pastel pink hair tucked beneath his heavy arm.

Being alone in a crowd like this doesn't concern me as much as it used to, doesn't gnaw at me like it did when I was young and foolish. Before I slapped a ring on my finger to try and fill that void. I've spent most of a marriage wishing desperately to *not* have to put on a show of pretend coupledom when I was out in public with Mandy, and the rest easily repeating the lies about how much of a shame it was to be flying solo while my adoring wife was off traveling the world.

There were countless days I dreamed of nothing more than to have my peace and solitude restored.

Now? Tonight? Watching all these cowboys cuddle up and look like they're ready to hang the moon and the stars for their girls?

Fuck this.

The most beautiful and infuriatingly headstrong creature I've ever met is sitting five feet away from me, and I can't do anything except ignore her.

I've moved onto something stronger than beer, having to focus on biting my tongue and drinking my goddamn whiskey. Turns out tonight's biggest challenge is ignoring the urgent sense of need to draw her into my body and feel her soft curves fitted against me.

"Did you bring your fancy camera getup with you, sugar?" Storm stops his assault on Briar's throat for half a second and gestures at the skyline, turning into a flare of brilliant orange, deepening to a shade of royal purple along the mountain range.

"Not tonight." I shake my head. Though now he's mentioned it, I almost wish I had tossed my equipment in the backseat just to have it on hand. Never mind, there's always gonna be another impressive display in the skies over Crimson Ridge to chase after on another night.

"Who's got a fancy piece of equipment? And why is this the first I'm hearing about it?" Sage's voice chirps in, and my gaze flicks over to meet hers. The sparks and dancing flames hit her dark eyes, making them glow like two golden orbs.

"Hasn't your boy here mentioned his favorite little hobby?" Storm cocks an eyebrow my way.

"Oh my god. Sage, you have to see his stuff. Beau is really

talented." Briar pipes up and I'm immediately regretting the day I ever made friends with Stôrmand Lane on the pro tour.

"It's nothing." I shift my weight and pick at some fluff on the blanket I've got draped over my lap.

"Heartford here is more than just that ugly slug of a thing on his face. He's got an online account for his photos and all." Storm carries on.

Briar nods and goes all soft smiles, looking at me as if taking photos is something more than just a silly little thing I do for fun. "He's got incredible photos of the ranch. That one you took of Teddy in the river is my favorite."

"Why is this the first I'm hearing of it?" Sage arches perfect eyebrows my way.

Layla decides to really make a nuisance of herself and hops into the conversation with a drowsy yawn. "He's got a secret account, an incognito profile."

"Can you blame me? I don't need any old weirdo on the internet snooping around. Privacy, ya know," I grumble and keep my eyes on the ground, feeling the back of my neck heat. It's not that I care about close friends knowing, but the only reason I shared the photos with Briar in the first place was because of her horse. It's more the fact that I can't decide whether I want Sage to know or not, and it doesn't really make sense either way.

At the mention of Teddy, Briar starts animatedly talking about horses with Layla, which fortunately lets the chatter drift away from the topic of me and my photography.

I'm not really paying all that much attention to the flow of the conversation, at least they didn't harp on about it too long. It's only when I reach over to nudge Storm's boots out the way and grab myself another drink, that Kayce's voice floats over the crackle of the fire.

"Christ, Heartford, you've got the world's biggest fucking blanket over there; quit being a selfish bastard, and share with Sage."

CHAPTER 14

Sage

My eyes drift over the cowboy who settles back, reclining at leisure against an impressively large rounded hay bale. He looks my way, and there's no reading his stony expression.

Meanwhile, I've got my arms wrapped around my stomach, trying to deflect the attention I've unintentionally brought upon myself by sitting here with chattering teeth.

Would there be anything more mortifying than admitting how distracted I was earlier, so much so that I left any warm layers I had intended to bring for my Devil's Peak sleepover sitting in a neat pile on the bed back at my cabin? That I was too busy trying to focus on *not* thinking about the fact I'd be once again sitting in the front of Beau's truck with him, while he's all broody and quiet and turning me inside out without knowing it.

"I'm a big girl. I'll be fine." Scooping my hair over one shoulder, I twist some of the strands. "It's my fault for forgetting to bring warmer clothes tonight. I've been lured in by Crimson Ridge being all heatwaves and sweating my mascara off down at the ranch."

"Want me to run up to the house and grab you something warmer?" Layla offers. "I can see your goosebumps from here, Sarge. Don't tell me you're not shivering in your boots."

From the corner of my eye, I see Hayes start to move where he's seated on the tailgate of one of the trucks. A country gentleman, ready to strip the shirt off his back. "Here, take this. These bones are more used to the mountains than yours are."

There's a cough, followed by a raspy clearing of a throat from my other side.

"Plenty of room here." Beau looks a tad murderous while taking in my frozen appearance, and certainly doesn't say it with any warmth in his tone. Even so, he flips the corner of his blanket up, extending an invitation for me to go toward him and settle there.

My heart leaps into a gallop. This seems like a terrible idea, considering how much of a puddle I turn into while in close quarters with the man.

"It's all yours, Sage," he says those words evenly, without any hint of what he might be thinking, and maybe that's what prompts me to move.

Perhaps I'm pettier than I ever knew myself to be, because I'm suddenly very interested in snuggling myself beneath that blanket he's using. And screw him for the way he manages to be such a tightly sealed fortress, acting like we're complete strangers. Here I am, battling not to reveal every single inner thought written in my expression, to not give away the dirty little fantasies I carry around about this man, and he's able to act as indifferent as they come.

So, my feet are moving, and I plonk myself down with a flutter of my eyelashes, and a polite smile in the direction of my boss, who I definitely did not have another toe-curling orgasm while thinking about this morning.

Truly, my efforts should be deemed worthy of a Best Actress award.

If I was in charge of the script to the cowboy movie I'm currently seated in the middle of, the dashing older gentleman next to me would be offering to cuddle for warmth. You know... that cute, swoony moment where the couple who have been at odds finally agree to compromise in the face of the night air and a dire need to share body heat while wrapped up in a plush blanket.

Sadly, for my overactive imagination, Beau Heartford has clearly understood the assignment where his public image is concerned. He's the perfect example of a wedded man.

The guy couldn't make it more obvious that he isn't paying me any mind. He might as well have constructed a pillow fort between us and planted a flag on his side, clearly indicating a territorial divide to under no circumstances dare consider crossing.

It's comical really, in an infuriating way. Here we sit, sharing a blanket in front of a cozy bonfire, with heat and a gentle rubbing of thighs and shoulders against one another whenever either of us adjusts our position. When only a few short nights ago, we stood breathlessly close and he stared at my mouth while clasping hold of my wrist, seemingly without any intention of letting go.

Until his wife's phone call, that is.

He's doing all the correct things. As a married man—or at least in the eyes of those here who don't know the truth of his circumstances—his disinterest in my presence came complete with a gruff apology when I first sat down, and we innocently bumped elbows. I swear to god, he nearly leaped up to run off and join the nearby cows the first time his jeans brushed up against my bare thigh.

No matter, I know this tune. I'm nothing to him, and he's only a gorgeous fascination I need to shake off. Even if we did share another of those moments that feel so damn electric between us, he's still my boss. He's clearly not interested in acting on anything. I'd like to consider myself clever enough to make sure my guard stays up and my radar for frivolous, unattached fun remains on point and uncompromised.

In fact, half the crowd here tonight is certainly more than

capable of showing me the side of Crimson Ridge that shimmies to life and boot-scoots around a dance floor after dark.

"Tell me more about The Loaded Hog." I lean forward and pin the group of cowboys and cowgirls, the rodeo crowd who are accompanying Kayce, with a smile. "What does a gal like me need to know before I jump into the arena with the other so-called *Chaos Twin*?" I make a V with my fingers and point between my eyes and his cheeky expression over on the truck tailgate.

Hayes chuckles. "Can't ever turn that brain off, huh? Got that workaholic blood in your veins? Guess you and my brother will have that in common."

"A little market research goes a long way... I'm nothing but a utility knife. Consider me prepared and ready for every angle and opportunity for promotion."

"The old girl is sweet, but has long needed a glow-up," Brad says while leaning up against Flinn, as the two share a tumbler of whiskey between them.

"The previous owners didn't give a shit for a long time. Let any old assholes in, especially the kind who were happy to spend big but only have an interest in looking for trouble. Ultimately, they were in the game for a quick buck and that was all it was for them."

Flinn nods. "This is a small community... if you're going to have a place like the Hog, you want to make sure it's safe for everyone."

"There's something to be said about creating a place you can feel proud of, that you'd happily go there any day of the week, not just because it's the only choice in town, ya know?" Kayce cracks his knuckles. "I'll also be the first to say that since Hayes took over, I've been glad to have somewhere that makes it comfortable whether you're drinking or not."

"You know..." Hayes runs a hand through his hair. "There's that summer fest starting this weekend in the main street. Kicks off tonight. Live music, food trucks, shit like that. I was planning to go give a hand behind the bar later on, but if you want to come down and take a look around, you're more than welcome to join us?"

At my side, I swear I feel a wave of tension roll off Beau, but whatever. He's occupied talking with Storm and I'm probably just imagining things.

"Layla and I have a hot date on the agenda for tomorrow." I give an apologetic smile. "We're cuddling horses and knocking out a killer website, so I'll have to rain check."

Kayce stretches his long legs out in front of his camping chair. "I'm driving, Sage. Gotta be back up here for an early start tomorrow, so you can hitch a ride back with me if you do want to go down to Crimson Ridge."

"Head down to town and light it up if you want, Sergeant, but I'm tapping out. You know where your room is, and I'll leave the door unlocked for you to creep in at sunrise." My best friend gets to her feet and yawns. "Just don't go putting on anyone's hat, or they absolutely *will* try to get you pregnant." She smirks at me and kisses my forehead. Colt is right behind her, ever the besotted, burly shadow taking care of my best friend.

Once they're standing, that's the signal for everyone else to start moving on for the night, like a mob of cattle, it would seem.

Storm tosses Briar over one shoulder and strides off in the direction of their truck. "Later motherfuckers." He calls into the gathering darkness, amid the shriek of protest from the woman hanging upside down. She buries her face in his shoulder and shares her own farewell mixed with a muffled apology.

The others start chatting among themselves, making plans to head back down the mountain. Everyone seems to be saying their goodbyes, and I'm left weighing my options.

A night of dancing and music and fun down in Crimson Ridge?

Or... remain here, where a certain cowboy is also planning to stay?

I'm stranded, surrounded by an ocean of indecision and temptation, and I don't dare put a toe in the water, lest I find myself unable to resist diving headlong into the jaws of all sorts of very, very wrong ideas.

Although, it would seem that the cowboys in these mountains move much faster than my brain after a couple of whisky neats. In the time it has taken me to assess my options for tonight, chew the inside of my cheek, and dart sidelong glances at the man I'm currently sharing a blanket with, they've packed up and are ready to head out.

Kayce swings into the cab of his truck and hollers my way.

"You coming or what, Sergeant?"

CHAPTER 15

Beau

How I've held it together for the past few hours, I don't know.

Sage has me upended. Thrown off my game.

She disarms me at every turn, leaving me clinging on like I've only ever known during the grimmest of rides. Those sickening moments when a bull decided to try and roll on me, and I knew it could all end in disaster any second.

I *want* to be relaxed around her. The guy I want to be is charming, and could freely flirt with her, in the way I allowed myself the tiniest glimpse of that first day we met. But instead, all I'm left with is a brain that won't shut the fuck up about all the worst-case scenarios.

So instead of being able to be the nice guy I wish Sage could get to know—the real me—inside my chest there's a snorting, snarling thing, and it desperately wants to snap vicious jaws at these young bucks with their ideas to take Sage out for a night in Crimson Ridge.

Of course, the girl can do whatever she wants.

So I keep my eyes trained on the fire as everyone decides to head off. I've got my spot right here to lay my head, and certainly won't be going anywhere with this amount of liquor diluting my blood.

"We'll show you a good time, Sergeant." Kayce starts the engine. "And pinky promise I'll have you back up this mountain ready for your day with Layla."

I know the two of them are just friends.

I know that.

But the Hayes boy? Offering her the shirt off his back? Absolutely the fuck not.

Hearing their promises and possibilities, the thought of Sage being out tonight with them, makes my chest tighten. I know firsthand the kind of fun that a rodeo crowd will usually attract and indulge in... my jaw works, chewing over the words that rise up.

"Oh, I'm sure all those cowboys could show you around," I mutter, keeping my focus on the fire.

Sage stands over me, looking down with that mane of silky dark hair flowing over her shoulders, acres of smooth brown skin, and her denim cut-offs with boots that are determined to kill me.

"Cowboys, cowgirls..." She shrugs and hits me with a sly little cock of her head to one side. "I'm thinking maybe I should go see what this town has to offer for a night of fun since it's been all loved-up happy couples here."

Bass thumps quietly from inside the waiting vehicle.

But, Sage hovers. It's just enough of a moment's hesitation that I really can't decide whether to be an outright asshole and force her to leave, or whether I'm going to break and do something utterly selfish.

"Are the keys in your truck?" she asks. Looking so damn gorgeous, with her plush lips flushed darker thanks to the chill on the breeze.

"You're not driving anywhere," I growl. "Considering the whiskey you've taken on board tonight." Not that I've been monitoring what she's been doing, but I know I've had enough to drink that it was never even a question about going anywhere before morning. She's my employee. Only natural I put the same rules in place for her.

Dark, pretty eyes narrow my way. "I need to get my things out of the backseat, but thanks for the *dad-mode* reminder."

Sage spins on her heel and I stab my fingers into my hair with a heavy exhale. I don't know how to wrestle this creature into submission. I don't know how to do anything except try to lock the door that I should never have dared to touch. Little did I know that day when I ran into her on the sidewalk would permanently alter everything I thought I knew about desire and attraction for another person.

Getting to my feet, I grab one of the larger pieces of wood hanging out of the fire, prodding the remains of bright orange coals and lingering flames burning a low glow in the darkness.

My life in the arena was a million micro-moments. Split-second decisions, reading the way a bull might decide to flip beneath me, frantic heartbeats to see me through an eight-second eternity. Landing safely, boots crashing into the dirt, only to await a score where one fraction of a number might determine whether it was me taking home the winning buckle, or some other guy.

What am I supposed to do with an onslaught of craving that keeps wrapping me tighter and tighter? There's no counting down. There's no walking away from it at the end of the night. It stays, embedding itself in my bones, and I'm not sure that I want to be rid of the feeling.

In my marriage, I've felt starved, trapped in the darkest, most grim cellar.

With Sage? It feels like tasting something sweet and good and hopeful for the first time. Yet, I can't dare to allow a single drop to pass my lips.

"You guys head out without me. I'll set Crimson Ridge alight another time." Sage calls out with a laugh. My pulse double bounces when I hear the previously idling truck pull away amid teasing and boos from the occupants inside. Headlights play briefly over the nearby trees, and the hum of the engine begins to fade.

She's not leaving.

"You're staying out here? No tent?" She stares me down.

"Told Colt I'd keep an eye on the fire. Make sure it settles overnight without a fuss." Rubbing my hands over my jeans, I have to take a deep inhale while looking out at Devil's Peak, painted in an indigo hue against the velvety sky.

"Beaumont, *hmm*?"

"Add that to your roster of names."

"Sounds about right... shoulda known your full name would be something old-fashioned and grouchy."

"Yeah, well, not all of us are good time, golden, party boys without a care in the world." Once again, I'm reduced to a grown man growling at a pretty girl, because it's all I seem to be able to do when she gives me that sass and attitude. The side of Sage I *want* to play with, I *want* to push back, and I certainly *want* to see just how much she enjoys when someone does give her the kind of consequences she's tempting and seeking.

"Oh, that's right, you've forgotten how to have fun."

Turning to face her, my focus immediately drops to take in her figure. Sage leaning up against that hay bale, giving me an alluring stare is a breathtaking sight. Glittering eyes framed with a thick smokey liner, enhancing their beautiful almond shape. Eyes I shouldn't be paying such close attention to.

"I'm not boring." My teeth clench, and I've taken a step closer before I can stop myself.

"Coulda fooled me, Mr. Rodeo Star."

Goddamn it. This woman. Her energy sucks me in, and once again, I've stepped nearer without thinking. We're so close, her backed up against the bale, and our bodies now hidden in long shadows. With only a low light cast by the remains of the bonfire, we're both concealed, with nothing but a carpet of stars starting to poke holes through an inky purple sky overhead as they wink at my misfortune.

"Out here being a thundercloud ready to rain on anyone who dares think about having fun. The kind you wouldn't recognize if it jumped up and slapped you in the face." She darts her tongue out to wet those enticing lips.

Leaning closer, I press one forearm high above her head. Sage is all spitfire and teasing words, with a shimmer to her eyes that I'm losing the willpower to not outright stare at. My eyes roam her face, tracing the delicate curve of her cheekbones, down to the cupid's bow sitting right above that pretty as sin mouth of hers.

"I might be a little out of practice now, but in another lifetime, I would have been able to show you the ride of your goddamn life." The words roll like the first rumble of thunder between us.

"In another life, huh?" As Sage says the words, I see her mouth tip up at the corners. Ever so pleased with herself for loosening the knot keeping my self-restraint in place.

I've officially lost hold of my damn rope as I lower my head and allow the tip of my nose to skim her jaw. "There wouldn't be any other ride you'd need."

I mean every single fucking word.

"Where has this big game suddenly come from, cowboy?" Sage doesn't move. I'm not even sure she's breathing. It's like she's just as painfully aware as I am that we can't be this near, we can't be like this. Despite that, for whatever reason, she's allowing me to get oh, so perilously close, while still maintaining a fraying thread of separation.

"I said I was a bit out of practice, baby. Not that I didn't know what I was doing."

My pulse thunders in my ears, because all I want right now is to angle our mouths together and finally, fucking finally, have the chance to taste her.

"Beau—" Sage breathes my name, ushering it as a quiet warning. A reminder to both of us not to forget ourselves entirely.

"This isn't allowed to happen." My brows knit together, and yet I still linger right there, with only millimeters between my lips and the spot above her pulse point I could suck down on.

She hums a soft agreement. "We can't."

"I'm your boss..."

"Pretty sure that ring on your finger is the bigger issue."

Of course, she's right, and we both know it. I step back, pushing off the hay bale, and scrub a palm over my mouth. "You should probably go inside." My eyes don't stray from hers.

"You should probably stop looking at me like that." The devilish thing she is, Sage smirks. Now this girl knows the truth, and I can't decide whether this feeling ballooning in the pit of my stomach is relief or the worst kind of *I'm fucked* sensation.

"What the hell am I supposed to do with you? When you look like that... when you walk in wearing shorts like those..."

Sage interrupts me. "Are you blaming my choice of clothing?"

"No," I shake my head and drag a palm over the back of my neck. "I'm blaming myself for losing any sense of which way is up or down when I'm around you."

"What if I didn't mind?" She lets her head tip back a little, raising her jaw and hitting me with deeply hooded eyes framed by those goddamn thick lashes. "What if I wouldn't mind you getting a little reckless with me and letting go of that control you're clinging to, hot stuff?"

"Goddamn, Sage."

Her eyes dance with daring and temptation and the sorts of games I need to learn to walk far away from. "What are you gonna do? Put me over your knee?"

"You're not a child," I grunt.

"No, I'm not." Her tongue runs slowly over her bottom lip as she studies me and reads me like a fucking book. "But I am a hot-blooded woman who very much enjoys being treated to a spank or ten by someone who knows how to handle me."

I'm so beyond fucked. Because I want her.

I want to show her exactly how capable I could be when it comes to handling her. The way she's looking right at me, this girl can see straight into my every depraved thought.

"Don't tell me you aren't feeling this, too." She challenges, and

I'm damn near on her again. Crowding Sage with my bulk, I stand over her, looking down at those perfect, pouty lips.

"Fine. You wanna hear it? You wanna hear me say the words... that my marriage—the one where in the eyes of the public, all but our first child's name had been picked out—is over. All of it's done. Except, I'm not *free*." My voice is thick with desire and the strain of trying to explain something that I shouldn't even be saying out loud. "The only thing stopping me from fucking getting my hands on you, Sage, is this ring still stuck on my finger, and my own damn morals that are hanging by a thread. Are you happy? Is that what you want to hear?"

Sage lets her eyes bounce between my own, and my mouth, and her expression softens. The sight of her so close has me exhaling through my nose, blowing out a long, resigned sigh. The truth blossoms with each thudding heartbeat, that there are so many other ways I'd prefer a night like this to go between us.

"You captivate me, Sage. You capture me." Without thinking, I take a lock of hair and rub it between my thumb and forefinger, studying the soft strands beneath my callouses. "I'm a man with a hundred racing thoughts at any given time, and only a scattering of limited words. Somehow, I don't know how you do it, but you twist that and make it feel like all thought flies out of my head, and there are suddenly words on my tongue."

She hums, and it's such an alluring, sweet little purr.

"Got things you wanna say to me, cowboy?"

"Too many words I shouldn't say, but goddamn want to, like you can't even begin to imagine."

"Sounds like we've got a mutual affliction, then."

I let out a groan. Fuck. Is it even worse knowing there are hidden thoughts lingering in this girl to match my own?

My throat bobs as I swallow, willing my dick to stay the fuck down. "So that's why I have to... I have to just be your boss, baby."

"My *very* married boss."

"Yes. Your extremely fucking married boss." My voice is gritty, uttering the words I hate that I have to say. However, there's no telling the disaster I might bring upon her if I allow this thing to grow any further.

"Ok." There's disappointment in the way her lips twist, but I know just how smart this girl is. "Sensible to a fault, huh?"

A grunt escapes me, and the whiskey has loosened my tongue to the point that I'm saying shit, that by all rights, should never be allowed to fall between us.

"Sage, I can't stand the fact I'm tangled in this messy carcass of a relationship. I shouldn't be considering what it might be like to knock on your door night after night, but all I want to do is slip through the dark and seek out your cabin. When it's far too late, all I can think about is you, and that day I first saw you. It's infuriating and it's terrifying because I'm about one second away from throwing caution aside and forgetting myself whenever I'm around you."

"You're sounding less sensible by the minute." She nibbles her bottom lip.

I shake my head. The allure of her lips curving over those words, it catches me in a place where I'm painfully aware we're out here in the dark on top of this mountain where no one in the goddamn world would know... except for the two of us.

"Christ. You gotta go inside before I do something to really fuck up your life, Sage."

Like taking a swift kick to my gut, I step back, putting distance between us. At least enough to prevent myself from pawing her right here and now.

Her eyes linger on me. That stare of hers assesses everything in the way she so capably does. Except, where I'm so used to how whip-smart Sage is with words and quick retorts, she takes in the sight of me battling all the ways I want to immediately go back on my words—to instead see what it's like to swallow down her moans—and leaves me hanging in silence.

When she finally speaks, it's words I don't want to hear, although, for both of our sakes, they need to be said.

"I'm working on the Devil's Peak website with Layla in the

morning. I'll catch a ride back from her tomorrow sometime." She digs out her phone and turns on the flashlight, collecting the all too familiar duffel bag that once used to be mine. An item that, much like my every thought, now belongs to her.

"No need to wait around for me, hot stuff."

CHAPTER 16

Sage

FLEUR:

Did you take that cute outfit with the yellow stripes with you to hillbilly town?

You mean my dress with the sunflowers that you ruined last summer? No. I didn't because it has a giant grape juice stain down the front.

PIA:

Told you she wouldn't forgive you for that.

FLEUR:

It wasn't me!

PIA:

I've got screenshots from when you snapped me in a panic about how to soak it properly.

Sarge, you tell me when and where, and I'll deliver the evidence.

. . .

Christ, you're a savage, P.

Can't decide if I'm terrified or proud of you.

Sorry, Flower-pot, but you lost all wardrobe-sharing privileges long before you ruined my dress.

PIA:

Remember the necklace incident over winter?

Not to mention the mascara...

FLEUR:

Oh my god. What did I ever do to you? I thought we were never going to mention the mascara.

I fucking knew it. You were squirming like a little toad when I hit you up.

"Mom borrowed it." My ass.

I MIGHT BE GIVING my little sister shit, but I'm grinning as I type out the words. Those two hellions are more than enough to keep my parents on their toes. Especially Pia, who is some sort of genius mastermind. I swear that girl knew how to pick every lock in the house before she turned eight after teaching herself by watching videos online.

On the other hand, Fleur is the dreamy, forgetful, cuddly soul who would rather have her head in a book, or the clouds, than be in touch with reality.

I quickly type out a follow up reply.

> Got any good alien documentaries for me to watch? I'm gonna need some of the good stuff. Find me something super addictive, please, and thank you. That thing you sent me about the Little Grays was wild. I was up 'til three a.m. with that one.

This is our thing. My sisters and I have a weakness for all things paranormal conspiracies and alien cover-ups, and they're forever sending me things to binge watch. I've secretly grown to love it as I've gotten older. When I moved away from home, at first a pang of worry followed me around that they wouldn't want anything to do with their older sister once I became an adult in their eyes.

There's always been a nagging sensation I've carried around. An uncomfortable feeling that because we don't share the same biological father, I'll somehow end up pressing my nose against the glass to their life, stuck outside looking in on their adorable nuclear family.

Chalk that up to abandonment issues and being the oldest child. A perfect storm of never feeling good enough, while also refusing to be seen as weak for needing anyone's help.

Hello, Sage, it's your therapy bills calling.

With ten years between us, it meant that by the time they were hitting their final year of grade school, I was intent on flying away. I was pursuing grand adventures on my own as an adult. We fought hard and loved fiercely while I was still living under the same roof, as three sisters are always going to do. Having Layla virtually live with us gave me not only a best friend, but a sister who was ahead of me by just a year at school. She seemed like a godsend when the twins only ever seemed to piss me off.

Layla arrived with her green eyes and copper curls and became part of our life after moving in next door with her aunt. So, of course, we all adopted Aunt Evie as our own by extension, and until coming here for the summer, I'd been visiting on the regular, more frequently so on Layla's behalf since her move to Crimson Ridge.

We've all found it tough to acclimatize to the cold, hard reality that Aunt Evie doesn't recognize any of us now. Dementia can officially go fuck itself.

FLEUR:

I'm on it.

But… cute cow photos? I'm begging here.

PIA:

Be real. She's probably not paying the itty bitty baby cows any attention.

I've seen your browser history, Sergeant.

Chaps. Cowboys. Daisy Dukes.

Hey… hey. May I remind you, I am here in a professional capacity only.

Also, I've already had to threaten Flower-pot to keep outta my wardrobe. Don't make me tell Mom about your secret collection of ninja stars stashed in the wall behind your bed.

PIA:

Bitch.

You wouldn't.

Then keep your nose out of my browser history next time I'm home.

That's a little stalkerish, even for you.

FLEUR:

Mom wants me to tell you she misses you btw.

She wanted to video chat, but I said you were busy...

Look at you. Buttering me up by running interference.

FLEUR:

You know I love you.

REMEMBER.

Baby cow pics, pretty pleeeeease.

I'll spam you later.

Gotta run.

Love you both. Stay out of my old room.

THEY BOTH FLOOD my screen with weird memes that only kids their age would understand, and I swipe out of our group chat.

Even though I'm in my usual position, working from the dining table at the main house, I can tell there's a whole lot going on outside. It's a hive of activity around the ranch today, with cattle arriving that will form the mainstay of the herd Beau intends to run here.

I should probably get my ass out there and start documenting everything. Over the past week, since the night of the bonfire, my employer and I have developed a silent understanding that we're ignoring the obvious. We're pretending like our conversation and closeness—our admission to one another of just how dire a predicament we're in—that night on top of Devil's Peak never happened.

There's a glimmering light, a soft glow of a candle flickering in the back of my mind that wants to burst into a roaring flame.

Beau told me the truth, but also confirmed the worst in the same breath.

Even though he's equally as compelled by this thing as I am, there are too many complicated lines and unwritten rules, and I'm guessing external pressures on his part. Enough to firmly put a halt to anything that might happen between us.

I'm no expert, but having a marriage front and center in the public eye to be picked apart must be a nightmare to navigate. An impending divorce is already stressful enough a prospect for regular ol' couples splitting up, without the opinions and judgments of strangers who have no idea about a single thing in your life. Add in all those snide comments, snarky click-bait gossip sites, a rabid fanbase who all seem to worship the ground that Mandy Spires deigns to trot her designer high heels over, well… I can see why Beau is so quick to shut down any tiny idea that there might be something hanging in the air between us.

Yet again, I'm caught reminding myself that none of it matters anyway, because I'm here for a summer of *fun*. Moping after my married-and-incredibly-untouchable boss simply isn't part of my agenda for my time in Crimson Ridge.

Sage Maloney doesn't pine after a mustache she cannot make the acquaintance of.

No. She dons her bad bitch boots, channels her inner rockstar, and lives her life to the fullest.

When I make my way out into the stifling heat, the ranch feels like it has sprung into high definition technicolor. Until now, she's been a lazy cat stretching and worshipping the sun. Today, there are horses and cowboys and plumes of dust kicking up beneath the hooves of the animals being brought in by transporter.

It's riotous and filled with pulse-thrumming excitement.

At first, I hang back from the pens where they're working. I see a couple of guys—including Beau, who, of course, my eyes are oh, so easily lured to—overlooking the cows lined up nose to tail inside a chute, and others on horseback who are working to split them in different directions once they're released out into open space.

Layla loosely explained things to me. Apparently, there's a quarantine process they need to go through first, with vet checks she's going to carry out after a few weeks. Once that time has passed without any issues cropping up, their passports will be stamped to confirm them as the newest ranch residents. Cow-citizenship to Crimson Ridge proudly confirmed.

After taking some wide-angle footage and photos, capturing the overall feel of the moment, I stroll closer. The ranch is filled with excited anticipation amidst the bellows and rumbles of the cattle. This has got to be a milestone moment for any property, and I'm grinning as I draw nearer to where all the action is happening. I'm honestly really happy for Beau that his dream is unfolding. Every inch of this place has had his influence on it, from where he's spent days building and mending fences, to the care he's taken with preparing the stables, to planting trees that will eventually grow to provide cool shelter for the animals in blazing hot summers yet to come.

We might not cross paths much in the course of our days, but his determination to build something special here is obvious, even as an onlooker who is supposed to be doing anything *but* looking his way.

"Sergeant." The gruff voice of Stôrmand Lane floats across from where he works in tandem with Beau to look at the stock before they're released. "Make sure to get my best side." He hits me with a look that sums up his unique brand of wild charm.

Scrunching my nose up, I shrug. "Look. Sometimes in this game, you gotta make a silk purse out of a sow's ear..."

His chuckle is infectious as he pretends to scowl at me.

"Wanna hop on a horse and get out there?" He jerks his chin in the direction of the other riders.

I don't have a chance to reply because I'm snared by blue-gray eyes and rendered speechless for a moment. Beau looks every inch the hard-worn cowboy in his hat and, holy shit, a pair of chaps to leave me more than a little light-headed. What is it about a cowboy's wranglers wrapped up in that additional package? Holy hell. It's like someone decided to make it even more complicated to focus on anything except the way his chaps act as an eye magnet. They draw my gaze straight to a groin and ass I very much wish I could become more familiar with.

Swooning over chaps aside, it's Beau's stare that keeps me pinned down in the dust where I stand. It takes a few flutters of my pulse and a hasty swallow to understand a possible reason for his intensity. At first, I can't figure out why a deep furrow lines his brow, bringing about a kind of sternness in him that makes my pulse skitter around erratically. That's when I see his attention flicker to the source of what has got him looking my way with such ferocity.

My hat.

As realization settles in, a smile creeps across my face. I haven't worn this in front of him, yet.

Evidently, the *cowboy hat* rule is alive and thumping its chest like a caveman in these mountains.

Does he think I'm wearing someone else's hat?

Preening satisfaction hums a tune in my veins. I shouldn't feel so damn smug at the immediate and visceral reaction from him, but all things considered, with how torn up I've been over this man lately, I'm thinking this is about the best damn purchase I've ever made in my life.

"Plenty enough bodies out there already as it is," he grumbles at Storm. "I'm sure there are better sight lines from here, anyway. You know. For the photos and crap."

I wrestle back my beaming grin and carry on, busying myself with the job of recording and photographing. All while soaking up the sensation that there are most definitely a pair of eyes that keep drifting my way. God, I really am a terrible person because I'm eating up every second of this powerful feeling.

There's no denying that I love being watched, and right now, this man is satisfying that craving beyond all measure.

Following the outer rail of the pen, I head in the direction of where the cattle are being split off into smaller herds and secured in separate grazing pastures. It's such a gorgeous scene—mountains rising up out of the landscape coated in a purplish haze, sun streaming down, and the glossy coats of the horses who have been brought in for today's work.

I'm in the happiest of zones, caught up in the process of taking some close-up footage when the snort of a horse approaching brings my attention up from the viewfinder for a moment.

"The place looks better with some cows. It was like the pantry was bare before."

Kayce draws to a stop just beside the railing I'm perched on and leans forward in his saddle.

"Don't let the boss catch you chit-chatting." I tease.

"Me? Not a chance. Though, he and Storm are over there gossiping like a pair of clucky old mother hens themselves."

"Is everything going ok? It's all going to plan, I mean?" As I gesture in the direction of the cattle, his horse swings closer and stretches its long neck my way, taking a good look at the camera in my hands.

"Yeah, man. Other than it being hot as balls today, everything's fine."

"When do you next head off to be flung around on the back of a bronc?" I click off a few rounds of close-ups on the cattle.

"Soon... these next few events are close to Crimson Ridge. This part of the circuit, we don't have to travel so far, which is great for those of us working part-time and also going in to compete for the prize money."

"Best of both worlds, huh?" Shielding the camera screen I flick through a few images and love the way the light is hitting perfectly with the mountains fading away in the background. Today's shots are going to be perfect, I can already hear the *cha-ching* of cash rolling in with these kinds of visuals adorning the website.

"Honestly, now? I'm grateful to get to do what I do. Maybe at one time years ago, the dream was to shoot for the top, to go after the buckles and the big arenas like Beau and Storm did in their day, but this feels like a good fit."

"Careful. That sounds a little wise, Wilder."

He chuckles and scratches at his jaw. "Don't tell a soul. Folks might get the wrong idea and think I've grown up."

"Wait. Can you... stay right there..." I quickly snap a few photos when he looks out over the scene before us and unknowingly strikes the most perfect of cowboy poses while in the saddle. Who would have thought that my best friend's loser ex could actually turn his life around? I get on well with Kayce, especially now that he's quit the drinking and hanging around with bullshit people. He's got the makings of someone who might actually turn out to be a good one after all.

"Am I the new poster child for this ranch or what?" He lets out a wry laugh.

"I'll talk to the boss. You polish up half-decent. I'm sure we could use your services in center stage."

"Beau would much rather be behind the camera than in front of it. He won't complain."

"So I hear." I run off a few more sequences of fluffy cow ears and wet noses.

"Has he shown you any of his work yet?" Kayce asks.

He hasn't, and I've been fighting a silent battle with myself to not rush off and hunt down this secret photography account he has. "I don't exactly think it's been a high priority on his to-do list." Shaking my head, I focus on looking very interested in what I'm doing. Not at all like I'm instantly imagining how panty-melting Beau would look with those calloused hands dexterously handling a camera and lens.

"Fair call. Guy's got more than enough on his plate. Speaking of, I'll be seeing you around a bit, kiddo. Even though these cows will be happy enough out here and don't need much tending to at this time of year, I'll be dropping by to check on the herd." He ruefully clicks his tongue. "I've also got Teddy to sort out."

"Why?" My brow creases.

"Oh, Beau didn't tell you?"

"Tell me what, exactly?"

Kayce readjusts himself in the saddle. "Him and Storm, they're off on a bit of a bromance road trip. Between the two of them, they're gonna pick up a few horses for the ranch and the therapy program. Reckon it'll take 'em about a week or so."

One of the other cowboys whistles and calls Kayce's name.

"Gotta go earn my keep, I guess. Watch how a pro does it." He smirks, and guides his horse back in the direction of the others.

Leaving me to mull over whether it's a blessing to be free of all things Beau Heartford for the immediate future, or whether it's going to be impossible to ignore the gaping hole left behind if he isn't here on this ranch.

CHAPTER 17

Beau

SAGE:

We have a big problem, boss.

I blink, reading back the message that has just arrived. My mind races with the possibilities of everything that could have gone wrong back at the ranch. Cattle escaped. Stock injured. Teddy breaking someone's ribs. Any number of eventualities could be the reason for her message. My brain immediately wants to skip to picturing all kinds of worst-case scenarios.

Did she burn herself again?

Gritting my teeth, I try to swallow back the tension. Kayce would surely have called if shit was truly bad, if there really was a crisis, wouldn't he?

We do?

What's wrong?

Are you ok?

I'm not exactly sure how we're gonna solve this...

You look like you're about to crush skulls in every single one of these photos.

A close-up image comes through next, cropped to show just my face half-hidden by the shadow from my hat brim. Scowl firmly locked in place and my jaw clenched like a steel trap.

Dragging my hand over my mouth, I'm partly hiding the fact my lips want to twist into a faint smile, partly exhaling with relief that Sage is teasing me. There's an odd sensation squeezing around my ribs that she's choosing to send me a message at this time of night.

I like it far too much. Even though we shouldn't really be texting each other at all.

Am I not allowed to look serious?

No, not when you're giving off the vibe of kicking puppies at noon, followed by landing your fighter jet by dinner.

Another mustache joke? How original.

Do you get a discount on aviator sunglasses when you flash that top lip?

I'm gonna go right ahead and ignore all of that, by the way.

Back to the photos.

I'm sure you're exaggerating.

Hand on my heart. I'm not sure I can do my job when every single one of these photos are going to scare your potential clientele away, Heartford.

Before I can think of anything remotely clever to say in reply, she's already sent a follow-up message.

How's the cowboy road trip going?

"Your shot. Or else I'm gonna be forced to get you sloppy drunk like that time in Houston, just so you'll whisper all your secrets in my ear, sugar."

Stôrmand goddamn Lane rubs chalk over the tip of his pool cue and blows me a little air kiss.

Shoving my phone back in my pocket, I hate that it's so effortless to chat with Sage like this. I'm excruciatingly aware that even if I wanted to respond, it's a terrible idea for me to allow any kind of *conversation* to remain ongoing.

Being playful? Asking me how things are? Veering into topics beyond the business essentials we need to communicate over? It could potentially spell doom for both of us if I start replying to anything of that nature.

"Everything ok back at the ranch?"

"Yeah. It's fine." I line up the nearest ball and miss the pocket, horribly. My head is far, far away from this backwater country bar.

Mentally, I'm in Crimson Ridge, sneaking glances at the way she sits with one knee tucked up, bites her lip, and scrunches her nose while completely absorbed in her design process.

Storm chuckles. "Then what's got you itching to check that phone of yours again? You look like you've got ants in your jockstrap."

"Just take your goddamn shot already."

"You never properly thanked me, you know." He crouches to survey the table and the array of scattered balls from eye level.

"What for?"

"For finding you someone to get that big ol' ranch dream of yours off the ground."

With a sharp snap of his cue, Storm sinks his shot easily, then walks around the table to figure out his next angle.

"Who?"

"Sage. The girl's got some pretty epic talent... you should consider yourself lucky I didn't just snap her up—"

My shoulders tense, heart pumping faster as all I hear is her name, and it's coming from the mouth of the man who was notoriously fond of women in all the years we were on the pro tour together.

"Back off, Storm." My teeth clench. I'm gripping the pool cue so hard it might snap clean in two.

He looks up at me from his position, leaning forward with a tattooed left hand braced beneath his stick and brows furrowed. But instead of continuing to take his shot, he straightens up, then points the tip of the cue my way.

"Woah there... Briar is my everything. You know we're extremely happy..." His voice drops low in warning.

It happens right before my eyes; his expression morphs from one of being mildly pissed at me, to becoming the smuggest fucking asshole who ever walked the earth.

"Oh, *shiiiiiit*. You're into her, aren't you?"

My ears are ringing. The thud of my pulse intensifies in the side of my neck. All I can do is scowl. Storm coughs into his fist, choking on his own glee.

"Fucking hell, sugar. You look like you wanna come over here and shove that pool cue somewhere. Got it real bad, huh?" The man across from me raises his eyebrows suggestively. It's taking everything in me not to readjust my grip on the stick beneath my palm and side-swipe him across the jaw with it.

"Christ. You're the worst, you know that? Just play." I grunt and jerk my chin at the white ball he'd been lining up only a moment ago.

"Oh, hell no." He crows. "Screw any more rounds of pool. This is a big deal... a revelation like this calls for shots, or getting an entire bottle to celebrate, or a round of cold ones at the very least." Storm blows out a low whistle. "Damn, Heartford, you're walking around with a giant goddamn boner for your one and only employee."

I tug the brim of my cap lower, my attention flickering around the empty bar, before I hiss at him. "Would you shut the fuck up?"

Storm's blue eyes dance, all mischief and merriment at witnessing my utter misery in this.

"Does she know? Is that her texting you right now?" The mile-wide grin on his face is just asking to be wiped off.

"She knows. And will you piss off if I say it is?"

The glittering look in his eyes is a dangerous prospect indeed.

"What does she think? That hideous thing on your face hasn't scared the girl back to the city?"

Christ. I blow out a breath and tilt my head to the ceiling.

"Aw, look at you, all flustered, like a schoolgirl with a crush."

"Screw you." There's no escaping his inquisition now. I'm gonna have to grab him by the horns in order to ride this one out, and hope to hell I make it from the arena in one piece. "She's on a contract for the summer." I'm trying to figure out how to salvage this disaster.

"Perfect, so she's only looking for something brief and fun?"

God. There's no hope, this wreckage is plummeting straight for the bottom.

"No.... well... I don't know." Shit. I drag my cap off and run my fingers through my hair before wedging it back down. "Whatever. It doesn't even matter, anyway."

"Something happened between you two already?" Storm is a dog with a goddamn bone.

"No. Nothing." I shake my head and slump onto the stool at my back. "Besides, she knows *nothing* is gonna come of it, because it damn well can't."

"Why not?"

I frown at him. "Are you serious? You bloody well know why."

"This is completely different. You're not your father."

"Is it, though?" This feels like wanting to climb out of my skin. "I fucked up and married someone I didn't even know. This isn't anything but my fault, and I might not have any feelings for that woman, but I still jumped in with eyes wide open."

Storm rests his ass against the edge of the pool table. Our match long since forgotten now that we're into this.

"Your judgment is more than a little clouded by your own personal experience, wouldn't you say?"

I dig the heel of my palm into my eye socket. Jaw clamped down. Throat working overtime. How do I explain the way this feeling has ruled every decision I've made for so many years?

"My shit is different to yours. I did the wedding thing with my eyes wide open and sober as a judge. Not blind drunk and being taken advantage of. I made them, and myself, a promise. I swore I'd *never* be like him, yet here I am..." My words falter. Out of a force of habit, I'm fucking paranoid about someone overhearing us—even though the only other soul in this place is the gray-haired bartender with a hearing aid who is too busy playing word puzzles while sitting behind the bar to pay us any mind.

"I get it. You don't want to let anyone down. But have you stopped to think about the fact they wouldn't give a shit? Tessa and your mom. I sure as hell know those two women would rather see you flawed, doing the best you can, and *happy*."

Reaching for my half-finished beer, I drain the glass, mind racing as I gulp swallow after swallow. My goddamn father, the rodeo star of his time, who played the stand-up family man with my mom when Tessa and I were young... only to one day not come home after one of the stops on the tour ended.

The lying, cheating asshole had a whole other life.

A woman he'd been seeing—semi-living with—for years.

Turns out, while he'd been living out the highs within the rodeo arena, he'd found time to provide for another woman, another child, with a second on the way. My mom had no idea about any of it.

Finding her crumpled, brokenhearted, and sobbing on the kitchen floor at one a.m. was a core memory imprinted on twelve-year-old Beau. One I carry to this day.

No one should have to hug their mom and feel that raw pain. Agony and tear-stained distress caused by the very man who taught me how to saddle a horse properly and took me to my first rodeo.

"I promised them." I shake my head, throat thick with the fresh wave of that particular memory. "I told Mom and Tessa I'd never be like him. I'd never do that to a woman. And more importantly... I promised myself."

Storm narrows his eyes on me. "So where does that leave Sage?"

My shoulders drop. Where *does* that leave her? The brilliant girl who deserves so much better than to be caught in my web of bullshit.

"Nowhere. It leaves her nowhere, other than being a woman who works for me for a couple of months. That's it."

He twists his lips in thought and brings one hand up to ruffle his hair.

"What's that look for?" I glare and shift uncomfortably, because I know Stôrmand Lane, and he's got the exact expression on his face—a guarantee of trouble—the kind that has nearly landed my ass in lock-up one too many times over the years.

"Figured you were a smart guy, Heartford. Now? I'm not so sure."

"Well, I've *always* known you were an asshole. So, spit it out."

With a glance toward the bar, he raises one eyebrow, then strides over to interrupt the man engrossed in his crossword. From where I sit, I watch as he nearly startles straight off his seat when faced with an actual customer to serve. Especially one of such an imposing size. Storm points to the shelf, and the man fetches down a bottle of whiskey and a pair of glasses.

After paying, he strolls back over, looking mighty pleased with himself.

"Have you worked it out yet?" he asks, while pouring us a glass each.

"Fuck you with this cryptic bullshit. Enough already."

Storm hands me the drink. His tattooed knuckles bearing the

name of the girl he fell so hard and fast for he didn't know which way was up anymore.

"Let me spell it out... nice and easy for you, sugar." Clinking his glass against mine, he knocks back a long sip and hisses. "You're out there on that ranch alone, aren't you?"

I bring my glass to my mouth and allow the whiskey to slide down my throat with a burn that seeps straight into my veins.

"So, other than a pesky moral standard you've set for yourself —which is benefitting absolutely no one, least of all your blue balls—what's to stop you from indulging this little curiosity?"

I nearly choke on my drink, brandishing the cursed ring I always have to wear while out in public. "Did you forget the part where I'm fucking married?"

"A technicality. One that is only a stone's throw from being finished, right?"

My eyes roam the empty room. "Mandy would be out for blood. You know I'd be trapped forever if I so much as looked at another woman." I hiss through gritted teeth.

"You know how to be careful, I'm sure."

A snort bursts out of me. "Well, aren't you just the poster boy for fidelity?" I tip my glass at him while rolling my eyes.

He shrugs, pausing with the glass lifted to his lips. "Hey, hey. All I'm saying is don't cut your dick off to spite your face."

"Pretty sure that's not the saying," I mutter into my whiskey.

"If you're both liking the idea of what's under each other's hoods, then what's the harm in indulging a little curiosity? Best-case scenario, you're rid of that nightmare of a woman in a couple of months, then you two can give things a real shot. Worst-case, fun-time gal chews you up, spits you out, and decides to float off to greener pastures after summer. At least by then, your dick will have finally remembered what it's useful for... other than having your soft little palm tugging frantically on it every night."

I glare at him, without knowing what to say. I hate that he's making sense. I hate that he's messed with my reasoning so quickly. I hate that I'm tempted to do exactly as he's suggesting.

Stôrmand Lane is the worst motherfucker to exist, because now that seed has been planted, I'm watching it sprout almost immediately. Stupid, irrational goddamn ideas have started laying down roots unbidden, entirely uninvited.

"Well... either you take my advice, or you don't. Whatever angle you come at it, I think we'd better toast the fact your cock hasn't withered away out of neglect. Let's give that 'stache of yours a proper drink to celebrate."

Storm grabs me by the shoulder, all devious smirk tugging on his lips and mischievous eyes.

"Here's to not feeling guilty, for having a pulse, and fucking *finally* being into someone that isn't your own fist."

CHAPTER 18

Sage

COCK RING:

Are you still at your computer?

My phone vibrates on the nightstand, bringing a little heat to my cheeks when I see who's name is illuminated on-screen. After the brief exchange we had a few hours ago, Beau disappeared faster than a skittish horse. Just when it seemed like he might be open to talking, the conversation evaporated in front of my eyes.

Rolling my lips together, I quickly tap out a reply. He's lucky I'm even entertaining him dragging his ass back to my inbox at this extremely late hour.

Nope. I'm being good tonight. In bed and reading a book.

More precisely, I'm mid-way through devouring a chapter involving an extremely hot four-way and knotting. A girl can only but live vicariously through her favorite monster fucker literary masterpieces.

Ok.

Good.

You work too hard, you know.

Beau takes an eternity to type his next message, with dots bouncing on the screen and then disappearing over and over. I'm deeply intrigued to see what speech he seems to be busy penning via text. Is he about to give me some lecture, or a complex set of instructions for mucking out Teddy's stall tomorrow?

That's probably what I should have done.

Gone to bed early, I mean.

A laugh escapes me. Nope, it's not boring-boss-Beau texting me... this feels a whole lot like a man who has discovered a way to ignore his moral compass. I shouldn't be so gleeful at the prospect of a man entangled in the complexities of marriage and divorce texting me, but here I am. Apparently, I'm a slut for a cowboy who is potentially very bad for my health.

Have you been drinking, hot stuff?

A little.

It's Storm's fault.

Well, he is pretty to look at.

I'm not surprised it only took one bat of his eyelashes to render you incapable of resisting his charms.

He's not that pretty.

Well, ok, the asshole is. Always has been.

I see that he's typing something straight away, and my teeth catch my bottom lip as I wriggle back against my pillow, eager to see what he has to say.

Do you think he's nice to look at?

A little flutter occupies the space where my heart resides. Which is apparently between my legs these days.

Jealous?

I don't know if it's a good idea for me to have my phone right now.

The guy currently in charge isn't good at following the rules. Not like sober Beau.

What if I like the guy who wants to break a few rules?

Fuck. Don't tell me that.

Definitely don't tell him that.

Why not?

I need to ask you something.

Okayyy...

Why didn't you want me to shave my mustache?

Truthfully.

My lips tip into a smile, and I drum my nails against the bedsheets. There's a devil within me who wants to taunt Beau's inner demon. A naughty little troublemaker who wants to pry apart that tough shell and see what secrets he's got going on. What might I be able to lure out of this man if he can be convinced to come play my game?

I just know he's got a hidden freaky side he keeps locked away, and the fact he's drunk texting me has effectively swiped a forearm across the entire table of defenses I had put in place against this man.

What I *should* do is put my phone on do not disturb, then immediately plunge my horny ass in that outdoor tub with my monster smut and favorite five-speed tentacle dildo as a distraction. Which was the flavor of evening plans I had intended on, all of two minutes before his text arrived.

Fuck it. No overthinking this; he's the one who initiated an after-dark rendezvous. I chew the inside of my cheek and hit the video call button.

The phone rings once, then connects with a muffled rustling noise filling the speaker. Except, rather than Beau's handsome face, like I'm hoping to see, it's only my own peering back. A blank screen occupies the place where his video is turned off. Looks like he's not keen on doing this face-to-face, but he *is* willing to accept my call.

Or at least, the alcohol is.

"Truthfully?" I arch an eyebrow into the camera.

"Truthfully… I shouldn't be answering right now. Or texting you." His voice is low, roughened, and hella sexy. A clink of ice cubes punctuates the silence as he sips a drink on the other end of the phone.

Goosebumps dance across my shoulders, because the thought of Beau Heartford reclining in his bed with a whiskey in hand, while watching me on his phone, might just have unshackled a dangerous creature inside me.

One I have little, to no, interest in taming tonight.

"We're just talking," I say, while propping my phone on the bed so that I can keep both hands free. Settling back against the headboard, with one hand, I scoop my hair over my shoulder, and stare down the camera at the invisible man who quietly watches me.

"I have two weaknesses I probably shouldn't tell you about."

My fingers drag up the cotton of my baggy t-shirt, tracing the swell of my breast leading to my collarbone. "I'm certifiably weak for cute girls with tattoos who could ruin my life... and men with mustaches. That's the reason I didn't want you to shave yours."

There's another clink of ice against the side of a glass before Beau makes a noise in the back of his throat.

"Jesus."

I tilt my head, fighting back the smirk that wants to settle on my face, hearing the obvious effect I'm having on him, all wrapped up in that one gravelly word. "What about you, hot stuff?"

He pauses for a moment. "Are you asking if I have a thing for men with mustaches?"

I sink my teeth into my bottom lip. Oh, hell, I'm in a world of trouble if Beau is going to hit me with that panty-dropping charisma. I've witnessed a tiny glimpse of what he's capable of, and I'm in treacherous waters if there's more where that came from.

Softly shaking my head, I click my tongue.

"Considering you used to climb on the back of rampaging bulls as an idea of a good time, I suspect you don't have any. So, indulge my curiosity. What's your weakness?" I comb my fingers through my loose curls. "Although if it *is* hot as fuck facial hair, I've got some great accounts I can recommend you subscribe to."

He clears his throat before speaking.

"Apparently tonight it's Stôrmand Lane convincing me to play him at pool..." Beau hesitates, and a crackling tension extends across space and time while I'm left hanging before he continues. "And the prettiest girl I've ever laid eyes on, who video calls me when I'm all alone in my hotel room."

His voice oozes with sex as the words we both know Beau shouldn't be saying, make their way to dance across my skin like it's his fingers running a drugging path straight down my body.

Damn him for being the worst kind of forbidden fruit. Yet, I can't seem to find it within myself to stop this, to put a halt to this madness we're tiptoeing closer to the precipice of.

"Cowboys like you… must spend a lot of nights alone in hotel rooms?" My pulse thumps between my legs, and I shift my weight, squeezing to try and ease the growing ache building there.

Beau makes a noise that is part rumble, part agreement, and a whole lot of immensely hot. But he doesn't answer. Without requiring a drop of alcohol, the right dosage of recklessness surges through my bloodstream tonight.

Reaching over, I pluck my hat off the place where I've had it hanging from the wooden headboard.

"Who's fucking hat is that?" The demand comes fast and gruff.

I'm basking in the glow of knowing I've got his undivided attention. Smirking at the camera, fluttering my eyelashes, I rub a forefinger over the rim. "You like? It's cute, huh?"

"Don't try to be coy. Who does that hat belong to?"

"You know… I don't remember."

"Sage."

This man could bring me to orgasm by saying my name in that tone of voice alone, I'm almost certain of it.

"Don't burst an artery. It's mine. I bought it for myself, with my money, because I loved it and I wanted it. Happy?"

He's back to silence again now, but wicked tension continues to ripple between us like a fire line all the same.

"Do you watch porn, Beau Heartford?" I reposition myself in front of the camera, sitting upright with my back against the pillows, using the shadowy light and angle to my best advantage. Staring at the camera positioned on the bed at my feet, it feels too damn enticing having his eyes on me this intently. "All those nights you spent alone in your hotel room. How did you unwind by yourself after coming off the adrenaline high of the rodeo, *hmm*?"

"Jesus Christ." He sounds pained, and immensely turned on. "I —I don't know if it's a good idea for me to answer that. None of this is a good idea."

"Do you want to stop talking? I can hang up." The fluttering pulse in my neck matches the wings beating in my stomach, hoping for what his answer might be. Yet, I still feel like there's every possibility the stern, grouchy, closed-up version of Beau is going to make his appearance and shut this phone call down faster than a fire marshal at an overcrowded nightclub.

"I'm married, Sage. Maybe it's only on paper. Even if it's over. That legality, or... fuck... technicality, still exists." He exhales with a heavy rasp, his words not exactly slurred, but they're drowsy coming off his lips. It's the sexiest sound, hearing him let his guard down, allowing me to have the version of him *not* strung together so tightly for once.

I can just picture his hard-worn fingers threading through those dark curls of his. Can see in my mind's eye the way he scrubs his hand over his mouth, highlighting that strong jaw, his mustache, the salt and pepper stubble when he hasn't shaved.

"There's an answer to that question that I'm supposed to give you... but it's really fucking hard to think straight, or remember a single thing when you're giving me those eyes."

I'm a peacock preening my feathers, shamelessly glowing from head to toe.

"You're a good man, Beau Heartford. Maybe a little *too* honorable for your own good."

"Don't I fucking know it."

"You don't want to come this far and get caught allowing those impossibly high standards you've set for yourself to slip, now, would you?" I click my tongue.

"Takes one overachiever to know another."

God, I love when he meets me like this. Ready to dance in the flames.

"Have you ever been tempted?" Cocking my head to one side, I let my eyes linger on the camera.

"Tempted? To cheat? Or tempted by *you*, Sage." He growls, and it doesn't fucking matter how far away this man is; I feel a shudder roll straight down to my toes. "Because those are two *very* different things. The first, no. Never. The second, I'm barely hanging on by a goddamn thread. I'm getting closer to snapping the longer I'm around you."

My tongue runs a line along my bottom lip, and I swear to god, even though I can't see his face, it's as though I can feel him track that movement through the phone screen.

"Is it cheating if you're not here?"

He remains silent. It's so fucking sexy I can't breathe.

"You don't have to watch, but I like it when I know someone might see. Maybe that's my third weakness... having an audience."

As I say the words, I become bolder. He hasn't ended the call. If I know anything about this man by now, he's likely caught in his own head, battling all the reasons why we shouldn't be as attracted to each other as we seem to be.

So, I make the decision for him.

He's suffering through wanting me? Well, I'm going to show him just how much I want him, too. In the worst kind of way.

Sliding my knees wide, I give him an unhindered view of my panties below the loose hem of my t-shirt. From this angle, he will be able to see the strip of fabric covering my entrance—he will have an unhindered view of the soft material seated directly over my pussy.

"You're just watching, baby," I murmur as my fingers trace the soft swell of my inner thighs. "Maybe you'll let yourself enjoy this. Maybe you'll wrap your fist around your dick and touch yourself for me. Or, maybe you'll be a good boy and wait 'til I'm done, then get yourself off after."

All I hear over the blood rushing in my ears is another chink of ice cubes. There's every possibility that after tonight's show of unbridled exhibitionism, I'm forever going to feel my pussy clench upon hearing that particular sound. With each sip he takes of his drink, Beau is successfully imprinting the sound of whiskey on the rocks in my memory. A damn reward for being the perfect performance... just for him.

I walk my fingers along the edge of the fabric covering my soaked entrance. The panties I have on are white cotton, so guaranteed he'll be able to see what awaits to be discovered there straight away.

In the camera, I notice it myself. A darkened patch of wetness giving away all my secrets where this man is concerned.

The material is absolutely drenched.

"You don't need to know that I'm thinking about you while I'm playing with myself... while I'm stroking my pussy late at night, wishing it was your hand between my legs." As I keep my gaze fixed straight down the lens, I drag my fingers over the spot just above my core, before shifting up to seek out my clit.

A hum of pleasure escapes me. The throbbing ache there is so delicious when I give a little pressure, fondling myself ever so slowly. Through the camera, I can see my hardened nipples poking against the front of my t-shirt. With each shift of my hand, rubbing and circling across the damp cotton, that fabric drags over my sensitive tits.

"You don't need to hear about all the little daydreams I keep having about that night on Devil's Peak... when I wanted you to say fuck it, wanted you to slip your leash and let your hands find my waist."

My weight sinks further into the pillows at my back the longer I keep stroking and playing. I like how this angle looks on the camera. While there's nothing *showing*, it's the act of the tease that makes it so much hotter. A shadowy crease at the tops of my thighs. A peaked outline of my nipples. A deeper flush to my mouth. It's sensual and erotic and plays right into the side of me who loves to put on a show for an appreciative audience.

"No, I don't think you need to know that I can't stop thinking about what might have happened if you'd pushed me up against that hay bale, like a true cowboy. For your mouth to suck down on my neck, to nibble that spot... you know the one... that special little place that acts like a mute button for the brain."

There's absolutely no way to know what Beau is doing. My only certainty is that the call hasn't ended, and if that's the case, then he's still watching. Knowing he's in this with me, allowing me to indulge this side of myself, well, that sets my blood aflame.

I glide my hand down the side of my panties and keep my eyes locked on the camera. No going back now.

Hitching the fabric, I slip my fingers beneath and brush over my swollen clit. "I'm not gonna tell you that I wish you would turn up at my door. I'm not gonna tell you just how hot it would be sucking your dick while I use a toy in this spot right here." My breathing quickens as sparks shoot through my limbs, and my fingers rub firm circles.

God. I'm so close already.

"All you're doing is watching me push my fingers into my wet pussy."

Slipping my hand lower, I press forward when I come into contact with my slippery arousal. Can he hear just how slick I am? It certainly sounds loud enough to my ears; lewd, wet sounds of my two fingers easing into my entrance fill the empty room.

The scene on camera is only a partial glance, a half-covered sight of my core. My panties show off my pussy where they're pulled to one side. The softness of my thighs tremble as my climax draws nearer.

All I can think of is *him*. Of this man lying in his bed hundreds of miles away, staring at my fingers frantically working beneath that soaked material. Is he joining me in this? Is he stroking his dick to the sight of me? What does Beau Heartford look like with stiff cock in hand, caught up in the temptation of watching something as forbidden as this—someone he's convinced himself he shouldn't have?

Imagining all that... I'm just about done for.

"I know we can't." Sliding my fingers up to seek out my clit, the ache there is desperate to be relieved. "... this is too complicated." I press down and circle hard, the wave rising and racing toward me now. "... we have to forget this ever happened."

My words begin to falter.

"But, fuck, do I wish... wish things were different." I gasp as pleasure swells. Surging to claim me with a roar in my ears and sparks forming behind my eyes.

My climax crashes, erasing everything, leaving me speechless. It takes everything in me to keep my eyes fixed on my phone, where I hope to god he's transfixed. I hope he's seeing every shake and tremor roll through my limbs. I come so fucking hard, my pulse pounds a frantic beat, and I'm damn near panting.

A curve touches my lips, because that felt so sinfully wicked, and yet so incredible. I'm floating and glowing all over as I drag my hand out of my underwear.

With a soft hum of satisfaction, I bring my knees together and clamber forward to lean close to the camera. Before reaching to pick up my phone, I let myself tilt my head and cast a dreamy look at my invisible playmate for this devious little game. If there was ever any doubt that my halo has long since been misplaced, I cement things in that regard. Bringing my hand up, I run my tongue along both knuckles, then suck down on my fingers.

That's it. That's the itch scratched, I tell myself as I taste my arousal.

While I'll never know what it's like to have Beau in the way I want, he just gave me a way to act out a little forbidden fantasy. And that will have to do. It'll have to be enough.

As I pull my fingers from my mouth, I let my teeth sink into my bottom lip for a lingering moment. Perhaps I'm waiting, giving him an opportunity to say *something*... to my disappointment, he doesn't.

Silence hangs around me as I watch myself on the screen.

"*Mmm.* Now that's certainly a memorable conversation, Beau Heartford." With a wink, I reach forward and pick up the phone.

I'm under no delusion; this man won't break his rules. Not for a girl like me. So I allow my thumb to hover over the red circle and give a little smile. One that tells him that I know tomorrow, in the cold light of day and with veins free of whiskey, he'll be back to how things have to be in his mind.

"Good night, Cock Ring."

CHAPTER 19

Sage

"God, your tits are incredible." I pout. *Not jealous at all* of my best friend's blessings in that department.

Layla swats me in the face with one lazy hand, while her other holds the straw cowboy hat covering her eyes. I prop myself on my elbows, lying on my stomach in the middle of our lineup of towels set out on the grass beside the river.

"Look, if I have to share those marvels of nature with Colt for the rest of our days, then give me this." Tugging my sunglasses down my nose a little, I peer at Layla's sun-kissed skin in all her topless glory. Her shoulders shake with a little silent laughter as I mutter my abject disappointment.

"Do I need to worry about you going into heat while stuck out here on your own?" She lifts the hat slightly to side-eye me from beneath the brim.

"Maybe? I have been reading a lot of shifter smut lately... howling at the moon is pretty cathartic."

Briar and Sky snort from where they lie, sunning themselves on the other side of me. These girls haven't yet met all the different sides of Sage Maloney. Layla knows my antics well enough to be assured that I'm not actually joking.

"How long until you have to start wearing clothes again, rather than strolling around half-naked at every opportunity?"

I flop onto my back and take in the wispy streaks of clouds barely touching the brilliant cobalt sky overhead. "I'm not sure. Although, wouldn't *that* be a sight for all your cowboys? Imagine them turning up here today, only to discover the four best sets of titties to bless Crimson Ridge enjoying some time out in the sun."

That's what the past couple of hours have consisted of. The perfect lazy summer day spent at the river. We've floated, swum, picnicked, and alternated all of that with lounging like a pack of lizards on our towels.

One perk of a ranch with not another soul for miles... we can have our very own undisturbed, topless fun in the sun.

"When did Storm say they'll be getting back, Briar?" Sweet, pink-haired Sky sounds half-asleep as she lifts her tattooed arms to shield her eyes.

My foolish ears prick up, even though I keep trying to talk myself out of being overly interested in the answer. That is one little detail I truthfully do not know. Beau has gone zero-contact since that night when things took a turn into a territory I can only assume crossed one too many lines for his liking. There's been an echoing silence in that place where, for the briefest moment, we might have shared something tangibly enticing.

So, all I could do for the past week, which has almost blurred into two, is keep my head down and sink into my work. I've been in regular correspondence with Tessa, of course, but her brother—my boss—has avoided me. He's even gone to the extent of passing occasional messages through her and Kayce when he turns up each morning to check on the cattle and take care of Teddy's needs.

Talk about driving the nail home with efficiency. Beau might have let the liquor convince him to watch my little show, but he's decided to shut himself away once more. This time, it really feels like I'll spend the rest of my summer on this ranch without any further interactions with the guy.

"When we talked last night, he said maybe a few more days. There's a rescue horse Storm said he'd visit to take a look at for me, to see whether she might be a good fit for the therapy program. But it's kinda a detour out of their way." Briar twists around onto her front and digs her phone out of the bag beside her towel. "Look at her sweet face... I'm really hoping it'll work out. She's called Willow."

The pony on screen is a miniature, with a white nose and spunky mane. When I pinch the image to zoom, I can see a chestnut patch covering her shoulder.

Sky croons and coos, peering over my shoulder, before I hand the phone along to Layla. "If there's anyone who'll sweet talk her, it'll be Stôrmand Lane." Sky adds.

"With those two out on the road together this long? We'll be lucky if we don't end up with ten dozen horses trotting back to Crimson Ridge after them. Beau's just as much of a horse-whisperer as Storm is."

Why yes, I'd swish my tail and gladly prance for that man and his mustache, too. So I'm no better than a filly seeking a good home, apparently.

As I pass Briar's phone back over, she gives me those dark eyes, always so filled with curiosity. "Have you watched any of Beau's old competition videos yet, Sage? He was really good, you know. Right up there with Storm."

Layla giggles from beneath her hat. "Oh, we know all about your love of watching rodeo footage, city girl."

Briar goes beet red, and it has nothing to do with lazing in the sunshine for hours.

My lips curve. "*Mmhmmm*. So we've all heard. Any more *family emergencies* to be taken care of lately?"

Briar groans, burying her face in the towel. She's absolutely never going to live down the fact that we eventually discovered *exactly* what she and Storm got up to in the bathroom at The Loaded Hog the last time I was in town. While we were out for dinner and all. Who would have thought quiet little Briar Lane would have a devious side to match the likes of Storm?

"I'm going to make sure to be very careful if I ever need to use the restroom at that bar." I readjust my sunglasses. It's too much fun watching her squirm as I keep teasing. "Maybe I'll suggest with their rebrand we could have some special signage made up to indicate the best 'quickie friendly' stall to use? Or consider investing in more robust countertops? Add in extra mirrors to really compliment the experience of getting railed cowboy-style?" I reach forward with both hands, grabbing an imaginary ass and thrust up with my hips.

Poor Briar moans behind her fingers, mortification covering her face, while the others are busy shrieking with laughter.

"Hey, hey... remember, the whole point of today was to leave your phone back at the cabin and get you to *stop* working." Layla gasps through her mirth and nudges my ankle. "I didn't pry your phone away from your talons and snarling fangs, risking life and limb, only for you to start chit-chatting about your clients."

"I only threatened to eat your soul once. Don't be so dramatic." There's no way I'm going to admit how bad my fingers have itched not having a phone with me today. Probably the biggest sign I needed this cold-turkey digital detox.

"Same rules apply to Sky, too. This is a chance for both of you to get your heads out of constantly working. The world is not going to end if you take a day off and don't answer five hundred emails or notifications, all before noon."

Sky groans. "I know. Luke confiscated my phone last night, so I wasn't even allowed to peek at it before coming out today."

"Mr. Rhodes really is the whole package, isn't he?" I tilt my head and grin at her.

The color of Sky's cheeks matches her hair. For someone who is confident in her own way, she becomes adorably bashful where talking about her cowboy is concerned.

"Alright, bitches. Since I'm banned from mentioning anything work-related, I'm gonna dunk my ass in that river before I officially cook like a rotisserie chicken out here." I push myself to a sitting position and hook the tie of my bikini bottom to reveal the deepening shade of brown and a paler line along my hip beneath the material. Hello, summer sunshine, you beautiful thing.

"I'm coming." Briar pops up.

Pretty soon, the four of us are back soaking in the crisp, crystalline waters, letting the afternoon float away on hour after hour of laughter. With nothing to do and nowhere to be as the sun tracks a path across the Montana skies.

Something that feels like we all needed, in our own separate ways.

"Are you sure you don't want a ride back to the house?" Layla slams the tailgate of her truck closed. "It's not exactly a short walk."

My best friend comes over to where I'm still happily occupying my prime sun-baking position, lying on my towel. She stands blocking my rays while shaking her copper curls out, then ties her hair up in a bun. Today's sunshine has brought all those cute freckles dusting her nose out to play, and she looks every inch at ease with life surrounded by these mountains.

I'm beyond happy she's found herself and made her home here with Colt. After having worried about Layla for so long—especially during all her years working herself to the bone to take care of her aunt. Even though I miss not permanently living nearby, it settles something in my heart knowing just how well loved and looked after she is.

My girl deserves all that, and more.

"No way. I'm here until that sky blushes pink and the sun dips behind Crimson Ridge." I cradle my chin with one fist, and smile sweetly up at her. "Besides, I've got a hot date right here with this Kindle and four book boyfriends who I don't have to choose between. So, shoo, and leave me in peace to enjoy my cornucopia of perfect dick, while you head on back to go save a horse… or whatever it is you and Colt spend your evenings doing."

Layla shakes her head and smirks back at me. "Ok. Don't go loitering after dark, Sergeant."

I pout. "You know those are my prime hours for having a bit of fun." I make the sign of the cross. "But for you? I promise, no after-dark rituals or fraternizing, Freckles. I'll text you once I'm tucked up safely in bed."

"Bye, Sage. We love you." The other two call from the truck as Layla climbs in, and my party for one commences. It's still stinking hot, and if anything it feels like the air only grows heavier as the light turns more golden.

Tiny beads of sweat glisten over my shoulders, occasionally rolling down my cleavage, and the ground is utterly baking beneath my towel. This is the kind of ranch-life summer scene to swoon over. Cicadas chirping, the scent of earth and grass, and the sound of trickling water for company.

I'm a little jealous of all the people who will get to stay here and spend time in this very spot for seasons to come. Even if it is with something as boring as fishing in mind, it's a picture worth appreciating for the way she poses like a mountain beauty queen under these endless skies.

My skin tingles with that touch of stinging sun really beginning to make itself known, and I'm about ready for another dip to cool off thanks to the baking heat and insanely hot scene I just finished reading.

Just as I get to my feet and gingerly pick my way across the rounded pebbles on the riverbank, I hear the sound of a truck engine cutting across my patch of solitude. Did one of the girls forget something?

Stepping in just enough to cover my ankles, the cool rises up from the soles of my feet in a blissful flood of relief.

Except, when I turn to wave, expecting to see the familiar sight of the Devil's Peak Ranch logo and Layla's smile, it's a white truck approaching instead.

Oh, shit.

My heart leaps into my throat, and I whip back to face the willows clinging to the opposite bank. What the hell is Beau doing back now, when Briar thought they'd be gone for another few days at least?

I tilt my head up to the heavens and let out a rueful chuckle. Of course, this would be our first interaction—me wearing nothing but my skimpiest bikini bottoms. Oh, well. It's thoroughly on-brand for *Sage.* This cowboy should probably have figured that out by now.

Using one arm to cover the girls, I start wading out into the river. Probably best not to assault him with a full frontal of hard nipples at this time of the day.

Behind me, the truck grinds to a halt with a spray of gravel, followed by the sound of a door slamming.

"What the hell, Sage?" Beau hollers my way.

I keep wading forward into the water, which right now, judging by his tone seems like the best place to plunge into and leave him to stew out there in the sun. "Oh, hi, boss. Didn't know you'd be back today." I shrug and glance back over my shoulder.

A cowboy ready to wring my neck shouldn't be so unbelievably hot... but, here we are. 'Pissed off bull rider' is a mighty sexy look on Beau Heartford. Unfortunately for him, the expression he's wearing doesn't produce the desired effect on me that he's evidently after.

I'm no woman who will fall in line at his heels like an obedient little puppy. It only tempts my devilish hellcat side, the part of me that immediately wants to flick her claws and push his buttons.

"I've been looking for you, trying to call you, and you weren't goddamn answering," he barks.

When I turn around, he's standing beside my towel with arms folded across his broad chest. There's an immediate smile tugging on my lips because I'm doing the same, only for very, very different reasons.

He's being extremely good and doesn't miss a beat at my almost nakedness. Cowboy here isn't looking anywhere below my eyes.

"You were?" I tilt my head to one side. "Oh, shoot… I left my phone with my fucks to give. They're somewhere back at my cabin."

"Sage." His brows furrow heavily. "Now isn't the time to play cute."

"No, it isn't. It's my day off, and the only game I'm playing is one that involves a swim and a nap. Maybe if you'd checked in with your *assistant*, you'd know my schedule."

His nostrils flare.

My pulse kicks.

Fuck you, Beau Heartford, for being the ultimate temptation. Have a taste of your own medicine.

"Get out of there."

Oh, this man knows nothing about the inner workings of my hard drive. Tell me to do something? My stubborn streak just rocketed like a shooting star, boldly carrying me to do the opposite.

I back further into the water, enjoying every second of his eyes flaring at the sight of my taunting grin. "Nope. I think I'll carry on, as you probably should, feel free to go on about your day."

"Don't you ever know when to not turn everything into a joke?" Beau's jaw is so tight he looks set to grind his teeth to dust. "This place is a working ranch. You could have been out here somewhere… could have been injured."

A wry laugh puffs past my lips. "Well, as you can see, I might be a little sunburnt, but other than these pesky tan lines, I'm fine." Other than the fact I'm currently arguing with my boss while cupping my breasts and attempting to avoid a nip-slip… yeah, totally fine.

"This isn't funny."

"Sure looks like it from here."

"Get out of the water." He takes a step forward, spreading those wranglers into a wide stance.

"Why?" I sink further below the water, shivering under the intensity of his focus.

"Because..." He lifts his cap off, then sinks strong fingers into his hair. This man has only been gone a couple of weeks, but seems to have a different energy to him. A grittiness beyond pesky details like those dark curls being more unruly, and the fact he's got some darker stubble going on along that tense jaw. Of course, it only makes the mustache situation even hotter. Screw him.

Ruffled, rugged Beau is a sight set to drive me wild with wanting something I can't have.

Definitely a good idea for me to stay submerged. Even if my pussy is loudly complaining, insisting I paddle back on over to the bank to get a closer look.

"Because?" My tits are below the water now, but I keep my arm in place. "I must have missed the part of orientation where my boss has rules against swimming after sundown. What are you gonna do?"

"Just... just get your ass out of the river, woman."

"*Mmm*, I think I'm perfectly fine, and I think I'm a big girl who will be perfectly ok continuing with my plans to enjoy a pretty sunset and a swim."

"*Sage*."

Nope. I'm not going to let any man tell me what to do. Especially not one who I have no commitment to, beyond our professional arrangement. Even though we've steamrolled past anything remotely *professional* with our late-night phone call. Whatever.

"Bye, Heartford. I'll see you in the morning... don't wait up."

I spin around and plunge below the surface. The cool, rippling water swallows me up and soothes my overheated skin. As air bubbles trickle from my nose, I feel my pulse fluttering away on hummingbird wings inside my chest.

The last thing I need right now, is to spend any more time staring at Beau Heartford.

As I dive a little deeper, skimming below the waterline, I feel a pressure wave slam into my back.

A rough grip closes around my ankle and tugs. Hard.

The act drags my body back through the water, unrelenting, continuing to reel me in until my spine collides with a solid mass.

Beneath a punishing hold, I pop up, breaking the surface. A hiss and a splutter bursts out of me like a drowned wildcat. "What —What the fuck?"

A deep growl is right at my ear, filling my senses. Taking hold of me so that I'm unable to move when I'm pinned against Beau's strong torso.

"You should come with a fucking warning."

CHAPTER 20

I've officially lost my grip on reality.

"You should have a damn sign hanging around your neck." My mouth presses against Sage's wet hair.

I'm inhaling that scent of *her* mixed with all the familiar notes of summer swirling in the air. Hay and wildflowers and the rushing water merge to give me the same feeling as being drowned in warm rain. My hands find her hips beneath the surface, and I'm so goddamn hard for this girl. Completely and utterly lost, surrendered to the relentless ache to have her. To be near her. So wildly frustrated, not just with Sage for giving me a heart attack, but the endless reminders of our god-awful circumstances. To the point that I've long since forgotten all the very reasons I shouldn't be acting on this impulse and yearning.

"I've got horses to settle in, the herd to check on, and I'm spending time I don't fucking have combing every inch of this ranch looking for you. Expecting to find you broken or bleeding somewhere... and instead..." My teeth pin her shoulder as I fist the ties of her tiny bikini bottom.

I can't even say the words out loud—of pulling up in the truck and seeing her looking like my every dirty fucking fantasy standing in the water damn near naked. Wildflowers and geometric patterns climb up Sage's thigh, scaling the swell of her right hip, leading to the side of her stomach. Of course, the ways this woman continues to be so effortlessly tempting and damn sexy keep mounting. Of course, she has a tattoo covering an ocean of flesh that is hidden away from sight until the opportunity arises to see her bared like this.

An urgency thunders in my veins, raw and desperate. My chest feels like it's being ripped apart by the pounding going on inside my rib cage.

"That sounds like a *you* problem." She hisses and tries to wriggle out of my hold. Here in the deeper water, she floats without being able to get a foothold, trapped and out of her depth as I easily stand my ground.

What the fuck am I doing? I'm fully clothed, plunging into this swimming hole without a second thought. Following after her, all because I've been driven beyond the brink of what I thought I knew how to handle. This girl has consumed every single aspect of my days and nights for over a week—in reality, for far longer than just the amount of time I've been away from the ranch—and I'm done trying to wrestle with myself anymore.

She's so damn soft beneath my touch, and the feel of her writhing against my body, fighting me to get away, officially undoes any last semblance of restraint I might have had.

Sliding one hand across her front, I feel her stomach cave beneath my touch. Sage lets out a noise that matches my agony. She knows just as well as I do that we can't be here like this, and yet there's no stopping where we're headed.

I grab her chin and tilt her face forcefully to the side in order to meet me. It only takes a split second, but I'm defenseless against all the ways I desire to bust past that forbidden boundary between us.

My mouth sinks against hers.

As I kiss Sage, I catch the briefest flash of honey in those dark eyes, and a cursed protest disappears beneath the force of my need for her. Those wetted lips I've imagined tasting in so many different moments are pillowy soft, so sweet, tinged with the heat of her fiery embers and sparks she's intent on kicking back my way. I'm hungry for every single one of those devilish noises and wicked flames I should know better than to be lingering here with.

Sage growls into my mouth, and it's a sound that races straight to my cock.

I dive forward, drawing her tighter against my body as I do so.

"You." *Kiss.* "Drive." *Nip.* "Me." *Suck.* "Fucking." *Lick.* "Insane."

With each word, I draw back enough to speak against her lips while keeping a fiercely tight hold on her. Not trusting my hands to resist wandering straight to the most intimate parts of this girl. The moment I allow my fingers to leave her jaw and waist, I'll be in even more peril than I am currently. There's too much of Sage on display right now for my brain to comprehend.

Does she have any idea the things I want with her? From her? The filthy fucking thoughts I've been plagued with since that night? Ever since I first laid eyes on her with that gaze tempting me into all kinds of trouble.

I pinch her bottom lip between my teeth, and her feistiness dissolves into a noise that spells my absolute ruination. A moan of frustration laced with pleasure escapes her, and I feel my cock thicken inside my jeans.

"We can't do this." It's more of a plea than anything that she gives me, as I back us toward the riverbank, stopping once we're shallow enough for the water to lap at my hips.

Spinning her around, I cup her face with both hands. "I know." *I fucking know.*

My lips trace her nose, her cheeks, back down to the corners of her mouth. I fucking need to taste her properly. This time, when I sink against the seam of her mouth demanding entrance, there's no stopping or pausing. A surge of fierce satisfaction roars straight through me when I press my tongue forward, and Sage kisses me back.

Her tongue slides against mine, and we're lost to the tangle of hunger swirling between our bodies. She makes the softest growling noise, a moan that I greedily drink down as her fingers curl into fists, bunched in the front of my sodden t-shirt.

"We shouldn't." Sage is a better person than I'll ever be. Reminding me of the exact words I've so determinedly tossed aside, as I let my mouth begin to roam freely. Working my way along her jaw, I'm biting and sucking a trail following her pulse point.

"I can't fight this, baby. I'm not supposed to crave you, but I can't find any more reasons not to." Goddamn, I'll get down on my knees and beg this girl right here, right now, if that's what she needs.

"Beau. You're *married.*" Her fists stay clenched in my shirt, but she rails harder against my torso. An act that shoves me away and clutches me near, all in the same action.

"Say the words, Sage. Tell me you don't want me anywhere near you." My palms skate down her shoulders, following the curve of her spine, as my lips keep descending to seek out her collarbone. Goddamn the feel of her soft breasts brushing against my torso is like heaven. I'm torn between the need to keep descending her body, to take them into my mouth, and the desire to feel her properly.

"Tell me you don't want to know what my touch feels like." I hum against her sun-kissed skin.

"Oh my fucking god."

"Tell me to stop right now. I'll walk away." My voice is low and gritty to my own ears while my teeth graze back up the column of her throat. As I pursue that tender patch of skin, my tongue laps at her pulse, tasting the faint hint of saltiness and sweet fragrance there.

"You're the one who had all the rules. Don't do this to me." She breathes, arching her neck to give me better access. "I'm not gonna be anyone's second prize."

That drives me further down this path of self-destruction. I sink my hands lower, palming and squeezing her ass beneath the water. "There's no putting you anywhere but front and center in my mind, baby. Did you think there would be anywhere else for you after taunting me out of my head with that little show of yours? Did you honestly think I'd be left doing anything but fucking my fist non-stop? You've got me so goddamn wrapped up in you, I'm out here forgetting any reason why I shouldn't even look at you."

"So what? You think you can just put your hands on me and murmur some pretty words, and I'll give you what you want?" Sage's hips chase my seeking, needy touch, even as she keeps sparring with me. This girl is clinging on with the same fervor I've been afflicted by. We're both as fucking twisted up by this thing as each other.

In no reality should I be considering what I'm about to do. But there is a version of me who can't think of any reason not to give us exactly what we're craving.

"Oh, you talk a big game. Do you like the idea of me making you feel good? Think I can't feel the way you're grinding your hips for more?" I slip beneath the edge of the fabric and my pulse thrums at the first glimpse of her softness—of her; wet and warm and so eager to meet me in this. "Do you want to know just how good it will feel when I give you what you've been longing for?"

"You have no idea what I need, cowboy." Sage's fingernails dig into my stomach through the thin cotton she's still got a death grip on.

Sliding my hand beneath her ass, I hitch her thigh, hooking her leg as high as possible, and damn near groan at what I find. It only takes the slightest nudge of that material to discover the slippery evidence waiting there for me.

"*Mmmfuck*, baby. Your sweet little pussy gives away your secrets. I think you'll like my fingers well enough when they know how to find that spot you love so much." I press lower, and she's so velvety soft as I reach that hidden junction of her thighs to begin toying with her entrance. "I'll bet no idiot boy you've been with has ever bothered to take care of your pussy like I know you need. Never stroking that spot only your toys get to.

None of them bothered to make the effort to get you off perfectly, did they?"

Sage lets her head sink forward against my chest, moaning louder as I start to explore. Pressing two fingers just inside her channel, holy fuck, I'm so painfully hard imagining what it might be like to finally feel her wrapped around me. My dick throbs with urgent need, and tight desperation takes hold in my groin. I'm not exaggerating when I say I've been struggling to go half a day without needing to relieve that tension. Only *she* has that sort of power over me, an all-consuming chokehold where I'm constantly lost to memories of the way she worked herself on camera.

"Fuck you, Beau." She lets out a pained noise of pleasure, clenching around me. She can't bring herself to stop this and I can't bring myself to walk away. So it looks like we're both selling our souls at this moment.

Her teeth bite down, and it's the hottest fucking thing.

Leave me covered in her marks. I'd gladly have Sage brand me head to toe with her bruises and scratches.

"No, I think those boys were all too busy fumbling around. Idiots who think the only way to please a woman is to ram them with cock and don't even know how to *properly* make a woman come." As I speak, I keep slowly sinking two fingers inside her. Curling and stroking, I keep that rhythm, rubbing against her inner walls until Sage's back arches and her thighs begin to shake.

"That's it, baby. Give me all those dirty little noises." I squeeze her ass, lifting her higher to open for me, dragging my knuckles through her seam, seeking out her swollen clit. "Do you know how impossible it was to avoid thinking of the way you looked on that camera? I've spent a whole week, supposed to be discussing horses and livestock, and no matter where I went, I kept getting hard at the memory of your wet cunt swallowing your fingers."

It shouldn't feel so satisfying to bear witness to the way her body jerks as I brush that sensitive little spot. It shouldn't be the softest, most delicate petal beneath my calloused fingers. There are a multitude of reasons I should tear myself away from this girl, and yet I can't find it within myself to let her go.

With a final firm stroke over her bud, I reluctantly drag my hand away. Not because I'm ending this, but rather that I've got plans for Sage. And for that, I need her out of this river.

This girl wanted to push me over the edge? Well, I'm plunging straight for the depths of ruin and dragging her down with me. My breath saws in and out of my chest as I sink my fingertips into her soft curves.

"You think you could get away with putting on that kind of performance and not face any consequences? You're going to lie there and take your punishment because I've been in agony all week long. Now it's my turn, baby."

CHAPTER 21

Sage

You're going to lie there and take your punishment.

I'm not sure who this cowboy is, and what he's done to lock away the Beau I've gotten used to being around. One thing's for certain, I'm in endless trouble with the way the man before me looks ready to consume me whole.

Beau is everywhere, surrounding me, still clutching me impossibly tight against his body. Meanwhile, any place his hands and torso and—oh my god, his wet jeans and t-shirt—aren't pressed hard against my figure, it's like he's replaced my blood with a tingling, pulsating sensation.

My lips sizzle with the scratch of his stubble and bristles of his mustache lingering there. I can still taste the warmth, a hint of coffee and mint from his mouth covering mine. My breasts ache, heavy and full after the way my nipples have dragged against the wet fabric plastered against his front. Not to mention, beyond all of the ways my body has just been swept up by Beau, he's left me with an unbearable emptiness and need between my thighs after playing with me so expertly.

I lick hastily over my lips, tracing the spot where he was a second ago with shallow, panting breaths. And that's when his palms skate down the slope of my waist, following the invitation to reconnect with my hips.

He's got a wildness to him, a desperation, and it's so fucking hot.

Those calloused hands, firm and wanting, reach beneath me. Beau picks me up in one rough movement, wrapping my legs around his hips. Water sluices off my lower body as he starts to walk us out of the water.

"What are you doing? You can't just—" I'm horny and incredulous. I've never had someone manhandle me quite like this before.

Beau doesn't stop. "Oh. I can. And I will."

As his steps hit the shingle, he stoops to collect my towel, holding me against him like I'm a goddamn feather.

"Beau..." I keep protesting. Because this is about as far from anything I might have expected from him. It's reckless. Sheer madness. He can't possibly be considering stepping across this line with me.

"No, Sage," he grunts, and keeps striding up the riverbank. "I've driven since before dawn to get back here."

As he speaks, I feel every one of his gritty words rumble straight through his soaking-wet chest and into my own. He refuses to set me down, or let me go, and proceeds to unhook the hinges on the flatbed.

"I've struggled with a head full of impure thoughts about the pretty girl staying in the cabin only fifty paces from my bedroom. I've spent the past hour going out of my head worrying about your safety. If it isn't already clear, you're on my mind permanently, and I'm about done with denying all the ways I'm needing you." The hinges clank loudly as the tailgate falls into place, and that particular noise sends a shudder straight down to my toes.

My stomach swoops in time with the realization that he's not simply tossing me into the backseat and locking me in his vehicle.

This man has other plans in mind.

He deftly flicks my towel to cover the metal below me, followed by depositing my ass on the back of his truck, then cages me in. There's absolutely no escaping this moment.

"Right now, the only thing I need is your permission. Or are you going to be stubborn as fuck about that, too?"

Beau stands between my knees, with water droplets coating his tanned skin, white t-shirt clinging to his muscled frame. The see-through cotton has partially hitched up on one side, revealing the trail of dark hair disappearing below the waistband of his dripping-wet jeans. Those stormy eyes of his are hooded as he stares me down with enough force to have me shivering even though the setting sun bakes our damp skin.

This cowboy looks like sex and temptation... and heartbreak.

He's the worst decision I could ever consider agreeing to.

"What are you doing?" I swallow hard. "You're—you're married."

"Are you telling me no?" He palms the sides of my ass, then hooks the waistband over my hips, tugging slightly against the sodden fabric.

"W–What are *we* doing? Beau, this absolutely cannot happen." My eyes can't stop bouncing all over him. He's so hot, so ruggedly powerful, and that mouth of his is right fucking there.

He strikes with the ease of a man who handles livestock and hauls hay bales on the daily. A cowboy who spent a career on the back of a bull. Flipping me onto my belly, it's an act that spins my world and leaves my barely-covered ass on display for him. "Is that a no, or do I have your permission?" He repeats, and this time, his voice has dropped so low and seductive that I think there will be nothing left of me after whatever happens next except for a wisp of smoke once my blood has self-combusted.

I bite my lip, heart shuddering inside my chest.

"Go on. Use your words, Sage. You do love to run that pretty mouth of yours, don't you?"

"Fuck you." I pant.

Asshole that he is, Beau knows that he has me trapped. A rich, dark chuckle comes out of him, and his fingers toy with the edge of the fabric. Taunting me. Teasing me. Being the wickedest of temptations with something he knows I'm already lost to.

"I'm waiting." He skates his flattened palm down the curve below my ass cheek. Every inch of skin he makes contact with comes alive, absolutely hypersensitive to his stroking exploration.

I'm torn in two. When did this man suddenly wrench free of his restraints? Until now, he's been unable to escape those bars he'd been locked behind. And why am I so completely enraptured by him, to the point that I'm willingly turning a blind eye to all the reasons why I should be stronger and tell him to stop?

Squeezing my eyes shut, I let the word loose on the warm evening air.

The single pin drop moment that might ruin both of us.

"*Yes.*"

Beau makes a satisfied, desirous noise and roughly yanks my bikini bottoms down, stretching them tight over my upper thighs.

"I think you like being bad," he murmurs.

"I think you like being bad with me." I'm so painfully aware that he's fully clothed, and I'm splayed out here naked, draped over the back of his truck with dust and the lingering scents of hay and leather floating all around me.

His palms roam up over the swell of my ass, and he groans while squeezing a handful on each side. "You have no idea."

My pulse is a stallion, galloping mile after frantic mile in the side of my throat. Yet, rather than acting swiftly, this man continues to stroke my damp skin. It's like he's stalling. As I shift my weight, I'm left wondering if maybe now that we've reached this precipice, he's about to reconsider everything.

Oh god. Is he about to prevent this from going any further?

"Did you touch yourself while you watched me?" I purposely taunt, with a breathy gasp. Shoving him to the edge of reason, because I'm not going to hang here in this torment on my own any longer. "Did you stroke your cock while watching me put on a show, or were you too afraid of what it might mean if you gave in?"

That earns me exactly what I'm after.

"Goddamn it, Sage." Beau sounds pained and desperate as the first crack of his open palm lands on my bare skin, making me jerk. Heat blossoms immediately, racing from the site of the sting to throb in my clit.

"I couldn't stop watching you." Another smack follows on the other side. "You had me trapped, even though I should have ended that call before it went as far as it did. You had me nearly unloading without a single stroke."

As he says those final words, they come out through gritted teeth when he gives two quick blows, one after the other, and then his palm soothes over the sting. The way he glides his touch over those spots of heated flesh simply melts my brain.

I want more.

"Did you have your dick in your hand?" I gasp and claw at the towel.

"The whole time." *Smack.*

"Fuck, that's so hot." My body jerks and arches and begs for him without restraint.

"What the hell am I supposed to do with you, my naughty girl?" Beau gives me one more imprint of his palm before finally delivering what I'm panting for. He dives a hand between my legs, sinking his fingers back into my weeping, clenching pussy.

"I'm not anyone's. I'm certainly not *yours*." My spine bows as I outright moan.

"You say that now, but you will be."

"That's rich..." I'm frantically trying to widen my legs but can't because of the bikini restraining me from simply opening fully for his touch. "Coming from the man who has a ring on his finger... who has a *wife*." As I gasp out the words, there's something I can't explain that happens to my body. This infuriating man curls his fingers and expertly strokes my inner walls, leaving my mouth dropping open on a whine.

"What I have is an *ex*, she's a divorce just waiting to be finalized. A signature on a page erasing her from my life. That woman is a shitty decision from my past, just like I'm sure you have a trail of broken hearts littering the streets in your wake, beautiful girl."

"I'm not interested in excuses." I claw my fingers for purchase as he strokes me so damn perfectly. "Don't—Don't give me some sorry story about being neglected as a husband, and so you've decided to stray."

"I've already told you, it's not like that." Beau draws back slightly to drag his fingers through my slit. This time he moves slower, but no less ruthlessly to liquify my body and brain into pure, glimmering pleasure, just for him. "I need you, Sage," he murmurs.

God, I can't handle hearing him say that. "I'm not interested in settling down, either. Don't think you can sweet talk me."

When he pushes back inside, my words falter. I damn near bite my tongue in half just to stop the slutty noises that want to escape my compressed lungs.

"Why does it have to be you?" My breathing hitches, and my forehead drops.

Beau fucks me with his fingers, and my body rocks back and forth, draped over the tailgate of his truck, leaving me nearly losing my goddamn mind. I want to fight this. I want to protest everything, and yet, I'm helplessly caught in a web of obsession over him.

Selfishly, I can't bring myself to deny us any longer.

All I can do is scrunch my eyes closed while allowing the pleasure to keep building. With each movement of his hand, my clit throbs and begs for his attention.

"One time." I whimper.

He makes a noise that sounds so smug, so wicked, like he's just won another world championship. "Just this once, *hmm*?"

"Yes." My teeth clench. I'm so close and hate that he's wound me into this frenzy.

"We both know that isn't going to be enough, baby."

Holy fuck, I can't seem to stop gripping his fingers harder and harder each time he calls me that.

"Until you aren't married anymore..." I gasp as he sinks deep, tightening around his fingers. "That's already one terrible decision I have to live with myself for making."

"You're not the one to blame here, Sage." His words are soft, in contrast to his rough handling of my body. "I'm the one in the wrong place at the wrong time. A man who should know better than to even think about looking at you. But I can't survive another goddamn day."

I exhale a shaky breath, a whimper of pleasure. "Then you'd better make this worth it, cowboy. *One. Time.*"

CHAPTER 22

Beau

Sage tells me yes, and it's like the split second when the bucking chute opens. Everything surges forward, launching into action, with heat and tension boiling in my blood.

She's got me going out of my head with a feral need to *fuck* and *own* and show this girl what she does to me. My pawing and grabbing at her is fierce and determined. I'm not lying when I say I need her.

It's driven me beyond the point of no return.

I strip her bikini bottoms off, damn near tearing the skimpy, wet fabric from her body in the process. Sinking straight to my knees, I cover her with my mouth from behind.

Sage is the sweetest goddamn thing. Her pussy feels so unbelievably soft and delicate, and I drown in the way she unfurls as my mouth roams between her thighs. All that fight, all that angst between us, simply disappears in the warm evening air like sparks flying and crackling high into the sky.

I feel like I'm fucking soaring, getting to taste her, lick her, and show this girl everything I've kept hidden away until now. My dick is hard as steel, throbbing with the need to be inside her, to feel her wrap around me like she did my fingers.

There's no drawing this out. I'm starving for the second she detonates, and it's going to be right now, so I can taste every sweet, slick drop. Sage makes the most beautiful noise above me as I shove my tongue inside and seek out her swollen clit with my fingers, working hard and fast. Her body clenches and trembles, then falls over that edge for me as I groan against her cunt.

"Goddamn." I lick her as far as I can reach, running long, slow strokes everywhere I can.

Sage moans. "Holy fuck. This is wrong." She sounds like the exact opposite of what she's saying is true.

"Doing the wrong thing turns you on, doesn't it?" I drag my mouth across her heated skin and get to my feet. Placing another kiss, this time over her spine, I help her to turn over and guide her to sit upright.

When Sage meets my hungry gaze, her cheeks are flushed. Those lust-blown eyes she gives me are the deepest, darkest pools to dive into. She's so fucking stunning, that urgency for her grips my chest and squeezes.

"Damn you. Why do I enjoy it when you're like this?" Her chest shudders with the comedown from her climax. The sight of her breasts, full and rounded, with tightly furled nipples, is so beautiful. All I want to do is worship every inch of this girl for days, weeks on end, and not come up for air.

I stare back at her and start to rid myself of the soaked t-shirt clinging to my skin.

"We both like it... because you and me? We're wired the same way." I drag it up over my head, then toss it to land with a wet slap in the flatbed of the truck. "We feel like we always have to be in control, but if you find that person you'd willingly give up control for..."

"Who says I'd give up anything for you?" Sage's eyes flicker up and down my stomach, and I can't deny how fucking incredible it feels to have her stare at me with open desire.

My hands work my jeans, but my eyes remain fixed on hers the entire time. "I think you're curious. You don't always have to be the one to hold tight. You deserve to have a safe place to let go. It doesn't make you any less strong, Sage."

She huffs, eyes flicking back and forth across my own. "What does it say about you, cowboy, that you're here with me like this? After everything you told me about why we *can't* and *shouldn't*?" Her nipples furl tighter as she loses the battle with keeping her gaze on my face, and drops her eyes to watch my hands shove my jeans over my hips, then push the waistband of my briefs down.

"It means I'm so fucking weak for you, Sage."

Taking myself in my fist, I stroke slowly from root to tip, trying desperately to keep my damn head.

Her plush mouth drops open. "Oh my god, you're pierced?" Sage throws her head back and lets out a wail of frustration. "Why are you so hot? Why am I being punished?"

"You like the look of my dick?" I step closer, heart hammering.

Those rich, honeyed eyes flare when her chin dips back down. "Are you serious? Look at that thing. It's so fucking sexy."

She bites her bottom lip as I stand there, more than a little dumbstruck by the stunning, confident creature right in front of me.

"That's the cruelest punishment yet... you've just shown me the greatest toy to ever play with, and I only get to take it out once, then I have to put it back?" Sage widens her knees and gives me a look that tells me I'm immensely fucked, because I haven't even been inside her yet, and I'm already making plans on how to bend my own rules.

"It doesn't bother you?" My throat bobs.

"The only thing bothering me is that I need you to stop teasing and get inside me, right fucking now." Sage damn near growls.

I'm wedged between her spread thighs, and her glistening cunt is right there—so close all I have to do is press my hips forward, and I'll feel her for the first time.

"Beau." She kills me with a seductive rasp and sultry look from behind a heavy curtain of lashes.

Just as I'm about to seal our fate with this, I freeze. My stomach clenches. What the hell am I doing? "Fuck, I don't have any condoms out here."

"I don't care. Fuck me raw." Her answer is immediate.

My cock jerks beneath my hold, hearing how certain she is. "Jesus Christ."

"You need my clear results? I haven't been with anyone since I was last tested."

My blood has been replaced with a herd of broncs, kicking and bucking and racing in every direction.

"I'm—I'm clear, too. But I get it if you don't trust—"

"How long has it been?" Sage licks her lips, and her ass lifts a little, moving those hips of hers a fraction closer.

My dick throbs, sensing just how near her drenched entrance is. A groan comes out of me, and I drop one palm to hit the tailgate beside her hip, bringing our mouths to hover just as close. I drag my nose to trace her jaw and drink down the noise of need and frustration she gives me.

"You wanna know how long?" I murmur against her skin. Allowing my lips to explore, I suck her earlobe into my mouth for a second. "A very..." I kiss the side of her neck. "Very..." Sage arches to give me better access to the spot just below her ear. "Very... long time."

"Then you'd better shut up and get inside me."

Sage reaches down between us, covering my fist with her own, and she gives me the final confirmation, the final thread of rational thinking severs, and my pierced tip notches at her core. We both suck in ragged breaths as her slickness, her unbelievably hot entrance welcomes me in.

"*Ffffuck*." I plant my mouth over her thrumming pulse and press forward. Holy fuck, she's soaked. Everything blanks as my dick slips inside, and this girl is the silkiest, softest thing wrapped around me.

I haven't done this with anyone in so damn long. Never mind the fact the last person I did have sex with forever ago is a woman who fills me with regret upon simply hearing her name.

Goddamn, this is the most incredible sensation. A rolling wave of heat pours through me with each steady roll of my hips.

"Oh god." Sage's hands fly to the back of my neck, threading into my damp hair. She holds my mouth against her throat, angling herself, guiding me to sink deeper. "That fucking piercing." Her teeth graze my pulse point on a moan.

She enjoys it? If I wasn't already ready to risk it all for this girl, knowing that it feels good for her is gonna unravel me real quick. A thought rushes at me, of the horrified look on Mandy's face when she learned I'd had it done. The type of reaction that couldn't be further from the one the girl currently wrapped around me like a dream. Sage's response to the sight and feel of my pierced cock is everything I could have hoped for.

The noises Sage makes as I push further into her velvety channel tell me just how incredible this feels for her, to match the way she feels like heaven for me. There's no pretending or performing. She's lost to the pure overwhelm of sensation, just like I am.

"You're so wet, baby. Christ, you feel so good." My tongue runs across her skin, tasting her and wanting to keep swallowing down every one of those tiny whimpers of pleasure she keeps giving me.

A tingling, tightening sensation zaps straight down my spine, and I seek out her thighs. Digging my fingers into her flesh, I draw back a little, then thrust forward. As I sink all the way to the hilt, we both groan in unison. Now, we're single-minded, simply chasing after that urgent need for relief. Sage's nails sink into me, clinging tighter to my nape as she lifts her hips, encouraging me to continue driving as deep as possible.

"Fuck—Fuck, right there." Her soft little rasp and needy moans shoot straight to my balls as I pump into her over and over.

"Jesus. Keep gripping me like that." I'm having to focus on anything but her walls rippling around me, and her soft, full breasts right there begging for my attention. Squeezing my eyes shut, it's all so fucking good. I'm pressing hard into her flesh, using a punishing hold to pin her hips right where I want. Driving forward repeatedly, tension builds low in my spine.

"Beau... holy shit... I'm so close." Sage gasps, and I feel it. I feel her tightening, and goddamn, I can't get enough of how incredible this is.

"Where do you want me to come?" I grit my teeth, fighting tooth and nail to not burst right then and there.

"Make a mess, come inside me." She yanks on my hair. "*Please.* Make a fucking mess of me."

"Jesus. Fuck." Hearing her demand that with a loud moan is my absolute ruin.

My mouth dives against her breast, sucking one of those tight nipples past my lips as I slip a hand between us. It only takes a few firm circles over her clit, and Sage loses it completely. Her body shakes, and then she's crying out with pleasure as her orgasm takes hold, with her pussy gripping me in rhythm with each shift and thrust.

It's such a beautiful thing to witness, seeing and feeling this woman give over her everything.

I can't hold out anymore. My balls draw up tight. All that searing, urgent pressure explodes through my groin, leaving me grunting and panting and gasping against her soft flesh. The force of my release thunders in my ears as my cock sinks as deep as fucking possible and unloads.

Jets of cum shoot out, filling her channel, slicking everything to become overheated and slippery between us. It feels like I keep pulsing, jerking, over and over. All my blood is in my dick, every single brain cell has flown out of my head, and the entire world around us evaporates in a mist.

I'm not a religious man, but I'm pretty sure I just found the woman I'll never get past having such a powerful, craving desire for. To willingly worship every day.

We blindly seek out each other's mouths. With sloppy kisses and murmurs exchanged as our hands roam freely, gliding over hot skin. I'm pretty sure my soul leaves my body, feeling her continue to clench around my length, encouraging me to remain buried inside. Her pussy keeps gripping me, as if she doesn't want me to draw away.

I can't move.

I don't ever want to move from this spot.

I'm already addicted to feeling her. To having those nails scrape my back. To the way we mold together so goddamn perfectly.

And I'm already thinking of all the ways I can have her again.

CHAPTER 23

Sage

My fluttering pulse has hardly subsided by the time we pull up to the ranch buildings in Beau's truck. Neither has the intense throbbing between my legs.

It's official. I've been rendered speechless, boneless, barely more than a limp noodle where my body used to be.

After fucking me senseless, the cowboy beside me has been quiet since leaving the river and making the short drive back across the property. I guess neither of us really knows what to say after the whirlwind of everything that just happened. A force sweeping us up and unceremoniously dumping us out in the deepest depths, leaving the two of us to figure out how to navigate a safe return. Now that we've clawed our way back to shore, there's a peaceful little silence, but it's *silence* all the same.

Just the windows rolled down and the sweet evening air winding around where we both sit. A gentle, warm breeze caresses my skin to match the cloud of bliss I'm currently floating upon.

One time.

Well, shit. What a singular, mind-altering occasion that proved to be.

I'm mentally cursing myself for making that foolish statement, right before discovering the equipment Beau's secretly been packing.

My pussy is still sobbing in disbelief at that particular revelation.

He parks the truck, and overhead, the sky has transformed into a cloak of rich purple velvet. A few pink streaks fly high above Crimson Ridge in the distance, and I wonder if my sanity is soaring carefree and giddy up there somewhere. She's clearly abandoned me to this cowboy's clutches this evening.

That is, I guess, up until now. Because this is over.

I'm sure it's not exactly going to be straightforward to look my married boss in the eye come tomorrow morning. Not now he's had his face buried in my pussy, and I can feel his cum seeping down to slicken the space between my thighs. All of that horny, sex-fueled tension has finally been relieved, which means this is one-hundred percent the best decision for both of us.

I gulp down any lingering protests to the contrary, and smooth my hands over the cotton sundress I was able to throw on before leaving the river. Beau is still stuck wearing damp jeans, but found a dry shirt somewhere in the back of his truck.

"Thanks for the lift." My fingers curl around the door handle. And my throat feels a little coarse.

"*Mmhmm*," he hums, no hint of what he's thinking discernible in that noncommittal sound. Climbing out my door, I catch sight of him sliding out his side at the same time.

Rounding the front of the truck, he's right there, all long strides and hands tucked in his pockets. I duck my chin as I walk past him, because how the hell do I do this part? What is there to even say? Abandoning any attempt to figure it out, I shake off those incessantly whirring thoughts and make my way in the direction of my cabin. The sound of a summer night follows me, with crickets humming, just like the shadow of Beau's large frame tracks after me along the path.

He walks me right up to the door, and my cheeks develop a little extra heat to them when we pause beneath the covered porch and he's right there at my side. Except, Beau is back to being his wordless, confounding self.

I twist the handle and flash him a brief smile. "Ok, well, goodnight. See you for coffee at 0800 hours, boss." Then, I push inside.

I've hardly stepped across the threshold when one long arm shoots out above my head, blocking the doorway. Beau's shoulders fill the frame.

"I'll let you get what you need," he says, jerking his chin in the direction of my room.

There's no question in his voice. It's just a flat-out instruction, and I'm left craning my neck to stare up at him, as my stomach does a series of flips.

"I've got everything. So, I'll just..." I point to my bag and towel currently in my hand before hitching a thumb in the direction of my room and bed. Meanwhile, my heart starts skittering around inside my chest, because the look currently on his face is one I don't know how to interpret.

Beau reaches out to catch me by the waist, his thumb sliding up to my ribs. With a firm line set in his jaw and ocean-deep eyes, he begins to walk me backward.

"Where do you think you're going?" His voice is low. That tone winds a coil inside me upon hearing his words float out all smooth and rumbly into the stillness of the night.

My lips twist the tiniest fraction. "To bed?"

He makes the sexiest, velvety noise of disagreement. "You're in my bed, baby."

"I don't think that's my place."

"It is." His eyes flash.

"Shouldn't we consult those marriage vows?" I sound incredibly breathy for a woman who strode away from that vehicle, confident that I'd close my cabin door and lock away our secret. One that was to be kept between the two of us, the mountain sunset, and the tailgate of Beau's truck.

Bringing one hand up to cup my jaw, Beau slowly thumbs the fabric of my dress with the other sitting on my waist. He studies my features with a slight furrow to his brow. "The vows that don't mean shit? The piece of paper I've done nothing but punish myself by sticking to, while the other party in that arrangement did whatever the fuck they wanted?"

All I can breathe and think is *him* as those warm palms hold me close, and everything in his energy crackles with an intensity, a damn forceful insistence that feels like he won't allow me to leave his side. I'm not sure that I want to, either.

He shakes his head. "Sage... I've been nothing but faithful all this time, and now that I've met you? None of that even goddamn matters anymore."

"But—" This is leading us firmly into territory that I don't know how to navigate, or wade through.

"There's been no one in my bed. Not for years." Beau's eyes go so damn soft when they gaze down at me. If there was a true weakness I might have for this man, that expression right there is enough to have me forgetting everything I know about myself and our circumstances, and what it might mean if I agree to this.

"Years?" My teeth catch my bottom lip as I melt into the way he holds my face so tenderly.

"Yes, *years*, baby. Let me have this. Give me this before I go insane with needing you. *Please*."

I attempt to hide my smile away, try to resist the urge to simply throw all caution to the wind and climb all over him at the outright pleading in his tone. Instead, I take a deep breath in an effort to keep my cool and give him a tiny nod in agreement beneath his palm.

Feeling the moment I relent seems to satisfy him. He reluctantly lets me go long enough to hastily gather up a few things for this impromptu sleepover.

"Wait—" As I zip my bag up, I tilt my head to one side. "What about the horses?"

"What about them?" He drags a hand through his hair, eyes fixed on me as he musses those wild, partially damp strands and drives my ovaries to whimper with how sexy he looks.

"You said you had horses to settle in."

Beau pokes his tongue against the inside of his cheek, raking his gaze down my body. "We do. Four new ones."

"Can I meet them?" My lips curve into a tiny, pleading grin.

He exhales heavily and scrubs a resigned palm over his mouth. "Fine." The heated expression in his eyes says this additional detour is anything *but* fine.

I step into his frame, going onto my tiptoes, and when he dips to meet me, I let my lips brush over his, forming a smirk against his mouth as I do so.

"Thank you. That might even earn you one more look at my pussy, hot stuff."

Beau lets out a delicious, dark chuckle. "No question, that's absolutely happening more than once before tonight is over." Before I can evade him, he drags my bottom lip between his teeth, slowly tugging in a move that makes my clit throb, and successfully pulls my brain apart at the same time.

"The deal was one time."

Beau slips his hand over mine, then threads our fingers together to begin leading me in the direction of the barn. "One time, huh? That sure as hell sounds like a strange way to say *one night.*"

My bag is lifted from my hands, and he drapes the duffel's strap across his chest in the way he'd likely done hundreds of times before... when it was still his bag. God, I'm a fool who can't wipe the grin off her face. This grumbly cowboy has succeeded in turning my legs to jelly and my blood to sparkling stars.

Swallowing hard, I realize that he's not only holding tight to me, his fingers interlaced with mine, but he's taken possession of my overnight items, too. Apparently, Beau Heartford isn't risking any chance of me slipping away this evening.

This could possibly be the worst idea I've ever contemplated agreeing to.

But then again, I never was very good at being the good girl.

We reach the barn, and as soon as we step inside under the

warm glow of overhead lights, I hear the added noise of the stable being halfway full. There are more snorts and shuffles, a stronger scent of hay, and a richness fills the air that is unmistakably the additional bodies now calling this place home.

As we make our way from stall to stall, Beau introduces me to each new horse. The whole time, he can't stop touching me, and I damn near swoon off balance with how good it feels. I'm a slut for soaking up every tiny fraction of his attention, each micro-point of contact between our bodies.

Beau keeps his arms wrapped around me from behind, covering my spine with all his warmth and strong torso damn near enveloping me like my very own cowboy blanket. When we stop to look in on each stall his voice rolls through my back as he tells me about them one by one, alternating between resting his chin on my head, then stooping down to feather kisses along the slope of my neck.

Goldie. Clover. Dusty.

"They're gorgeous. I'm sure they'll love their life here," I say, staring at the prettiest set of long lashes batting my way. Dusty is a bay gelding, while the other two are chestnut mares, so I'm told.

Although, I wouldn't place a lot of faith in my brain to remember much beyond the way Beau's mouth feels pressed against my ear. I'll probably have to get him to repeat all this tomorrow so I can take notes, and actually, you know, do my job.

"*Mmm.* I think you might look pretty gorgeous in the saddle."

There's nothing but a riot of wings where my stomach used to be. Internally, I'm a complete mess of sensation because this man is exposing me to a side of himself that I'd do very well to forget immediately.

I cannot go past tonight with memories of Beau's stubble and mustache tickling my throat as he talks about his horses in that dulcet, low register.

"You said you had four horses?"

"Here." Beau squeezes me even tighter, and steps us toward the next stall.

Staring back at us with curious eyes, and an elegant, long neck, is a bluish-hued gray horse with a dark mane and ear tips, along with pretty dappled spots covering his back.

"This is Mist. He's going to be my guy for most of what I do around here. We'll need a bit of time to get to know each other, to see how we get along and start talking the same language."

I smile, looking at the creature before us, who snorts and bobs his head as if agreeing with those exact sentiments. His neck dips my way over the door, and I reach up to run a hand along his nose.

One of Beau's big paws lifts off my body—coming up to cover my hand, dwarfing mine, as we both stand there admiring the beautiful horse—and I'm entirely unsure how to process this moment. It feels like a whisper in the quiet stillness of whatever late hour it is, a tender moment where our fingers intertwine, and Beau encourages me to explore and brush my touch over Mist's forehead and soft ears.

My pulse is doing rapid-fire somersaults in the side of my neck.

"He's a good boy. A Blue Roan," Beau murmurs. "I've had my eye on him for a while, just been waiting for the chance to finally bring him home."

"Sounds like you've got yourself a new bromance. Better bring your best dating game, Heartford." Any further reply I might have had gets cut off when the cowboy at my back lets out a wicked noise, and starts nibbling on my neck. Leaving me to falter over my next attempt at words.

He makes a pleased hum, all too satisfied with himself, as he draws both our hands back down to wrap across my stomach. "What was that switch you were talking about? The one that turns your brain off? Is that it right there?" Beau nibbles and sucks again, doubling down in his efforts to completely scramble my senses when he kisses the spot just below my ear.

"You're dangerous after dark," I whisper.

"You have no idea." His rumble is gravely and oh, so deadly to my sanity.

"What if I want to sleep in my own bed?" The words are hardly past my lips before Beau is walking us in the direction of the double doors leading out of the barn.

"Then I'll follow you there," he says, so self-assuredly. If I didn't know this man had been a professional athlete, a rodeo star, there's no hiding that cockiness in his tone.

Goddamn him, without hesitation, I'm lapping up every second of this overindulgence... of this relentless presence and roaming glide of his touch. It's like I'm the center of his universe, and unfortunately, I'm the kind of creature who enjoys that degree of undivided attention a little too much.

"Run out of things to argue with me about, pretty girl?" He chuckles, knowing he's won and I'm officially a blissed-out little kitten, contentedly purring while curled in his arms. "We done? Can I take you the fuck to bed now?"

There is no way I should be nodding.

Not in any plane of existence, should I be agreeing to this.

And yet, I do.

"Take me the fuck to bed, Beau Heartford."

CHAPTER 24

Beau

One solitary night.

One opportunity to get this out of our systems.

Sage thought we were going to stop after *one time?* Like hell I was ever going to let that happen. As the seconds and minutes and hours ticked by, time passing long beyond the midnight hour, we continued to get lost in each other. While tangled in my bed sheets, one time turned into a multitude of times. A cascade of positions and earth-shattering climaxes, the likes of which are going to be forever ingrained in my mind.

Sage is everything I never knew I needed. And there's no way this girl isn't going to end up as mine.

I've just got to figure out how to get us through these next couple of months... to work around the issue of carefully extracting myself from the one major obstacle standing between us. Most importantly, how to do so without potentially harming Sage, or dragging her into something that isn't her shitstorm to contend with.

Goddamn, I've got to measure my footsteps so lightly, I'll have to spend the next few weeks walking on fucking eggshells at every turn.

This girl is mine. I've been craving her and undeniably needing her this entire time, and I don't care if it's only been one night exploring each other's bodies. I couldn't give a shit if it might seem like I'm leaping in too fast, too soon. We've had a special kind of spark glowing between us since that very first day on the sidewalk.

This attraction between us has been building relentlessly. There's not one day gone by since Sage first collided with me, bursting into my life, that she hasn't occupied my thoughts like a fever dream I never want to be woken from.

Now, I've got the task on my hands of not letting that budding flame flicker out if Sage doesn't take to the idea of waiting for me to sort my mess of a life out. She's already told me she doesn't want to commit to anything, which adds another layer of complexity to whatever this is. There's no evading the reality that we're drawn together, inexplicably so, beyond something as fleeting as lust. This right here is no fickle desire; it's as solid and sure as how it feels to be grounded in a saddle.

Which is probably why I'm still clutching her tight, and have no intention of allowing her to leave this bed. As soon as she does, this spell will be broken, our race against time will have run its course, and I'll be left with only a hollow feeling in the spot beside me. I'll be cursed with the sight of an empty pillow. Whereas, right now, it's a place her head looks so natural to be occupying as she stares back at me from beneath heavy-lidded eyes in the faint morning light.

"Not getting up bright and early to go put on a pornographic showcase in the workout room?" Her voice is raspy with sleep, and heat surges low in my stomach.

I roll in her direction and settle myself to cover her soft body with my own. Bracing myself on my elbows, I push her silky hair back off her forehead and let my gaze roam all over those stunningly beautiful features of hers. Rueing with each heavenly stroke that I'm not going to be able to trace her warm skin with my fingertips like this tonight or tomorrow or however long it'll be. Until the second our time comes back around, and I can prove to her just how good we are together.

"You say I need to come with a warning... but I'm telling you, that weight lifting routine of yours is a hazard. Definitely put a lock on the door if you're gonna be out here flexing these abs when you've got guests staying in the future." She grins sleepily at me while poking the side of my stomach, and fuck my life, there's no doubt that I'm already lost to her.

"Can you blame me? I've got to watch your ass running around in skin-tight shorts. A man's gotta find some way to get rid of that frustration." I meet her soft smile with a smirk of my own.

"Just give me your credit card and ten minutes online. I can find you some handy toys to help with that."

A laugh escapes my lungs, and I drop my head down. I can't resist dragging my mouth along her body, seeking out those perfect breasts. I'll probably die a little on the inside each time I have to see them covered.

"Can I be honest for a moment?" I kiss her sternum, continuing to map her softness beneath my lips.

"Always." Sage threads her fingers into my hair and arches her back. "I'm finding the talkative version of my boss quite a revelation." She hums, content to let me wedge myself right here between her thighs, yet again.

"Watch that smart mouth." I nip at the side of her breast.

The laugh Sage lets out is a sound I want to drink down every single morning for the rest of my life. "Go on then. Tell me all your secrets, hot stuff."

"I've never done something like this," I murmur against the curve of her stomach.

"Mr. Heartford." She gasps with a faux-scandalized look widening her eyes. "Don't tell me I popped your cherry?" Her fingers sink a little tighter into my hair, holding my gaze.

"Christ." I exhale a chuckle and give another gentle nip with my teeth. "No. *This*... not exactly a one-night stand... but..." I don't want Sage to get the wrong idea about me. She needs to be under no uncertainty. I'm not that guy. I'm not anything but hopelessly gone for the girl currently looking back at me with honeyed streaks to her brown eyes.

The girl who looks like all my future mornings and nights, and every moment in between.

"Aw, look at you. Mr. Chivalry, right until the final orgasm."

"How do you expect me to leave you alone? Now I know how sweet your pussy is."

"You said it yourself. We can't. There are much bigger things at stake here, cowboy. So we've got it out of our systems."

"You're in my veins, Sage." The confession comes out of me, firm and resolute. Holding her eyes, I crawl back up her body and lean my hands on either side of her head. "Baby, there's no getting you out of my system."

Just as I'm contemplating a final round of demonstrating to Sage just how good we fit together, her phone pings with an incoming text.

She lets out a groan and rolls onto her side, stretching to reach for it. Suits me just fine. I take the opportunity to shift my weight and position at her back, spooning my girl from behind; brushing her hair aside, I kiss a wet line along her nape and shoulder.

Sage reads the message while I keep up the assault on her with my mouth. "I've got to go."

My eyes flick over her shoulder to read the name on the screen, and I make a low noise. Like hell I'm letting this girl go spend the day with the likes of the Hayes brothers while she's all revved up.

"How long do you have?" One hand reaches around to cup her tits, and I start playing with her nipples. She's still a little tender after all the attention I've lavished on them since last night, and her body jerks as I pluck at the stiffened peaks.

"Beau..." It's only a partial protest. "I'm just confirming what time to meet. You know it's my first pitch of the rebrand. I have to get my shit together if I'm gonna dazzle them."

"Oh, I don't doubt that you'll be anything but remarkable," I murmur, uninterested in letting her go until I've satisfied this insane need to have her shatter for me one final time.

As I keep working the side of her neck harder, my palm slides from her breasts down the soft swell of her stomach. When I reach the heavenly spot between her thighs, I slowly press against her pussy, parting her to dip a finger into her wetness. Seeking out her swollen clit, I start to glide firm circles as Sage writhes and whimpers beautifully for me.

"I can't stay in bed with my boss all day."

She's not telling me no, and that signals all the green lights for me to see this through. As I keep rubbing and dipping through her slickness, I see over her shoulder the follow-up text, confirming their meeting time. It's not for a few more hours, which is about the best fucking news considering the fact I'm desperate to keep her trapped beneath me for as many infinite minutes as I can cling to.

"Beau." Sage gasps my name, as tremors start taking hold of her body.

"Sorry, I'm busy."

"This isn't funny. I have to shower and get ready."

"One last kiss, baby," I whisper the heated words in her ear.

My girl shivers with a little moan of pleasure.

That's all the invitation I need. It's like I'm a man starved for air, not like I've already had my mouth on her too many times to count through the night, as I roll onto my back and drag my girl to straddle her luscious thighs over my face.

"What? No..." Sage huffs with a hint of a whine edging her voice when she has to brace herself against the headboard above me. "You said this was a one-time—one-night only thing."

I look up at her beautiful body from beneath her pussy, raking my eyes across every single curve and inch of smooth skin. I'm doing my utmost to commit every single part of her to mind, because I'm gonna have to hang on tighter than I ever did to the back of a bull in order to survive what comes next after she disappears from this spot.

Blowing gently over her pussy, I keep my eyes locked on hers. "You haven't left my bed yet, I'd say it still counts as one night."

Any more talking at this point is gonna take up far too much precious time. My hands are demanding, hungrily seeking out the flare of her hips. Dragging her down to my mouth, I set about working her hard and fast.

"Fuck. *Fffuck.* Oh god." Sage shudders and moans above me, letting lose every raspy curse and sexy as fuck sound, completely unrestrained, as her arousal coats me and I get goddamn lost inside her cunt.

"That's it, full weight, baby." I bite down on her inner thigh, before roaming my mouth to lick and swirl my tongue and suck down on her clit. I draw that pouting bud between my lips and drink down every single one of Sage's responses.

I devour the way every time my mustache grazes her clit, her eyes roll back in her head.

"Holy shit. I'm so sensitive, I can't—" She cries out and humps my face at the same time.

"Fuck yes. That's it. I know you can."

"I'm so close." Her gasps fill the room.

Another text comes through, cutting across the thudding of my pulse and ache of my straining cock. Before Sage can register the sound, before she can come back into her head, I slap my hand to the side and steal her phone.

Keeping a punishing grip on one thigh so that she can't escape the position I need her to stay in, I see it's from Hayes asking if she might be available to come in earlier after all.

Not happening.

"Passcode," I growl against her core.

"Why?"

"I'm buying you some extra time."

Her features slacken with pleasure as her hips keep grinding over my mouth.

"Fuck. Fine..." She gasps out the numbers and continues riding my tongue like the perfect girl she is for me.

I type a quick reply, all while keeping my mouth dragging over Sage's seam.

"Beau... what... what are you saying?" One of her hands sinks into my hair while the other keeps bracing herself on the bedframe.

Smirking against her pussy, as I let my mouth drift back to focus in on her clit, ruthlessly working her now, I show her the message I just sent.

Sorry, I'm needed for a breakfast meeting, and my boss is demanding that I get there immediately.

"Oh god." Above me, this perfect fucking dream of a girl moans loud and unrestrained. Yeah. She gets off harder than ever being naughty like this. I toss the phone aside and finish her off. As Sage's orgasm builds into that peaked crescendo I'm addicted to witnessing, I bring my fingers around to tease her ass. The feather-light press of my fingers back there, just as I suck down on her clit, sends her tumbling over the edge.

My tongue keeps lapping at her, massaging slowly and reverentially through her come down as Sage's body sags and trembles with the intensity of her climax. Her sweet whimpers and fingers twisted so tight in my hair are everything. I just want to draw this out, keep her floating in this very place, where time fucks off and leaves us alone. Why can't I simply turn every one of these seconds into the eternity they used to feel like whenever I was holding on for grim death in the arena?

Eight seconds used to last forever.

Now? Now, each second is a cruel, lightning-quick thing that slides by all too rapidly, accompanied by thundering heartbeats and the flutters of her heavy lashes as she stares down at me with panting breaths.

"You really do like being bad with me, don't you?" Sage is perfectly flushed, her nipples hard and darkened with arousal. She's a goddess with her thighs clamped around my head, and I'm scrambling to think of another reason, any other means possible, to drag this out.

But this time... this time, it really is over for us.

Utterly blissed out, Sage shifts off me. The moment she goes to slide out of the bed, my hands linger on her body, dragging and stroking heavily over her curves. As I lie here with all the blood from my body in my groin, my floundering heart is busy trying to crawl out my chest to follow after her.

She swipes up her phone, and looks at the message again, then nibbles her lip and hits me with the kind of mischievous grin cast back over one shoulder that seals my fate.

"I can't believe you sent that."

"Don't say I'm not a good boss. I just bought you the time you need to *prepare*." I push up onto my elbows, and her plush, soft lips are there to meet mine straight away. Sage kisses me deeply, tasting herself, humming straight into my mouth.

"Thank you," she speaks against my tongue. And I don't think she's talking about the text on the phone. "I'm gonna shower. Is it ok if I use yours?"

"Sure." I shift my weight, and as she pulls back, headed for the bathroom, my legs are already swinging over the side of the bed. Every cell in my body has zero interest in being separated. The only desire I have is to follow after her, to relentlessly pursue my girl.

Sage backs up, gloriously bare, shaking her head and holding out her palms. "Nope, no. Down, cowboy. You stay over there."

"I need to shower, too." A grin takes over my face. With hungry eyes, I devour her body, dragging over her nakedness from head to toe.

All that does is earn me another shake of her dark hair, and she points at the bed disapprovingly. "Absolutely fucking not. Don't move."

And with that, my girl collects her bag and disappears into my bathroom. But not before sticking her head back around the door, gifting me one last glimpse of her beautiful eyes and perfect ass.

"You're on your own now. But feel free to think of me while you stroke your dick, Cock Ring."

CHAPTER 25

Sage

Pulling into the parking lot of The Loaded Hog, I've got my windows down to let the warm summer breeze glide across my skin, and hopefully blow away the sex hormones clinging to me like cotton candy clouds.

Good lord, I've had some fantastic nights in my life, indulging in a whole lot of decadent fun, but nothing can hold a candle to all the ways Beau Heartford just upended my world.

After parking, I quickly check my reflection in the rearview, scrutinizing myself for any smudged mascara or pesky love hearts that might be hanging around in my eyes, long overdue for their checkout time.

What might be most depressing in this scenario is that I'm going to have to lie through my teeth to Layla... and Briar... and Sky—which sits awkwardly on my conscience even just thinking about the idea. It's not like I can tell anyone a single detail about my night. I can't even tell my best friend about the most incredible sex I've ever had. *Shit.*

A fact that is indeed a crying shame, because that cowboy certainly knows how to use the equipment he's been blessed with. It's honestly doing his dick a disservice to not be able to publicly, and enthusiastically, sing the praises of his ability to find *that* spot, repeatedly.

Talk about a revelation. There's nothing more disappointing, after a bunch of flirting and talking a big game, than to discover that getting down to business can so often involve fumbling hands and failed orgasms.

Where Beau and I are concerned, we crash land firmly in the category where our chemistry between the sheets is explosive.

Goddamn him and his slutty mustache for making me come harder than I've ever been able to, with or without the assistance of a battery-operated teammate.

A flood of heat rushes between my thighs, recalling every stroke and scratch of his mouth beneath me this morning.

Nope, my pussy and I are not spending any more time thinking about the vision of him staring up at me while sucking down on my clit until I couldn't stop shaking.

I take a moment to check my phone, immediately feeling a plummeting feeling in my stomach when I open my inbox to find a flood of messages from Layla.

Um. Hi.

You dirty little liar.

So much for "I'll let you know I'm home safe." Since you never actually messaged me, I'm going to assume you either went full wolf shifter and slept naked under the stars, or your memory got wiped by aliens.

If that's the case, here's your reminder that you have an important meeting today.

(Good luck, by the way).

Shit.

Sorry!

Humblest apologies being accepted, or do I gotta grovel my ass up to Devil's Peak?

I might have gotten a little over-cooked in the sun and forgot to check my phone. But I'm fine, and about to toss my brilliant ideas at The Loaded Hog... so fingers crossed you don't hate me and maybe feel like smooching a horseshoe for good luck for me?

God, one night, and I'm already making up lies to my best friend. Even when Layla was first sneaking around with Colt, she at least told me there was someone, even if she avoided telling me the details of who it was.

As I'm scrolling through a few last minute details to refresh myself, I see there are some new messages from my sisters. It's nothing in particular, just some cute photos of them and their friends hanging out together in their school uniforms. Seeing their faces sends a further double-dose of worry through me, because no matter how much I might want Beau, what would it do to my family if this got back to them?

They might not realize just how much pressure I feel on my shoulders to do everything perfectly, and maybe it was never their intention, but it's always been there. Coming from a family of successful academics and scientists, while I've always been the creative free spirit? Yeah, the subtle pressure has always hung around my head that I should be following their path.

When I told them I wanted to start my own marketing and PR agency, they were supportive, as they always are. But the lingering feeling never quite goes away that they are expecting me to do everything *right*.

Would it crush them entirely to know I've made the choice to fall into bed with a married man? Especially knowing what my mom went through to make the decision to walk away from a terrible relationship. She would be so disappointed. I can already see her face lined with worry and sadness at me being the wild child who has once again failed to live up to expectations.

My selfishness when it comes to desiring Beau can't be enough of a reason to let myself get caught in a complicated situation. We've made the correct decision ending it after one night. Even though it's going to be insanely hard to be around him from here on out, I'm determined to do the best I can with this job.

Tessa is counting on me. My family keeps telling me how proud they are of me. The twins look up to me.

Christ. What kind of role model am I being for my younger sisters by messing around with a man who is legally still married? Putting to one side all of the pieces Beau has let me know about, there is a very real scenario that paves the bottom line here. He isn't single, and he certainly isn't a man who I should be allowing myself to be distracted by.

Let alone, how hard would my family take it if rumor got out that I fucked my boss? That Beau fooled around with an employee? Shit like that sticks, and couldn't be worse for my reputation starting a new business. Even if unproven, it might become a lingering shadow following me around, the kind to undo all the hard work I'm putting in here to make the ranch a success as it opens its gates to the public.

Glaring at myself in the mirror, I give myself the bottom line... time to pick my jaw up off the floor, wipe the drool from my chin, and dust off this post-multiple-orgasm daze I've been afflicted with.

I've got a client proposal to nail, and all going to plan, an event to host that'll knock Crimson Ridge's cute lil cowboy booties off.

Slipping out of the truck, I scoop up my things from the backseat, clutching everything against my chest. I've got all the tools I need to wow this particular Hayes twin. *It's showtime.* The moment when I need to throw my shoulders back and shake off the events of last night. I'm moving forward, starting right now.

We certainly got it out of our systems, and it had to end. That's the reality of the secret we now share. Life carries on.

CHAPTER 26

Sage

As I'm making my way to the bar's front entrance, a voice calls out my name.

"Out back, Sage."

"Ahh, it's Chaos himself." I spin on my heel to find the familiar scruffy, sandy head of hair and grin of Chaos Hayes stacking empty beer kegs by the back door. He's got his wild mane tied in a topknot and wears a black tank with ripped jeans, revealing all those rodeo athlete muscles. I've already had the chance to admire them up close on the day he was out at the ranch helping unload hay bales. He's exceedingly pretty; I'll give him that, but doesn't spin my teacups.

"Come through this way. My brother's inside. I'll stick around and help interpret the grunts and scowls if you like?"

"Don't worry, I'm prepared. Everyone knows a wild creature comes gently when there's a tasty treat on offer." I fish out the bag of candy from my duffel and rustle the contents.

"Smart girl."

"This is what you do when you're not wrangling broncs? You wrestle kegs pretending they're cute little baby cows?"

"More like ropin' unruly patrons to get 'em out the door at closing time." He winks, gesturing with those ingrained country manners for me to go inside ahead of him. "Nah, my brothers and I are just trying to help out in the places we can. Wes is mostly too busy, not to mention goddamn cranky, what with taking over our family ranch. Cam loves flashing his Sheriff's badge around, so he's more likely to scare customers off than actually be useful. But we can all see the potential in the place, so family does what it does, and we're pitching in."

"Four brothers running a cowboy bar? Well, that's our marketing campaign right there." I laugh. "Let me get my notebook out. How many of you are already taken, and how many of you can I truss up to dangle like baubles in the window?"

"Oh, you haven't heard about the Hayes curse then, have you, ma'am?" Chaos smirks at me.

"There's no curse. You're all just assholes." A rough voice meets us as we enter the main bar area. Stools sit upside down on tables, legs pointed toward the ceiling like a sea of dead ants, and the sour tang of beer tickles my nose. At least the floor isn't sticky now, unlike the last time I was here when it felt like walking through tar.

I glance around, not seeing anyone at first. Then, a scruffy head of dark hair appears. A man stands up from doing something below the cash register with a towel slung over one shoulder. I'm not sure what's more striking about him. The tattoos up the side of his throat, the green eyes, or the bad boy aura he wears. One glance and I know this kind of cowboy. He's the type who smells like reckless decisions made while pressed up against the wall of a back alley at three a.m.

"Twins?" I point back and forth between the two men, who look like they couldn't share a whisker of DNA if they tried.

"Knox here *wishes* he was a Hayes... but we won't hold it against him. We picked up the nickname after one too many nights out being young, drunken dumbasses. Back then, we had nothing better to do than be country kids starting fights and borrowing tractors after dark... not necessarily in that order, either." Chaos folds his arms and clicks his tongue. "This scowly shithead got dropped on our doorstep covered in fleas, and he's been my besotted little shadow ever since."

"Get fucked." Those green eyes narrow, and he flings the towel at his *brother's* face. "You a coffee drinker, ma'am?" He jerks a stubble-covered chin toward what looks like a shiny new spaceship of a machine.

"Almost exclusively by the gallon." I stick out my palm. "Nice to meet you properly... outside of the emails flying back and forth. I'm Sage Maloney."

"Pleasure, Sage. Thanks for working with us." Knox shakes my hand—it's all no-nonsense with this cowboy—and then points to a stool waiting right-side-up at the bar. "You? Don't even think about sitting your ass down, fuck face. Polish those glasses." He whips a growl at Chaos, who holds up both palms in mock surrender before flipping his hands around to present him with two middle fingers.

"You'll be sobbing into your pillow soon as I'm out of town for the next leg of the rodeo circuit, bitch." Chaos grins broadly, but steps behind the bar and starts picking up the glasses one by one with his ass resting against the back bench.

"Give us both barrels. What have you got planned for the place?" Knox is quick to make my coffee and slides the cup my way.

"Thank you... I'll be singing your caffeine-dispensing praises far and wide, by the way." As I take a large sip, I tap the screen to wake my tablet up and spin the proposal around.

Knox leans forward on his forearms, working his knuckles, and his brows pull together as he studies the visual mood board I've compiled. Chaos joins him, bumping shoulders to jostle for a closer look.

"That's fucking cool." He spins a glass around on a cloth and raises both eyebrows, glancing between me and the screen.

"Thought the Hog could use a bit of a modern gunslinger look with the logo and signage... but it'll still fit with the ideas you had for introducing a distillery and being more than just a late-night dive bar."

I sit up a little straighter and point to the visual I made of the neon sign: a pig with belt buckle slung jauntily on its hips, cowboy hat in place, and wink to complete the look.

"Eventually, having something like this lit up outside would be a great PR opportunity... folks love an icon to take photos of. Once they do, that becomes free organic marketing. Locals typically love having something to be proud of, and out-of-towners always tend to remember a visual landmark much easier than a name."

Knox rubs a thumb over his jaw and keeps silently listening.

Chaos lives up to his reputation, poking and prodding at the screen to zoom in and look closer at different parts of the design.

I talk through my ideas for how they can tie in the visuals while gradually adapting what they already have here, and then we get to the point of the concept where I pitch them my thoughts on an event to launch their rebrand... officially.

Once I finish, feeling a little like I've just talked their ears off without pausing for breath, I gulp back the last of the coffee, which has long gone cold.

"How long do you think will be needed to make it happen?" Knox fixes me with a look that doesn't exactly tell me what he's thinking, but I'm fairly certain he's the type of straight-shooter who would give it to me plain and simple if he didn't like the concept.

"I've talked to a designer who needs about ten days to fabricate, deliver, and install outdoor signage. The other parts are mostly building excitement online, which happens through word of mouth." I tick off my fingers. "Having a reason for folks to come check the place out. You could have tastings of a new menu, live music during the afternoon to set the tone, and a focus on a family-friendly atmosphere. Using the height of summer for something like this will always work in your favor."

"She knows her shit, bro." Chaos flashes pearly whites my way.

"I like the staggered approach." Knox twists his lips, thinking hard. "There's some practical shit, renovations, and messier projects we'll tackle in the off-season during winter."

"Might as well make hay while the sun shines, huh?" Chaos elbows his brother. "Get her dolled up now, then we can work on the other shit behind the scenes."

Knox runs one hand through his hair. "Think it looks like the Hog is about to have a makeover." His green eyes don't give much away, but I'm inwardly squeaking with the thrill of knowing they're happy with the concept.

Play it cool. Play. It. Cool.

I'd worked my ass off for this—probably going over and above, but whatever, I'm *extra* to the core—so to nail it the first time feels incredibly satisfying.

"We can leave it in your hands? All the frilly party shit?"

I grin. "*Frilly party shit* would be my honor. All you gotta let me know is a budget to work with, and I'll take care of the rest."

"Send us some numbers. We'll make it work."

We continue to chat a little more. The guys and I hash out some of the practicalities around staffing, catering, getting in a band, and how they want to set up the space.

As we're wrapping things up, I get to my feet and shake Knox's hand again. He might be on the quiet and gruff side, but he's got a clear head on him for running this place.

"If you're open to the suggestion..." I hover before making a move to leave. "I think bringing in a photographer for the event would be well worth it, even if it seems like a big chunk of your marketing budget. One afternoon and evening would easily give a year's worth of stills and video footage to repurpose afterward. My advice is that it's money well spent."

Knox tips his chin. "Go for it."

"Do you have anyone locally you'd want to use?"

"Let me check." He picks up his phone and sends a quick text.

Chaos is still working his way through the glassware, and even though he's obviously more at home out on a ranch from what I've seen of the man so far, he seems to be committed to helping his brother in this.

Knox frowns, reading the reply he just received.

"Shit. It's peak wedding season. They're booked out for the next few months."

An idea bubbles up, one that I really should ignore. However, my pussy is clearly still reluctant to vacate the driver's seat where my decision-making is concerned.

"Let me just..." I mutter, digging out my phone.

Can I make use of those photography-nerd skills you've been hiding away?

It's for the Hayes boys. The event at the Hog.

There will be food and whiskey in it for you. Promise.

COCK RING:

Sure.

My grin widens when I see his reply come through immediately. Followed by four words that leave my blood humming merrily to his tune.

But it'll cost you.

CHAPTER 27

Beau

"Mmm. You like that spot right there, do you?"

I receive a forceful nudge from a whiskery nose, followed by a demanding snort for my fingers to continue scratching beneath Mist's jaw.

"I'm supposed to be mucking out your stall, you handsome prick," I mutter, and he really doesn't give a single fuck. His eyelids go droopy as he looks damn near ready to put every single one of his twelve-hundred pounds to use by falling asleep on my shoulder.

I've tried to spend as much time as possible out here with him lately so we can get familiar with each other. Not that Mist is my only reason for being so preoccupied with the horses and the barn and all kinds of other crap that I've been giving my attention to around this part of the ranch.

There's a girl with silky hair, glittering dark eyes, and a sultry little smile powerful enough to leave me forgetting my own name. A particular brand of temptation, who I very much need to remain apart from, for as much time as humanly possible.

I mean, we're not avoiding each other's company entirely. Something of a silent compromise extends between us in the hazy morning light when she appears from her cabin to steal my pot of coffee and settle down at her computer. Followed by a weary sort of convergence across the kitchen island at the end of the day after we've both worked our asses off. For me, it's out with the cattle, seeing to mundane tasks like mending fences, and working with the horses. For Sage, it's her continued work on the ranch PR and the upcoming event she's up to her eyeballs in organizing.

We'll share dinner together in the evening—I don't trust Sage not to simply forgo eating a proper meal in lieu of how hard she's working to get everything ready for The Loaded Hog's big relaunch—but afterward, I don't linger at the house.

I cook. She talks to me about all the little details, the myriad of aspects she's effortlessly coordinating; listening to her run over her day is like a cool breeze to soothe my frayed nerves where our current circumstances are concerned. Then, I spend most of my night back out here, sitting with the horses, and staying as far away as possible from the girl I've fallen for, yet cannot risk being near.

After the kind of night we spent entangled together, I knew I was undeniably fucked. It hit me like a ton of bricks the moment we saw each other again for the first time—as soon as she returned to the ranch following her meeting with Hayes. Sage came into view, and the squeezing sensation in my chest collided internally with immediate recognition. With a stifled groan, right alongside a rush of blood to my groin, reality slammed into me at that very second... I needed to become *extremely* fucking busy on this ranch for the foreseeable future.

Absolutely no good can possibly come of lingering in that house after dark, when all I want to do is drag Sage against me and have her in my bed all over again.

The need to reach out for her is damn near overwhelming.

So, here I am. Indulging Mist's demands. Staying far away.

Fuck this. It's hell.

At least all this time I've spent with the horses has been as good for them as it has been for me. Briar and Storm certainly had the right idea about establishing an equine therapy program. I'm their first unplanned beneficiary of the immensely calming effect grooming and fussing after all of them brings. Gives me a perfect solution to keep my hands from wandering places they shouldn't.

Turns out, I can walk in here with a mind spinning so relentlessly, it feels like smoke and burning rubber have replaced my lump of brain matter, only to see Willow's muzzle poke out and snort at me... and somehow all that chaos ebbs away.

Of course, the tiniest little terror to make this ranch home, has an attitude the size of the entire state and a personality to match. Storm calls her *Duchess*. He's not wrong there. She might be all of knee height compared to the others in this stable, but trots around as if she's twenty hands high.

As I'm checking on their feed and water for the night, my phone vibrates in my back pocket with an incoming notification. Never in my life have I enjoyed carrying a phone. I gladly handed the responsibility for responding to calls, messages, and anything remotely related to social media to Tessa for years while I was on the pro circuit.

That was until Sage came along with her smart-ass quips and the occasional teasing message she sends me during the day. It's nothing particularly damning. She's intelligent enough to know having written evidence on my phone—to leave even a hint that there's something more between us than a purely professional working situation—would be a terrible idea.

So, instead, she settles for roasting me about my mustache, or asking me questions regarding the ranch. I guess it helps with what she needs and is currently working on. Since I'm nothing but a hindrance where technology is concerned, if I can help out in some little way, I suppose that's something.

Only, it isn't her words gracing my world in the middle of the afternoon. The sight on my phone screen is an email subject line that turns my stomach sour.

My thumb immediately stabs at the contact number I detest having to call, but seeing the latest bullshit from her lawyers is more than enough of a reason to forget about civility and forced politeness via email exchange. As to be expected, the voice who picks up the phone is not my wife.

"Hello, Mr. Heartford."

"Zeb. I know she's right there. Put her on the call." My fist clenches tight, along with my jaw.

"Oh, just give me one second. I'll see if Mandy is available to talk." Her assistant makes a show of covering the speaker, and there's a series of muffled whispers before the phone gets passed over.

"Beau, so good of you to get in touch, honey." Her cloying voice drifts down the line, all sing-song and pretending to be anything but a cold-hearted, calculating fame-seeker. "You must have a great intuition for phoning me right when I'm right in the middle of something..."

No way is she going to wriggle out of this conversation. "Cut the shit. Why is your lawyer emailing me complete garbage?"

"Oh, didn't I text you about that? Must've slipped my mind." She breezes. "Look, I know we said three more months—"

"Two." My grunt cuts her off. "We agreed to *two* more months, and you know it. Those were the terms." The final severing of the head from this miserable, toxic situation. The finish line to my years upon years of being trapped in this. Finally, now that my pro career is over, I was able to get her to agree to mutually beneficial terms. And now we've seen out the obligatory window, things are scheduled to be announced publicly via a carefully curated press release.

Always with the goddamn calculated steps, where this woman is concerned. But at least that's the final one of them that I have to take. I'm so close to freedom. I can taste it like a fresh hit of ocean salt hanging in the air when your toes sink into the sand.

Mandy sucks in a breath through her teeth. "See, the problem is, it's gonna have to be longer. That's why my lawyer thought we should send over an email outlining everything, to let you know the specifics."

My neck prickles. What the fuck did she just say?

"Not interested, Mandy. What the hell? Why are you coming at me with that kind of bullshit?"

"You know how tirelessly I work, and well, to be honest, this is what my career needs before we go upsetting so many fans. I've got some important tour dates coming up this year for my next album, and then we both walk away, easy." She says it all so lightly, as if it's the simplest fucking thing in the world, and that it shouldn't even cross my mind to think otherwise.

I couldn't give a flying fuck about her fans, or her album sales. "How much longer?" My ears are ringing like I've just taken a boxer's fist to the temple.

"Not much, just a little extension, honey. Hardly anything, really. Think of it as just a tiny little extra piece woven into our story."

That almost makes me choke. There is no us, and there certainly is no story I wish to hang onto memories of. In fact, I want to purge my life of this woman's presence as quickly and as efficiently as possible.

"How. Much. Longer?"

"Just until next summer."

I think I black out for a second before rounding on her with a violent hiss.

"A year? What the shit, Mandy?" She's got to be fucking joking.

"What's another twelve months when it means you get to keep your little ranch to play around on, and we part ways without a messy legal battle through courts and lawyers and public disagreements over assets? Neither of us wants that, Beau."

"You agreed this would be settled sooner." I seethe, teeth gritted and every muscle drawn tight. I feel it rising, the helplessness and frantic pounding beneath my skin. Not only does she want to stretch this out, but now she's threatening my ranch, too? Yet again, she's going for the jugular, because she knows legally she's damn well entitled to half of everything.

She is well aware of exactly how much of an idiot I was when I signed away my life. When I didn't stop for one second to think about things like joint assets or division of property. Fuck, I was such a naive piece of shit back then.

"Well… things change. You know what this industry is like. I've got the opportunity to tour with my new album, and you know I could really use—"

"Don't start. I'm not interested in hearing it. What I do know is that you're a leech and an attention seeker."

"Beau." She scoffs over my name. "Don't be like that. You're telling me you'd rather we do this the hard way?" Her nails rap against something solid in the background. "Contested divorces can really drag out, you know. Not to mention how going that route will tie up all our joint assets… which includes property."

Tilting my head back, I mouth *fuck* and scrunch my eyes.

"Are you still there, Beau?"

I drag a heavy palm over the back of my neck.

"Fine. But we're putting this in writing, we're signing a contract spelling out precise dates, and there won't be any other crap like this you pull. You understand me?" It's always been this way. Mandy knows exactly how to ensure I say yes, how to exploit my biggest weakness, and how to make everything bend to her will.

"Got it. Crystal clear. Thank you for always being such a wonderful husband. I'll get my lawyer to send over documents and we'll square away that date for you, so there's no need to fret. I know how you worry."

"I expect to have paperwork with your signature already on it before the end of the day." I damn near crush my phone when I bark down the line before hanging up.

As I stand there, it feels like I'm being swallowed alive.

Torn apart piece by fleshy piece.

Every cell of my skin itches and feels like I need to scratch at myself to escape this suit I've been forced to inhabit. It clings to me in a way that feels somehow boiling hot and freezing cold at the same time—both extremes are burning me, and I can't get away from the searing pain.

I'm panting. Almost light-headed. Fumbling with my phone, I dial Tessa. I just need to hear her voice. Just need to have that point of contact with someone who understands. She's so good at being there for me, so good at being the voice of reason. A place of calm I can shelter while my brain and body slowly return to a place where I don't feel like my throat is going to close over.

As the phone rings and rings, my chest grows tighter and tighter. Followed by the dreaded moment it goes to voicemail.

"Tessa, fuck, call me, please. I need to talk."

I hang up and immediately try again. Same result.

As the beep of her voicemail sounds, I squeeze my eyes shut and yank on my hair.

"I could really use you right now. Be smug forever. Whatever. I don't care, but I need... I need your help, ok." Everything feels like it's spinning, spiraling out of control. The words taste like ash on my tongue. I fucking hate feeling this way. It feels like the goddamn weakest thing in the world to have a brain that can't just *relax*.

A small cough comes from behind me. Whirling around, I come face to face with Sage standing in the middle of the barn, cradling her tablet and camera. Her eyebrows are up in her hairline somewhere, and I don't know how much of any of that she fucking heard.

"Hey... so... sorry to kinda intrude..." She shifts her weight, then gestures at the stalls. "I'd been planning to do a photoshoot with the horses, but I can come back another time." Her brown eyes bounce over me, but I can't meet her gaze because I don't want a fucking pitying look. It's my mess to deal with, and I can't handle the idea of this girl seeing me collapse under the weight of my own bullshit.

"How much of that did you hear?" I swallow thickly.

"Just the bit about your sister having something to be smug about." She gives a slightly forced smile. "Can I help? You know I'll never turn down an opportunity to be smug."

"It's fine. Normally, I'd talk to Tessa."

Sage rolls her lips together, then casts her eyes around the barn. "Hey, so you remember how you helped me when I nearly flambéed my entire arm? Maybe that's our thing. Having each other's backs when we'd rather eat dirt than ask for help."

"I'm not on fire." Air doesn't even feel like it's reaching my lungs. They're so tightly squeezed by the invisible band cinched around my chest.

"Yeah, but your brain is." She narrows her eyes, looking me up and down, then strolls over to the workbench lining the wall. "What about a little bit of mutual appreciation?" Sage pushes some tools aside, sets her things down, then hops up to sit her ass on the benchtop.

I stay stock still, watching the cotton of her sundress gather around her thighs before my focus bounces up to find the plush curve to her mouth as she smirks at me.

"Statistically speaking, people who have an orgasm every day live longer, calmer, more peaceful lives."

All I seem to be able to do is give her a stern look in return. Why is she prepared to put up with my dark cloud? How much more perfect can this girl be to walk in and find me tangled up inside my own ball of misery and yet look past all that?

Sage treats me like there's nothing to make a fuss about.

"Look, all I'm saying is that if you've got your dick in your hand, I bet your brain would shut up real fast."

Her eyes sparkle. A challenge laid down right here in the middle of this barn.

I swallow heavily, searching around for words on a long pause. "I can't just whip it out right here."

"Why not? It's your property, your business." Sage tilts her head to one side, swinging her legs.

"Pretty sure that violates every code that exists for bosses and employees."

"Ok, but say we're not at work right now... it's tequila o'clock somewhere. Which makes it dick-out-o'clock somewhere, too."

"Are you trying to kill me?" She's got me damn near choking as mischief continues to roam freely all over her expression.

"No, but I am trying to blow your mind... or at least let you blow off some of that steam."

She settles herself on the workbench, leaning back on both hands, and spreads her knees, parts them ever so gently, but only just wide enough that my brain can't do anything except fixate on the shadowy spot where her thighs meet beneath the fabric.

"*Mmmm.* Come on. Indulge my curiosity. You've had the chance to watch me touch myself, let me see you. Why don't you fuck your fist for me, cowboy?"

The only sound I register is the thudding of my pulse. My dick has already started thickening, hearing her raspy purr and being surrounded by the scent that will forever stick with me long after this girl ups and leaves this ranch.

It's that thought. Knowing that I'm going to have to let her leave once this summer is over, that has my hands moving. Fuck it. We hardly had a chance to start with, and now this bomb Mandy has dropped? With swift fingers, I work to unbuckle my belt, and as the metal clanks, I see her body respond—an immediate shudder taking hold. Sage bites down on her bottom lip, eyes going glassy as she watches me from that perch.

It makes me feel a surge of something purely primal. A flare of anticipation burns white-hot through every inch of my bloodstream as those honeyed dark eyes descend on me. Is this what Sage felt when I watched her that night? When not even the wildest bull could have dragged my eyes away from devouring the sight of her. Was *this* the sensation coursing through her veins?

Sage smiles, teeth still digging into the plump swell of her lower lip as I wrap my hand around my length. I can't fucking believe that she wants this, wants to sit there and soak in the sight of me. To enjoy watching as I play with my cock and my piercing, all while continuing to lengthen, thickening inside my fist.

"When did you get that?" Her gaze eats up the way I thumb over the head, pushing the metal back and forth, and goddamn, this is so unbelievably hot. So reckless. I have absolutely no interest in stopping where this is heading.

"Storm and I had a stupid bet years ago." I stroke myself from root to tip, heart hammering a furious beat. "Whoever lost the buckle that year had to get their dick pierced. Whoever won had to get a piercing, but could choose where."

Her grin takes center stage. "He suits a nose ring."

"You'd better not be complimenting another man while drooling over my cock... not while imagining me tapping the back of your throat."

"Are you gonna do something about it, Heartford? Make me?"

This fucking girl. I grunt and tug harder, wishing like hell I *could* take her up on her taunting.

"What would you do... if I was thinking about someone else while sucking you... taking you as far back as possible?"

"Jesus Christ. You don't wanna know."

"World champion, *hmm*? There's a competitive animal inside you, isn't there? And you're keeping him locked away so no one will see that side of you."

My fist shuttles faster, and tension pools low in my spine. "I'll fucking show you just how competitive I can be if you dare think about anyone else while you're stuffing your fingers in that tight cunt for me."

Sage's eyes flash with a challenge.

"You wanna watch?"

"Hurry the fuck up." A groan of desperation escapes because her pussy has been all I can think about.

She looks mighty fucking pleased with herself. "God, I love that sexy noise you make when you're getting close." Her palms skate along those lush thighs, dragging the hem of her dress higher, bunching a pool of soft fabric at her waist.

"What do you think my tongue would feel like around the tip, sliding over that bar?" Her eyes grow more hooded the moment she dips a finger beneath the seam of her panties, then swirls over her clit. "I can't believe I didn't get to blow you at least one time the other night." Her breath hitches in time with that torturously slow way she fondles herself, and I'm captivated by how filthy this moment is.

We're separated by ten feet, and countless layers of longing, yet it's like I can taste her sweetness on my tongue.

She isn't wrong. I'm regretting not finding time for that particular game myself, but it was only due to the fact I was far too obsessed with being sheathed inside her, or getting my mouth on her.

"Do you like that feeling? What's it like for you when it gets sucked and pushed back and forth? Does that make your toes curl, cowboy?"

"Ffuuuuck." My jaw tightens, and heat flashes down to my balls. "I've never had that."

Sage's fingers stop moving briefly. Her lips part on a choked noise. "You're kidding?"

"Wish I was," I grunt.

Her gasp fills the air, and she's so goddamn pretty, resuming the attention on her clit, getting closer and closer to the edge, just as I am. "No one has had that piercing in their mouth? That's gotta be a felony in at least fifty states."

"You offering?" Each glide of my palm works me harder and harder, and every time my hand strokes over the metal at my tip, I'm fighting for my life because I just want her mouth. I want her wrapped around me. I just want to pump into her and feel her walls flutter as she writhes and bucks against the sheets.

As she begs and taunts, it sends me into a place where all I want to do is pin her to the mattress and fuck as deep as possible.

She takes it all. She urges me to go harder. *Please, Beau. I can take it.*

"Holy fuck. Don't tempt me with a good time, cowboy. I'm trying to be good over here, and you're giving me *that* look."

"I think you're trying to be anything but."

"Yet, you've got your dick leaking all over your hand, baby."

"And your pussy is weeping for me."

"She absolutely is." Sage whimpers. "She's crying at the sight of a piercing that hasn't been shown the kind of lovin' it deserves."

"Sage... goddamn." My balls tighten, and I have to talk through clenched teeth.

"That's it. Keep going just like that. You look so hot I could die."

"Fuck." This time, my groan is purely feral for her. "This is torture. You're over there looking like a dream. I can see how wet you are, and all I wanna do is fuck you raw. You have no idea how bad I want to slip inside your pussy again."

Her tiny little moans are breathy and desperate and the sweetest sound. "You are. I can feel you pushing in, but I'm tight, which means you gotta work hard for it." She absolutely kills me, starting to play the game ruthlessly now. "Beg a little. I bet you can feel me, even all the way over there."

Heat surges through my groin.

"*Mmmfuck.* Yeah, you can feel me squeezing your dick, can't you? Feel how close I am when I make that noise you like the most. That point when I'm moaning louder because your fat cock is all I can think about, and you're filling me perfectly."

A pent-up, gritty noise finally bursts out of me. "You'd better be nearly fucking there."

"God, you get so deep. You keep tapping that spot." Sage's eyelashes flutter, her fingers circle frantically, and I know we're both seconds from losing it.

Blood pumps like gasoline through my veins, my cock swells with each shuttle of my fist growing more forceful, more urgent.

"You're gonna milk me dry, aren't you? A slut who wants to be dicked down and filled with my cum so badly you're out here being a fucking cock tease."

"Holy shit." She gives me the hottest goddamn sound of pleasure in return for the utter filth coming out of my mouth. "I am —god, I am—" Her glittering eyes stay locked on mine as I watch the flood of pleasure claim her. It's so damn intoxicating. She's an addiction I can't shake, and I devour the way her body convulses as she moans through her orgasm, continuing to massage her clit.

"Jesus. Sage. *Fuck. Fffuuuck.*"

I groan as all that intense build-up of tension bursts at the base of my spine. My cock pulses and erupts all over my fist, leaving my skin coated and hand making slick noises as I stroke myself through it.

I don't know what just took over. Why I said that to her. Where those words came from is beyond me, but Sage looks so beautiful and dreamy, and she clearly doesn't mind.

"Goddamn, hearing you talk me to filth and put on a show is a lethal combination. Maybe I need to get you to record yourself so I can play that back sometime." Her hum is soft as she floats along on the lingering wave of her climax.

Struggling to collect myself, to find any sense of sanity or words, I settle for pulling my t-shirt off in order to clean up the mess I just made.

"These horses just got a lot more than they bargained for by moving here." Sage grimaces. "Should I go and apologize? How do I say, 'Sorry for flashing you my kitty, but it was totally worth it?'"

While Sage looks like a queen, I'm still trying to regather my soul. How can this girl find it so easy to be playful and joke around while I just want to tackle her into the nearest pile of hay and taste her? I want to swipe up her fingers in order to lick them clean. I want her cum on my tongue when I cover her soaked cunt with my mouth. I want to tear that dress off completely and part her soft thighs. I want to hook her legs over my shoulders as I drive my hips forward until my cum coats every inch deep inside her.

"Do you think they'll judge me for enjoying being a bit slutty? Do horses kink shame?"

That makes me chuckle as I bunch up the now cum-covered material into a ball.

"They're gonna have to get used to being around Storm and Briar." I shake my head.

"Ohhh... I forgot those two go at it like rabbits. Honestly, good for them. Well, at least I don't feel so bad now." Sage slides off the workbench, tucks her dress back around her thighs, and then walks up to Dusty. When she gets there, she raises up onto tip-toes to lean over the door to her stall. "Sorry, bud, I think you're gonna have to invest in a pair of earmuffs when Stôrmand Lane is around."

Tossing the t-shirt aside, I set about doing my jeans and belt back up. My mind might have gone as placid as a lake, but I still don't know what to say to Sage right now.

"What do you need help with out here?" She beats me to it, hitting me with a look over one shoulder.

I swallow thickly. "Nothing. It's all taken care of. You... you can just head back to whatever else you were doing..."

"C'mon, now. We just worked off a bit of tension, might as well make myself more useful than to just give you some bonus memories for your spank bank."

I scrub a hand over my jaw. This fucking girl. "You did not just say those words in the middle of my ranch."

She grins broadly at me, shrugging that bronzed shoulder. "So, what's the lowdown, boss? Time for horse shit scoopin'?"

Christ. I can't think straight anymore. Apparently, my brain just took up residence in my dick.

But as much as I'm offering for her to leave, I don't actually want her to go. Memories of being in here with her that night, of my arms being wrapped around her and drawing down deep lungfuls of her scent and warmth occupy my mind's eye. Well shit, if I can't reach out to hold Sage or touch her the way my hands demand to, then perhaps we can still spend time together in another way.

"The girls need to stretch their legs, and I was going to check on the cattle before sundown. Are you feeling up for a ride?"

Sage's lips twist. "Careful. That sounds borderline flirtatious, Mr. Heartford."

I drag my cap off and ruffle my hair. "I'm sorry—"

"Please. I'm just teasing you. I'd love to get out on one of these pretty ponies. If you can hold my hand on what to do, since I'm a tad dusty on all the bits and pieces and straps and thingies."

My lips tug at the corners. "Ok, well, three things. For one, you can't work on a ranch and go around butchering the language like that all summer. You'll give us a bad name among cowboys for miles around. Second, you and I both need to get changed."

Sage rolls her lips together to disguise a laugh while looking at my bare chest. "I don't think I'm the problem here."

"You're not going horse riding in something that flimsy, unless you want to be chafed to bits." I gesture at her sundress and bare legs. "Thirdly, come with me. You can learn how to saddle Goldie over here."

It might be far less than perfect, certainly not how I want to spend tonight with her, but it'll have to do.

And something eases further inside my chest, knowing that I can steal her attention and smiles and sharp wit for an evening. Even if it ultimately isn't the way I'm craving to be connected to my girl, at least I can have her all to myself.

CHAPTER 28

Sage

I'm a sleep-deprived, caffeine-fueled gremlin in her element.

Today is the day. The Loaded Hog officially opened her doors, with new signage proudly installed and a fresh look on the inside. She might not be my baby, but I couldn't be more proud.

Ignoring the minor detail that I'm functioning on about four hours of sleep, and I can't remember the last time I ate a proper meal—pretty sure it might have been the grilled cheese Beau shoved under my nose at around one a.m. After burning the midnight oil on repeat all week, I could easily be mistaken, days and nights have somewhat blurred together.

I've been doing so well, too, throwing every single cell and scrap of creative energy I could muster into getting things ready for today. My talents have stretched as far as perfecting the art of stuffing goodie bags at the dining table until my eyes nearly fell out of my head in the early hours of this morning.

Being preoccupied has been my only lifeline.

Because try as I might, I can't stop thinking about him.

Even though I absolutely have to shake this sickness, this neediness that keeps on grabbing me by the throat when I least expect it.

Ugh. Do not think about my one night with Beau Heartford, having his hand wrapped around my neck while he fucked me slow and deep and murmured how pretty I look when I come.

Don't think about that day in the barn. Don't think about how his cheeks flushed, and his eyes rolled back in his head. Don't think about the way he talked you through it in the sexiest, roughest voice imaginable. Don't think about *that* moan he let out without realizing he did. Is there anything hotter than a man moaning?

Especially... whatever you do, Sage Maloney... do not for one moment think about how that cowboy, for all intents and purposes, touched himself for you and then took you on a date afterward. I mean, it was all very 'keeping hands to ourselves,' but even so.

Horse riding and sunsets overlooking the ranch and a mustache to swoon over?

Good lord, I am fuckity-fuck-fucked.

"Welcome to the Hog." My smile remains plastered on my face as a group of cowgirls stroll in, dressed in pretty pink boots and denim skirts. Their eyes light up with a first glance at the table I've got set up just inside the door.

"Here's your complimentary swag, ladies." I hand them one each, then hold up the stash of bracelets—ones I sat up long into the small hours, threading together while watching UFO documentaries earlier this week. "And here's a little memento as a thank you for coming to celebrate with us."

They ooh and ahh over the contents of the gift bags, then burst with laughter when they read what's spelled out by the tiny letters strung together of their new friendship bracelet.

"*Finest Wranglers.*" One giggles.

"*Rather Be Ridin'.*" Another gives me a wink. "Ain't that the truth."

"*My Hat. My Rules.*" Their other friend laughs. "These are so cool, thank you."

"You're very welcome. Remember to take some photos over there, and tag the Hog when you post them on your socials... we're running a giveaway." I point toward the photo booth. As I lean forward to brace a hand on the table and point through the crowd, the tiny shift in my weight gives me a prominent reminder of the extremely naughty little secret beneath my dress.

One that leaves my thighs squeezing together as I turn and greet the next wave of incoming guests arriving for an afternoon at Crimson Ridge's hottest new attraction.

The event has been smooth sailing so far. With live music playing out in the garden area, games, and face painting for the little ones. Crowds of all ages have shown up in support of the Hayes brothers with the bar's relaunch. The place is humming and electric in a way that feels incredible to witness firsthand.

"Where do you want these, Sergeant?" Kayce strolls over, box in his arms, delivering me a fresh supply of bags to hand out. Behind him, carrying a second box, is another cowboy, one who I haven't met so far, I don't think.

"Handsome, and somewhat useful when you're not on the back of a horse... why thank you. Just come and set them down here." I gesture to the spot on the floor next to where I'm standing.

The two golden-headed cowboys are quick to help, and as I give out a handful more friendship bracelets, I feel Kayce linger by my side. He's busy being a sweetheart, setting up the bags on the table for me without having to even ask him.

As my eyes tick up, I see the other man hovering nearby.

"You should ask for his number, you know." I nudge Kayce's boot with my own. "He's totally checking you out. One hundred percent digs what's beneath those jeans, Wilder."

Kayce keeps his head lowered and methodically rearranges the lines of party favors. But I see blush hitting his cheeks and the back of his neck. The cowboy, who always has a smart joke or a grin from ear to ear, looks adorably flustered. His Adam's apple bobs, and he shakes his head.

"Don't know what you mean."

I chuckle and take the opportunity to give his shoulder a little squeeze. "You ever want to talk about it, or need someone who understands what it's like to be forever confused by your own damn self? I'm your gal."

Kayce doesn't give me a reply, but straightens up and brushes his hands over his jeans. Just as he goes to walk away, just when I think he's about to disappear off into the growing crowd, he pauses.

Clearing his throat, he looks around at the entrance to confirm there's no one within earshot, then dips his chin. "When did you first… I mean… how did you know you were?" He shoves both hands in his pockets and stares at the toes of his boots, chewing the inside of his cheek.

"When did I first know I was bi? Pretty sure I took one look at *that* gorgeous librarian searching for ancient relics, her dashing treasure hunter, and realized a whole lot of things about myself. Talk about one little movie about Mummies being my entire sexual awakening."

I nudge his elbow with my own. Except, our all too brief conversation starts and ends right there when I hear Layla call my name.

"Sure you're ok?" I ask as quietly as possible.

This time, his familiar golden boy grin and blue eyes flare back to life, ticking up to greet mine. He shrugs. "Just figuring some stuff out. Nothing I can't handle. But thanks… you know…"

"What're you two gossiping about?" Layla squeezes up beside me. Sky has joined her, too.

"Kayce offered to get up there on stage with Chaos and give everyone line dancing lessons." I give him a waggle of my eyebrows.

"Christ. You really live up to your nickname." He rolls his eyes. "Sergeant's orders, is it?" He salutes me, then starts to walk away backward, smirk firmly locked in place.

"Don't forget to lose the shirts and grease up those abs," I call after him. "And don't think you'll escape being filmed, either. You know I've got viral views to collect like a dragon hordes treasure."

Layla picks up one of the friendship bracelets and lets out a soft laugh. "Can you please give this one to Luke?"

Sky peers at the letters and lets out a snort. "*Horse Daddy.*"

"Can neither confirm nor deny, I might have used you two for inspiration on some of these. Also, do you know how impossible it is to keep it non-slutty after midnight? I was fighting for my life not to start making them all dirty."

"Gold stars for keeping your mind out of the gutter, Sarge. They're such a good idea, you know." Layla kisses my cheek. "My genius girl."

As she and Sky help out for a moment, chatting to the next round of people who stroll through the door, I feel it. The unexpected sensation makes me jerk, and I nearly bite my tongue in an effort to strangle the noise wanting to fly from my lips.

A text comes through, vibrating in my back pocket. When I carefully pull my phone out, I have to take a deep breath through my nose seeing the words there on screen. Trying my utmost to play it cool without giving away a single hint to my friends standing right there of what's happening.

COCK RING:

Payback time begins now.

"Can we get you a drink? Or something to eat while you're still working over here?" Layla's voice is enough to have me locking the screen and stuffing it back into my pocket with cat-like reflexes.

"You know I get a little extra naughty—I mean, perfectly well-behaved—when tequila is involved." I bat my eyelashes pleadingly at her.

"Food first. Then you can have your horn dog devil juice." She shakes her head at me. "I'll get the kitchen to prep you something."

"Love your work." Blowing a kiss, I'm quickly back to distributing bags and bracelets and chatting to newcomers.

All the while hanging, dangling, teetering on the precipice of expectation. Not knowing when the next round of *payment* is going to be collected.

I don't have to wait long before the familiar presence of Beau makes an appearance. He's enough to set my hormones all aflutter, in his best jeans, a plain white t-shirt, with a camera bag slung over one shoulder. As he walks toward me, those strong hands lift his cowboy hat off, and the motherfucker looks like he's some sort of living, breathing, slow-motion rodeo movie montage strolling my way.

He's even got a smug look creasing the corners of his eyes. A look that says *I know what your pussy tastes like*. The kind of glance that spells a whole lot of danger for me, because I *love* the kind of game he's playing. Even if we are absolutely bending all the rules to the point where they might simply explode like glass hitting concrete.

There's so much trouble in the hint of his lips twitching when he closes the space between us. We could very easily slip up and reveal something unintentionally, and maybe that's what makes this entire situation even more desirable for me.

Well shit, have I got a lot of miles to run tomorrow morning to burn off this friskiness, or what? Probably should remember to book in with my therapist at the first possible availability, too.

"You must be the photographer." I cock my head to one side. "Has anyone ever mentioned that you look exactly like that washed-up rodeo dude? Beau Heartford? Heard he used to spend more time grooming his mustache than actually getting on the back of a bull."

A miracle occurs right before my eyes. The world's biggest, boyish grin spreads across his face, and oh my fucking god, I don't know if my knees are going to buckle right here right now.

"Apparently. Heard he's an asshole who hates coming to things like this, though. Guess you must be mistaken, ma'am."

We stand for a moment as a couple stroll up to the table, and I run through my little meet-and-greet patter, before sending them in the direction of the photo wall.

"What's that look for?" I narrow my eyes on him, because Beau is giving me the kind of expression I refuse to interpret for myself.

"Nothing." He shrugs, and hooks a finger over the edge of one of the bags, peering inside to take a look. A long, thick finger that I know can turn me to putty in his hands. "You're very good at this." A heated expression flickers up to hold my own.

"Kinda seems that way, doesn't it?" My lips curve, and I glance around the room. This cowboy is ruthless, and I'm having to be the epitome of professional, even while he's tormenting me. "If you can make sure to get plenty of crowd photos, maybe ask a few groups if they'll let you take some up-close shots? The band, kitchen, the bar staff... anything that will sell this place a hundred times over will be perfect."

Beau follows my line of sight, and nods as he assesses the scene. "Are you sure you're feeling ok, Sage?" he murmurs as he drags his phone out of his pocket. "You seem a little on edge?"

The smooth tone of his voice is immediately followed by a slow, rolling, buzzing sensation building in my core. As he taps on the screen, the speed increases ever so slightly.

I work down a heavy swallow and have to adjust my stance because, holy fuck, that setting is my kryptonite.

Beau taps the screen again, ending that particular glimpse of pleasurable torture—for the moment at least.

"No wonder you're strutting in here looking like an emperor." Clearing my throat, in an effort to not sound like I'm already panting for this man, I reach for my bag sitting on the floor and rifle through the contents. "I can ride this game out all night long, you know."

He chuckles, and it's the most delicious sound coming from somewhere deep inside his chest.

"We'll see about that."

"Do your worst, Heartford. Remember, you only get to collect your payment if you actually take photos... and no half-assing. I expect you to do a proper job of it." Letting my eyes tick up to meet his, there's a twist to my lips as I lay down the ground rules.

That's when I notice he's not looking my way. I catch his side profile; he's got one hand dragging through his hair, looking a little wide-eyed while casting his attention over the crowd.

For a moment, I feel a pang of guilt hit me square in the chest. Realization pierces me like an arrow that this might be all too much for him. Being around so many people in this sort of environment? Beau has played it cool until now, but I would hate to force him into something that makes him want to shred his own face off.

Just as I'm about to offer an option, to give him the alternative of an easy-out by simply leaving, he shakes his head with a wry laugh.

"You know... I just can't get my head around the fact there's a room packed full of guys and girls who are all gonna want to get in your pants."

That's what he's tangled up about? Well, in that case, my inner demon just received a high-voltage dose of mischief surging through me, perfectly timed just as the band kicks into a more raucous song.

"I'm an equal opportunist. What can I say?" Shrugging a shoulder, I fish out the secret item I'd kept hidden inside my purse until now.

With my most innocent of eyelash flutters, I hand the friendship bracelet over to Beau.

"Here, I made one just for you... I'm wearing something special tonight, and now you can too."

CHAPTER 29

Beau

Turns out, the promise of tormenting Sage for hours on end is the perfect cure for any apprehension I might have had about spending the afternoon in a crowded bar.

Sure, I've had to put up with a steady trickle of autograph hunters and selfie seekers. Of course, there have been the usual whispers and questions. Assorted looks and enquiries about whether Mandy is here with me, or not.

Normally, I'd be shrinking away from it all. Yet, somehow, having ninety-nine percent of my focus on a beautiful girl—with her siren-red sundress fluttering around her thighs and black boots to match her silky raven hair—has dissolved any of that usual sense of panic I would feel in this type of environment.

Even though I can't reach out for her, like my palms itch to do, we're still secretly connected, in the most intimate kind of way.

As I sit here, my thumb rubs a caressing stroke back and forth over the friendship bracelet wrapped around my wrist, with its pink beads and tiny white cubes with letters on them. My very own custom-made one.

Cock Ring.

I have to wrestle back the urge to grin like a fool at the very feminine, delicate piece of handmade jewelry sitting against my hard-worn skin. And the devious little phrase she's spelled out. That familiar heat builds low in my stomach, at being in possession of the knowledge Sage went out of her way specifically to make this.

The fact that in amongst all the late nights and never-ending list of preparations she was coordinating, Sage was thinking of me.

Goddamn, why does it have to be even more time, a seemingly unending trudge through the darkness, before I'm free of my marriage? This is the cruelest fucking blow, to know that she and I fit so naturally together in so many ways, and yet I have to keep her at arm's length. Or at least, try my fucking hardest to.

Although, I already suspect, with a lingering sense of reckless foreboding sitting in my gut, that I'm perilously close to doing something tonight that might upend all of that.

Resting my ass on a barstool, I let the shutter click repeatedly, capturing a rapid-fire succession of frames featuring people gathered on the dancefloor. The light is low, a golden tinge to it, with replica antique bulbs dangling overhead. The mood is high, the room filled with a kind of uniquely summer-time ease, while the band keeps the patrons happy.

In amongst it all, I see Sage with her friends, who have pulled her to join them now that she's long finished with the welcome station and party bags. They're following Chaos Hayes, who has a shit-eating grin on his face as he shakes his ass and leads a series of line-dancing steps, leaving the girls howling with laughter the entire time.

But it's not so much the other bodies filing up in rough lines across the wooden floorboards that have any of my attention. It's easy enough to keep my eye focused through the viewfinder, so no one would know who I'm actually looking at as I click off round after round of photos and watch her expression the entire time.

Every moment her wearable vibrator hits a different peak of the setting I've currently got it adjusted to, I see it. The slightest change, a minor falter in her movements as she battles against giving away the wicked little secret beneath her dress. The app she uses is loaded on my phone, and it's been as simple as tapping the screen here and there throughout the afternoon and into this evening. One easy press of a button to have complete control over the sensations gripping her body. All while Sage has continued to go about her business without giving away a single hint of what might be going on.

It's sexy as fuck.

She's the ultimate temptation in all this, because even though it might have been a stupid game—a smart-ass request for payback once she called in this favor by asking me to be the event photographer—I'm damn well edging myself just as hard as I'm edging her. Imagining the state she's currently in? Yeah, that has my cock eager and twitching.

"You're not a dancer, Beau?"

A gruff voice interrupts my fixation on the girl I'm not supposed to crave so incessantly, and the way her expression keeps flickering ever so slightly when those waves must roll through.

Lowering my camera, I see Knox Hayes flick a towel over his shoulder as he spreads both hands to lean on the bar.

That has me easing back on the stool, feeling much more smug than I have any right to after getting that last look at Sage's face attempting to fight back a shudder. But fuck it. She agreed to this game. "Nah, I'm good right here, thanks. Though I'll take a cold one since you're over this way, if you don't mind."

"You betcha," he grunts, flicks the cap off, and slides a bottle across the polished bar.

"Congrats on everything. You boys sure know how to burn the candle at both ends." I take a sip, and as my throat works, I see Knox cast a watchful eye around the packed venue.

"She's a work in progress."

"Between the ranch and here, you're gonna be busy."

I don't know if it's a moment of humor as such, but Knox gives me a raised eyebrow. "You'd know all about that."

"Sure do." Shaking my head, I set the beer down. "You let me know if you need to talk sponsorship or anything like that."

"Appreciate it, Beau." He looks as if he's about to say something else, but before he can, there are more people needing to be served, so he's gone with a quick nod my way, disappearing as fast as he arrived.

As I drink my beer, I can't help but mull over why tonight feels different. I had wondered if I'd spend the entire time suffering from the worst kind of prickling jealousy. At first, I worried that I'd struggle with being here due to the fact that Sage is so gorgeous, ever so single, and surrounded by a whole host of hungry cowpokes. Except, to my surprise—and asshole that I am, my unbridled glee—I'm not worried at all about other guys or girls aiming to catch her eye. They can flash pretty smiles and charm all they like... I know every single ounce of her focus is gonna be on me.

Every part of Sage is going to be hooked on the way I'm controlling her body. With one slide of my finger across that phone screen, I can send a bolt of pleasure straight to her core, and that knowledge alone is a heady fucking feeling.

She willingly gave that power to me the moment she loaded the app on my phone.

As I nurse my drink and keep on taking photos, I see out of the corner of my eye the second Sage decides to quit the dancefloor. The group of girls head in the direction of the bar, followed by their cowboy shadows materializing out of thin air at the same time. Colt, Storm, and Luke had been sitting over in one of the booths, yet they're here within a heartbeat of their girls taking a step in this direction.

Sage's dark eyes lock with mine for the briefest second as they walk over before her gaze drifts, and she veers away to the other end of the bar to talk to Hayes. That only provokes me to pull out the app and switch up the setting. Keeping a subtle eye on her side profile, I see the tiniest jerk take hold of her body, and her knuckles grab the lip of the bar tightly.

Yeah, she'll have to work extra hard to avoid giving away the game now.

The guys are busy chatting, happy to leave me taking photos, and equally keen to avoid any being taken of themselves. They caught a glance at me whipping my camera out, and proceeded to run like calves about to be roped. They're keeping me at a wary distance, so I get up off my stool and wander over to a quiet spot near the entrance to the bathrooms. Leaning one shoulder up against the wall, I'm busy scrolling back through some of the photos when I sense her follow me over.

"That's the best you've got, cowboy?" She hisses at me over her water. A damp sheen highlights the blush painting the apple of her cheeks. Another thinly disguised shudder rolls through her frame when the wearable hits the more intense sequence of vibrations it's pre-programmed to run through.

Hiding a smirk, and feeling right about done with being the good guy any longer, I pretend to hold the camera's digital preview screen up so she can see the photos. To anyone who might happen to look our way, it'll appear like I'm getting her approval on whatever is shown there.

"Meet me at the truck. Right fucking now." Gritting my teeth, I can already feel my dick aching and rapidly hardening, just thinking about how turned-on she must be.

"I can't. In case you haven't noticed, there are eyes everywhere." Her head jerks in the direction of the bodies clustered at the bar.

"And not to mention that our friends are all right there." There's no missing the way her eyes fixate on the wedding band I'm wearing. And fuck, if I can't stand the fact I need to have it on. I'd gladly melt the thing down and eliminate it from my life entirely.

In no scenario can I resist Sage anymore. I've sealed this for myself, and have to find a way to get her away from all these people.

"Then I'll keep turning the setting on that thing higher and higher until you do." Tapping the camera's button, I scroll through photo after photo.

Sage peers closer at the camera, feigning indifference, then scoffs. "I could easily just remove it."

I make a noise that tells her just how sure I am in the certainty of knowing that the opposite is true. She's too easy to read. The flush high on her cheeks evident from the layers of pleasure both the naughtiness and inherently public nature of all this is bringing her. Where the wild bravado of this girl is concerned, she won't back down from a challenge, of that I can be guaranteed.

My voice remains low before I shoulder my bag and walk off in the direction of the rear exit.

"You could... but I know you won't."

MUSIC PULSES QUIETLY into the night air when Sage eventually appears a few minutes later, ducking around the back of my vehicle in the parking lot. She wraps her arms across her stomach, casting a furtive glance side to side in the dark, but I already know there's no one else out here. Or at least, no one who will be able to see us hidden on this side of my truck.

I rest my back against the door, with one knee bent and the heel of my boot hooked on the running board. Keeping my eyes locked on my phone, the brim of my hat hides her expression from me, but I catch a glimpse of her black boots stepping closer.

"Need something, baby?" I tilt my head to take in the gorgeous sight of her, strung out and about to lose her goddamn mind.

"Just needed some fresh air." She scrunches her face as another wave hits.

I push off the paneling, stepping around in order to crowd her body until both shoulders hit the back door. "You're so goddamn stubborn, you know that?"

"Told you I could handle it." Now that we're out here all alone, her breath hitches in sharply, and there's a more obvious tinge of desperation dripping off that wicked tongue.

When Sage is fully pressed up against the side of the vehicle, I take the opportunity to show her my phone screen. Confirming for her that the wearable is now turned off. I know that final setting will have left her toes curling, even if she's fighting tooth and nail to avoid giving a single hint away, refusing to show how badly she's affected. Crouching down to my haunches, I let my fingertips run along the patch of bare skin on the inside of her thigh, tracing a feather-light stroke over that sensitive flesh. A delicate place that makes her go weak when I let my mouth drift forward to map that particular spot.

I remember every seductive, raspy little noise she made that night when I gave her exactly this kind of treatment.

Sage sucks in a whimper, attempting to stop it dead in its tracks before quickly looking around. She immediately tries to shove at my shoulders. Her tiny fists ball up in an attempt to push me away. "Stop it," she whispers hoarsely. "We're right out in the open. What are you doing?"

"I have to see," I murmur, pushing the soft cotton of her dress up around her waist. Once my fingers find the edge of her panties, I fix my eyes on hers and very slowly start to inch them down over the swell of her hips.

Sage's mouth hangs open, plump lips beautifully parted, looking down on me like an absolute dream as I peel the drenched fabric down. And instead of fighting, she allows me to continue dragging the waistband lower and lower.

The whole time we remain locked here, in this silent moment of illicit desires being fulfilled, my pulse thunders, and I'm just so goddamn close to losing my mind. I can't keep pretending I'm not entirely obsessed with her, and it's agony to know just how long I'm going to have to wait before I can officially make Sage mine.

"I know exactly how much this turns you on. Being out here where someone could see you being a complete fucking slut. What if I spun you around and simply bent you over out in the open? How hard would you grip my dick when you come, I wonder?" My words are a barely there thing, dangled on the warm night air in the spot right above her cunt. Allowing each gust of my mouth to hover oh so close elicits the exact reaction I'm seeking. She squirms perfectly for me and pants harder.

Of course, I can't, and won't, do any of that. I'd be out of my damn mind. But playing with her imagination? Toying with that fantasy and stoking the embers smoldering inside her? I think that's gonna be the thing that brings us both the greatest moment of relief since we've been fighting the temptation to cross that line once more.

"So pretty." The material hugs her soft thighs, and the sweet scent of how wet and aroused she is fills my senses. "You have the prettiest pussy, baby." My whispered words leave her shuddering and shifting her hips perfectly for me as I reach between her thighs and carefully ease the toy out.

Sage's figure sags, bracing herself against my shoulder as I slip it from her panties, then blow ever so gently over her glistening seam. All I want is to stay exactly like this, looking up at her and watching the pleasure wash over her features. All I want is to imprint the memory of exactly how perfect she is.

"Beau..." Her nails sink a tighter hold on me. A warning. An invitation. An urgent reminder that the longer I stay here with her exposed to me like this, the greater the risk that someone might appear from out of the heavy shadows. My truck is parked in the furthest corner of this lot, but that doesn't safeguard us from anything when there are so many people milling around the bar enjoying a humid summer's night.

"Goddamn, Sage. What are you doing to me? I'm forgetting all reason. Damn well can't remember why I'm not supposed to just maul you in front of every single person in that bar. To prove to every girl or guy trying to talk to you, that you're not theirs to look at."

She reaches forward with a hooked finger, tipping the brim of my hat back a fraction. "And I'm not yours either, remember?"

There's a glimmer in her eye that I recognize immediately, the same one I saw that night in the barn. The same expression that tells me this girl is willing to meet me in this and screw the consequences. We're both just as entangled in this web and can't seem to find it within ourselves to stay away, to put a stop to craving one another, no matter how many times we attempt to define the line in the sand.

Sage wets her bottom lip and lifts her hips ever so slightly. "You know something?" She gives me a raspy little purr. "I really... really... love eating pussy."

A groan escapes my throat, and my cock jerks. Hearing that breathiness in her voice and visualizing that about this girl has me fucking dying already.

"... but I love having my pussy eaten properly even more."

Oh, it's fucking on.

I don't even know how it happens, but I've got her panties set back in place, the door open, and have tossed her wearable somewhere in the footwell in all of a heartbeat. Sage is climbing into the backseat with my hands shoving against her ass to push her ahead of me before my brain registers this is happening. Her spine rests up against the opposite door as I crawl after her and seal us in, chasing after this perfect goddamn creature. I don't waste another second. Fisting my hat, I reach forward and place it on her head.

Seeing it there, hell, that unlocks something purely possessive inside me. I've never in my life felt this kind of unhinged, immediate urgency for another person.

Sage catches sight of my expression, and licks her pillowy, tempting lips as her fingers play over the felt brim shadowing her eyes.

"I'd better not catch you tampering with my birth control, cowboy." She spreads her legs as wide as possible, giving me every inch of her as my shoulders wedge between her knees. "I've heard a rumor you bull riders get extra feral seeing your hat on a gal. Want 'em knocked up real quick." Her fingers sink into my hair and I feel the biggest rush of relief at having her touch me. Like a calming breeze winding through my tense muscles, which doesn't make any sense at all because I'm equally coiled tight and so fucking wild for her. I'm so painfully aware that I shouldn't be daring to do this right now, yet I can't think of any reason to walk away from my girl.

Using two fingers, I hook the side of her panties, tugging them out of the way, and I place a soft kiss against her soaked pussy lips. Absolutely goddamn starving for her sweetness to be coating my tongue. "Don't need to worry about that. I had it taken care of a hell of a long time ago. Besides, you're the one ordering me to fill you up, last I recall. *Make a mess of me*. Wasn't that your demand?" I let my tongue roam all over her. She's so sensitive, so swollen. Each stroke of my mouth and brush of my mustache has her thighs quivering around my head.

"*Mmm*. It's fucking hot." Sage lets out a soft moan. "Bet you hated every second your fat cock pumped deep and emptied inside my pussy."

"Jesus Christ, Sage." I have to bite down on the inside of her thigh, damn near choking on her dirty mouth.

"What did you expect? Edge me like that for hours, and I'm a whole lot of extra nasty. Especially with your tongue doing the thing." She yanks on my hair, dragging my mouth back to where she wants me, and of course, I don't dare try to tease her any longer.

"Just like that?" My teeth nip her soft flesh before sinking against her. I'm relentless, licking and devouring every shudder and whine Sage makes as she dissolves above me.

"Oh god. Yes. *Exactly* like that." Her body trembles, and it only takes a few more swirls of my tongue before she detonates with a beautiful cry, her little budded clit pulsing, and the scent of her arousal fills this back seat.

"*Mmm*. You're sweet like honey when you're gushing for me, aren't you, pretty girl?"

My veins are burning, set alight, and I damn near shoot everywhere in my jeans at the way she tastes. It's always so unreal getting to have her, like a waking dream, and I can't stop. I need more, and I need her right this fucking second.

I grab her by the waist and twist us in an awkward tangle of limbs until she's straddling my groin. Dimly in the back of my mind, I can feel the small circular outline of my ring pressing into my thigh from where I cast it aside the second I set foot outside the bar. Hidden away in my pocket, the indentation forms a dull thump of a reminder of just how messed up it is that I keep chasing after Sage like this.

Yet, I can't find it within myself to stop. My length throbs as I fumble with my buckle and fly.

"We can't. Not out here. Anyone could see." Although, as Sage says those words, she's not moving off my lap. Her eyes stay fixed on the spot where my dick comes into view when I shove my briefs down.

"Tinted windows," I grunt as I fist myself, pull her panties aside, and guide the head to her swollen entrance.

Sage moans as my piercing glints in the space between our bodies, before dragging through her slickness.

"You're so fucking bad for my health."

Her perfect tits are right there, with hard nipples poking through the fabric, and it takes everything not to start sucking on them and soak the thin material.

"I can't quit you." I keep my eyes fixed on hers as I move her to sink down on me. And she's so slippery, absolutely drenched, easily welcoming me into her silky soft channel.

"This is too risky." Her walls flutter around me the deeper I press inside.

"But it's a turn-on for both of us. I'm in a world of trouble when it comes to you, baby. Because I need you every goddamn day. I need this. I need to be near you... to be touching you and tasting you."

Shallow, panting breaths fill the air as she sinks down to take all of me, and we're fully connected. Her pussy ripples, sucking me deeper, and I let out a groan at how incredible she feels impaled on me. She's so unbelievably sexy, seated in my lap wearing my hat, swallowing every inch with her dress rucked up to reveal the crease of her thighs. It's like everything drops away, anything outside of this truck simply ceases to exist—disappearing like a wisp of smoke. All I can think of is *her*.

"God, you feel so big like this." Her fingers curl up the back of my neck, and it's so tempting to lean forward and drag my mouth over her neck, the ultimate test of strength not to cover her in bites and bruises. "I know we only had the one night. But I missed this. I missed you." She breathes harder and clenches around me.

"*Fffuck*. Baby. I've been going out of my mind every day not having you. I've nearly caved so many times, you don't even wanna know." I squeeze her hips and drag her down as firmly as possible to grind on me. "Ride me slow. Give me every little bit of you. I don't want this to be fast or frantic. This is how you can imagine my hands being on you if I could when we're out in public." I slide my rough palms around to squeeze her ass cheeks and rock her body gently, and we both let out a low groan at how incredible it feels.

"Are you trying to get us caught?" She gasps as my piercing rubs deep inside her pussy. "We shouldn't—can't stay out here so long." Those words turn into a plea when I grip her ass even tighter and use that leverage to thrust my hips up into her ever so slightly.

"I swear to god, my truck has smelled like you ever since I picked you up from the airport, and now it's gonna have the scent of your cunt in here drive me wild, too."

Sage's eyes have just started rolling back in her head, her channel squeezing me tighter and tighter when a loud buzzing starts up from somewhere on the seat beside us.

Her pussy spasms, and she gasps. "Shit. Oh, my god. It's Layla." She tries to push herself off my length, and I growl, keeping her pinned there as her phone continues to ring.

"Take the call." I fumble to grab her phone and hand it over.

The effect that has on her body is something I've never experienced. I'm having to bite back every need to flip us and start pile-driving her hard and fast, because this girl just gripped me like the tightest fist imaginable.

"H—Hey, Layla." With her free hand, she digs her nails into the back of my neck, continuing to let me rock her body back and forth over my cock.

Through the pulsing rhythm of blood rushing in my ears and my groin, I'm acutely aware that the windows are fogging up as she straddles me and tries so very hard to be quiet, straining so hard not to give away our secret. As I keep working her, the muffled voice of Layla and background music blares through the phone.

"No, it's ok, don't... don't come find me, I'll—I'll be back in a few minutes." Her mouth forms an o shape as her eyes go wide, and I feel the tremors start to take over. She's right on edge, and I'm a greedy bastard who needs her to shatter immediately. I crave this side of Sage, all flushed and gorgeous in my hat, while strangling my cock. I'm ravenous for her to unravel at my hand.

My thumb dips into her slickness, finding the swollen bud right there begging for my attention, and I start rubbing circles over her clit.

"Um—Yeah, sure—Just wait. I'll be right there."

A smirk plays on my lips. Yeah, she fucking will be.

Layla says something else, and I see the struggle painted all over Sage's beautiful features as her pussy starts squeezing me to death. As I increase the pace, pressing harder on her clit, she falls apart. "Oh—Ok—See you—One minute." The second she hangs up, the phone drops onto the seat, and Sage doubles over with the force of how hard she comes.

"Good fucking girl." I keep massaging her through it, and I'm not gonna survive much longer. "Keep riding me. Fuck, Sage. I'm so fucking addicted to you." I groan as she whimpers and humps my hand and pulses around me, dragging me straight down with her. I'm defenseless. Lost to all those beautiful moans and scattered curses, her scent, the heat of her rippling channel.

"*Ungghhh.*" My dick throbs and balls draw up tight, and that surge of tension that has been building and building damn near blinds me as I unload. Cum shoots forward, my length kicks, and I'm pumping her full, with all the filthiness of her words from before echoing in my mind about how much she enjoys it just like this, too.

Neither of us can move, but I know we don't have long. We might be able to steal a few lingering minutes, but certainly nothing like the drawn-out, languid type of moment to decompress that I wish we could indulge in.

Sage hums and lets her fingers stroke my neck. "Honesty moment?" Her voice is dreamy as fuck.

"Always." My throat feels raw. Like I've released some sort of primal noise at the same time as unloading inside her.

"I don't want this."

I swear my heart stops dead in the center of my chest. The engine stalls and I start freefalling through space and time with a deafening silence.

"Hey, no, not like that." She shakes her head at the sight of my crestfallen expression saying it all. "I mean, I like you, hot stuff... but I don't *want* to be attracted to you while it's complicated. I've always swerved the other way when anything feels too serious or like it's gotten too intense. Once, I had a guy send me a dozen roses unprompted, and when I tell you, I blocked him so fast I nearly broke my thumbs. I'm not built for commitment. Certainly not if someone is already part of a complicated as fuck package deal. Absolutely not someone who is *married*."

By the time Sage has finished speaking, my emotions have gone through a loop on a roller coaster. I've now got a stupid damn grin on his face. Maybe it's because all the blood from my body is currently in my cock, still buried inside my girl, but I'm grinning at her through the darkness.

"Did you listen to any of that?" Sage huffs and rolls her eyes.

"Sorry, I only heard the part where you said you like me."

She tugs on my hair. "Of course you did. It's this fucking hat, isn't it? Scrambles your cowboy brain cells."

I let my palms rest heavy on her hips. "Ok, here's *my* honesty... Sage, if it isn't clear, I'm not trying to pin you down and brand you or clip your wings. Putting all of my crap that still needs to be resolved aside for a second—I just want to be with you. Does it have to be more defined than that right now?"

"Well, considering we're lying to our friends and hiding in the parking lot. Yes. It is more complicated than that." Her teeth catch the inside of her cheek.

A heavy exhale rushes out of me, and my hands roam over her softness, gliding beneath the fabric of her dress bunched up around her waist. I hate this. "I want to take you home, right fucking now."

"Unless you want to be front-page headlines in the morning, you need to take yourself and that fancy dick of yours and head back to the ranch. *Alone.*"

I shake my head, rueing everything about the fact she's right. "This is so wrong..."

"What is?"

"I'm supposed to—" There's so many ways I'd prefer this moment to look. I'd much prefer to fuse our mouths together, but there's no chance in hell of doing that without leaving a very obvious sign that Sage has been out here with *someone.*

Sage laughs a soft little noise that bounces around the inside of the truck. "What? Walk me home hand in hand, buy me flowers, and be the sweet guy?"

"Watch that smart mouth, pretty girl. Surely I should at least be able to take you home if I've just fucked you senseless in my truck?"

She smirks. "Thank you for the orgasms, hot stuff. Now, I'm a big girl, and I can drive myself back to the ranch later."

"Text me when you're leaving so I know you're on your way," I mutter.

"Bossy."

"Well, I am your boss. And judging by the fact you just tightened like a fist around me, you get off on knowing you're being a risky slut, fucking the boss in the parking lot."

I can't get enough of the way she's looking at me like *that,* with my hat perched on her head. But, this has to end, and she has to go back inside.

"God, this side of you is dangerous."

"Apparently, you like it?"

"*Hmmm*. I'm still deciding—"

I thrust up into her, giving a final warning. "I'm gonna let you walk back in that bar. I'm letting you go for now, even though it's against all of my better judgment. But don't even think for one second about finishing that sentence while my cum is dripping down your sweet thighs."

CHAPTER 30

Sage

Rhythmic chirps of insects rise and fall as a wave of sound on the night air. The noise reminds me that it is, in fact, long past the witching hour when I should have shut my laptop and called it a day.

Arching my back, I yawn and do a big feline-like stretch, then promptly sink down to bury my nose in the soft, masculine scent of Beau. His giant t-shirt is all I've got on, other than my underwear, while I sit on the porch outside his bedroom. A secluded spot to overlook the undulations of this ranch from as they stretch out beneath darkened skies.

Am I completely lost, drifting rudderless in the midst of the ocean, where this cowboy is concerned?

Clearly. I've willingly tossed my map and compass overboard along the way and disappeared to a place where it's all too easy to escape into a fantasy. A hideaway where we're able to be together and don't have to worry about anything beyond the reaches of this property.

Since the night at The Loaded Hog, we've given ourselves over, surrendered in the most effortless way to this thing. There wasn't even a question otherwise. The moment we fell into the backseat of his truck together was like we shattered any remaining illusion we'd been clinging to that we might have had a hope of denying ourselves this thing any longer.

I pulled up to the ranch at whatever hour of the morning it was by the time the event wrapped up, climbed straight into his bed, and haven't slept anywhere else since.

So, now, we're indulging all that longing and curiosity. On repeat.

I'm doing my best to ignore the pangs of guilt that bubble up every so often. Beau has reassured me that he's on a fast-track to a divorce. And while I had been determined to *not* allow him near me until he was undeniably, one-hundred percent single, I'm clearly not very good at following my own rules. My boundaries were nothing but fairy floss dissolving under the force of a single heated glance and quirk of his lips.

For him and his ocean-deep eyes, apparently, I willingly ignore the standards I set for myself.

Gnawing on my thumbnail, I cast another eye over the open email from Tessa currently pulled up on my screen. I've filled out the necessary details, and now all that remains is for me to attach formalities like relevant documents and press send.

As I'm busy re-reading the note she included with the job application, I hear a shutter click. My head whips up to find Beau standing there, freshly showered, wearing a pair of low-slung sweats. He lowers the camera, and I see, in the other hand, he's carrying a bottle of whiskey.

"Didn't you say you were finished working *before* I headed to take a shower?" He arches a disapproving eyebrow, then deposits everything on the coffee table and settles down beside me on the outdoor couch. Those calloused palms immediately seek out my waist, dragging me onto his lap.

I'm too busy juggling my laptop and talking myself out of licking his bare chest to do anything other than let him manhandle me like this.

"You're looking for new clients already?" With brows knitted together, his eyes flicker over the screen.

"That's the life, hot stuff. Who takes care of the eldest daughter? She looks after her own damn self." I shrug. "Actually, since you're the resident rodeo star and all, you'll give me a stellar reference, won't you? Promise I'll suck your soul out through your cock as many times as you like in return."

His fingers pinch my hip and he makes a rumbly sort of protest.

"Tessa sent it to me as an exclusive before the pro tour announces the role publicly." What sits on my laptop is a PR opportunity she has already put my name forward for. A golden prospect that comes complete with an impressive retainer paycheck and luxurious added trimmings. Effectively the dream for someone like me. Not only that, but it would open up an endless horizon of opportunities to grow my client portfolio.

The only catch is that it starts this coming fall, and since it's attached to the rodeo tour machine, will require being on the road traveling the entire time. Where my thoughts about this man are concerned, I have to ignore the ramifications of such a detail. I can't allow my lust-fueled obsession with Beau to rule my decisions about my career. The cold, hard reality is that once summer is done, my work here will be, too. There's no skipping off into the sunset, giving him heart eyes while patiently waiting for him to become available. And even if he did, would I dare want to commit to something *serious* when I've already proved that I'm no better than the 'other woman' in this scenario?

How do I know I'm not forever going to be the second choice? The easy option who will allow herself to be cajoled and charmed with promises of 'one more month' while their separation drags on and on. Leaving me stuck, forced to lie to everyone who matters to me?

As much as I enjoy being with Beau, I have to think clearly, and not let sex be the passionate, wild creature at the helm of my destiny.

That's when I realize he hasn't said anything in reply. So I close my laptop and lean over to set it down beside his camera, then hook my arms around his neck. I might be resolute in making smart decisions for my future, but that doesn't mean I have to be anything but a slut who craves him all night long in the here and now.

"You know what's more interesting than boring old client applications?" I muse, as I study his strong jaw. "Having a drink, since you've so generously brought me one."

Beau reaches for the bottle, uncaps it, and hands it over. He's still not saying anything, but then again, I've gotten used to his unique brand of silence. It usually means there's too much noise going on inside his brain. Somewhere along the journey, it all gets bottlenecked, and doesn't manage to actually make its way out of his mouth.

Whereas I have the opposite problem. Things tend to drop out of mine all too freely.

I change positions, clambering to sit astride him, and run a finger across his bottom lip before tilting the bottle. He keeps hooded eyes on mine as his chin tips backward, allowing me to pour a shot of the amber alcohol into his mouth.

His Adam's apple bobs as he swallows it down, and the fierce intensity behind his stare locked on me sends goosebumps flying in every direction. Stern, silent Beau is one of my many, many favorite weaknesses.

"Ok, now your turn." I give him a taunting little smile and hand the bottle over. He lifts it out of my grasp, and I don't know quite what I was expecting. I hover, anticipating the moment he'll lift it to my lips and tip my head back. Instead, he raises it to his own mouth, wraps his lips around the open neck, and takes a swig. As I sit perched over his groin, I feel his hand slide up my spine until his fingers dig into my hair. With a sharp tug, his grip tightens, and he yanks my body to the side. The shock of how quickly he strikes leaves my mouth dropping open with a gasp. He takes control of every aspect of my universe.

His strong body looms over mine, and with a devilish look in his eyes, Beau spits the whiskey into my mouth.

Well, shit.

I was well and truly prepared, and willing, to be a whole lot of naughty for Beau Heartford tonight. This cowboy had just guaranteed I'll be extremely fucking filthy, just to please him. My blood sings with excitement, and I gulp down the delicious burn lining the back of my throat.

As I dart my tongue out to wet my lips, Beau devours the tiny movement, then swoops in to take my mouth. He tastes like whiskey, the faintest hint of spice, and the way he slides his tongue against mine is deliciously slow and sensual. He sucks every molecule of air from the space around us, and the longer he kisses me, the more I feel my bones melt into a rich, honeyed liquid state.

After he successfully turns my mind to jelly and leaves my pulse thumping between my legs, he finally relinquishes my mouth.

I'm a starry-eyed kitten, ready to nuzzle against his chest and be his perfect little pet.

"Did you know, I've been down bad for you ever since that day on the sidewalk?" Beau takes another sip of whiskey, this time handing me the bottle as he works down a swallow.

"Some places I can go and no one knows who the hell I am. If you're not into rodeo or country music..." He winces slightly while saying those words. "You wouldn't know my face. But out here? It's damn impossible."

I take a long drink and let him keep talking.

"You didn't have a clue who I was. Couldn't have cared less. And it was the first time I ever felt attracted to someone so instantly."

He wraps a hand around mine to briefly drag the bottle to his mouth, then pushes it back my way.

"You terrified me, because I *couldn't* want you. I didn't have the right to desire you—I still don't. Not when I legally have a wife. But she never saw me the way you do. She only liked the way a rodeo star fit her brand. That's all I ever was, a glorified accessory to suit her image."

I let my fingers play over his face, stroking his skin and brushing against his stubble and facial hair. "Can I ask you something? Why did you do it? Why marry and stay in it, if you weren't happy?"

Beau lets his head sink back against the cushion. "Loneliness. A stupid idea that I was supposed to have already found my person."

His hands slip beneath the t-shirt I'm wearing, gliding up my bare waist to brush strokes over the sides of my ribs with both thumbs.

"Each time I contemplated getting papers drawn up, another sponsor would arrive, another win would go my way. Suddenly, there I was, a world champion, and the spotlight shone even brighter. If I'd picked that moment to end a marriage that hundreds of thousands of so-called *fans* were living vicariously through, well, I was dumb enough to be scared of what it might do to tank my career. That fear felt damn well real enough at the time, so I chose to focus on what I could control. I buried myself in doing the thing I was blessed to do, and shut the hell up about something that was my own fault. Running away wasn't gonna fix anything."

Beau exhales, looking at me with an apology swimming behind those blue-gray eyes.

"Mandy knew my greatest secret; my truest fear was never inside the arena or what might happen to me if a ride went wrong. She knew my deepest shame was becoming my father. It still is. The thought that I would be considered no better than him, was enough to stop me from ever attempting to end things or walk away before now."

My heart squeezes hearing him talk openly like this for the first time. Giving me a tiny insight into what he's been through and blamed himself for.

"Take it he wasn't a good guy?"

He shakes his head. “The worst kind of cheater. After seeing what he did, I made a promise to all the women in my life—to my mom, my sister, even my gran—that I’d never be the disgusting son of a bitch he was. So, I was trapped. If I broke that commitment to Mandy, then I would be letting down the women who mean the world to me. And if I stayed, then so what? All I’d do would be to burden myself with living a lie.”

“That’s not a life, though. Wouldn’t they rather see you happy?”

“Sure. Maybe on some level. But they deserved better than to be dragged through a media frenzy, to be hounded by gossip, to be snapped by paparazzi looking to make a quick buck. They never asked for the fame my career brought to their doorstep, and I couldn’t face the prospect of them being caught up in an ugly public conversation about me or how all the men in my family were the same.”

“Mine might not be exactly like that...” I take a breath before carrying on. “I’ve got myself one of those deadbeat fathers, too. But my *real* dad? The guy who actually raised me? I would go to the ends of the earth for him in return for what he’s done to take care of me and my mom. She was strong enough to walk away from an abusive relationship after spotting the signs that were there early on, and I constantly feel like I’ve got to live up to the standard she set for me, you know? It feels like the least I can do, to try my best to never let her down.”

We sit together, sharing another few drags of whiskey and exchanging the kind of silence that echoes so unbelievably loud in the wake of everything the two of us have taken a moment to say.

“Why did you keep my bag?” Beau hits me with a narrowing of his eyes.

I take a hasty gulp. After how freely Beau has just shared, I’d be a terrible person not to do the same for him in return.

Wetting my lips, I can feel the blood whooshing in my ears. “I kept it because I liked you, ok? Probably too much, considering how quickly that moment came and went. It was the first time I'd felt anything like that... I don't know how to describe it. You snuck in and lingered. It was this sense that I'd tasted something I might never get to have ever again. So I hung onto it, because it felt like I wasn't ready to say goodbye to that feeling."

I gnaw on my bottom lip and shift my weight.

"Ok. My turn for an interrogation." Reaching for his camera, I lean back in order to peer at him through the viewfinder.

He's far too close and blurry, but at least I feel like I can avoid talking about my utterly complex, tangled string of feelings where he's concerned.

"Do you regret being famous?" I put on a fake interviewer's voice.

Beau chuckles. "Part of me, absolutely, yes. But I can't pretend that I don't love what the rodeo gave me. So many people go through life never getting to live their passion. How could I regret that? Even if I wish the fame didn't come with it? That would be fucking selfish of me."

"*Hmm*. Good looking *and* philosophical. That earns you a bonus round, Mr. Heartford." I press the button for the shutter, and feel his hands come up to cover mine. He adjusts something on the lens, then guides it back up to my face.

This time I can see his handsomeness all too clearly.

"Why photography?" I take a couple more photos, now focused on his eyes.

"At first, it gave me something to use, a coping tool, if you want to call it that, to try and help when I felt overwhelmed. Focusing on details and settings and stupid shit. The kinds of things most normal people don't want to be bothered learning." His hands glide up and down my back as he talks in that low, steady tone.

"Normal has always seemed incredibly dull to me."

He lifts one hand to scratch at his jaw. "So I ended up spending a ton of my free time when I wasn't training or competing at events fucking around with a camera until I managed to get all those tiny pieces correct and kept refining it, ya know."

"You are *such* a Virgo, Mr. Perfectionist." Taking a few more snaps, I let the shutter click on repeat, honing in on the veins popping on the back of his hand.

"I was blessed to be touring some of the most beautiful places in the country. Having my camera and a reason to get away from the crowds and the noise, well, it saved me more times than I can count."

"What's your favorite thing to photograph?"

Beau takes another drink, his eyes getting that look about them when he's far away. Thinking of another place, another time, another moment in his life that had so many layers to it before I came along.

"Sunsets are always the one thing I'm constantly chasing." Readjusting his weight beneath me, he brings a hand up to play with some loose strands of hair framing my face, rubbing them between his fingers. "You know nightfall is coming, but there's so much color there, and it's a different painting every time. The sky is so vast and unpredictable. That's a gift for a photographer. You could set up your tripod in exactly the same position every single day, waiting for the exact same time of evening, and never take the same photo twice."

The heat of him seeps beneath my shirt, warming my skin, and I don't think I've ever felt so *safe* with another person. Another miserable realization that against my better judgment, I might just have allowed my heart to crack open and allow him to sneak inside. Just when I'm potentially about to secure a future for my business that will take me far, far away from this delicious closeness and temptation to trust someone for the first time.

His throat bobs, and he reaches for the camera, gently prying it from my hands. An act that leaves me feeling naked and vulnerable all of a sudden. This heartfelt confession time was all well and good when I could stare at him through a camera, and keep that shield in place. But with one swift move, Beau just disarmed me.

"It's kind of like how I feel when I look at you. I never know how you're going to surprise me." He cups the back of my neck and proceeds to obliterate any lingering thoughts I might have had about *us* and how we're at the mercy of being at the wrong time.

Beau speaks against my mouth before kissing me with an achingly soft glide of his lips.

"You're my sunset sky, baby. Bright and mysterious and beautiful all at the same time."

CHAPTER 31

Beau

Kissing Sage has never felt as important as in this moment. To have this, just the two of us, when I can try to demonstrate just how deep my feelings for her run.

She really, truly is the one I'm chasing after. The part of my life that feels the most miraculous, and yet she's also slipping through my fingers at the same time. How am I supposed to show her all the ways she's important in my life? How could I expect a girl as driven and talented as her to want to throw all of that away?

All I am is the ex-rodeo star, a married man. That can't possibly be a reason for her to entertain giving up an opportunity like the one she's been offered.

So, I let my mouth cover hers, slide our tongues together, and surrender to the connection of our bodies. Because maybe that's all we'll get for now. Who knows when our time will come back around? Who knows when it might finally align in the skies, the moment I can convince her to take a chance on us? To be mine?

My hands roam everywhere beneath the soft cotton of my t-shirt she wears, and each time I dip lower to squeeze handfuls of her ass, she arches into my hold. Her teeth nip at the corners of my lips, and she lets out the sexiest little moans.

Fuck. I'm entirely gone for her. Swept up and unable to do

anything but pray that by the time I've sorted my shit out, she might still give me the time of day.

Allowing my fingers to slip beneath her underwear, I fondle her ass and play a little more boldly. Guided by the way her body tells me exactly where she wants my touch, I press and rub against her tight rosebud entrance.

"Please say you're into that? *Please*?" Sage pants against my mouth.

My dick throbs. "Are you?" I say hoarsely. Hardly daring to believe this is where tonight might go from here.

"*Mmmm*. Extremely." Her tongue licks up my throat.

A dark groan rumbles between us. "How are you even real?"

Ever the wild thing sent to torment me, Sage slides a hand down to my groin and cups my erection. "Has it been a while, hot stuff?"

Using her other hand, she keeps on playing with my stubble, dragging her fingernails over my jaw while squeezing my cock. Just to really send my brain flying somewhere up into the sky overhead, she pushes that luscious ass back against my hand.

"How about... it's been never." I swallow hastily.

"What?" Sage gasps in horror. "Oh, you poor baby." Another firm grip of her palm has my stomach knotting with heat and desire and need.

"I—I don't want to hurt you." I dig my fingers into her flesh and admit the part I'm most hesitant about. Logically, I know plenty of people enjoy... this... while piercings are involved. But with my girl, the last thing I want to do is risk causing her pain in some way.

"You won't. Lots of lube. We'll take it slow." Her mouth works a line along my jaw. Nipping and sucking on my overheated skin. "You gotta let me give you this."

"Isn't this usually the other way around? Pretty sure it's normally the guy pleading and convincing the girl to give it a try." My voice is gritty, coarse-edged with the effort of keeping a level head right now.

Sage's tongue glides over her bottom lip and then leans forward to nibble mine with a sinful little noise.

"Well, luckily for you, I'm not like anyone else you're gonna meet."

No, she's absolutely right there. No one is ever going to come close to matching this woman. There's no one else except her, and it's going to be the greatest challenge I'll ever face to make sure our future looks like thousands more nights with her pressed up against me like this.

"We need my toys." She sinks her teeth into that plush bottom lip.

My heart feels like it's about the pump straight out of my chest. Somehow, I find a croaky answer for her. "Ok."

"Probably that sexy as hell tub as well." Her little hum is accompanied by rubbing me harder through my sweats.

"Do you want me to wear a condom or something?" My brain is in my dick while simultaneously still struggling to grasp where this is going.

"Always with those cowboy manners." She giggles. "No. I know you'll be gentle, and I want you to feel everything right there along with me."

"Are you sure?" I'm battling to form actual words the more she keeps cupping and squeezing me and determinedly works me into a frenzy.

Sage finally gives my straining cock one last dose of attention, then brings both hands to cradle my jaw, kissing me deeply until both our breathing turns ragged. I feel like I'm floating when she pulls back and gives me a look that could have me handing over my entire soul within a second.

This incredible girl climbs off my lap, swipes up the bottle, and crooks a finger my way.

"You want this ass? You know where to find me."

I'm not sure there's any force in this world powerful enough to prevent me from following my girl.

Standing just beside the outdoor tub, with only the stars and moonlight for company, along with the soft glow of warm light spilling from Sage's cabin... I'm feeling nervous as all hell.

How is it that she can be so endlessly confident and sure of herself, and right now, I'm second-guessing every move?

Sage stops in front of me, a shimmer to her dark eyes, and has her hands full with items that are beyond anything I might have imagined. The curve gracing her lips is that same look she slayed me with the day on the sidewalk. Daring me to touch, goading me into her game, to see how far I'm willing to dance with her.

That day, I couldn't do anything. I couldn't dare step across that line.

Tonight, there's no hesitation.

Reaching forward, I lift the enormous goddamn tentacle dildo from her hands and hold it up at eye level. Raising one brow, I watch her face split into a broader grin as she shrugs a shoulder innocently while standing there holding lube and another smaller cylinder-looking vibrator.

"Look, sometimes a girl just wants to be extra full. It'll make it feel even better for you, too."

"Christ." The hand not holding the giant sex toy scrubs over my mouth. Sage tilts her head to one side, catches her bottom lip between her teeth, and waits for my brain to get up with the play. My cock is a steel fucking rod, and my thoughts are definitely stuck on the image she just painted of being *extra full*.

Working down a swallow, my mind finally blinks back online.

I reach for the rest of the items and set them all down beside the tub, quietly studying the way Sage's chest rises and falls a little faster. Her nipples are hard points poking through the front of her shirt, and I drag a finger over the swell of her breast. She gives me the horniest little noise when I make contact with the tight bud and pinch down.

"The bullet vibe..." she murmurs. "Wanna get that warmed up

for me? Setting three is like heaven in a teeny tiny vibrating package."

There's no need for a second invitation. I swipe it up, and as soon as the soft buzzing starts, a shudder takes hold of her body. I set about running it across her breasts, moving back and forth, until she's clawing at my waistband.

"You need to be naked. Like, right this second." She pants.

"Well... I need you soaked." I drop my hand down and roam the vibrations over her covered pussy, while dipping my head to start kissing her neck.

Sage starts shoving at my pants, determined in her efforts to move things forward, and I chuckle as I suck down on her earlobe.

"These toys get you all riled up, *hmm*?"

"You'd find out if you weren't taking so goddamn long about it." Her huffs at me are adorable.

"I already told you, I enjoy being able to take my time with you, baby." I hook the hem of the t-shirt and drag it up over her head. Once she's bare, I let the toy play over her budded nipples and drink down every whine of frustrated pleasure she gives in return.

Letting my attention move lower on her body, I crowd her backward to sit on the lip of the tub and get my mouth on her perfect tits. As I do, I rub the toy across the front of her panties. Sage is damn near vibrating herself as she clings to my neck and guides my head to keep sucking and teasing her breasts. My tongue glides over her nipples, swirling and flicking, and I allow my teeth to graze the pebbled, stiffened peaks.

"Want to get wet for me?" I draw her breast into my mouth and damn near groan at the way she sinks her nails into my nape.

"What I want is your dick deep inside me." She tugs on my hair, then widens her knees as far as possible so I can hold the vibe tight against her core.

"That's why they call you *Sergeant*, huh?" I tease, before helping her shift her weight and drag her drenched panties down, tossing them aside. "Gonna show me how demanding you are?"

She swings her legs over and climbs into the water, beautifully naked and oh so soft, hitting me with a flutter of her lashes over one shoulder as her smooth skin dips into the tub. "For that piercing of yours, cowboy? I'm always a good little slut."

I quickly shove out of my sweats, preparing to clamber straight in after her, when Sage stops me. Kneeling by the edge, the position puts her right at eye level with my leaking dick. From behind that seductive little look she gives me and that position on her knees, I already know she's got plans forming.

"Let me suck you." Sage reaches to take the toy out of my fist, and holy shit, I feel a bolt of heat zap along my spine. Since the night in the back of my truck, my girl has been eager to play with my piercing at every opportunity, and well, who the fuck am I to tell her no? Goddamn, her mouth is incredible, and she seems to get off on this just as much as I do.

Her plush lips wrap around me, and I let out a groan as she flattens her tongue to run a wet glide along the underside of my length. As she teases me, lapping and dragging her mouth right back to the tip, she reaches forward to run the vibe gently over my balls.

"Jesus. Baby, you're trying to kill me." I stroke her hair and jerk with the intensity of the sensation before I feel her shoving that hand forward the same moment she works my tip. Her tongue slowly pushes my piercing back and forth while encouraging me to widen my stance. The second I follow her silent command, I feel it. Her fingers and the vibrations rub over that stretch of hot, smooth skin behind my balls.

"*Ffffuck*, baby." My cock throbs in her mouth, and I stifle a rough noise in the back of my throat. "That's too good. Keep that up and you're gonna make me lose it too quick."

Sage peers up at me from beneath those thick lashes, hitting me with a mischievous glint in her eyes that tells me she'd definitely do her worst to make me blow right here and now if only she wasn't so determined to fuck long into the night.

Her tongue laps to flick my piercing one final time, then lets me go on a wet pop. A trail of saliva hangs between her lips and the barbell, which I reach down to swipe with a thumb.

"You're trouble." My pulse races as fast as my blood is damn well heating the longer we play this game.

"I think you kinda like my trouble."

"I do," I murmur, letting my thumb drag her bottom lip down, utterly caught by how fucking stunning she is. Especially like this, with water lapping at her waist and the moonlight glinting off the rippling surface. The droplets covering her arms look like tiny shimmering stars coating her brown skin.

Sage remains kneeling, but shifts to a spot just beside the table where her other toy waits. Showing off the arch of her spine as she does so.

"You want it like this?" I climb into the tub and position myself behind her, immediately dropping my mouth to kiss a heated trail along the slope of her shoulder. Handing over the bullet vibe, Sage doesn't waste any time, taking it from my grasp and reaching down to shove one hand between her thighs, she uses it to start circling over her clit.

"God, yes." Relief coats her voice when the sensations her body has been waiting for start to take hold.

My hands are so damn desperate for her. Roaming to wrap around from behind, I glide gentle palms up her stomach, squeezing her breasts, then pinching her nipples. Each second I get to explore her body feels like another opportunity to memorize every single thing about my girl. Every slight shiver, each response is stored away, even though I can't be certain that I'll have enough time to learn every single touch her body craves.

With one hand cupping her breast, I reach between us and fist my cock so that I notch at her entrance, but that's where I pause. As much as I'm consumed with the need to simply push forward and drive inside her body, I hold it, allowing just the barbell and swollen head of me to stay there.

Sage immediately tries to fuck herself back onto me, and I hum with satisfaction, my lips brushing over her ear.

"Need more?" While continuing to torture her tits, I get lost in the way her pussy keeps squeezing just the sensitive head of my dick. In an effort to latch onto every whine and agonized moan she gives me in return, I keep kissing her neck.

"Do you want just the tip?"

"More. I want more."

"You want all of me, trouble?"

"Fuck you. Yes, please." Sage pants. "*I do.*"

"Such good manners." I let my teeth graze the side of her throat, and she's so unbelievably wet and slippery. "Since you look so pretty when you come..." This time I slip my way inside, and she's like a silky glove as my cock pushes forward on a slick glide. Fuck my entire life, Sage detonates before I've even fully sunk to the hilt.

I simply hold there, buried deep in her pussy, while my hands stroke and tug on her nipples. Teasing in exactly the way I know drives her out of her head with how sensitive her breasts are after she comes. "Fuck, I love how you squeeze me like the tightest fist. My dick just wants to live inside your cunt, pretty girl."

"Beau." Her walls keep rippling around me. "Don't make me wait."

"Oh, you're desperate for that monster cock, *hmm*?"

She whines and lets her head drop forward between her shoulders. "I want to feel you."

"You're the sexiest goddamn thing." This time I slip out and reach for the massive fucking tentacle. Sliding the length through her arousal, I make sure to rub back and forth a little before wedging it inside her, inch by inch, as Sage moans and bucks into my hold.

"Oh god. Yes. Keep going. More. Push a little further." Sage whimpers with a series of demands, letting me know exactly what she needs. Each time she does, it sends a thud straight to my balls, hearing her be vocal about how I can best go about making this perfect for her.

"Stay like that... keep working that needy clit, baby." I kiss her shoulder and reach for the lube this time. Drizzling a generous amount over her ass, the moment I start to spread it around, she immediately pushes back on me.

"Play a little bit first. Your fingers will feel so good." She gasps as I stroke over her hole, and Jesus, my hands can't stop kneading, squeezing, grabbing to spread her wide, knowing her pussy is already full.

We're both desperate as I slowly work over her nerve endings and carefully press forward with one finger until I feel her muscles relax allowing me inside.

"Is that ok?" I stay like that, gently toying with her and already feeling how goddamn tightly she's going to grip me. "Fuck, you gotta tell me if it's too much, ok?"

"I'm fine—it's perfect." Sage's words are breathy and pleading.

I gradually build up to adding a second finger and have to squeeze my dick with my other hand to settle down because she's clenching around me so damn hard. That toy filling her channel makes everything so much more intense, and I can tell by the way her body shudders she's building toward another release.

"Please. Please. I need you—I need—" Sage's begging morphs into a cry of pleasure as she falls apart, and I feel every wave as her muscles ripple through her orgasm and then relax even further. Her grip intensifies on my fingers as I sink two fingers up to the knuckle and nearly fucking lose it in anticipation when her ass clenches around me, and her moans keep fluttering softly into the night.

"Christ, you're so beautiful. You feel incredible." I croon in her ear as I ease my hand away, and know this next part is gonna ruin me. She's destroyed everything I thought I knew about myself and put me back together with her fire and spark and passion.

God, how could I not want to give this girl anything but the entire fucking world?

I quickly lube myself up and shift my weight forward. The water sloshes around us and adds to the sensation playing over every nerve ending as I guide my tip against her ass.

"Tell me if you need to stop." I stroke her skin and wait a moment because I don't even know if Sage is back in her body yet.

But she nods and gives me a dreamy little glance, looking back at me over her shoulder. "Just take it nice and slow." She moves back against me. "Since you love going slow, hot stuff." Those long eyelashes drop to form a hooded gaze over her flushed cheeks.

I grip my cock and push against her, taking my time to ease forward until I feel the tip and my piercing slip inside and nearly choke with how unbelievably tight she is.

"Goddamn, you're gonna squeeze me to death. Relax for me." My girl makes a soft little noise, and I can feel the vibrations playing through the water and her body as she keeps using the bullet. She bears down ever so lightly, and I press a little further forward.

The more I gradually, ever so slowly, fight my way inside, the more I nearly fucking die. She's the hottest, tightest furnace wrapped around me, and she was goddamn right. I *can* feel the toy stuffed inside her pussy, and I don't know how long I'm gonna last like this.

Sage moans and shivers beneath me, keeping the vibe working over her clit. It's all I can do to grit my teeth and curse softly as we keep slowly moving together, allowing me to sink forward a tiny fraction at a time.

"Baby, you feel so fucking good." I try to remember to talk to her, to check in. "You're gripping me so hard. Just ease back for me." I'm damn near done for. I've never experienced anything like this, and Sage trembles with beautiful noises, letting me know exactly how good it feels for her.

My grip against her soft flesh tightens, bruising her hips, but the more I do it, the louder Sage gets, and the more she pushes against me, begging.

With a long groan and panting breaths, my hips sink forward to meet hers. My length pulses as I'm finally there, fully seated inside her, and a roaring fills my ears. I'm barely hanging on, my brain hardly functioning when all I can think of is how hot her tight little hole is. And Sage is a vision, a limp-boned, blissed-out thing of beauty beneath me.

Leaning over her back, I tilt her head to let me kiss her, to take her mouth until she sobs into me.

"Beau... fuck me... let me feel you." Her murmured words are ragged, just like my own breathing. And she outright pleads for me to move.

I slowly slide back, then carefully shift my hips forward, and all I can do is drink down every clench and shudder and whimpering sound of pleasure beneath me.

We shift together, and the heat and slickness and intensity of how full she is—how the ridges and ripples of that fat toy rub against me through her inner wall—it all leaves me spun out of my head.

My dick thickens. My balls ache with a desperate, coiled desire to unload into her.

"I can't hold it, baby. You're so tight. I'm so close." With each measured thrust forward, that pressure continues to build at the base of my spine.

"Please. Oh fuck. I need you." My girl lets out a shuddering moan, and her body starts to convulse as her orgasm sweeps through. Every wave, long and undulating, is heaven as she contracts and clamps down around me.

"Christ, baby. That's it. God fucking damn. *Unghhh.*" I pulse my hips with shallow thrusts forward until I lose all rhythm, and the blinding sensation hooks in place right there behind my eyes as my climax bursts, so heated and slick between us. I'm gasping for breath as my length keeps throbbing, and cum pumps in thick spurts, filling and marking her while branding me all at the same time.

"Oh god. *Ffffuck.* I can feel it. I feel *you.*" She sobs out the words before slumping beneath me, and I fumble to take the vibe out of her grasp. Turning it off and tossing it aside, I then band her against my front. My dick feels like it's being wrapped inside the tightest fist and squeezed relentlessly.

My mouth is everywhere I can reach, kissing every inch of damp skin possible to trace with my lips. I'm pretty sure I tell her I'm obsessed with her. That I can't lose her. I don't even know what I'm saying.

Keeping myself seated inside her, I reach down to slip the dildo out gently. My girl trembles at the feeling, and I ease it from her body as slowly as I can.

"I just want it to be me and you, baby. I need it to just be the two of us." I nibble over her ear and neck and hang on tight to her softness, holding her fiercely against my chest.

There's a raging torrent, a flood of confessions I want to whisper in her ear. A dam strains to hold back the words, waiting to explode beneath the weight of my need to let her know exactly what she means to me.

I'm so overwhelmed by it all, so compelled to tell her how I feel. Except, that's the most irrational thing I could do. A confession drenched in sex, shared during the aftermath of a mind-altering climax? This beautiful creature would undoubtedly laugh in my face and roll her eyes.

If I'm going to share anything so deeply important with her, it's not going to be in the heat of the moment. Certainly not as a direct result of this being the first time I've experienced anything even approaching this level of intimacy and trust before.

Sage doesn't need me to unload a waterfall of emotions, to complicate this more than it already is. Anything my foolish damn heart wants to shout from the rooftops has to stay locked away.

My girl just needs me to hold her and take care of her.

That's what she needs. So that's what I give over.

Along with my entire goddamn heart, in secret.

CHAPTER 32

Sage

LAYLA:

Sage Maloney. I swear to God, if you don't answer your mother's texts... that woman is about to get on a plane to Montana this evening.

She keeps messaging me, and there are only so many times I can cover your ass by telling her you are "busy working" without sounding like you have actually been abducted by those aliens you love so much.

I wince at the sight of Layla's messages arriving. I've very much been guilty of avoiding my mom's phone calls and texts. But considering the circumstances, I am genuinely busy with client work... I just have a cowboy-shaped distraction filling my evenings to now plan accordingly for.

Beau Heartford proves to be an extremely powerful form of motivation to work my ass off in order to be finished by the time he comes back in from his day around the ranch.

I'm sorry. I'll call her tomorrow.

Promise.

I'm busy rifling through Beau's drawers to look for one of his t-shirts to steal for after I get out of the shower, when I see the next flurry of messages arrive.

Ok.

That's it.

Are you really gonna make me haul ass all the way down this mountain to get the truth out of you?

I'm a patient woman. But enough is enough.

Who are you knocking boots with, and why have I had to wait since the night at the Hog to be dished any details?

I swear to god, my stomach hits the floor as I jump out of my skin. Spinning around, I've already leaped to the assumption that Layla is standing right behind me.

My cheeks flame as I feel like I've been caught red-handed—quite literally, with my hand in the cookie jar. Except the only cookie involved is mine, and this kind of jar comes with a magical piercing capable of having me scream my cowboy's name.

Fuck, I hate that I'm continuing to lie to not only my best friend, but my family, too.

Sadly, no one.

I'm sorry, I genuinely am just snowed under with these contracts.

You know me. Ever the perfectionist and full-time workaholic.

Besides, I've landed a gig with the big boss dog rodeo circuit.

I haven't had a chance to fill you in, but I'll dish up all the juicy details when you're down here next.

Shut up. That's incredible.

I'm so proud of you, Sarge.

Chewing the inside of my cheek, I watch as Layla's sweet words of congratulations continue to roll in. She drops any continued line of interrogation and instead simply shows up for me as a supportive best friend.

As I exhale heavily, a quiet sense of dread is already sitting heavy in my stomach in anticipation of the next time I will see my friends. Because it will most likely be in the presence of the man I need to pretend to have about as much interest in as a horseshoe.

I swipe a t-shirt and close the drawer with my hip. As I bump it closed, the whole thing rocks by accident, and I hear a clatter on the top. Shit. A box pushed away at the back topples onto its side, and the wooden top flips open.

In that moment, all those prickly feelings of guilt roar into a bonfire, with my morals and tattered boundaries providing the fuel for the flames.

Coming face to face with Beau's wedding ring was the last thing I expected, and yet, of course, he keeps it *somewhere.* Even if he never wears it normally, he does when out in public, like the night at The Loaded Hog, before he took it off.

Now, I know where it lives. Hidden away, shoved out of sight, in this nondescript wooden box on top of a tall dresser in his walk-in.

As I stand there clutching the soft fabric of his shirt, my brain flies to a memory of the last time we stood in here together. I was almost on this exact spot, as we were getting ready to spend an evening soaking in the bath.

Beau leans forward, bending to kiss my collarbone, and my fingers drift up to weave through his hair in the way I'm entirely addicted to. With his mustache scratching my skin, he lets out a long breath.

"Don't remind me, I need to get a haircut sometime soon."

"I like this wild boy look on you." I pout. He suits it, and compared to old photos I've seen of him during his pro years when his hair was trimmed much shorter, this more rugged, tousled mess seems to be much more his speed.

"I hate having to sit through small talk. Invariably, it turns into a circus if people start wanting to get chatty and ask for photos." He straightens up and drags his fingers through his curls, immediately making him look more disheveled and so sexy I could melt.

"Well, aren't you lucky I learned to save money by doing my own hair. Have you got some scissors and a comb?"

Beau rummages in one of the cupboards and pulls out both items. I take his hand, dragging his grumbling ass behind me into the bathroom, and prod at him to sit on a stool in front of the mirror.

"Welcome to Sage's Styles and Snips. Let's get you trimmed up today, sir." I pretend to flick a cape around his chest, then look at him in the mirror and squeak. "Oh my god, look, it's Beau Heartford." Letting one hand fly up to my mouth, I start fanning myself with the other. "Can I sit on your lap and get you to sign my titties?"

He shakes his head, but can't catch the tug at the corner of his lips before his smile gives him away, and I laughingly nudge him to ditch the shirt. Once he's all bare-chested and, of course, utterly gorgeous, I set about combing through his strands. We figure out how much he wants to trim off. It's hardly anything, which makes me immensely happy.

After we've stayed in comfortable silence for a while, with only the snips of the scissors and rake of the comb through his hair echoing around the tiled bathroom, I float an idea.

"We should throw a thank you for everyone who's been involved with helping get the ranch off the ground. I've been thinking of an event that could double as a solid PR exercise, and I think that's the perfect late-summer marketing for this place. It doesn't have to be a big deal, but it'll allow the word to spread."

"You know these things much better than I do." Beau looks at me as I fuss with his hair.

God, I love having his eyes on me far too much.

"It'll be super cute. Like one of those movie moments. I can just see it… music, good food, pretty lights, a bonfire… we'll get her looking amazing. This ranch deserves a grand gesture."

"A grand gesture?"

"Yes. She's a star in her own right. Giving her a party, a proper one. That's what she deserves—along with finally settling on a name, by the way."

Beau grunts. "Yeah. I'm working on it."

"No, you aren't. You're too busy playing with horses and cows all day long. Let me help you. We can brainstorm over dinner tomorrow."

"Sure." He studies me in the mirror for a moment. Those blue-gray eyes track my fingers sifting through his hair. "Didn't pick you as one for the sappy, romantic movies. What with all that ET conspiracy stuff you fixate on."

"I'm a sucker for a grand gesture. You know the scene in the movie where the girl thinks it's all over, that she's down for the count… and then…"

"And then what?"

"It's silly. It's not one thing in particular… but it's that energy of the moment, you know? The romance of it all. The willingness to lay yourself bare for someone, to leave it all out on the field and risk it all. That's the high stakes of one character offering up their heart to another. You know it's pure romance when it sends chills down your spine and makes your stomach flip."

"Sounds more like you're describing a horror movie."

"Shut up. Of course, you would think that, Mr. Virgo. But some of us are romantics at heart. The best movies have the *grand gestures. That's what I want for my life. I'm not going to be the girl who settles for mediocre."*

"No. No, you're not, Sage."

Recalling the way he said those words. So low and steady, brings a cold dose of reality to slosh over me like a bucket of trough water. I said it myself, no settling for second place or mediocre.

Do husbands ever leave their wives? They always say they're going to, but do they ever actually go through with it. What guarantee do I have that everything is going to be wrapped up in a neat little bow, supposedly, by the time fall comes around?

Occasionally, my mind wanders off, daydreaming a little too freely. I drift to a place where my brain convinces me that things might be able to happen, that the two of us might find a way to make things work. Except in every one of those cute little rose-tinted scenarios, the question always rears its head... would I settle for a man, or would I keep needing to roam freely?

Does my guarded, hardened heart dare stop to consider opening up fully to someone else the way Beau has tempted me to?

And ultimately, when I've circled back around to the realms of practicality and doing the next best thing for my business and career—what does life look like once I've left Beau Heartford behind?

CHAPTER 33

Sage

"I'm yet to be convinced that this isn't a scheme to dump my body over a cliff. I swear I was only joking all those times I teased you about the 'stache. I haven't got any money to give you, but I'm prepared to be extra slutty if you agree to spare my life?"

Beau's deep chuckle drifts my way like a melody on the evening air, mingling with the sounds of horse hooves against the dirt trail and their gentle snorts as we climb higher into the hills overlooking the ranch.

"How's that inner control freak handling a little adventure?" he calls back over his shoulder.

"Frankly, quite terrible. She wants to know where we're going and what the hell we're doing riding horses all the way out here when it's going to be dark soon."

"What if I promise her I'll kiss it and make it all better?" Turning in his saddle, Beau catches me blatantly staring at his ass. Well, if he didn't want me to drool over him in a pair of wranglers at every opportunity, then he really should know better than to ride a horse in front of me by now.

He's every inch the picture of relaxation. Reins held loose in one hand, the other rested on his jean-clad thigh. From the faded cap to the way the cotton of his t-shirt stretches across his shoulders, down to his worn boots, he looks like a cowboy destined to be among these mountains day in and day out. Beau is so achingly sexy in the waning daylight, it lures me into a fantasy of wanting to forget myself entirely and beg to stay here for a lifetime.

It's the most unimaginable prospect, for someone as ambitious as I've always been, the thought of days spent doing exactly this—riding horses and counting the first stars as they appear one by one in the pink-tinted sky overhead—feels like something a version of me has been wanting and never realized it until now.

Then, there's the other side of me. The hustler. The woman with a business to grow and a client portfolio to expand.

She doesn't know what to make of any of this, because nothing could have prepared me for the way Beau Heartford has blindsided me with his quiet charm and rugged appeal.

This cowboy was certainly *not* in my five-year business plan.

Goldie is an absolute sweetheart to me, allowing my amateur horse skills to be mighty relaxed, considering that I'm tethered behind Beau and don't have to do anything more than avoid slipping sideways out of this saddle. As long as I can cling on and handle the unfamiliar burn in my thighs from using muscles I didn't know were there, the beautiful horse beneath me is the one doing all the work, really.

We keep climbing higher and eventually reach a clearing with a sweeping view over the ranch below. Instantly, something giddy makes itself known—a certain feeling about coming here raises its head. Beau obviously had this location in mind, and I wonder how often he has spent time in this particular spot with Mist. Both man and horse appear to be perfectly in sync, pulling up to a halt beside a couple of large conifers as if this is a well-trodden path for the two of them.

He swings out of his saddle in a practiced move that yet again causes my ovaries to sigh. Coming around to stand beside me, he gives Goldie's neck a pat and shares a soft murmur of praise with her as he does so.

"Are you sure you're not bringing me out here as a sacrifice to appease the mountain hillbillies?" I narrow my eyes at him. "They won't want me. I'm certainly not virginal, and I'm far too opinionated to be considered a peace offering."

Beau shakes his head and takes the reins from my hands. "No. I think I'm stuck with you."

"Can you please tell me what we're doing out here now?"

He taps my thigh, gesturing for me to turn in the saddle so he can help me down. I hoist my leg over in a far less smooth motion than he just demonstrated. Each glide of his heavy palm up my waist and indentation of his fingers feels like the kind of caress I'm going to be chasing forever more. Having Beau's steady hands to help me to the ground feels like the taste of something I've been forging my way forward without. Now? He's shown me a glimpse of what it's like to have someone who so effortlessly provides a solid foundation to rely on.

As he sets me on my feet, I'm pressed between his broad chest and the horse at my back. Scents of masculinity and leather mingle with the tinge of sweet hay that follows Goldie around wherever she goes. Truth be told, it all makes me more than a little giddy.

Beau doesn't take his hands off me, just lets his thumbs glide up and down while bracketing my rib cage. With each slow stroke, I feel like my tank and thin sweater are going to incinerate and flutter away in little puffs of ash. There's a heartbeat pulsing in my clit after only a few seconds of having Beau's undivided attention, and I'm already devastated that activities of horseback nature don't allow for flirty little sundresses. The kind of mid-thigh temptation I could widen my legs ever so slightly while wearing and encourage him to slip his hand beneath. I'd be very interested in a scenario where he pushes a thick digit or two inside and fingers me while we stand here against a backdrop of mountains and the tiniest sliver of the moon hanging low in the late evening sky.

His eyes bounce between my mouth and my chest, and I suspect we might be thinking much the same kind of horny thoughts as one another.

"You look hungry, cowboy." I drag my teeth over my bottom lip. "Maybe it's you I should be afraid of. Maybe it's *you* who wants to eat me alive out here in the wilderness?"

A wicked look flashes in his eyes, like a spark of a storm forming on the horizon out at sea. "Baby, all you ever have to do is ask." Then he raises one hand to swipe his thumb over my bottom lip, slowly tugging it out from beneath my biting hold. "But first, you gotta work for it." Creases form at the corner of his eyes and this man looks like the dictionary definition of temptation where I'm concerned.

I swallow and push at his stupidly toned stomach. "I've clearly done my job *too well*, and taught you too many tricks, Heartford."

Beau hits me with one of those lopsided grins that makes my thighs clench, then moves away, leaving me swaying ever so slightly. "Help me unpack, trouble." After leading Goldie to follow after him and hitching the horses, he casually tosses words over his shoulder. I float over to his side where he begins to unpack from the saddle bags, handing me a collapsible tripod and his camera bag, before gesturing with his chin toward a grassy area in the clearing.

"We'll set up over there."

"It seems a bit dark for taking nudes." I tilt my head at him and then promptly squeal as I evade his swat in the direction of my ass.

"While I know you love to be the star attraction, baby, I'm gonna teach you to take some photos of the night sky. We should be able to see the Milky Way with tonight's forecast."

My heart does a little flutter when I look back and see Beau walking toward me with an armful of rolled-up blankets and a thermos. This looks an awful lot like a date, and while we haven't exactly talked about anything relating to being *together*—beyond the way we can't seem to stay apart even when we know we are supposed to—I'm caught off-guard by the sneaky preplanning this man has put into our evening.

"Looks like you intend to be out here all night." I clear my throat and crouch to set everything down like I'm carrying a baby bird. Without a doubt, Beau's camera is very expensive compared to my second-hand model, which was all I could afford at the time, but it does everything I need it to.

"Taking it slow always produces the best results where the stars are concerned." He busies himself setting out the blankets and I'm worried he'll be able to hear my heart pounding in amongst the stillness of the night air. Sex is far too easy with Beau. Flirtation and fooling around are effortless where he's concerned. But this? I'm not sure my heart can handle knowing he's gone to these lengths to bring me out here like this, when he could have easily spent the evening taking photos by himself, like he usually does.

Not when I already know I'm leaving.

Before I can fully descend into a flaming tailspin and spiral to crash in a heap of emotional confusion, he's beside me, crouched down to set up the tripod and camera with practiced hands.

I was right. Seeing Beau handle a camera while oozing smooth confidence in every tiny action is unbearably sexy. He renders me more than a little weak at the knees while his veined hands and corded forearms flick buttons and manually adjust settings, before fixing the camera in place on the tripod.

Jesus, there is something so hot about a capable man.

"Now we wait." He tilts his head to look up, flicking his eyes from mine to the skies overhead, then back to capture me. I don't know if I've been properly breathing this entire time.

"You don't need to look through the lens?"

Beau shakes his head and shows me his phone screen. "Best not to touch the gear. It needs to hold steady, otherwise you just end up with a blurry mess. I use a remote to control the shutter."

"Of course. He's got a fancy cock, and a fancy camera. No wonder you were oh, so comfortable having control of my wearable, if this is what you spend your nights doing." I roll my lips together.

That drags one of those low, rumbly laughs out of him that manages to turn my insides to liquid each time I hear it.

"Come here." He stands up and hooks the belt loops on my jeans, tugging me into him with a move that leaves me fighting back the urge to let out a slutty little noise of need. "I'll let you play with my fancy camera, and if you're really well-behaved, you might earn the other piece of equipment I've packed for you."

Licking my lips, I wrap my arms around his back and tilt my chin to look up at him, allowing my body to go a little boneless as I sink against his frame. God, I love how it feels to be pressed up against all that strength and warmth. "Consider me highly motivated and dedicated to the task at hand, boss." I let myself rub against his groin and savor the groan he lets out in response.

"Christ. I promised myself I'd be good and not try to get you naked within five minutes, and you're making that fucking impossible, you know?"

My lips curve. "Shame I can't add that sort of talent to my resume."

I'm tumbled down onto the blankets before I have time to protest being manhandled, and Beau doesn't give me any choice but to follow his demands. Strong, guiding touches move me to lie tucked against his chest under the crook of his arm, and he brings up the controller for the camera on his phone so we can both see.

I shamelessly nuzzle into his side, stealing a deep inhale of his scent as he taps a couple of different settings on the display.

"Each shot is usually about thirty seconds for the best result." He tucks me closer, gluing me to his side—as if he can't stand the idea of there being any fraction of space between our bodies. "Gives enough time for the camera to capture the light, but doesn't start to get blurred with the earth spinning."

"*Hmm*. We really are just floating on a rock in space, aren't we? Wonder if we'll spot any aliens?"

"Well, I know there's no place in the universe I'd rather be than right here. So I wouldn't be surprised if whatever is out there flocks this way." He says it with a low voice that extends right through every cell in my body. A hook digs in behind my ribs, pulling me further into the depths of this man.

I don't want to look at the deeper meaning behind that admission. This is Beau's escape, his private little slice of paradise. It's not because I'm here with him.

"Here." He shows me what to do. "Use that to select your point of focus, then tap when you want to take the photo."

It's hypnotic as I follow his instructions, then lie watching the image, waiting with bated breath as the shutter clicks on the tripod set up. Quietly counting the heartbeats until the sound comes again and the image preview shows a carpet of stars set against a dark, jagged outline of the mountain tops surrounding Crimson Ridge.

"There are so many more than you can see just looking with the naked eye." I let my attention flicker over the photo. There seems to be an endless array, hundreds of thousands of pinpricks of starlight glittering back from the screen.

Beau makes a quiet noise of agreement from somewhere deep inside his chest, and I feel him nod above me.

"Take as many as you like. We've got a while to wait yet 'til the best part of the show."

We lie together in silence as I poke at different locations, choosing some of the brightest stars to try focusing on, letting each slow-motion whir of the camera fill the quiet.

There's something lulling about it. Beau wasn't joking when he said everything about this process moves at a slow pace. Between the length of time it takes for each photo to form and the stillness of the evening, it feels like time slips into a zone where it has no meaning.

"It must be a relief coming up here," I murmur after playing with the camera for a while.

"Not exactly. You see, ever since the day I helped out a stranger... and lost my bag to them in the process... I'm usually trying to concentrate on taking photos. And instead, I'm stuck thinking about this girl. Now I've got her in my arms, and I'm struggling to believe it's not all a dream."

Pushing up onto my elbow, I give him an arched eyebrow. "You don't think I'm real?" I have to focus every ounce of attention away from the fact Beau just casually mentioned thinking about me as much as I've been unable to stop thinking about him since our first meeting.

Consider me an unmitigated slut for being in the spotlight of his mind's eye. If there's anything I know by now about being the object of his unwavering obsession, it's that I'm greedy for having his focus on me.

"Ask me anything, and I'll show you I'm real enough." I wet my bottom lip, heart zooming around inside my chest. "As long as you give me an answer to a question in return... oh, and a piece of clothing." I flutter my eyelashes at him through the darkness.

"This is much more interesting than having to sit out here in the dark all alone." His smirk is evident in his tone as he readjusts himself to lie back with both hands resting beneath his head. When he gazes up at me, there's a faint quirk playing over his mouth that I can make out through the shadows.

"Did you always know you wanted to run rings around everyone and start your own business?"

"Isn't that every eldest daughter? Trying to carry everything and be perfect at all times?"

"No answering questions with more questions." He clicks his tongue. "Boots. Off."

I huff and roll my eyes, even if he can't see the full extent of my expression. Shifting my weight, I slip my boots off and toss them aside.

"Fine. My sisters are the bit of good that my parents can look at, but I could never shake that feeling that I'm always the reminder of a bad time. The product of a crappy relationship that my mom had escaped. I always felt like the outsider to their bubble who was going to get cast aside for being too much to handle. So I always knew I wanted to do something for myself, to take care of myself." I chew the inside of my cheek, heat flushing up my chest at how vulnerable it feels to admit that out loud. "Besides, I got fired from my first three jobs out of high school for questioning too many things, so I figured out kinda early on I was virtually unemployable."

Beau adjusts himself to bend one knee while he lies back, listening to my confession, and looks every inch the cowboy heartthrob sent to destroy me.

"Jeans," he says in a low command, and heat rushes to pool between my legs.

"That was only one answer." Despite my protest, my fingers are itching to pop my button and tear my clothes off for him. I also love that he's not making a big deal out of this. It feels so effortless to share pieces of me I've never told anyone before, and I don't know how to rationalize that inside my mind.

"Ah, but this is what happens when you don't follow the rules. Lose the pants, pretty girl."

Damn him for the way his voice always dips into that lower octave when he calls me that. It's like he's speaking directly to my pussy, and I become far too pliant at his instruction.

"Who's being bossy now?" Getting to my feet, I turn around and take my sweet time. Ever so slowly, I flick the button, then let the zipper fall with a hum that cuts across the quiet, before hooking my thumbs and shimmying the waistband down to slip over the lower curve of my ass.

The entire time, I feel Beau's eyes drilling into me with wild ferocity.

When I bend at the waist to lower them further, I take the opportunity to glance back and fully indulge my own rampant arousal. To my sheer pulse-thumping delight, Beau has one hand palming himself through his jeans, and I can see the way he cups his erection.

"You don't play fair." His tone is full of raspy need.

"And you wouldn't want me to, either." I give him a little smirk before bending right down to touch my toes, and he lets out a deep groan.

"I have more dreams than I should admit to about that ass."

When I turn back around and make a show of letting the material fall from my fingers with a soft thud to join my boots and socks, he's shifting his hips. It sends a shiver racing down to my toes with excitement at how much he enjoys my body.

"If you're a very good boy, I might even let you fuck me there later." Unable to resist, I climb to straddle his groin, and the feel of him is so intoxicating against my delicate skin. The roughness of his jeans, the hardness of his cock pressing beneath me, how his calloused fingers immediately settle on the outside of my thighs as if that's the only place they should ever belong.

"Fuck," he grunts, and I bite back the way it feels particularly satisfying to unravel his composure with a single mention of messing around with my ass.

"Ok, hot stuff. My turn for the deep dive into your psyche." I run my palms under his shirt, feeling the heat of his skin and dusting of hair over his lower stomach. "When did wedded bliss first start falling apart?"

Beau squeezes my thighs for a moment, and I'm chewing the inside of my cheek as I let him mull his words.

"Two years," he says quietly. "Maybe even quicker than that. I feel like I blocked so much of it out. But definitely, by two years in, we effectively started living separate lives in different cities all the time. Although, I knew *something* was off after only a few months. Once we'd done the legal marriage stuff, it was like she turned into an unrecognizable person. But I was so busy with training and competing I willingly turned a blind eye."

Beau glides his palms up and down my skin and exhales a long breath. "Now I know Mandy well enough to know that the woman I dated in a whirlwind and stood at the altar waiting for was a sham. The charming, sweet, adoring persona she's good at putting on isn't who she is. That was the bait, and I fell for it."

"Thank you for telling me." Letting my fingers curl against his torso, I flash a small smile. "May I have your shirt, please?"

Beau heaves himself to sit up and flips his cap off, before reaching behind to drag the shirt over his head in one fluid motion.

I swipe it out of his hands before he can toss it aside, bundling it up and pressing my nose into the warm scent the fabric carries. Well aware that this is dangerous territory—to be lingering in a needy little bubble of wanting every little detail of him.

"Your family has always supported you? No matter who you dated?" he asks softly. There's a hint of concern evident in that question, which makes me smile into the fabric coated in his scent because I can already hear his willingness to leap to my defense against anyone, no matter who.

My inability to stop feeling giddy over this man is once again a massive issue because he's not being *that guy*. The jealous asshole, or the insecure idiot, where my attraction to women is concerned.

Nodding quickly, I hum in agreement. "Always. They're fiercely supportive, and never once made me feel like my queerness wasn't completely normal. But I always feel like there's subtle pressure there, not related to my sexuality, but for me to bring home Mr. or Miss Perfect. The standard is set so high by my parents, and I'm forever raising that bar for myself seeing their relationship, whether I consciously realize I'm doing it or not."

Beau's gaze holds me through the darkness as he starts slowly hooking my top. A shudder roams freely through my limbs as he lifts it up my stomach, grazing my skin with his knuckles, setting every inch of my body alight just for him.

"Well, they're correct. You only deserve perfection, baby."

CHAPTER 34

Beau

Sage's divine softness shivers at each point of contact with my touch, and I feel like I'm having an out-of-body experience. Her stomach caves as I drag the material off, leaving her nearly bared to me.

"You're goddamn heaven, baby. So beautiful." The groan in my voice disappears into a dark hum of desire as I lose the battle to keep my mouth off her.

Still sitting upright, I cup and squeeze her breasts together, covering the thin lace with my mouth and sucking down on one hardened nipple. My girl moans quietly and holds my head there, grinding harder on me with her hot, wet pussy perched over the steel bar in my jeans.

"I like this game better." She arches into my mouth as I bite down. "Much, much better." Her breathy voice hitches as I suck hard on her tits through the soaked fabric.

"You've got one more question," I murmur against the softness of her breast. Using my teeth, I drag the material of her bra down to expose her pebbled nipples before flicking at the tight bud with my tongue. "Unless you're gonna be a dirty girl and rub that soaked cunt on me until I blow in my briefs." My teeth catch the stiffened peak, and I give her the tiny little nibbles that she loses her mind for. Whining and rocking her covered clit against my belt buckle, Sage chases that added friction her body is hungry for.

"Why can't I be sensible around you? I've never been this person." She gasps as I draw her nipple into my mouth and suck down harder.

I can't get enough of any part of this girl's body, but her tits are my obsession, I swear to god.

"Sage, every time I think there's a chance I might be able to function without thinking about you every two seconds, I fail." Cupping and squeezing her roughly, I pinch down on the wetness covering the hard buds, before nipping the outer swell of her breasts. "I think we're both suffering from the same issue."

"You think about me, hot stuff?"

My dick pulsates with need, tight and threatening to burst through my fly of its own accord.

"You know I do." *Lick.* "All the damn time." *Bite.* "I can't *stop* thinking about you, trouble." Running my tongue in a slick track straight up her throat, I pause with my lips dusting over hers. "And I don't want to stop, either."

She makes a frustrated, whimpering noise. "I'm not waiting for you to get these off." Her hips lift. "Take your cock out right now."

"Slow, baby." I remind her, and that drags another of those impatient noises from the back of Sage's throat. Pinching my teeth down on her bottom lip, I then suck on the spot to ease any potential sting. Moving in the darkness, I fumble to get rid of the barrier formed by my jeans and briefs. Sage unclasps her bra, letting her rounded tits bounce freely, and tosses it to join the rest of her clothes as I shove the waistband as low as possible. Letting my rock-hard cock stand tall between us, I drag my knuckle back and forth over the front of her panties.

"*Mmmfuck.* You're a mess. This pussy is drenched and so damn needy." I rub and press harder over the material as I fist myself and give a couple of firm strokes. With how much I'm already leaking, we're in as much of a state of desperation as each other. It's like our bodies know the way we fit together so perfectly, and that sensation of being joined is all I goddamn want.

I don't want to let her go. Ever.

"Let me taste you first." She wraps her soft hand around mine, pressing her thumb down on my tip, swiping up precum, and dragging it over my piercing.

"Jesus. Fuck." My cock throbs beneath her touch. "Then you better rub that sweet cunt all over my face while you suck me down."

"God. This would be so hot if we could use your camera and film it." Sage slides the metal bar back and forth one last time with a wickedness in her sultry voice, before moving around and positioning herself on hands and knees, wrapping her perfect, biteable thighs around my ears.

Then her sinfully hot mouth is on me, and I don't have any reply for her little game of temptation. It would be insane of us to even consider it, but it's like she just set my blood on fire at the mere flicker of that single idea. I've never wanted to risk anything like that—not with a career in the public eye—and yet if this girl asked me to, I'd hand her the power, turn that tripod around, and agree to whatever she asked for, without hesitation.

Wrapping her lips around me, she runs her tongue along my shaft, teasing the barbell each time she eases back to the tip, and I'm feral. Letting my mouth close over her panties, sucking hard through the fabric until she's even more soaked between the combination of her arousal and my saliva. Then I'm nudging the material aside, using my tongue to roam over every part of her pussy. Tracing every ruffle and swirling along the seam of bunched fabric between her entrance to her clit and back again.

I could get goddamn lost in this closeness, the intimacy of skin-to-skin contact, the scent of her, and having our mouths on each other. Fuck taking photos. Fuck anything we came out here for in the first place. All I want is the sensation of her quivering and bucking and flooding my tongue with her cum.

All I want is for Sage to feel treasured and worshipped, like she can let go without worrying if I'll be there to catch her or not.

My balls tingle as her spit drips down to coat me. Sage gets sloppier and sloppier, making sweet, greedy noises around my length. Her lips trace down to the base of my shaft as her sounds of pleasure grow louder. Each one of those porny little moans she keeps letting out vibrates through me as I swell inside her mouth, and my balls tighten at how incredible she feels.

"*Ffffuck.* You need to come the fuck all over my face." I stiffen my tongue and dig my fingers into her hips. Shoving as far inside her cunt as possible, until she lets out a muffled squeal, I feel the ripples take hold. Her tongue laps at me frantically, and I know she's almost there. Using one thumb, I swipe through her arousal, then reach around, shoving beneath her panties to glide over her ass.

As soon as I press down on her tight little rosebud hole, Sage gags and makes a pleading noise with me buried in her throat.

With my tongue pushed deep inside her, tasting heaven, and my thumb rubbing hard over her back entrance, I feel her walls clamp down. She pulses around my tongue, feeding me her cum and soft little moans. The feel of her detonating is like a goddamn headrush, and it takes everything in me not to simply give in to the need to fill her mouth right then and there.

Sage pops off me with a gasp as I keep kissing her pussy and licking up every drop of sweetness she gives me, and I don't let up. I want this girl blissed out of her head and trembling. She's so goddamn perfect, and if all I get to do is give her orgasm after orgasm, then that'll have to satisfy my craving for everything about my girl for now.

Until a time when I can make her mine for real.

"Beau. Oh, god." She pants, forehead damp and slumped against my thigh.

I roam my hands across every inch of her bare skin that I can reach, still sucking on her and flicking my tongue. "Turn around for me, baby. Let me give you what you need." I growl against her core.

"I need you so deep." Sage whimpers as her swollen clit drags against my facial hair, and the gorgeous thing she is, does it again, arching her spine to chase the sensation.

"Keep doing that, and I'm gonna end up painting your tits and chin with cum, trouble." My groan gets lost somewhere inside her cunt as my dick jerks and begs me to let go and do exactly that. The visual alone is enough to have tension pooling low in my spine.

"Holy shit, that would be so hot."

"Decide what you want first... because you're playing with fire humping my face like a little slut."

Sage makes a wanton noise that goes straight to my balls. "I wanna be full of you. I want everything. You keep saying filthy shit, and I just want all of it."

But my girl knows what she truly desires because she climbs off my mouth and spins around to straddle me again.

"Good fucking girl. Lift your hips for me, baby. Let me pump this pussy until you're dripping like I know you're aching for."

Sage makes a tiny noise of relief as she rises onto her knees, giving me access so I can curl a finger to hook beneath her drenched panties, currently wedged between her pussy lips, tugging them to one side. With the other, I grip my cock and nudge the swollen head and piercing inside her soaked entrance.

She clenches around my tip immediately, like a goddamn dream.

"*Mmm.* Oh fuck. Oh my god." Her eyes roll back as she impales herself on me, sinking straight to the hilt in a slick glide. She's so soft, so silky, and an absolute fucking mess of swollen arousal.

"That's it," I grunt, feeling every single ripple and squeeze as her walls stretch to accommodate me. "Goddamn, I just want to be inside this pussy all the time. I'd have you wrapped around me all day if you let me. You look so perfect in my bed, naked and begging and soaked with how needy you are for my cock."

"Beau... fuck, baby... keep talking." Sage rocks back and forth, and I palm the softness of her hips, her thighs, her stomach as she tangles both hands in her hair above me. "I love it when you talk to me." Her whines, the sweetest notes of begging mixed with desire, fill the night.

Horny, out of her head, Sage, riding my cock gets anything she wants.

"I'm obsessed with you, baby. You wanna know how much? All I can dream about is having you. All I want is to be with you. I want to have you in my arms every night, every morning, and to be the only one to fuck you just right, the way I know you need it."

Sage squeezes me so damn hard I think I'm about to lose my mind.

"You take every inch. Look at you swallowing every bit of me. We were made to fit together, and you know it."

Her moans grow louder as her hips glide back and forth. It's slow, it's sensual, and I grit my teeth with the effort to hold off erupting and filling her until I'm dripping down her thighs because I don't ever want this moment to end. As I watch Sage arch and tip her head back, lost in the sensation of pleasure, the night sky overhead is a perfect, shimmering painting. The universe putting on a brilliant show of starlight can't ever compare to how spellbinding Sage is.

I'm so hopelessly in love with her. I have to bite back a thousand confessions that threaten to wrestle loose from my lungs.

Being buried as deep as I can get inside her velvety softness feels like the only thing I can think of ever wanting or needing. She's the only thing that makes me feel like me again, like I can breathe, like I can see a way forward for the first time.

"Oh—oh fuck—fuck." Her legs tremble, pussy tightening and gripping me to death.

"Christ. Yes. I need your cunt milking every last drop. It all belongs to you, my pretty girl. And you don't waste a single bit of my cum, do you? I'm gonna make sure you're full, and these panties are gonna keep me right there until I get you home, and then I can spill inside your tight little ass, too."

Sage lets out a low-pitched moan and snaps her hips faster, perfect breasts bouncing as her body shakes under the force of her impending orgasm.

"Fuck you. Fuck you for being this good. Fuck you, I need you to touch me. God, I need you..." Her sobs of pleasure melt into a shuddering groan as I give her exactly that.

"C'mon, give it all to me." I grit out, breaths frantic, as my stomach clenches and I fuck up into her with wild thrusts. "Stroking my cock like a perfect slut. Come with me, baby. I'm gonna come."

Circling her clit, the added pressure is Sage's final undoing. She detonates above me, convulsing and throwing her head back as her pussy spasms violently around my length.

"Unghhhh. Ffffuck. Baby." My release crashes into me, stealing my vision and my brain cells. I'm rutting up into her as my cock throbs and unloads over and over. With each jerk of my hips and shot of cum coating her walls, I feel the hot sticky slickness and unreal sensation between us when I pump deep inside.

Words leave my mouth, but I'm not even sure they make any sense. I tell her how beautiful she is. How much I need her. How I can't get enough of her hungry, perfect cunt. How she's going to take me all night until she begs me to stop.

Sage tells me she never wants to stop.

She clenches around me again and again, and I feel another short burst erupt deep inside her as my balls tighten up in response. She's got some sort of magical hold on me, one that erases any sense of which way is up.

Dragging her down to drape over my torso, I keep Sage still impaled on my length as I soften inside her, but only barely. I'm so savage for her it feels like I won't need any time at all to recover.

I take her mouth as she sobs little whimpers against me while I keep slowly rocking us together, guiding her through the comedown. My arms wrap her up, pinning every inch of my girl impossibly tight against my chest. We make out, slow and filled with so much need to be connected. It's the headiest feeling ever.

I'm high on Sage, and I don't think I've ever felt more certain that this is what I want. That I want her. I want to be wherever she is, for as long as I have breath left in my lungs.

CHAPTER 35

Beau

Sage lets out a peal of laughter as I flick the hose spray in her direction.

"God, you are a child." She grins at me. "These horses don't appreciate you messing around with their shower time."

We're outside the barn, with the horses hitched in the dappled shade, after going for a morning ride together. Now they're getting a well-earned cool off with a hose down, since the temperature is set to be roasting, and likely to fry everything in its path today.

"Oops. I didn't see you there." I shrug before turning the water to flick over her thigh again.

"*Hey*." Sage tries to evade the spray flying in her direction, and fails. "Don't make me wrestle you for that hose, Cock Ring. Remember, I've got the twins at home. I trained those two in the dark arts of battle. Don't think I won't bite as viciously as Teddy."

She makes a show of chomping her teeth my way.

I nonchalantly keep running water along Dusty's flank and back, before doing the same on the other side. As Sage finishes heaving the saddles over the fence railing and turns back around, I hit her with a squirt straight to the chest.

She stops dead, letting out a yelp. Those dark eyes flash as her gaze connects with mine, and I poke my tongue against the inside of my cheek. The weight of my gaze drags down her figure, and I see her nipples poke through the wet fabric clinging to her chest.

Sage lunges for the hose in an attempt to wrestle it from me, but I catch her around the waist and walk her, with the water still running freely in one hand, until she's backed up against the outside wall of the barn.

Caging her in place keeps my girl exactly where I want. Sage pushes and wriggles to try and get away, but it's only half-hearted. Her eyes stare back up at me, filled with deep pools of desire that reflect just how much I want to be carefree and wicked with her right here, right now.

Leaning one arm high overhead, I bring the hose up and allow the water to start cascading down her body. Her stomach caves, lips dropping open on a breathy little noise, but there's a glint to her expression. As her pupils dilate, I keep running water everywhere, saturating every inch, and the thin cotton of her tank goes translucent as it clings to her figure.

"Ready to fight me at every turn... but actually, you're just dripping wet for me, aren't you?"

She juts her chin. "You'll never know unless you make a move."

"Think I don't have moves, baby?" I shut the hose off, letting it thud to the ground beside my boots. Goosebumps scatter across Sage's skin at the sound, all while she keeps her gaze firmly locked on mine.

"How about I give you just a little taste of my fingers? Let's see if you can last eight seconds riding my hand without screaming my name."

As I taunt her, I hook the front of her tank and drag the dripping wet fabric down, followed by the soft fabric of her bra.

Sage lets her spine bow in an effort to draw me down to suck on her exposed nipples like she knows I always want to. I fucking love playing with her tits, but right now, I want to enjoy seeing her squirm for me.

Dipping my head, I blow across the tightly furled buds, then flick them, but that's all she gets. It sends a shiver of pleasure along her limbs, and I hum to myself with satisfaction.

"Is that all you've got? Eight seconds and all you can do is drool over my tits?"

She fucking knows just how much I love unleashing this competitive side with her. I flick the button of her jeans, lower her zipper, and fist the sodden material covering her pussy. Yanking her hips forward roughly, I don't miss the way excitement flares in those honeyed streaks of her eyes.

Sage likes it when I'm rough with her. It doesn't exactly come naturally to me to be that way... but for her? I'll damn well give her that side of me. The part that can always be counted on to be feral for my girl.

"Palms flat on the wall," I grunt, before spinning her around and shoving my hand down the front of her panties.

I've hardly sunk inside her, barely even curled my fingers and gotten up to my second knuckle, when tires crunch over gravel nearby.

Sage's fingers scrape against the wood of the barn wall, her body wriggling beneath my hold.

"Beau, someone's here."

"Shh. Just be quiet for me. It's only Storm. He'll go away if he thinks I'm not around."

Her cunt clamps down on my fingers as she whispers. "He absolutely will not."

"Isn't that part of the fun? Finding out if he comes looking for us?"

"Oh my god." Her hips shift, letting me stroke harder.

The vehicle draws closer, before coming to a halt, then the engine shuts off.

"Would you quite like him to see you with my fingers two knuckles deep inside this perfect pussy? How hard will you grip me... How loudly do you shatter when you've got an audience?"

This time, the sound is of doors slamming.

"*Shh*, baby. That's it." I rub faster, working that spot more forcefully, letting the heel of my palm massage her clit.

"Beau. You need to stop." Her eyes start rolling back as her pussy spasms.

"Do I? Or do I need to feel you get off on someone possibly catching us?"

"If they see me, they'll see you." She's squirming and panting so beautifully.

"Maybe I'm beyond caring." I press my mouth to her ear. "Maybe I'm so far gone that I can't find a reason to stop anymore."

"You're wicked."

"God, I love how you're soaking my hand, trouble."

Above the thud of my pulse and the recklessness that consumes me, the faint sound of voices drifts from the other side of the barn and grows louder with each second I finger fuck Sage ruthlessly.

"What a view. Those mountains look just like a painting."

I freeze. Every muscle in my body locks up, and my stomach falls through my boots.

"Oh my f—" Sage slaps one hand over her mouth.

"Shit." I yank my hand out and spin her to face me. My mind starts buzzing with a blaring white noise, droning static electricity, and I adjust her top quickly back in place, before moving to do the same for her waistband.

Her hands fly down to bat mine away. "Is that who I fucking think it is?"

With an inability to draw any air down in my lungs, my eyes lock on hers, and the side of my jaw pulses.

"Beau. Tell me your *wife* isn't standing out there."

Silence... it's all I've got to give. I don't have any words. My mind whirs too fast to process what the fuck is going on, because that voice is unmistakably one that still haunts me. Even when I've tried so long to forget it.

"Tell me you didn't invite her here," she hisses at me. And that's the piece that squares me up in the chute. It spurs me into a place where steely determination takes over. Seeing and hearing that frustration and hurt in Sage shifts me from the frozen tundra where I couldn't function, to now being back in my body with a wild rush of blood.

"Of course I didn't. Why would I do that?" I say, lifting my hat and stabbing fingers through my hair.

"Oh, I don't know, because you two are *married*." Her eyes are stony and hard, whereas only a moment ago, she was dreamy and surrendered to pleasure beneath my touch.

"Sage... I promise you."

That makes her let out a cold laugh. "Save your promises. You'd better go properly greet your wife."

I don't give a fuck about anything but this enthralling woman standing before me. Pinching her chin, I level her with a firm look, then press a kiss against her lips. Sage tries to duck away and protest against my mouth, but I hold her chin tighter to keep her right there, and I growl.

"Don't get any wrong ideas, or get this twisted, baby." I keep my voice hushed. "I'm going to go deal with whatever the fuck is going on. And all I'm gonna suggest—for your own sanity, because Mandy is a raging bitch—is that you take the afternoon off. Go see Layla, hang out with Briar, whatever you wanna do. I'll call you as soon as I figure out why the hell that woman is daring to set foot on my ranch."

I have to leave her, and I hate it.

"The only person I want here with me is you. So let me get rid of her, then we can talk, ok?"

CHAPTER 36

Sage

I've plotted ten different scenarios where I could slip something into Mandy Spires' morning matcha to give her a violent case of the shits.

Every day that she lingers on this ranch is another test of my powers to avoid wearing a snarl on my face and to keep my claws sheathed.

Who the fuck does this woman think she is?

Oh, that's right. She's legally entitled to half this property, and in the eyes of her hundreds of thousands of followers online, she's right where she supposedly *longs* to be—like a besotted wifey.

At her husband's side.

A ranch that at one time felt so vast, so expansive, has suddenly closed in around me. Everything has changed, and being here feels like the walls are constantly caving in. Mandy arrived with her assistant Zeb and five hundred pounds of luggage in tow, and has set herself up in the main house as if she owns the place.

I didn't stick around for long after her unexpected arrival. The possibility of making this woman's acquaintance while looking like a drowned rat is the sort of nightmare I'd rather gnaw off my own foot than endure. Although, I did linger out of sight just long enough to hear Beau damn near lose his shit, in a quietly-through-gritted-teeth sort of way. From the snatches of conversation, I was able to overhear between them, she planned this surprise visitation perfectly.

True to his word, Beau did call me and briefly talked through everything I needed to know. But there isn't much to say or do at all, other than to accept the cards as they've fallen. He checked on me, made sure I was alright, but other than a bruised ego to contend with, there's nothing that can be done.

We were a *one-time-only* thing that strayed into territory we both knew we shouldn't have set foot in. Now, here we are, blinking and disoriented with ringing in our ears, standing amongst the wreckage of what that looks like when it all comes crashing down.

Mandy's jet is supposedly out of service for maintenance, and the woman had already played her hand by live-streaming her arrival on the ranch for tens of thousands to see. There was no scenario where Beau could march her off his property without causing a painfully public scandal.

It's a waking nightmare.

In the meantime, I'm keeping to myself as much as possible, because being at the house while she's there is torture. Not to mention that after I took up Beau's offer of staying away, when I returned to my cabin, I found a bag left by the rear entrance. He'd filled it with an assortment of my clothes and things I'd left in his room, obviously having done a hurried sweep up to remove any evidence of *me*.

Why does this feel like the worst kind of breakup, when we weren't even together in the first place?

But there's one thing I know, and that's the need to be in control of my own future. Screw this bitch, I'm not going to shy away from going about my work. Even if it does mean having to put up with being at the main house while working from my laptop.

I've been for an extra long run this morning, and as I stand in the kitchen waiting for coffee to brew, I'm busy scrolling for a playlist to keep me dialed in with the type of focus not even Little Miss Country Music can fuck with.

However, it would seem that she's everywhere, and right on cue, she breezes into the kitchen while taking a video call. She's dressed only in a skimpy satin robe, with a mane of shiny, golden hair around her shoulders. Legs for days. Flawless skin. A waft of floral perfume drifts in with her like a flutter of petals cascading from the heavens.

If there's one thing I've discovered Mandy Spires excels at, it's looking a million dollars no matter the time of day. While I don't judge anyone for being all about their personal style—I shudder to think what this woman might have achieved if she put half of that energy into something beyond her fake tan and makeup.

"—tell James we can go ahead with the collab in studio." Mandy sweeps past, with one headphone in, holding the phone out in front of her. "But I need him to ditch whatever that god-awful haircut is he's been trying out lately. It adds at least fifteen pounds to him. And can we not find him a stylist who has half a brain?"

My eyes drill into the coffee, willing it to hurry the hell up.

"Good morning, Sage sweetie." She coos. "Look, isn't she just the cutest thing?" Before I realize what's happening, the phone is shoved in my face, and Mandy clasps me by the shoulders, dragging me against her fake tits so we're both in the frame. Looking back at us is a woman who appears to be a clone of the one smothering me. Except, she's got lips that have seen too much filler and a forehead that has clearly encountered one too many rounds of Botox.

"This is my agent, Coco. You two would get on so well."

Gross. This woman has no sense of personal space and seems to float around thinking that everyone is just a side character in her story.

"Hi." I rearrange my face into something that seems pleasant enough, and then point at the coffee. "Just gonna..." I slip out of

Mandy's hold. Great, I've got her stupid flower-bomb scent all over me now.

"She's such a hard little worker, that one. Such a cutie-pie." I hear Mandy say as she wanders to the fridge to pull out a bottle of water. I swear if this woman calls me *cute* or *little* one more time, I'm not going to be held responsible for the cutesy little blood bath this kitchen might turn into.

I manage to slip away without being dragged into any more unwanted hugs. Even so, her voice seems to carry through the entire open-plan layout of the house. My noise-canceling headphones are currently charging, and I curse beneath my breath that they've abandoned me at the moment when I needed them the most.

"... so wonderful to be back at home."

My hackles immediately stand on end. What the actual fuck? Surely this woman doesn't truly believe this place is *anywhere* where she is concerned. It's certainly not her home.

"I've missed Beau so much. It's just not the same without him, and you know how much I hate these long tours when we're spending so much time in different places."

The way her words roll off her tongue, so serenely, without missing a beat, leaves my stomach turning sour. This woman doesn't sound at all like someone who is about to wrap up a marriage and finalize a divorce. In fact, the longer I sit here stunned by her boldness, the longer I feel like I'm in a parallel universe.

Did I imagine everything?

Was I mistaken this whole time?

Have all the ways that I've been swept off my feet by Beau's charm and my attraction to him colored my understanding of things between them?

God. I really have been fucking this woman's husband.

I can't focus on the screen in front of me, and my fingers grow shaky. Try as I might to continue with the website editing that needs to be finished sooner rather than later, it feels impossible to concentrate. At this rate, I'm going to be struggling to meet my own deadline on this now that all I can think of is them together.

An entirely unwelcome and unwanted wave of images bursts through to occupy my mind. The two of them sleeping here under the same roof while I'm out in my stupid little cabin, none the wiser to whether Mandy Spires is spending her nights in the guest room or has curled up next to her husband, naked and oh so eager to make up for time spent apart.

My eyes scrunch closed. Is this the moment I need to call it quits? Is this the moment I need to pack up my things and haul ass up Devil's Peak to take up the open offer of a bed at Layla and Colt's ranch?

I've been staring at the images on my computer screen, lost in thought. It's a compilation of the cattle, with their fluffy tipped ears and wet noses, surrounded by the sort of gorgeous summer morning you can taste on your tongue—crushed grass and a sweet, warm breeze rolling straight off the mountains. Yet all I can think about is the way I felt at the moment I took those photos. How vividly I can recall the way Beau stood at my back with his strong arms wrapped around me, while the horses munched on grass beside us.

When I see these images, I *feel* him, and that's a giant goddamn problem I don't know how to crawl my way out of.

"Ugh, it's always torture when my agent needs to go over *so* many different opportunities all at once." My head snaps up, only to be cursed by the sight of Mandy sliding a chair out on the opposite side of the table from where I'm seated. She has that tone about her, the kind of wishful air to her voice where she's simply dying for me to ask her about what all these golden opportunities might be.

I don't take her bait.

"You know, I heard how incredible the job was that you did for that cowboy bar in town just recently." She bats her eyelashes and leans forward to rest the point of her chin on one hand.

"News must travel fast," I say. There's something in this

woman's energy that has my intuition pinging like a deep sea sonar. She doesn't seem to be at all concerned about my presence here, or at least hasn't made any mention of the fact I'm the only person on this ranch besides her husband.

I can't pick whether that's because she's used to a world where assistants spend every waking hour with their celebrity employer, or not. Does she truly not see it as strange, or is her indifference due to the fact she's quietly scheming. Behind the veneer of hugs and saccharin good mornings, like the one we've just shared in the kitchen, is this bitch cataloging every tiny detail?

"Tessa couldn't stop raving about all the ways you've been a godsend." Those blue eyes and blond curls seem ever so very vivid in the sunlight streaming through the window. It's worse that she's beautiful in a way that seems such a waste when her personality leaves so much to be desired. Mandy Spires will no doubt skip along a path paved in awards and accolades when far more genuine, talented people will be overlooked. All because they don't have that bombshell packaging music executives only need to take one look at before they start counting dollar signs.

It leaves an awful taste in my mouth that she's apparently friendly with Tessa. I didn't see that one coming.

"Thanks, I guess." The biggest internal battle I'm waging right this second is to carefully contain my facial reactions.

"She's the best sister-in-law I could hope for. Lately, she's done nothing but blow up my texts telling me just how excellent a hire you've been. Taking a chance on someone is just such a Tessa thing to do. That woman has the biggest heart. It just goes to show, there is gold to be found regardless of whether someone has the proof of whether they're actually capable."

Did this bitch just smile and tell me I was a pity-hire?

There's an inferno brewing inside me, with vile, hateful words that want to spit at her like poison darts, but instead, I sink my nails into my palms and think of an escape plan. I need to remove myself from this situation right fucking now, or my tongue is about to lash this reptile of a woman and probably say something entirely regrettable.

The embers are glowing ragey-hot, and my fuse is already starting to sizzle, so I need to move.

Before I can speak, Mandy is already pressing forward, carrying on in the way she's obviously so used to doing. Breezing straight past the part where she just insulted me to my face.

"So, while you're still here, I can't wait to have you on board with the album launch..."

This time, I can't bite my tongue any longer. "The album launch?" I cut across her words.

"It's going to be perfect. I can already see how we'll set up the outdoor area, with seating and a stage." Her wrist, wrapped in a gold charm bracelet, flicks in the direction of the floor-to-ceiling windows. "You'll be able to coordinate all the influencer welcome packs and get in catering, but make sure it's not someone from here. We don't need old-fashioned, sloppy presentation. I'm talking to my manager about live streaming the whole thing, so my fans can pay-per-view it all."

I'm very rarely left speechless. But faced with such a degree of audacity—in the flesh where this woman is concerned—I can't do anything but sit blinking rapidly at her.

"You're doing the album release... here?" Eventually, my mouth starts moving. Surely, I didn't hear that right. Surely, this woman is about to start laughing like a hyena and tell me it's all just a massive joke.

"Of course." She claps her hands together with a giggle that makes her sound even more delusional. "The fans adore it when me and Beau give them a little glimpse into our life away from the spotlight, and they'll be just so happy for us to share this with them."

This is like one of those moments when everything goes still. The momentary calm before the storm hits and decimates all that lies in its path.

Husbands never leave their wives.

It's not my place to pry, or allude to the fact I know details of their marriage. Or, at least, the version of events Beau has told me. If I can believe his side of the story?

"Since that sweet little *welcome to the ranch* event you're organizing is coming up, I'd say we should aim for about a month's time..." Mandy scrolls through her phone calendar, humming to herself.

I'm breathing heavily through my nose, while cursing violently inside my mind.

There are so many ways this is fucked up, none more so than the fact she's carrying on as if she and Beau are still very much a happily married couple. Then, there's the way this woman has steamrolled right through any boundaries about who I work for, or the nature of my business contract here.

Somewhere in the background, I hear talk of color schemes and lighting requirements, and that's when my phone starts ringing.

Cock Ring flashes on screen, and my heart lurches straight into the back of my throat. For about half a second, I consider declining the call. Can I be bothered remaining entangled in this? But then I'm struck by a mental image of Beau's calm eyes, and I fold.

"Sorry, I'm going to have to take this." I password lock my computer, then give her a polite smile that thinly disguises the fact I'd like to tear her extensions out and wrap them around her neck, before slipping outside. There's absolutely no way I'm going to stay anywhere within earshot of the main house.

Once I've managed to walk a few paces beyond the threshold, I answer the call, but don't say anything. I bring it to my ear and wait.

"Sage?"

"Give me one good reason why I shouldn't simply block your number?" Keeping my voice quiet and steady, I'm already halfway to the sanctuary of my cabin.

He exhales and curses softly on the other end of the line. "Fuck. Where are you? What has she done?"

"That's irrelevant." When I reach the door, I yank it open with a forceful tug and seal myself inside. Once the door clicks shut, I feel the air rush from my lungs.

"Can you come over to meet me at the cattle? I'm in the east paddock." The way his voice sounds haggard shouldn't make me feel better about things, but I'm stupidly clinging to a sense of relief that he sounds strung out.

"I don't think that's a good idea."

"Sage, I can't begin to tell you how sorry I am... hate me forever. It's the least I deserve." Even through the phone, I can see the expression that will be creasing his brow. I can picture the way he's standing with one hand dug into his hair.

"Are you still with her? How am I supposed to feel knowing the two of you are in that house together at night? That she's planning to live here from the sound of it." I hiss.

A heavy silence echoes down the line.

"She said what?" He speaks through gritted teeth when the words finally come.

"No. Answer my questions first. Or if you're not planning to give it to me straight, then I am blocking your lying ass right now."

"Sage, I know it doesn't look like it, and I understand why you might never trust what I have to say, but I promise you, we're over. We have a contract signed with our lawyers and all. It's just a matter of time—"

I cut him off. "Well, she certainly seems to think her circus roadshow can stop off here. And while we're at it, she appears to be under the illusion that I'm her obedient pet to order around."

"What did she do to you?" His growl rumbles through my ear. I hate the way he sounds ready to gallop in, leap off the back of his horse, and tear throats out for me. I deeply want to trust him, but I'm also too terrified of what it might look like if I allow myself to acknowledge I *do* trust him—all too easily, it would seem.

Letting out a long sigh, I flop down on my bed. "Nothing. But she seems to be under the illusion that I'll throw the album party to end all album parties for her right here at the ranch."

"Not fucking happening." His reply cracks through the air like a whip. “Please... It’s a lot to ask, but just give me a few days to get rid of her. I know it’s messy as all hell right now, and my life is more goddamn complicated than I could ever expect you to put up with. There’s nothing more I want than to be with you, and to figure things out, just the two of us.”

My throat tightens as he says those words. Sincerity flows out of Beau like the deepest well, rich and nourishing, when I let his voice wash over me.

And even though I say something in agreement, even though I’m vaguely aware that I’m nodding as I speak, I also know the truth in my heart. The lurking unease that comes with the risk of opening myself up to someone else, and the default setting I’m forever giving into.

The need to run. Because surely it can’t be this easy? It can’t be this good? Beau doesn’t truly want someone like me. Those words he’s saying are too tempting to slip under the spell of here and now. But that’s no guarantee he won’t wake up and realize I’m not worth the hassle of keeping around.

Too headstrong.

Too outspoken.

Too driven.

Squeezing my eyes shut, I send up a silent prayer, a desperate wish that it wasn’t this way, that I could learn to fully trust someone for the first time. There’s no other option, considering how Beau’s life is already complex enough without adding me into the picture.

I’ve already made my decision to move forward with my life, to take this next job, and that means it’s only a matter of time until I leave.

CHAPTER 37

Sage

"She just turned up... uninvited?" Layla's eyes go comically round at me from across the table.

I've just finished explaining the entire strangeness of Beau and Mandy's situation to her, Briar, and Sky. The girls turned up with their cowboys in tow to help with the setup for tomorrow night's event at the ranch.

Fortunately for all our sanity, Mandy has swanned off with Zeb after deciding to do some sort of brand photoshoot at a popular national park location a few hours away. Which means she's gone from the property, for a few hours at least.

Unfortunately, where my giant pile of secrets is concerned, it still doesn't exactly solve the problem that I'm lying to everyone about the illicit lines me and Beau have carelessly ridden across.

"That must be so awkward for Beau." To the other side of me, Briar muses out loud and scrunches her nose. "Mind you, there were plenty of women like that I used to run into all the time in LA. They really do think the sun shines out their own ass twenty-four seven."

"He's stuck letting her stay here." I shrug. "Apparently, it's complicated. Until they sort out their divorce, he can't risk it blowing up online and in the public eye."

"Fair enough. He's got the ranch to think of. I can't imagine he wants to have nasty shit spewed all over the internet right at the moment he's trying to get a brand new business off the ground." Sky nods, and points out what we need to be adding to the flower arrangements next as she talks. Thanks to owning her own florist studio, she's organized a gorgeous range of summer flowers. One of the ideas she came up with was for us to make flower crowns guests can wear and take home.

We're currently set up at a wooden trestle, elbow-deep in freshly cut blooms, airy fronds, and delicate greenery, while making up the arrangements. Over by the barn, the guys are busy draping festoon lights over the building's exterior and shifting hay bales into position to act as seating. Out of the corner of my eye, I notice it's just Colt and Storm. I know Beau was helping alongside them just before, but seems to have disappeared for the moment.

A rumble of a vehicle and clank of a horse trailer draw our attention from the mountain of floral art Sky has set us to work on. It's one of the Rhodes Ranch trucks pulling up, and Sky smiles sweetly in the direction of her cowboy behind the wheel.

"Daddy's brought the goods?" I tease.

"He's brought in a couple more new trail horses for me." That familiar deep voice almost startles me out of my skin when Beau appears just over my shoulder.

"Here. I figured if you're all as hopeless at remembering to stop for food as Sage here is, you could use some fuel." He leans a long arm over the table, pushes a pile of purple cornflowers out of the way, and deposits a rough wooden chopping block.

It's laden with a mountain of cheese and crackers and cold meat.

My cheeks immediately burn, because this isn't part of the plan. Beau is supposed to be staying the fuck away from me, and he certainly isn't supposed to be hand-delivering me snacks in the middle of the afternoon.

The others are suitably swooning over Beau Heartford being the charismatic dreamboat of a cowboy he is.

I keep my eyes firmly locked on the twine I'm busy wrapping and knotting. "Thanks." It's a quiet mutter. There's no way I can look at him without giving away our dirty little hidden secrets.

Even though my attention is elsewhere, the sound of clanking metal on the trailer and whinnying jolts me. *Shit.* I suddenly realize if there are horses arriving, then I'd better be doing my job.

"Crap, I'll be right back. I need to get some footage of this." Tossing the flowers down, I mutter in the general direction of the girls.

As I wipe my hands on the ass of my cutoffs, I feel Beau's size and brawn step in my way. One of those veined hands I oh so desperately want to have caressing my skin reaches out. Though this isn't anything to do with touching me, instead, he clicks his tongue softly and gestures in the direction of my phone.

"Here, give me that. I'll film the content and take photos. You keep doing what you're doing over here."

I'm rendered dumbstruck when he plucks it from my grasp without warning, then casually strolls off with my phone.

All I can do is brush my hair behind my ears and try to keep my breathing under control as three sets of eyes descend on me like lightning.

Turning back to my silly little arrangement of flowers, I unspool more twine and grab the scissors. With each passing fraction of a second, I feel their gazes pinball between me and the back of Beau's head as he heads over to the barn.

"Wait, so... Beau knows your passcode?" Briar breaks the silence.

I keep my eyes lowered, intently focused on what I'm doing.

"Sarge... how does your *married boss* know your phone passcode?" Layla drops her voice low.

The tips of my ears burst into flame. "Oh, you know." I tilt my head and yank the knot as tight as possible.

It happens in a blink. Layla and Briar look at each other sideways, and next to me, I feel Sky's fingers wrap around my elbow.

The three of them propel me to the farthest end of the table and huddle around me like a coven about to cast a spell.

"*Ohmygodyou'refuckingBeau*." Layla stabs a finger at me and gasps.

My eyes bounce between the three women looking back at me in shock. Like any of them can damn well talk, or judge, based on their past decisions when it came to cowboys they weren't supposed to look twice at.

Well, fuck. Looks like my dirty laundry is about to be aired after all.

"It's nothing." I shrug. "Just a stupid moment when we crossed a line, but everything is back to how it was."

"Holy shit."

"Sage. Are you serious?"

They have eyes out on stalks while whispering as loud as they dare.

"Don't have kittens. We fooled around a little. That's all."

"More than once?"

I bite down on my cheek, then wince and pinch my thumb and forefinger together in front of my face. "Only a teeny bit."

"Holy *shiiiiit*. Sage, this is kinda a big deal." Layla peeks over her shoulder to make sure we're still safely having a private conversation.

Briar's jaw is on the ground.

"Don't any of you dare give me that look. Considering the cowboy dicks you three slipped and fell onto, none of you can say a single word." I wave my finger in the direction of their faces. God, I wish they'd all stop gaping at me like that.

Finally, Briar picks her jaw back up and starts gushing. "I'm really happy for you guys... Beau is such a good—"

"No. Stop it right now." I shake my head and hold up both hands. "There is nothing to be happy for or to be giving me those swoony eyes over. He's married. Hitched. Ball and chained."

"But..." Briar looks crestfallen.

"I don't care if he's *almost* divorced, or whatever their story is...

the fact of the matter is, I slept with somebody's husband, and I can't make excuses for that."

Shifting my weight, I can't stop the guilt-laden words from bubbling up.

"And it especially doesn't matter, because it's done now, anyway. We scratched an itch and got it out of our systems. A bit of fun. That's all. Now it's over, and besides, I've got a job to do."

Layla stares at me.

"What's that look about?"

"Are you in love with him?" She asks, with softness welling in her big green eyes.

"*Pfft*. Be real. This heart has no room for love." I wave her off and hit the three of them with a carefully affixed smile. "You know me, if it isn't fun, they're not worth my time. And I am certainly *not* anyone's second choice."

Perhaps if I say it enough times, I'll believe it myself.

I want fun, not feelings.

And I certainly don't need to be overthinking what any of those tiny gestures Beau just did might mean... for me.

CHAPTER 38

Beau

TESSA:

Really wish I could be there.

I know you hate to take a compliment, but the place looks incredible. Sage sent me some photos.

Texts roll in from my sister, and I puff out my cheeks at the sight of Sage's name. It's been hell keeping my distance from her, and even more so since she's taken to leaving the ranch at every opportunity since Mandy arrived. Not that I blame her.

Between working with The Loaded Hog and Devil's Peak Ranch, she's got more than enough reason to be off-site in between the preparations for this evening. Once again, Sage has proven herself to be immensely capable and fucking brilliant at what she does.

I hate knowing that wherever she goes from here, they're going to hold on tighter than any cowboy trying to win a championship buckle in order to keep her talents.

My days have been long as fuck, rising before dawn and keeping my head down until the moment long beyond the point in time when the sun dips below the horizon. Then, after dark, I pack my gear and Mist to head off into the hills.

The entire time I spend seated beneath a vast, star-filled sky, with my tripod and camera for company, all I can think of is how much fucking better it would be to have her with me. Sage brings a vividness to everything she touches, and without her, the world seems to be only filled with pale, muted shades of color. Even the sunsets don't have the same intensity to them, because whenever I look through the viewfinder and run off a few shots, all I can think of is the night we had together, when I confessed that this is what she feels like to me. The night when I gave my heart over in secret.

Bet you'll be having the time of your life taking care of your broken boy. Who needs a party when you've got an out-of-action, grumpy bull rider to put up with?

Tessa's reply comes through straight away.

God. Don't remind me.

I swear, I love my husband, but Oscar is a terrible patient. Exactly like you used to be when you'd cry like a little bitch because you couldn't go hurl yourself in the arena.

Except it's worse, because I agreed to this in my vows, didn't I?

At least with you, I didn't feel bad if I slipped and accidentally smothered you with a pillow when you pissed me off.

Look, I'm not gonna judge the kind of shit you and Oscar like to get up to in the bedroom.

I can practically hear the way she tells me to fuck right off.

Tessa sends me an eye roll and middle finger emojis. I can't help but chuckle. My sister really has put up with the worst of me during my injuries over the years.

"Need another cold one over here?" Storm appears out of the soft glow of the fire and festoon lights, dangling a beer under my nose, and I swipe it out of his hand.

"Thanks."

He eases himself into the seat next to me, set back a little from the main crowd gathered near the bonfire and the music. I'd made my way over to this spot just before texting with Tessa in order to get a bit of clear headspace away from the overwhelm of talking to so many people. I mean, there's nothing wrong with it all—and other than one notable intruder and her wet blanket of an assistant—I'm glad they're here... it's just, a lot.

We sit in silence for a while. His eyes are where they always drift to these days, firmly fixed on the woman he's beyond head over heels for. Carefully watching on as Briar dances with Layla and Sky. Across the far side of the crowd, I can see the dark head of hair I'm not supposed to be looking at, yet I'm fucking weak and can't help but keep checking for where she is. Each time I see her talking and laughing and beaming that gorgeous smile, it makes me more and more fucking heartsick that I can't be right there in the conversation. To be beside her.

All I see is the curve of her lower back beneath that silky black dress, where my hand should be resting. The way her head tilts to one side in the exact position to find its home nestled in the crook of my shoulder. What I wouldn't give to be able to openly hold her, stare at her brilliance, and have every goddamn person in this world know I'm hers... and she's *mine*.

"So, are we talking about the thing you don't wanna talk about, sugar?" Storm tips back his beer. "Or are you back to lonely nights tugging on yourself to pass the time?"

"Fuck you very much. Just because you finally convinced someone to put up with your ugly ass, got yourself a smart goddamn mouth all of a sudden, huh?"

He chuckles. "You always did love the look of my mouth."

"Jesus Christ." A laugh bursts out of me as I scrub a palm over my face. "How Briar can tolerate your bullshit, I'll never know."

"I'm extremely charming."

"Yeah... *charmed* your way right in there, didn't you, Uncle Storm?"

"Screw you, Heartford." The toe of his boot connects with my leg. "But in all seriousness, are we talking about it, or did you manage to royally fuck everything up—even more than it looks like?" He tips the neck of his beer bottle subtly in the direction of Mandy's blond curls. The woman is swanning around in ten-inch heels as if she personally invited every guest here tonight, and they're lifelong buddies.

I exhale long and slow before leaning forward to rest my elbows on my knees, and my head falls between my shoulders.

"Fuck, man," Storm mutters, and I can feel him watching me. "You really know how to cockblock your own damn self, don't you? Briar tells me you two are perfect for each other. Something about it being meant to happen that she ended up here."

I shoot him a look.

"The girls know about the two of you, but that's it. Don't think we're going around telling anyone."

Air gusts from my lungs, at the same time heavy and yet weirdly relieved that our closest friends aren't being lied to anymore. Even if it's riskier, the more people who know.

"Sage deserves better." Is all I give him. No sense in getting into it, I've resigned myself to the fact the only woman I ever want to be with is probably gonna cut and run before I get a chance to make things right between us.

"Everyone here knows Mandy shouldn't be on this ranch. All those people she's bugging like a flea who won't quit, don't think for one second they can't see through all her crap. These are *your* people, Beau. They're here for you... and dare I say it, a lot of them are goddamn here for Sage, too. And I sure as shit can tell you who they ain't here for tonight."

Twisting the bottle in my hands, I tilt my head his way, meeting that piercing blue stare. "I don't want to lose her."

It's a gut punch to say out loud. The kind that hurts real good, because as I say those words—as I breathe life into them—it's like admitting that she's already lost to me.

Storm stretches his legs out in front of his seat as the music drifts our way on the night air, interspersed with the chirp of insects.

"So, how you gonna keep her?" he says finally.

"Sage isn't the type of creature who likes to be kept."

"Don't sell yourself too short. You're a catch. Fuck-off money, a big ol' ranch... I mean, it's a pity about your face. I suppose I can't blame her for not wanting to stick around and look at that disgrace on your lip every day, but..." He holds his stomach with a grunt of laughter when I smack him playfully in the ribs.

"I gotta deal with Mandy's crap first. I gotta get my side of the street cleaned up. How can I expect her to put up with the mess I've made? I'd never do that to her... but the selfish part of me doesn't want to let her out of my sight either."

"Have you told her any of this shit?"

"I've tried, but it's too hard with *that* sniffing around." I shake my head before jerking my chin in the direction of the wife I'm counting down the days to be long rid of. "I asked if she'd at least give me a few days, enough time to send Mandy packing back to whatever hole she crawled out of, and then we'd be able to talk properly."

Storm quietly sips his beer, but I can just about hear the asshole thinking.

"Want my advice?"

"Don't make me regret saying yes if I do," I grumble.

"Sage is like the horses who fight and run because they ain't got a single bit of evidence to prove they should give their trust to you." He muses, eyes drifting to where his girl tosses her head back with laughter. "Be honest. Tell her how you feel as soon as fucking possible. Chop your heart out and hand it over on a goddamn plate if you need to. Because if she's worth it like you say, then you don't even need the damn thing anymore. What good is it doing sitting like a lump of stone behind your ribs? If it belongs to her, it belongs to her, and she needs to know that without a single doubt."

Scrubbing one hand over my mouth, I feel that familiar squeezing sensation in the place where that heart resides. Like some force is already trying to do exactly as Storm says and reach inside my chest to tear it straight out.

"How long 'til this shit show is over?" he grunts.

"Which part? The bit where I get her to fuck off from my ranch, or the bit where I finally get to be free for good?" Drawing down another long sip, I swallow heavily, then hiss in a breath through my teeth. "Couple more days at most. Then she's gone, and the next time I'll see her will be through lawyers when the divorce is finalized next summer."

Even though that point in time feels like endless miles away, a light at the end of the tunnel flickers the tiniest bit stronger at knowing I've got the chance to be with Sage... properly this time. All I need is the moment to explain to her, to give her that undeniable certainty that I'm all fucking in where my girl is concerned.

So, for the moment, this is the way it has to be. Give Mandy what she wants in the here and now, so it can all be done. And this time, it'll be for good. She'll be eliminated from my life, and I can just taste that moment when it'll finally feel like starting afresh.

When I think of Sage, it doesn't feel like starting over. It feels like my life is finally beginning after being on pause and simply going through the motions for decades.

"Beau, honey?"

Fuck. My teeth are on edge the second I hear Mandy's voice call my name.

Storm makes a disgruntled noise. "You good?"

"Gonna have to be." I chew over the words like they're grit between my teeth.

"Let's get a couple of photos together." She sing-songs loud enough that I'm sure birds have been startled from their nighttime perches.

My jaw works as she totters over, wiggling her fingers at Storm in greeting with an overdone squeal.

I stay seated, trying my goddamn hardest not to give the game away by looking for Sage. It would only take a secretive glance, a quick flicker of my attention, to seek her out, and I'm sure this woman would scent blood in the water like a predator.

"Aw, Zee-Zee, would you look at him? Always so good at being broody and handsome."

"Can't it wait?" I take a steadying breath.

Mandy stops in front of me, clasping her hands together. "Pretty please? Just a couple of quick photos so I can post them for our fans." She rolls her wrist at me, and as much as I couldn't think of anything worse than to continue this charade, I've only got myself to blame.

Thoughts of news headlines, an explosion of outrage online, and comparisons to my father, crackle and burst in front of me like a scrimmage of reporters shoving flashbulbs in my face. I'm blinded by the looming threat of media vultures, wanting to protect the people in my life who mean the world to me, and the bitter taste of being unable to say *no* for the moment.

That time will come soon enough. For now, I'm at the mercy of smiling for another camera, another pose, another fake facade of the perfect marriage.

As I shove to my feet, the metal of my wedding band presses against the arm of the chair, digging into my finger. It feels hot and prickly to the touch, like it's going to embed itself with claws if I don't get the damn thing off real fucking soon.

"Make sure you stand over here so I can get the best angle." The instant her fingers brush my shirt sleeve, my muscles lock up. An urge to flinch is overwhelming, but I've had years of practice where this shit show is concerned. So I step to the right side of her and stand in the pose I usually take up in these sorts of moments. Both hands shoved in my front pockets to avoid having to put them anywhere near her, while Mandy wraps herself around my elbow as if we're the epitome of wedded bliss.

Zeb takes what feels like forever to get the photo. While I remain a statue, Mandy poses and pouts and asks for 'just one more.' My eyes are fixed on the camera lens as much as damn possible, but in between shots, I can't resist the pull to cast my awareness over the rest of the crowd. Most people aren't paying us any mind, but that's when I collide with honeyed dark eyes staring straight back at me.

A sharp stab of guilt tears straight through my gut. Seeing Sage witness this feels like the worst kind of betrayal of everything between us. It might just be a dumb fucking photo, a meaningless moment in time, but with each repetitive thud of my heartbeat, I see it on her face.

Watching Sage's expression turn shades of hurt and distrust might have been painful, but it's the next moment that absolutely kills me. It happens in a blink, when her point of focus drops to Mandy's diamond ring as it catches the firelight, the location of her claws sinking into the crook of my elbow. A tightness pulls at Sage's lips when she ticks her gaze back up to meet mine. The sight of indifference flickering across her beautiful face almost leaves me doubled over.

I'm caught blindsided. With my attention drawn away from where I'm standing, I don't react quickly enough to notice what's happening right beside me. Mandy forcefully tugs on my arm, jerking my body toward hers, and in that god-awful second, her lips meet mine.

My blood runs cold as I feel her force a kiss on me. The cloying scent of perfume fills my nostrils, and the sticky residue of whatever glossy lipstick she's wearing attaches itself to my skin.

Yanking myself away, I drag the back of my hand over my mouth. A dull roar rushes through my ears. Through a violent hiss, I manage to form words. "What the fuck are you doing?"

But Mandy isn't even looking at me. She's not listening.

Already trotting over to Zeb with poisonous fucking glee, she flaps her hands. "Did you get the shot?"

They huddle together, flicking through the photos, looking mighty goddamn pleased with themselves at successfully ambushing me like that. Instantly, my chest caves in on itself like I'm pinned beneath a two-thousand-pound bull. I search the crowd for sight of her, but as my eyes flick around, not giving a single fuck if anyone is watching my reactions closely, I can't see the only person who goddamn matters.

It's not until I turn my head that I notice her raven hair disappearing through the doors to the barn.

Swallowing heavily and scrambling to figure out how the fuck to race after her, I whirl on the two pieces of shit in front of me.

"Don't you *ever* pull that kind of crap again."

Mandy doesn't even blink, too busy editing and cropping the image on her phone. "Honey, you know the people want to see us together." She holds the screen up with a flourish, and it's like all the worst moments of this sham of a marriage collide in a violent explosion when I see that she's already posted the photo of us, the dreadful moment our lips touched. "All my best-performing content is with the two of us... *see*?"

The air crackles and vibrates with the fury rolling off me that I can't do any goddamn thing about this situation. And she's oblivious to it all, never stopping or pausing for one second to think about anything that doesn't benefit her personally.

"Isn't it all so romantic? I'm so glad I wore this color to match your shirt... and that new contour brush is working magic, Zee-Zee... I knew everyone would adore a couple's photo. See how they're eating it up." Mandy's eyes devour the sight of her notifications exploding. The fuel that feeds her addiction to fame and notoriety and makes her continue to act in a way that is unfathomably shallow.

All for the sake of the high that she'll forever chase and grow more and more desperate to attain as the years keep rolling by.

"Mandy." I clear my throat and keep my voice as quiet and

even-tempered as possible. "You've got exactly twelve hours to get the fuck out of Montana and never set foot in this town again. I might be willing to put up with your bullshit marriage contract, but don't think I couldn't disclose dirt on you if I chose to. You know as well as I do, that I could have done so if I wanted, and yet never have. Personally, I enjoy living a life with higher moral standards than stooping to your level. But get one thing straight, if you *dare* think you can come here and pull bullshit like that again, I'll gladly slap a restraining order on you, without giving a damn whether we're still legally married, or not."

She looks at me with an unreadable expression playing behind her eyes, still clutching the phone open on the tab exploding with love hearts and oozing with fawning comments. "I agreed to postpone a divorce. Not for you to have the freedom to force yourself on me. So both of you, pack your goddamn shitshow up, and I'll happily pay for a hotel out of town until that jet of yours is done being repaired." I lean closer and grit my teeth. "But my money is on the fact I could place a call your pilot right now, and he'd tell me there was never anything needing to be fixed in the first place."

"Beau—"

"No. Get the fuck out of my life, Mandy." My words spit out. "You wanna talk to me? From now on, you do it through our lawyers. That's the last bit of my hospitality and courtesy you'll ever see."

I turn on my heel and stride toward the barn without pausing.

Right now, I don't give a shit about anything but getting to her.

For Sage, I'd risk every fucking thing.

CHAPTER 39

Beau

"Better not be seen in here with me."

Sage doesn't look my way as she stands in front of Teddy's stall, scratching his nose. The fickle asshole has turned to putty in her hands. Standing there with heavy-lidded eyes, he gives me a sidelong glance as I approach under the glow of lights strung up overhead. A judgmental fucking look that tells me he knows all my sins. His nostrils flare, and the snort he lets out tells me that he doesn't think I deserve her.

Even the horses know Sage is the brightest glimmer of starlight on this ranch.

"I don't give a fuck." My heart pumps harder at the sight of her up close finally, after having to keep my distance all night. Sage's dress is a silky slip fluttering around her knees, raven, like the long mane of shiny curls hanging loose down her back. The most delicate straps cover her shoulders, contrasted with those black cowboy boots she could so easily crush my heart beneath if given half a chance.

Her attention remains on the horse, reaching up to the spot behind his ears. "Wouldn't want anyone getting the wrong idea."

"Sage." Pulling my hat off, I shove the other hand in my hair and dare step a little closer. "What you just saw was a setup. I didn't know she was going to pull that shit."

"Yeah, sure." Her tone is arctic, but then she croons something sweet at the horse who has bitten me more times than I care to admit. Yet here he is, mooning after my girl like a lovesick puppy, soaking up her touch just like he usually does with Briar. "Run on back to the party. Don't bother risking it all to come after me." A wry laugh comes out of her, and that knife still embedded deep in my stomach twists harder at the way her voice holds no emotion.

"Please, Sage. Just... let me explain."

"Desperate enough to risk sneaking around in public? Don't think that would fit the married man aesthetic very well." She shakes her head, and that scent I'll forever be chasing the hint of washes my way.

"I talked to Storm out there. Briar and the others, they know?" I venture.

That finally brings her eyes to mine with a flash. "I didn't tell them if that's what you're worried about. They guessed of their own accord because you acted like an idiot and took my phone. As if you were my boyfriend or something."

Sage says the words, and the air sizzles with unspoken emotion, with an energy that curls around me and is so wholly *her*. Filled with fire and determination, and the first hint that beneath that hardening of her exterior, is the Sage I'm beyond in love with.

"Am I not?" I narrow my focus on her.

"Jesus. Beau." She drops her hands from where she'd been patting Teddy. "You're not. We're nothing. There's nothing more gonna happen between us."

As her eyes lock with mine, I see a glint hidden away. A spark of challenge glitters at me, and this time, it's undeniably the dance we do. Sage isn't the type of woman who wants empty apologies, and she's got that feistiness to her that calls to the part of me only she has power over. She might very well be the only person who truly sees me.

"Try saying that again." My voice drops low and gritty as I step right into her.

"We're nothing to each other." She juts her jaw out. Pure daring is written all over her expression as she stands her ground and looks up at me.

"In case you need it spelled out, you're *everything* to me. Taking your phone in order to help out? Yeah, I'd do it all over again without question. I want to take care of you. And not only that, but I want to do little things for you, because that is my privilege to handle the simplest of actions if it will make your life easier. I want to help you, simple as that. While you're immensely capable and don't need anyone, you deserve to not always have to carry it around all the same."

She scoffs. "You don't mean any of that. Some pretty words you've rehearsed there, cowboy, but that's all. They're just words."

It's like she's just tossed a match onto gasoline.

"Meaningless. Fucking. Words." Sage glares up at me, and with each syllable she emphasizes, I feel my veins heat, blood pumping harder for the way she's pushing at me verbally.

My girl knows exactly what she wants, and she's not going to give me the easy option.

"Think I don't know how to show you otherwise?" As I let the quiet warning hang between us, I step closer, and Sage backs up. Another stride forward only does the same thing as she inches away, keeping the space maintained between us.

She wants me to chase her around this entire fucking ranch tonight? I'll hunt her until daybreak if I have to.

"You know I hate that I can't be with you out there, like you deserve. All I want to do is walk in the middle of that crowd and ask the band to play something slow, so I can dance with you under those stars."

"Good thing we're not together then, remember?"

Her shoulder connects with the door to one of the empty stalls at the far end.

"Oh, yes, we are." Keeping my eyes locked with hers, I pounce and wrap my palm around her waist.

"Nope." Sage is still all fire and snarls, but doesn't shove me off her. "Not while that ring is still on your finger. Or in that place where you so cleverly hide it." She says the second part with enough venom that I can only assume she's come across the spot where I keep it out of sight and out of mind until the painful moments when I have to put it on, like tonight.

"We. Are." I let my hand slide down to squeeze the soft curve of her hip and damn near groan at the relief of being able to touch her after what feels like an achingly long time.

A shiver dances across her shoulders when I sink my fingertips into the delicate fabric. My palm feels like it could burn straight through and leave an imprint there. I'm so desperate to hold her tight, so goddamn filled with the need to demonstrate just how strung out I am without having her near.

"Gonna leave it on? Make a proper mistress out of me when you do this with your wedding ring securely in place?" A curl tugs at her lip, chest heaving ever so slightly.

"That smart mouth of yours is asking for hell, and you know it, trouble." The fierceness of my grasp intensifies, and when I pinch down on the fleshy part of her hip, I see it. She needs this as much as I do. The honey in her eyes catches light, reflecting the festoon bulbs hanging high above our heads, and I walk us both into the empty stall.

As soon as we pass into the enclosed space, it's like all the brakes come off. Anything that might have been holding us back fails. We're careening straight for the edge, and neither of us has any interest in stopping this impending freefall.

"Planning to get your dick wet with your piece of ass on the side, then stroll back out there and play happy families with your wife?"

"No, baby." Lifting my hat, I set it on her head, and brush strands of hair away from her face as she makes a soft little growling noise. "I'm going to show you that nothing could keep me away from you. I'm going to prove to you that being without you is the thing that rips all the joy away. It's fucking misery not having you in my arms, and I'd walk away from this entire ranch, burn every single thing down right now. All you have to do is ask." As I stare, taking in the sight of Sage looking utterly breathtaking, I reluctantly let go of my grip on her body for a moment, but only to tug the ring off my finger before tossing it aside.

As the metal bounces and skids across the ground, until it collides with the wall, Sage's chest rises and falls faster.

"What if I don't want you?" Her voice grows raspy as my hands reach down and bunch up the soft fabric to gather just below her waist.

"Then maybe I gotta remind you just how good we are together, *hmm*?" I study her eyes. With each passing breath, I continue to hitch the dress, sliding it higher. "Keep lashing me with that sharp tongue all you want. I deserve it all. And I'll still have you moaning my name when you're falling apart for me."

My knee slides forward, parting her thighs and lifting so she's pinned by my bulk, her spine shoved up against the wall. The silky soft material gathers above her hips, and I'm in desperate need of being inside her. There's so much tension rippling between us; my pulse kicks relentlessly with impatience as I wrap her legs around my waist.

Sage darts her tongue out to wet her bottom lip. "Are you gonna make me?"

That drags a dark noise out of me, and I roughly shove one hand inside her panties. "You're fucking soaked for this." As my fingers rub through her slickness, my other hand comes up to wrap a heavy palm over the front of her neck.

Beneath the way I'm collaring her throat, Sage smirks at me. "Harder, baby."

"Jesus Christ." I plunge deeper, seeking out her drenched entrance. "Feels like you're all talk, but this pussy is a needy thing."

"Seems like you're the one doing all the talking." When I squeeze my palm a little tighter around the slender column of her neck, her subsequent breath hitches with pleasure, and I feel her squeeze around my fingers. "Here you are telling me you're gonna show me something real, and that's all you've got?"

With a ragged noise, I drag my hand out of her panties, fumbling to free myself from my jeans. My dick is about ready to burst, and there's no way I can wait to have my girl.

"Hold your panties aside." I keep my palm settled on the front of her neck and fist myself as soon as I've shoved my briefs out of the way.

Sage's dark eyes shimmer, and her flushed lips hang parted, as she makes me wait with throbbing dick in hand. She knows just how much power she has right now. This girl could leave me standing right here, no better than a fool with my erection held in my fist, and walk out of my life.

She darts her tongue out to wet her bottom lip, then reaches down to hook the lacey fabric, dragging it to one side in order to give me access.

"I hate that I want you." Her whisper dissolves into a soft, frustrated whine as I notch my pierced tip inside her channel. "This doesn't mean that I don't hate you right now."

"You don't hate me that much," I grunt, as I nearly goddamn lose my head when her velvety, slick channel starts trying to suck me in immediately. "I think your sweet little cunt quite likes it when you're fucking your boss."

"Oh, god." She tightens around me, hands flying up to cling around my neck, and it's fucking heaven to be connected to her.

"You're all I want, or need, baby." I shove inside her, pinning her hard against the wall. "This isn't like the times when those other assholes thought you needed to be given flowers or meaningless bullshit gifts. This is me giving you my entire fucking soul so you can do your worst—tear it to pieces if you decide that's what you want." My hips punch forward and in return, Sage sinks her nails into my scalp.

"What if I do? What if I shred you to pieces?" She lets out a gasp as my piercing hits the spot that makes her eyes roll back in her head.

"Fine by me. It's no use to me anymore. It belongs to you, trouble." I'm endlessly obsessed with how she looks, especially at this moment, with my hat on her glossy head of hair, and feeling her wrapped around me like the tightest goddamn little glove.

Sage is just about to say something when I feel her contract harder around me. Those lust-blown eyes widen, and I hear it too. Voices drawing nearer.

"... I thought I saw Beau came over here?" It's Zeb's voice, and I grit my teeth at the mere thought of being interrupted.

My girl swallows hard, her throat dipping below my palm. The fluttering of her pulse drums away on the side of her neck underneath my calloused fingers.

"*Shhh,*" I whisper and slow the movement of my thrusts right down to a lazy pace.

Her walls clamp down around me, and in an effort not to make a sound, her teeth sink into the plump swell of her bottom lip.

"Beau? Are you out here?" It's Mandy's voice now, calling out for me. Keeping my eyes drilled into Sage's, I sink as deep as possible, then pulse my hips to tap that spot. My dick swells with how fucking incredible she feels, and I couldn't care less if those two fuck faces walk the length of the stalls to discover us together.

The look on Sage's face is one of pure pleasure. There's no shame or confusion there; it's just us and our deep as-the-goddamn-ocean connection. The tiniest hint of a smirk plays on her lips when their voices come a little closer still.

I draw right out to the tip, holding there, and dip my head forward to whisper in her ear. "Do you want them to see you, my pretty girl? Do you want to make all those dirty fucking noises that drive me insane, or are you gonna keep quiet?" My cock sinks back inside her on an agonizingly slow glide. It takes everything for me not to erupt right then and there with how her body reacts. "I can play whichever game you want, baby. Tell me what you need.

Want them to know you're in here strangling my cock with your tight little cunt?"

When I pull back to watch her face, there's a battle going on within the rich brown of her irises and blown-out pupils. Sage clamps down and ripples around me with each steady, measured thrust I give her. Eventually, her head shakes ever so slightly, and that brings a ghost of a smile to the corners of my mouth that she just wants it to be the two of us. To keep this little secret to ourselves.

God, I love her so much.

We can't drag our focus off each other as her teeth bruise her bottom lip, and I keep fucking Sage right through it all. As I keep sliding in and out, oh so slowly, I'm entirely lost in her. The night air hangs humid and filled with the scent of us. Sweat dampens our skin, and my body lights up with the effort to stay quiet.

I can hear footsteps and talking in low voices as they linger and look in on some of the horses. Really, the only thing I'm paying attention to and straining to hear is if they move deeper into the row of stalls, but they don't. After a few minutes, they leave, and I release the groan building in the back of my throat as I sink all the way to bury my length inside my girl.

"Holy shit, that was so hot." Sage gasps, clenching and squeezing my length as I still my hips.

The blazing heat and tension building at the base of my spine is ready to damn well explode. I feel my blood turning an entirely feral shade for the sweetest thing wrapped around me. "Baby, I'm beyond caring about the rules. I've played by them my entire goddamn life, and all it brought me was heartache." I let go of her throat and brace my palm against the wall beside her head.

Sage pants and senses the urgency bubbling up, her thighs clinging tighter around my hips.

Dropping my mouth to her ear, my words are a prelude to the way I need this to go right fucking now. "This is the only good thing... you are the only good thing... so you'd better damn well wear my hat, shut up, and take my dick like my perfect little slut."

I slam forward and let the savage need for her to take control. Wrapping my palm beneath her ass to squeeze and hold her tight, I brace my weight on a forearm against the wood and drive deep, over and over.

"God. You're killing me... that mustache... *and* that filthy mouth..." Sage moans softly, air rushing from her lungs, and I feel those addictive tremors start to roll through.

"Yeah, well, you slaughter me whenever you give me those eyes, baby." Pressing my mouth against her ear, I feed her desperate, gritty sounds to accompany each of my thrusts.

"Beau—*Ffffuck*." Sage's fingers curl into my hair, and her legs shake.

"That's it. My pretty girl. Take everything. It's all yours," I murmur and readjust slightly to drop my hand between us, seeking out her clit.

As I roll over the swollen bud, I suck down on her earlobe before talking her through it. "Goddamn, I'm obsessed with having you and being yours, trouble. That's it. You're doing so well." She starts to claw at my nape as the wave rushes up to claim her. And as she falls apart I tell her exactly what I need her to know for certain.

"You're my future, Sage Maloney."

As her walls pulse around me, the force of her climax tugs me under. My hips stutter, and I grab hold of her body like I'm clinging tight to keep us together through a storm. I unload with a ragged grunt tearing straight out of my throat.

"Jesus. *Ffffuck*. Milk my cock with that pretty pussy, baby, just like that."

With each pulse of my dick, hot cum spurts forward, and I'm left more and more lightheaded by how perfect she fucking feels.

I wish there was a way I could erase time. Somehow go back and undo the day I ever crossed paths with the person I was never meant to be with.

All I want is for Sage to know that I might have complicated shit to figure out, but I've got no intention of letting her go. She's too goddamn precious to me. Not because this girl is fragile, but because she's the rarest kind of diamond there could be. Forged out of fire and unrelenting pressure and able to withstand anything that might come her way.

It's all hers. All my mornings, evenings, and every thud of my heart in between. She wants me to walk away from this place? I'll do it. Equally, she can have anything she wants here.

It doesn't matter what the question might be. I've already said yes.

CHAPTER 40

Sage

If there's one thing I know for certain this morning, it's that the sight of Mandy Spire's suitcases packed and waiting by the front door is as refreshing as a crisp spring morning.

Even though we couldn't spend last night together like we both wanted to, Beau made sure to take care of me after coming down from our secret moment hidden away in the barn. While it doesn't fix every challenge we have looming in front of us, being with him, and getting to spend that time physically reconnecting in the way we are so very good at doing, settled something deep inside me.

The man he is, Beau knew we both had to go back out there, and yet he took the time to help me tidy up and not look like the disheveled, freshly fucked mess he reduced me to.

Sneaking around with Beau Heartford shouldn't turn me on as much as it does, but I'm only human.

Which is precisely what my scratchy eyes are reminding me as I yawn and stretch, just about ready to angle my head and let the coffee machine run straight into my mouth. It's before-the-birds early, and I'm in dire need of caffeine before starting the inevitable tidy-up after last night's event. Especially before it gets too hot out there. I spotted Beau riding out on Mist, heading to check on the cattle like he tends to do before the sun gets out of bed and bakes us all with another midsummer's day. The care and attention he puts into every aspect of this ranch is something I'm so incredibly proud of him for; that man works so goddamn hard to take care of everything around here. I swear he'd go without food or water himself if it meant he'd be able to put his horses and cattle first.

My eyes squeeze shut, replaying his heated words and rock-steady hands on my body. Their lingering imprint clings to me like he's still right here at my side, even though he's somewhere on the other side of the ranch.

I'm trying really hard to believe him when he says that there's nothing between him and Mandy. That there's seriously nothing there, no love, it was never like that between the two of them.

Last night almost broke me. As the coffee brews, my mind spins back to the moment I was caught off guard seeing the two of them posing together for photos. Beau looking so unbelievably handsome, hands tucked casually in his pockets, and then the stomach-drop moment of seeing Mandy draped all over his arm.

I can still feel the aftermath of that sickening fall through the floor sensation, witnessing what followed immediately after.

That's when it happens. Slow motion, like some kind of diabolical reverse rom-com, where instead of the guy sweeping me off my feet, his mouth is sealing against hers.

Their lips lock, and I can't fucking look away as they kiss, bodies bending toward one another in a familiar way that speaks of years being tethered to each other.

Beau told me there's been nothing between them for an eternity.

Only, that does exactly nothing to reassure me that there isn't some lingering ember glowing between them after all this time.

How can there not be?

She's glamor and fame and eternal grace worthy of the big screen. She's old world charisma set in a halo of blond curls and flawless makeup, professional sculpting of cheekbones, with a nose picked straight from a catalog.

She's certainly not like me in any way.

All I could do was flee.

Every single complicated layer of ingrained fear tore through me at that moment. Being unwanted, abandoned, the gnawing sensation of only ever having a temporary seat at the table. Why would anyone want the *wild child*, the *troublemaker*, the girl who can't keep her mouth shut?

I'm only ever one misstep away from being left alone. I'll forever remind my family of a time when things weren't good, so why would it be any different in this? The girl who strolled in and caused shit because she couldn't keep her legs closed and her hands off her married boss. She's certainly not worth the trouble and hassle of keeping around.

And then, Beau gave me everything I didn't know I needed. Meeting me so securely in the surge of emotions I was trying to survive and giving me so much more than just sex. He showered me with intimacy and affection and somehow also gave me the dominant wickedness I crave being able to spar against.

He literally fucked me slow and steady until my legs were shaking, while his wife stood only a few feet away.

There wasn't a single hesitation in him. He was all in with me. Ready to throw away all that he's worked so hard to achieve. I still don't know what that means for us, or how we move on from here, especially when I've got a job offer set to carry me what feels like a million miles away from this place.

What would life look like if we could maybe make things work?

I greedily slosh coffee into my mug and cradle that precious dose of goodness between both palms as I make my way back outside. There's a spot where I love taking in the sunrise from, and tinges of pastel pink are starting to feather high above the mountain ridge line.

Except I don't make it outside at all. I've hardly left the kitchen when I come face to face with Mandy as she walks out of Beau's bedroom.

She's once again immaculately dressed, with full hair and makeup, even though the sun hasn't risen. But the worst part in all of this is the look she pierces me with. Casting a full sweep over me from head to toe with the sort of predatory smile reserved for scorned wives who have a vendetta to fulfill.

I don't have time to freak the fuck out about why she's wandering out of Beau's room at this time of the morning. I don't have time to spiral into a panic about him and her spending the night together. None of that has time to register because Mandy flicks her attention to the phone in her hand, then back to me and starts tutting.

"It's so disappointing when the smart girl becomes a dumb bitch, all for the sake of a man."

My stomach knots when she taps on that phone of hers and purposely blocks my path.

"One piece of advice, cutie pie. If you're going to fuck someone's husband, be a little more careful about your digital footprint. Leaving evidence lying around is such a rookie mistake."

She turns the phone screen around and starts swiping through a series of images. Ones that have all been taken of the screen and keyboard—clearly showing Beau's laptop. But it's the subject on the screen in each image that has my attention.

They're all of me.

All of them taken by Beau when I wasn't looking. Some are from moments while I'm working with my headphones on, some from when we've been with the horses, while others reveal more intimate scenes. Like the one Mandy pauses on dramatically that shows me sleeping.

It's nothing graphic or lewd. Not at all. Instead, the aching intimacy of this thing between us is plain to see. My naked shoulders above the white sheet. Hair spilling over both of our pillows. My head turned away while I slumber. It's a secret moment between lovers. The way it's been taken carefully captures me in such a raw way, the connection between us can't be denied.

"I wish I'd been able to find where he snuck off to last night, because I could place money on who he was with and what he was doing." She arches an eyebrow at me, as if she expects me to crumple to my knees and reveal everything in a guilt-laden confession.

"Couldn't say." I take a gulp of my coffee and stare her down. "But I'm sure he will be thrilled to know you're invading his privacy." I gesture in the direction of the stash of evidence she's clutching on her phone.

She flashes immaculate, polished white teeth my way. "What? A wife isn't allowed to check her email? There's nothing in this house that isn't mine."

My stomach turns into a pit of snakes, slithering and knotting together.

"The devil works hard, but the gossip mill on social media works harder." Mandy steps closer to me, and that fucking perfume of hers is so strong I feel like it'll be embedded in my pores. "I'll have so many stories going viral about you by noon tomorrow; you'll never book so much as a five-year-old's birthday party ever again. Screwing a married man and your boss? The scheming *other woman* determined to trash a happy marriage? You wouldn't survive the rumors of how you're nothing more than a pathetic buckle bunny. A groupie who lied to get this job, then seduced a good, honest man."

I stand there, trying to control my breathing as best I can, because everything she's saying—absolutely everything she's threatening—is as easy as she says. And her accusations of me having an affair with her husband are one hundred percent true.

"Who are these sweet little ones, huh?" She pulls up my personal Instagram and shows a photo with my sisters.

My blood immediately turns to hellfire.

"I'll cut you a deal, Sage. You're a woman with her own business, and I'm sure you will understand; a trade is a trade, after all."

There is no recourse for me in this. No evading the grim reality that Mandy Spires has found yet another way to hold court and control everything, to make us all dance to her insipid tune.

She checks her lipstick in the reflection on her phone screen. Dabbing gently at the corner of her crimson-painted mouth before lasering her eyes back on me. "I'll leave your family alone, and in return, you're going to stay the fuck away from my husband."

That smug, haughty attitude of hers, and the way she's pissing all over Beau like he belongs to her is the thing that makes me snap back. "Last I heard, he isn't your husband anymore."

Mandy smirks, and those coiled serpents ball tighter inside me. "For the next twelve months? Oh, that man most certainly is. Unless I decide to contest the grounds of our divorce for some reason... then, oh, I don't know... I'm pretty sure I could drag it all out for a very, very long time." She gives me a mocking look of sympathy. "Aww, did he tell you something different? What pretty little lies did he whisper in your ear just to get you to open your legs for him, I wonder?"

My mind races like the wind. I can't remember how long he said it was going to be until they were finished. I feel like this bitch has constantly made me doubt my understanding of things ever since her arrival.

A whole year?

Another twelve months of this? The risk of my family being dragged into her tangled web of toxicity?

What if it takes even longer than that? What if all those months drag on, and there's another extension, another round of legal battles, and suddenly one year turns into two, which turns into five, or more?

She witnesses my silence and carries on with that ugly, pitying look on her face.

"Don't tell me you thought Beau was *different* from all the other guys out there who will do and say anything to get their dick wet? Did you truly believe that a man like him was going to be the good guy? I've known him for ten years. You've sucked his cock for all of what... five minutes?"

Mandy gives me a mocking little pout. Meanwhile, I'm raging, storming on the inside.

"Want to see the document with his signature on it? He's all mine in the eyes of the law, not to mention the world, and you can guarantee I'll make sure he stays that way permanently if you don't take your whoring elsewhere."

"You would seriously trap a man like that?" I keep my voice steady, but it sounds hollow to my own ears.

"This isn't my first rodeo. Luck doesn't fall in your lap... you have to go out there and hunt it down. Life doesn't give you anything unless you're willing to do what it takes to succeed, and being Mrs. Beau Heartford sure does have a nice touch of added sparkle to it when those deals, album offers, and royalties roll in."

She lifts a shoulder and winks at me.

"Have a nice life, Sage. If I were you, I'd think very carefully about where you choose to lay your head between now and when you arrive at that new job of yours. Would hate to turn up and find they've already blacklisted you from their books."

Mandy gives a little scrunch of her nose, and blows me a kiss before disappearing through the house in the direction of the front door.

Leaving me standing surrounded by the racing thud of my heart, and the sickening knowledge that she's somehow managed to win.

CHAPTER 41

Sage

I've made it barely ten paces from the only café in Crimson Ridge, carrying a quad tray of iced drinks to take with me up the mountain as offerings for Layla, when I feel his familiar presence.

Looking up, I find Beau with his heartbreakingly gorgeous cowboy stance, one knee bent to rest against the side of my vehicle, cap flipped backward, and his attention on the phone in his hands. He hates coming into town, so I'm caught entirely unprepared to find him waiting for me on the main street.

I'm also swallowing hard. He doesn't know the truth about why I'm here.

As I draw nearer, his attention flicks up, and this goddamn man hits me with a crooked smile to have my heart simply upping and vacating my chest. He looks me over with a glance that leaves me turned completely inside out, having to concentrate on not stumbling straight into his strong arms.

I can't tear my eyes away from him, and yet I'm weighed down with regret all the same. An ominous drum beat thuds in time with each footstep as I'm sucked into his orbit while walking across the asphalt.

He looks lighter than I've seen him lately, like a burden has finally lifted from his broad shoulders. The sight of him with that spark glinting in the blue-gray of his eyes leaves me in agony that I'm about to be the destructive force to wipe away all that gorgeous ease that suits him so well.

"How did you know I was in town?" I swallow down the guilt and flash a smile.

"I know you always get your coffee on the way to go see Layla." He shrugs and reaches to take the tray out of my hands for me.

"Stalker." My teeth catch the inside of my cheek as I dare to look up at him, before turning my focus on digging the keys out of my back pocket.

"You're so damn beautiful, Sage," he murmurs, and I freeze for a second at the way his voice sounds too much like a man who is still riding the high of our emotional moment together last night. "Do you know how close I am to just saying fuck everything and kissing you right here and now? Why don't we just go somewhere? We could say screw it all and find somewhere far away from all this. They have ranches in Canada... Australia... and you could carry on working with your clients remotely."

My heart pounds harder with each word he says. This man is standing in the main street planning our future, and I'm about to tear everything apart. I blink furiously and let out something that resembles a laugh.

"Well, haven't you been busy this morning? Some of us are hard at work, and here you are, daydreaming about playing cowboy while jetting around the world."

"Sage, we're clear of Mandy. I made sure she knows her bullshit isn't welcome anymore. She's gone, and the album release ain't happening here. We can talk about what life looks like when you get back this evening. I just want to be with you without having to hide anything." He looks down at me with so much longing and hopefulness written on his face, it splits my chest wide open.

"Well, I'm happy to hear you sorted things out with her... but that doesn't change that you two are still tethered—whether you like it or not—for the immediate future, does it?" I'm wary of having this conversation right here, right now. I feel like the longer I talk about this with him, the more my resolve is going to be tested, when I absolutely need to make the decision for the both of us.

He must sense something in me, because he clears his throat and frowns. "Sage. I need you to trust me when I say it's over. I'm done with her shit. I can't even begin to tell you—"

"But what about it, Beau?" I huff out a quiet breath. "That agreement you're locked into for another entire year... the one that you never actually told me about?"

He looks at me with that light in him fading ever so slightly—the color of his eyes turning to a stormy ocean as his throat dips. "I'm sorry, I should have laid it all out in detail. She got to you, I'm guessing?"

I nod at him. "She knows. She got photos off your computer... of me."

Beau looks like he's churning up inside.

"*Fuck*. I promise I'll take care of it. Believe me, I didn't mean for any of this to happen, Sage. I tried so many times to find the right words to explain it all. And then it just felt wrong to drag you into my bullshit since it wasn't going to change anything."

"Well, it certainly feels kinda like being... I dunno, not exactly lied to, but like there were things being kept from me because you didn't want me to find out."

"Baby, no. I would never—" His brow knits together.

God. We can't do this here. This is exactly what I wanted to avoid.

"I know you wouldn't, Beau." I sigh, opening the door to the truck.

"This doesn't change anything between us." He watches me closely, still holding onto the drinks.

I can't help but laugh and give him a soft shake of my head. "Another year of hiding and pretending? How does that look? Keeping our distance while others are in sight and sneaking around endlessly in private." I reach for the tray and lift it out of his hands, making every effort not to brush our fingertips together, because if I dare let myself touch this man right now, it's only going to make all of this a million times harder.

"Look. The ranch is only getting busier. Last night was special, but we can't carry on like that. What if someone catches sight of us together... one photo... one grainy bit of camera footage... then it all blows up, and you're trapped by her for years? Another decade? She's already got enough at her fingertips to cause you all sorts of hell by refusing to agree to whatever you've got currently signed. No. I'm not going to run that risk. We're as bad as each other when it comes to trying to stay apart, and both knew the consequences the moment we ignored our *one-time-only* agreement."

This time Beau damn near growls. "You and I? We're end game, baby." Then he shoots his arm forward to block the driver's side so I can't climb into the truck.

"I'm in love with you, Sage."

My heart leaps into my throat, and I'm left rocked to my core. All I can do is look up at him with my mouth hanging open.

I can't fucking breathe.

He didn't just say those words.

Beau's eyes soften as he gazes down on me, and it's so goddamn reckless the way he's out here in the middle of the main street giving me those eyes and professing those words, and oh my god, this is exactly what I was trying to steer clear of.

He sees the hesitation and upwelling of uncertainty in me, and hums quietly. "Don't run from this. Don't run away from me. I know that's a lot to hear right now, and I don't expect you to say anything back, or even feel the same way. But you gotta know where my head and my heart and my goddamn everything belongs." He talks to me the way he does, caressing me with that gentle, dulcet tone of voice he uses when he's around the horses, the one that always leaves me melting on the spot for him.

The arm blocking my path disappears, and I don't think I can hear anything but a high-pitched ringing. Beau helps me slide into the vehicle while juggling the tray of drinks, and once I'm settled in, he rests both hands on the roof, dipping his head lower to look at me with so much sincerity and steadfastness rolling off him that I can't breathe.

"I love you, Sage." His words are rich and filled with promises of a life together that I don't deserve, because I'm a terrible person for what I'm about to do to him. "Please… just let's talk about things later, ok? Promise me you won't run?"

"Look… is this the conversation for the main street of Crimson Ridge? You're smarter than that, Heartford." I give him an eye roll and twist of my lips, when in reality I'm shriveling up with torment on the inside.

"I gotta go. Layla's gonna be out for blood if I don't deliver the caffeinated goods." Giving him a tender smile, I tap the drinks on the seat beside me. Then, say the three words that burn as they pass across my lips before shutting the door on my lie.

"I won't run."

LAYLA's damp lashes flutter at me as she sniffs and grips me by the shoulders. She studies me for a long second, before diving back in for another lengthy hug, crushing my lungs, while at the same time being the only thing that holds me upright.

"I fucking hate this kind of goodbye." Her voice quivers as she inhales another round of shaky breaths against my shoulder.

"Me too." My arms squeeze her tight as the drone of boarding calls sound over the PA system. "We gotta find a better way to do this shit next time… because I can't find industrial strength waterproof mascara to deal with *our* sort of farewells."

"Pretty sure I just left snot on your shoulder." She pulls back, eyes puffy and red, as she grimaces and wipes at my sleeve. "Sorry."

"The perfect memento." I reach out and brush over her wet

cheeks with a thumb. "Be good to that cowboy of yours, yeah? Make sure you treat that giant dick of his well and make me proud with your willingness to be his slutty little ranch wench."

She starts laughing and crying fresh tears at the same time. "Stop it. I'm already missing your ridiculousness."

"Also, word to the wise. I *miiiight* have stolen Colt's phone before I left and set a daily alert in his calendar reminding him to give your titties some extra lovin'... don't ever want to hear you say I do nothing for you." I grin, and Layla makes a choked snort of a sound.

"He won't have a clue how to turn something like that off."

"Thank me later, when he's out picking up horse feed in Crimson Ridge and gets a little note to remember you're overdue a titty fuck. Like I say... my gifts are coveted far and wide across many realms." I bat my eyelashes and readjust the strap on my duffel bag—inwardly feeling the stab right through my stomach as I clutch the canvas beneath my fingertips. "I'll message you when I land, ok?"

"Watch me hunt you down if you don't." Layla smiles through her waterworks, and blows out a long, unsteady exhale.

"Thanks for returning the truck for me." I drop the keys into her palm, then fold her fingers over the top.

She covers my hand with her other palm for a moment, face going soft with emotion. "He's gonna be heartbroken, you know."

The air hitches in my lungs, and I swallow down the lump wedged in the back of my throat.

"It's the best thing for both of us. He'll realize that."

Layla's expression reflects mine. A silent nod of agreement exchanged between us in the middle of the airport drop-off bay, confirming that we both know it's the truth. No matter how goddamn harrowing, this is the way it has to be.

"Go take over the world. Remember me when you're famous, bitch." She squeezes my fingers.

I blow air kisses with a great flourish and make my way into the terminal, leaving my best friend standing there wiping away the freely flowing tears with the heel of her palm.

Once I'm inside, that becomes my signal to transform into a robot. Hardly anything registers, except to go through all the motions. The whole time, I'm numbed to my surroundings. Checking in for my flight feels like I'm in a daze, barely registering anything, or anyone.

It's not until right at the last moment, while preparing to board my plane that I feel it. The call I knew was coming starts ringing in my bag, and without looking at the screen, I already know whose name will be there.

Cock Ring.

My throat burns as I take a grounding breath, then answer.

"Why the fuck is your cabin empty?" Beau's voice is heavy with anguish. "This sure as hell doesn't look like *not running*. In fact, it looks like you did the very thing you agreed you wouldn't do."

The chimes and announcements for boarding start blaring in the background, and I scrunch my eyes closed.

"I couldn't stay. We both know that. I'll finish the rest of the work I'm contracted for remotely. Besides, you've got things you need to sort out, Beau. And it's important you do it without me there to get in the way."

"Sage, it's not like that. No—"

I smile sadly to myself, feeling the heat pricking behind my eyes. "It's ok, hot stuff. You've been trapped in a broken situation for so long, you don't know what you want. You might think it is, but your heart isn't yours to give to anyone. Not until you've rediscovered what it means to be you, to take the time to find yourself, to figure out what you need..."

My pulse races and I push on before he can interrupt me. "I can't wait to see how high you fly, but my wings are spread wide, too. You told me yourself, you weren't gonna clip mine, and that means the world. But if we stay together right now, we're only gonna end up tangled and plummeting to the ground.

"Sage. We're meant to be." He pleads.

"Maybe? Or maybe you just like the idea of me." My voice is soft and I wish I could have kissed him one last time. I wish I could have said a proper goodbye, but then I would have been too easily swayed by him. "I'm different to her, so of course, I seem like the next best thing. You don't know for certain, and this is never going to work while you've still got one foot in your past. You owe it to yourself to know who you are without that shadow hanging over your head of your father's fuck ups. To know what life feels like without Mandy's toxicity."

"Please stay with me. *Please.*" His voice cracks, and I feel the surge of emotion rising higher inside me now.

"I was going to be leaving anyway for this next job. And as if that wasn't already enough of a reason to go right now, I can't risk my family getting dragged into my messy decision-making. I certainly can't risk my career. This is my life, my thing to be smart about, so I need to do this." I speak rapidly, knowing the only solution is to harden my heart to him if I'm going to make it through this, starting right this second.

"I know, I know you were going to take the job, but I thought we had more time before... that you weren't going to just up and leave." He croaks.

Even though it's the worst feeling doing this, I have to think of my sisters. I have to be sensible, over and above the allure of hiding out and stealing more days hidden away with Beau.

"We both know if we're around each other, it's impossible. We've already proven we can't resist being together. How many times have we broken our own goddamn rules? Look at how hard it's been spending only a few days apart... what kind of recklessness are we inviting in when it's a whole year? Not to mention that sneaking around is hardly the healthy foundation of anything. How do we know we're not just addicted to the thrill of someone catching us?"

His silent pain is a damn near visceral thing, burning and burrowing into my ear where I clutch my phone.

"I finally figured out what to name the ranch." When he eventually responds, Beau's voice drops to a low murmur.

It's too much. I can't fucking take it, that tone in his voice—the hurt I can goddamn taste like the salty tears running hot rivers down my cheek—as his words come through. It's enough to break me.

"I wish for a lot of things in life, Beau. Right now? I really wish we hadn't met in this timing. Another occasion? Another place? Maybe. You deserve to love freely for the first time, and to do it from a place that isn't hidden in the shadows. I really wish our stars were different. But perhaps that's how it has to be in the end. We're not promised the grand gesture, or the happily ever after in this life. Sometimes, we only get the stolen moments and the memories we carry with us, and that's gotta be enough."

He makes a guttural noise of protest, and I can picture him with head bowed, fingers threading through his dark hair.

"Why? Why did you leave without telling me?"

"I'm sorry. It was gutless of me, Beau. I know that. I'm not the good person you think I am. You knew I was taking this job next... the rest of what I need to do for the ranch I can email Tessa about. And beyond all of those reasons..." I swallow hard. "My sisters are young, and they're still in school. I've got my family to think of, just as much as you've worked so hard to protect your family, too. I respect how many times your decisions have been made with the only thought being to put others first. You told me yourself that staying in that marriage has been years and years of your life you've sacrificed to protect your mom, your sister... last night, we were way too impulsive... we played with fire and it was a rash decision."

"Sage—"

"Listen to me... I care about you, and that's why I can't bear the thought of you having spent all of that time punishing yourself for a mistake, living what amounts to barely a half-life for a decade, and then throwing it away just because I came along?"

My eyes sting as I bite back the emotion threatening to take over.

"Thank you for a summer I'll never forget. It was hella fun, hot stuff."

"No." Beau's grunt is desperate. "This isn't just fun for me, Sage. I'm—"

"No. No, you're not, Beau Heartford."

He curses under his breath.

"It's ok." Smiling through the tears, I imagine myself stroking a hand along his stubbled jaw, and I picture being able to go up onto my tiptoes to press my lips to his as I say the kind of proper farewell we should have had.

"Baby, when you're ready... only you will know when that is... if those stars ever align, come and find me in that sunset sky."

CHAPTER 42

ONE YEAR LATER

Beau

The early summer sun bakes down on the asphalt beneath my boots, sending up a shimmering mirage of heat as I walk into the airport terminal. Clutched inside my fist is a stupid goddamn piece of white paper with a name scrawled across it in black marker pen.

With each stride, I square my jaw and do my damndest not to fixate on the last time I walked through these doors almost a year ago.

I try to, and yet fail miserably. As I always do, because every single day in my life brings something that reminds me of *her*.

The sun beats down on the lonely, aching hole in my world where she's supposed to be. A life where I've had to endure making my own way through the changing seasons, the leaves turning golden, the brutally cold winds and snow drifts swirling in to consume the ranch, and eventually, the budding shoots of green poking their heads above the layers of melting ice.

I've had to sleep in an empty bed, remembering all the ways Sage filled my days with the kind of nourishing warmth, goodness, and laughter I've never experienced before.

As I draw closer to the arrivals area, there are only a handful of people milling around. This early in the day, the airport is quiet as a churchyard, and even though I don't feel that same tightness in my chest at the prospect of being *noticed* nowadays, it's still always a pleasant relief to simply be able to go about my business uninterrupted.

Especially since my thoughts are primarily occupied by replaying the same scenario from nearly a year ago. A mirror image of life, before everything flipped upside down, and the best thing that I could ever dream of strolled through those doors and into my world.

Then out of it again.

I clutch the sign a little tighter, keeping one eye on the door up ahead while opening up my texts. There are a raft of notifications waiting for me from Tessa that came in while I was driving.

Just had a call that the horse feed has arrived in town. Can you stop by and pick it up on your way back from the airport?

Also, totally forgot to ask you how your session went yesterday? Sorry, these pregnancy hormones are making me feel like my brain has upped and disappeared on me.

Sure, will do.

It went fine. That EMDR shit actually seems to be kinda working.

I'm so proud of you. Hell, and now I'm gonna start crying. AGAIN.

Why did no one warn me getting knocked up is ninety-nine percent crying over stupid crap?

Did you just call me stupid?

Zero out of ten for creativity. Your insults have gone down the drain.

Yes. But I meant it in a loveable, affectionate way.

There's nothing hotter than a man who goes to therapy. Remember that.

Whatever, baby brain.

Dots bounce on the screen as Tessa types, and my eyes tick up to the doors as I catch sight of them swishing open, but it's just an older couple tottering through, pushing a trolley of their luggage.

Oscar is at Frontier Days, you know.

Yeah, I saw the footage.

Sage is doing an incredible job. She's absolutely killing it with those montages and edits.

The videos she's been posting keep going viral.

I blow out a breath, and the usual grip of longing for her hits me as soon as Tessa brings Sage's name into the conversation, which she does at least half a dozen times a week. Especially since she figured something must have happened to make Sage leave so abruptly. Tessa only needed to take one glance at me in the aftermath to know the truth about how fucking cut to pieces I was over her being gone. My baby sister is nothing but a pain in my goddamn ass, and this whole getting herself pregnant crap has made it a million times worse. She's waged a continual campaign, goddamn keeping on at me about winning her back.

She's not dating anyone, by the way.

How would you know shit? You're sitting at home propped up with Trash Island reality TV, trying to choose a baby name.

Oscar keeps me in the loop. He's got all the hot tour gossip.

I've been on team 'get Sage back' right from the start, remember?

I'm still salty as fuck that raging pustule of a woman tried to make it seem like I was actually friends with her. If I ran into her, I'd gladly let my weak-ass pregnancy bladder leak all over her.

Just as her text pops up, the next wave of passengers start to emerge from the other side of the doors. Holding the sign up, I already pick out the dark head of hair before they've stepped beyond the threshold.

Brown eyes meet mine and drift quickly to the sign in my hand before he dips his chin in acknowledgment.

The guy is stacked. Broad shoulders and strong tattooed forearms. The kind of build that comes mostly with genetics, and gets chiseled thanks to working full time on ranches.

"Zeke Rainer?" I crunch the sign and shove it in the back pocket of my jeans before extending a palm.

"Just *Raine* will do." He reaches out to shake my hand with a gruff sort of nod. "I could pretend I don't know your face, but you're a little too easy to recognize, Beau Heartford."

"Don't I know it." I chuckle. The guy has got one bag with him and looks the spitting image of how I used to travel light when I was on the road all the time. "Call me Beau. You good to head on out?"

"Lead the way, boss."

My new hire isn't the type of guy to say a lot, and considering the headspace I'm in, that's more than ok with me. It's easy enough to let our spurts of brief conversation stay light. Rodeo. Ranching. The usual shit to casually chat about. He's just come back from a season in Canada, and the guy certainly has a wild grittiness about him that lets me trust, at one glance, he'll easily handle the winters here. That fact alone is going to be a godsend around the ranch.

"I've been managing alright with a few casuals onboard here and there, but it'll be good having someone like yourself to split the workload with."

"Tessa said over the phone that the summer has been completely booked out for months."

I nod. "I've got a young buck who has been managing the trail rides a couple of days a week during spring, but he's off on the rodeo circuit a lot of the time."

"And the equine therapy program you've got going on is growing?" He reaches up to run a tattooed hand through his unruly hair.

"It is. A friend of mine, our farrier, looks after the rescues for the most part. But between them and the other horses, we're up to capacity with the stables for now. Somehow, I blinked and ended up with too much bookwork and not enough time to spend in the saddle."

An easy silence stretches out for a while as the world slips past outside, and the breeze brings some relief from the mid-morning heat blowing through the rolled-down windows.

"The place has done well, considering it's only your first year?"

I have to swallow down the gut-wrenching sensation that comes with his astute observation. Because, yes, the place is flourishing and growing rapidly, and it's all thanks to the influence of one particular woman. Who hasn't been here to see any of the fruits of her hard work.

"Yeah, we have." My hand lifts off the wheel to readjust my cap. "It's at the point where we're underway with plans for new cabin accommodation to be built next spring. Already got bookings ready and waiting, they just keep on rolling in. We just gotta get the goddamn things built first."

Raine laughs, a low rumbling sort of noise, and scratches at his close-cut beard.

"You've certainly had your hands full, haven't you?"

I shoot him a sidelong glance, to be met with a knowing look. This man knows my career and knows enough about me. He might have been balls-deep in snow while north of the border, but I'm sure he'll be well aware of how things have played out in the world of *Beau Heartford* in recent months.

Resting one elbow on the window, I drag a hand over my mouth. "It's been a ride, and I'd rather go haul my ass onto the back of a bull than go through that kinda shit again."

"So it's onwards and upwards from here?" Raine adjusts his weight.

Yeah, it certainly looks to be that way, to the outside world at least. Mandy did her best to make the split turn ugly, even though we'd agreed to terms around public statements and joint media releases. Requests for '*privacy during this difficult time*' and other bullshit like that.

Yet, there were enough stories leaked here and there, the kind that feed the clickbait sites typically swarmed by social media trolls. No guesses as to where they originated from. Most of the articles were complete rubbish, fabricated smear campaign bullshit, and speculation about how the bastard husband of the country music star was to blame for our marriage falling apart.

My therapist had their work cut out to help me work through the overwhelm brought up by some of the nastier bubbles of online chatter. The ones centered on my father, and how it was inevitable that I'd follow in his footsteps to destroy a wonderful marriage. Strangely enough, having it brought up actually helped rip the bandage off crap I'd been stuffing down and trying to avoid for decades. Ironically, the keyboard warriors disappeared as quickly as they popped up. By the time the next round of the gossip cycle had shifted focus elsewhere, I'd managed to work through a whole lot of baggage that had been hanging heavy on my shoulders for far too long.

Thankfully, in amongst it all, no matter how much Mandy tried to manipulate things, her own scheming came back to bite her in a way I couldn't have seen coming. And it had nothing to do with me.

My *wife* was ultimately her own undoing. One of the album executives she'd started fucking around with had a spouse with claws even more vicious and vindictive than Mandy herself could ever aspire to possess.

Overnight, her label dropped her like a cold cup of sick. Within a week, she'd been ostracized by her management. And by the time the ink on our divorce papers dried, she was nothing more than a D-list celebrity squawking about Botox and plastic surgery to her rapidly dwindling social media following in order to pay the bills.

It didn't take long before I found out the truth of what Mandy threatened Sage with before she left. As her career vanished before her eyes, that woman was desperate to try and manipulate everything. To the point she couldn't resist letting me know of her own volition that she had pried around on my computer and found the photos I had taken of Sage.

My lawyer and Tessa damn near had to rope me to a chair to stop me from doing something stupid, discovering how she'd used her time at the ranch to invade my privacy. God bless my lawyer, who had already been amassing evidence of Mandy's infidelity over the years. A hefty file sat waiting to be unleashed, and that was enough to persuade her to hand over everything she had on Sage.

I didn't care if it meant giving away every scrap of leverage over my ex-wife. To make sure Sage was protected? I'd gladly do whatever was necessary. It might be considered foolish to trade years of accumulated proof in return for half a dozen screengrabs, but I'd give anything she demanded.

What it didn't do was shorten the duration of my agreement. That shit was binding enough that it guaranteed I remained locked into the rest of the year, waiting while the clock ticked down, to see out the stupid fucking duration of time until I was finally rid of Mandy Spires for good.

She got her share of property, a hefty sum of money; I got to ensure the ranch transferred solely to my name and couldn't ever fall prey to her selfish, greedy clutches.

As of right now? I'm a free man. Or at least that's what the paperwork sitting in my desk drawer says.

The painful reality is that I still feel like I'm trapped in an empty void, barely surviving the lack of *anything* from the woman I love beyond all reason.

The second I found her cabin cleared out that day, the echoing silence when she hung up the call. I was left standing clinging onto nothing but her lingering scent. That was the moment the ax fell, and whatever connection we had was severed entirely.

At first, I tried to stay in touch, but Sage never returned any of my messages—it was goddamn clear she didn't want me to stay in contact while we went our separate ways and sorted our lives out individually. Now, I'm permanently adrift. Stranded, wandering beneath endless skies and riding the ridges and valleys of a picturesque ranch. Yet I still feel like it's all nothing but hollow achievements if I never get to see her beautiful eyes smile my way at least once more.

To know for certain whether there's any hope, or if she's moved on with her life.

Sage is always with me, in these tiny moments, when I feel like I catch the faintest hint of her scent on the breeze. That wild orange sweetness that creeps up on me out of nowhere, and suddenly, I'm right back in the middle of a memory when she insisted on going to see the new horses in the barn that first night we collided together.

"Have you been around horses much?" I murmur over her ear. Physically unable to let her go. My hands feel like they belong on her body, in a way I can't even begin to explain. It's like the skin-on-skin contact with Sage grounds me and calms the whirlwind on the inside.

"No. Not much." She shakes her dark head of hair ever so slightly.

"You see Mist here, all horses, they have their own unique set of tells. Their habits, the tiniest shift of weight or stamp of a hoof, or flick of their ear."

"Sounds like a lot to learn."

"Well, it's worth putting in the effort. You gotta do the work to earn a horse's trust. They're not just gonna give it to you, and they're much too intelligent to let any old jerk ask them to do something."

"Fair enough. So how do you learn?"

"Time, mostly. Patience. Hours and hours of patience."

My head damn near spins thinking back to that night. Replaying that moment, and the darkest depths of irony that this year has been sent to test me beyond belief.

How true those words would come to be.

We pull into Crimson Ridge, and park up in the lot where I need to collect our order of bulk feed. When I check my phone, there are more texts from my sister, and the most recent ones leave me white-knuckling my phone as I read over the screen.

TESSA:

So, are you gonna sit there pouting like a bear with a sore paw? Or are you gonna do something about getting her back?

Remember, you told me yourself.

Your girl loves a grand gesture.

CHAPTER 43

Sage

"Sage Maloney, this is one of the biggest stops on the rodeo circuit. *The Grand Daddy.* You honestly expect us to believe you're going to hide away in your hotel room with takeout and be a hermit?"

Three sets of eyes peer at me through the screen. Everyone is currently at Rhodes Ranch for a BBQ, and the girls took the opportunity to video call while Briar and Layla are down from their isolated mountain world for the evening.

"I entitle this masterpiece: *rot girl summer, party for one.*" I shrug and wiggle my Kindle and tentacle dildo at the camera, leaving them all snorting and laughing. "Allow me to wallow and binge-read monster smut in peace, thank you very much. Now, I demand to know everything I've been missing out on in your horse-girl lives. Freckles, you're up first..." I pop a couple of fries into my mouth.

Layla gives me an exaggerated eye roll. "Don't think I'm not watching you, Sergeant. But since you're asking, and since you're all here to be able to let you know at the same time... the stables I worked at in Ireland got in touch and asked if I would be interested in coming back for a couple of months. I just booked our flights. We'll leave before fall."

"Holy shit, that's soon. As in... *really* soon?" Sky chokes on her drink.

"I know. We'd been planning to travel for winter anyway, so figured we could make it work. Colt is going to talk to Storm about helping look after the place until Kayce is finished on the rodeo circuit for the season." She looks at Briar, who is grinning back.

"Does that mean I get to come and look after your horses for you?"

"Pretty please?" Layla smiles broadly.

I sink back into my hotel bed, leaning against the headboard and let their conversation keep flowing on the phone screen. We end up mostly chatting about life in Crimson Ridge for the others, and very gratefully, the topic doesn't veer back to my life.

Or lack thereof.

As they talk about summer plans and their businesses, I'm struck by a wave of immense pride in all of them. They're living their dreams while also having the loves of their lives right by their side. And while I couldn't be happier for all of them to have achieved the kind of success they have, it certainly leaves a special kind of numbness, right down to the bone, that my business might be seeing the type of expansion I'd hoped for, yet no amount of client contacts and email inquiries for my services can fill the cowboy shaped cavity in my chest.

Since leaving Crimson Ridge, part of my coping mechanism has been to block everything to do with Beau Heartford and Mandy Spires. It took all of one night alone in a hotel the rodeo tour put me up in to be tempted to look them up online, and I practically had to fling my computer across the room. I'd drive myself insane knowing I had that sort of search function power at my fingertips, so an internet keyword blocker has been my best friend for this past year.

"We adore you and miss you, Sage." Briar's sweet voice pulls me back to the sight of my friends as we say our goodbyes.

"Miss your titties." I blow them all a kiss. "Bye, bitches. I'll send you some shots from the arena tomorrow night." Waving at them, I watch as the screen goes black, and they disappear. Once again, I'm left to the quiet solitude of another night in another town in another hotel room.

I've loved everything about the tour so far. The adrenaline of the competitions. The spectacle of each stop and energy of the crowd is a magical thing. Yet, it weighs heavy, because with every new place I go, and each day I turn up to work, there are ghosts of Beau Heartford I can't outrun.

His name is so ingrained in this sport, in this culture. Even when I'm trying my hardest to not think about the way his lips tip up with a smirk to send butterflies erupting in my belly, or his strong arms wrapping me up tight while lying in bed together, there's always an unexpected reminder of him that gallops in.

I'm considering whether I should drag my ass to go shower, or maybe I should hit the hotel gym for a late-night run on the treadmill, when my phone chimes.

LAYLA:

He's not here at the BBQ tonight. I just thought you might want to know.

And I'm serious when I say I'm watching you, young lady. The Sage I know doesn't mooch around in her room, no matter how much shifter smut she's got stacked on her Kindle.

Talk to me whenever you need to, ok?

I send Layla some kiss emojis, and really don't have the heart to respond to her note about Beau not being around. She's the best friend I could ask for, giving me that gentle reassurance that it's not like he's there, hanging out somewhere in the background of their call, entirely uninterested in speaking to me.

Not that I would blame him after what I did.

Although it doesn't exactly help to know that piece of information, because my overactive bitch of a brain instantly presumes the reason he's not there at the BBQ with all our friends is most likely due to the fact he's long since shoved memories of me in the trash. I've tried to stay indifferent to the year passing by, but I can only assume if his divorce went ahead without any further delays, then he may well already be single.

He may very well have moved on with someone new.

Ugh. That churns up a swell of awful, sour emotion deep in my gut. Thinking of Beau being with someone else is enough to make me nauseous.

Exhaling a heavy breath, my fingers ball into a fist and then hover over my inbox until I finally cave and open the thread of texts I've read and re-read what feels like a hundred thousand times. To the point that I could almost certainly recite them line-by-line.

COCK RING:

I know you probably won't have listened to my voicemail where I've said all of this out loud, so let me repeat it, in writing:

Please stay with me. Please let me show you all the ways you deserve to be loved.

I've lain awake at night thinking of how you're a woman who is far too good for a man like me, yet I'm here on my fucking knees, baby. I'm hoping you might give me a chance to prove to you how you don't just mean the world, but you're my entire goddamn universe.

I want you to have that crystal sun catcher you were thinking about buying so you can be showered with rainbows while you work. I want you to never have to cook another damn meal in your life if you don't want to. I want you to trust that when shit gets heavy, you can put it down and know I'm already right there picking everything up.

And that includes picking you up, too. That strong, independent, 'master everything yourself' collar you wear is gorgeous and sexy, and I'm so proud of everything you do. But let me be there to hold you when you just want to be soft for a moment.

Goddamn, Sage. I'm not gonna lie. This is killing me. I'd crawl across fire and burning coals just to have you stay. Don't let this be it for us. Don't walk away.

How can I prove it to you? Just tell me, and I'll do it. You want the stars? I'll fucking saddle up and rope 'em all for you, baby. I'll even throw in the moon if that's what your heart wants.

I love you, Sage.

I miss you so fucking bad.

The messages stopped after about six months. Beau tried. He really tested my resolve to stay away from him. Every single sweet line he wrote tempted me. I nearly caved so many times, having to throw myself into work to cope with the urgent need to hear his voice.

What was I going to be? His dirty little secret, hidden away in Crimson Ridge? Known forever more as the woman who broke up their perfect marriage? No, thank you.

It was what we both needed. I can only hope that maybe, there might be a day when Beau reappears in my life. But the more days that pass, the more the likelihood of that happening seems to dwindle like a candle flickering out in the evening breeze.

Stepping into my ensuite, I flip the shower on and start undressing. With thoughts swirling in time with the water flowing down the drain, I get caught in a memory of him. One of many that I tend to let roll through my mind's eye when I'm drowning in all the ways I'm missing him—his tenderness mixed with the kind of downright mischief he has to match my own.

"I'm not some filly to be tamed, hot stuff."

"You think I want to try and tame you?"

I nod and nibble gently on my bottom lip. Watching on from beneath heavy lashes, Beau slides his way down my body as I lie back, spread out beneath his bulk. God, I'm far too addicted to the weight of him splayed across my body like this. As he descends with a deliciously wicked noise, his nose traces between my breasts.

"Oh, you've got it all wrong, baby. I'm not interested in trying to do anything but hold on tight and not get thrown out of the saddle." Wet lips brush a hungry path, sucking my furled nipple through the thin fabric of my tank, and his mustache scratches over the sensitive curve of my breast. "I'm in this for the ride, the win, and the championship buckle."

"You're supposed to be teaching me how to take pretty photos of stars. Not whatever this is you're intent on." I scold him without any actual desire for him to stop what he's doing because, yes, please, and thank you, I'm addicted to orgasms given at the hands and tongue of this man.

Beau hums against me. A soft cowboy-esque purr of contentment rumbles from somewhere deep inside that broad chest of his the second my fingers thread into his hair. I'm so giddy with the noises he makes whenever I give him those kinds of small moments, the simplest things like brushing my touch over his brow or his jaw. And right now, I'm tightening my hold to guide him to exactly where I want his mouth covering my tits. He's far too expert at wielding that devious tongue against me like a goddamn weapon.

"Maybe I'm too wild, even for the great and mighty Beau Heartford to handle."

He slides further down my body, with the blanket we're sharing rustling as it pools around my thighs. My cowboy stares back at me with a calming gaze, deeper than a bottomless lake and more sturdy than the mountains we're surrounded by.

"Throw everything you've got at me, trouble. Do your worst. I'll climb back on even if I hit the dirt."

"What if I stomp on your heart?" I breathe out the words into the midnight air.

"Then it means I had the honor of getting close enough to yours."

My pulse kicks and flutters. Is he telling me he's in love with me? Surely not.

"You bull riders really are something else." I flash a coy grin at him and shake my head.

Beau's expression curves into a look of mischief as he deftly unbuttons my jeans, tugs them and my panties low on my ass in order to expose my pussy lips, before lowering his mouth.

"Make sure to hang on tight, baby."

CHAPTER 44

Sage

The crowd erupts into a deafening roar as the final barrel racer scores the fastest time tonight. I'm right at the barricade, watching it all unfold from close enough to hear hooves in the dirt and to feel the adrenaline pumping off both horse and rider.

Even though I'm being carried along on the wave of energy swelling and rippling through this arena, it's the end of a long ass ten days. The balls of my feet ache after being on the go from dawn until long into the night. Rinse and repeat. I'm hanging out for my next stretch of time off before we hit the next stop on the tour, and have already booked myself a massage for tomorrow.

I might not be one of the rodeo pros putting their body through hell night after night, but I'm running what feels like a marathon each day. All in my best boots.

This event has drawn a sell-out crowd, as it always does, which in turn fuels the competition. The cowboys and cowgirls seem even more keen-eyed than usual, prepared to push harder. So it's no big surprise to hear the time being called by the announcer is the best of the field.

Being the final night, there's extra entertainment being put on, and I know I'll need to get some footage of the crowd's reactions and the atmosphere. My posts always seem to perform best when I can add in some clips to show off the fans and supporters at the events.

Pulling out my phone, I do a quick check over the copy of the digital run-sheet, to make sure I haven't missed anything important while I've been down here set up to record the barrel racers. I think one of my favorite moments is seeing them in the run-up, just as they're about to let rip and hit the course. There's something electric in the air right before the final second, when the rider finally lets her horse unleash and fly like the wind. This is also why I tend to hang around at this part of the schedule a little longer than I should and invariably end up having to jog halfway around the arena to make it to the next place I'm supposed to be.

Fortunately for my hella sore feet, according to the schedule, tonight I can stay right where I am. Except, the longer I stand here with camera in hand, the seconds tick by without any action. Whoever is supposed to be coming out on stage hasn't appeared.

Whatever. There are technical glitches that pop up across every single stop on the rodeo tour, and the sound and stage team are probably scrambling in crisis mode behind the scenes. So I turn my camera onto the crowd and start shooting off some B-roll footage I can splice into clips of the event when I get back to my hotel later tonight.

Everyone else might be living it up long into the small hours, hitting the after-party, but I'll be pretzeled in front of my laptop editing video footage amid the debris of room service until my eyes can't stay open any longer.

Oh, so sexy.

As I'm panning a slow-motion clip along the stands rising up above me, I see the ripple of excitement hit. The split second when you can taste that bubbling of anticipation as it captures a mass of people. Noise builds, with cheers and whistles starting to erupt when the band strolls out on stage. I grin to myself, because it truly never gets old seeing a moment like that unfold right before your eyes.

A throaty guitar belts out a few notes, and I start to focus back to the main arena, ready to start running off some photos. But I've hardly turned on my heel when an all too familiar voice comes over the microphone.

"Hope everyone is enjoying their night out there."

I nearly drop the camera mid-shot.

My eyes flick to the big screens erected at the end of the stand because there is no way in hell I am hearing what I am hearing. This isn't happening.

Beau stands on stage, raising a hand to acknowledge the thousands upon thousands of people in the screeching crowd, with a microphone in hand. He's dressed to wrench my heart right out of my chest, in jeans and a plain white t-shirt. With that stone-gray cowboy hat on his head, the perfect color to bring out the blue in his eyes.

"I'm not supposed to be up here interrupting your entertainment, so I'll be quick about it." He rubs a hand over the back of his neck, and I don't know how I'm still standing. Seeing him up on stage like this, witnessing his face broadcast on that giant screen—the first time I've seen him in a year—it's like the man I'm looking at isn't real. He's tanned and relaxed-looking, even though he's on camera and talking to this enormous crowd.

"Some of you might recognize my face." As he speaks into the microphone, the crowd hoots and hollers his name. I see the closeup of his expression in the video image as the corner of his lip tips up, and he dips his chin to acknowledge the fans. A crowd cheering for him even after years of being away from the pro tour.

"I always thought the biggest regret in my life might be the day I read a bull wrong and ended up left for dead in the dirt. Sometimes, when one season ends, another presents itself, and you've gotta be man enough to know what to do about it. I won't say I ever get anything fully right, but there's one thing I know for certain." He pauses, and I catch the flicker of his eyes as spotlights play over his strong jaw. I see the moment his strong throat bobs. "My girl is in this arena somewhere. She's been touring with you fine folk this whole year, and I'm here to ask if you'd be willing to share her with me. Life ain't worth doing if it's without her, and if that means I gotta start living life on the road again, then hell, I'm about to beg someone to give me a job on this tour just so I don't have to spend another minute without my girl."

I feel someone lift the camera out of my unsteady hands, and I'm reduced to a trembling mess. This is an out-of-body experience. Surely, this man isn't standing on stage telling the world about us?

"Truth is, I've been in love with someone for a long time now, and I understand that some of you might judge me for that. But I'm here to get the girl back. The one who truly owns my heart."

A piercing wolf whistle comes from right beside me, and I turn toward the sound with what must be panic and confusion written all over my face, only to find Oscar Diaz in his full rodeo gear with my camera slung over his shoulder. His fingers are in his mouth, letting out another shrill whistle, before he waves his hat back and forth in the air.

I'm open-mouthed, struggling to comprehend what is happening. My eyes dart back to watch the big screen version of Beau search around for the source of the extra noise. As he does, the crowd behind me starts calling out in unison when they see what Oscar is doing.

My senses are almost completely dulled by the roar of blood in my ears, the commotion at my back seems like it's coming from somewhere far away.

Did I pass out? Am I hallucinating? Is this a cruel and terrible trick my mind is playing on me? Will I jolt awake thanks to a free-falling sensation any second now, only to discover it was nothing more than a fantasy brutally invading my dreams?

Beau hones in on where the sea of stamping feet and whistles are coming from. Locating the part of the arena where I'm standing, quaking, feeling like I'm about to float right out of my boots. He points in my direction and turns to toss the microphone to the guy with the guitar before they clasp shoulders. Then he jogs offstage.

I lose sight of him and don't know what to do with myself. The sweaty-palm urge to run away grabs hold as my stomach turns into a riot of fluttering wings. He can't possibly be willing to do this, not here, not causing such a public scene.

I'm not worth any of this trouble he might be bringing upon himself.

Oscar presses between my shoulder blades, pushing me closer to the railing, and Beau comes back into sight. He's jogging across the dirt of the arena, looking every inch the cowboy who spent a professional career in that very same spot under the adoring glare of spotlights and crowds and eagle-eyed sponsors.

He scans the crowd, looking for where the peak of commotion still thunders in my ears, matching the furious speed my heart is pumping at. With each step he comes closer, I'm teetering on the edge of bolting, but in the same breath, I'm glued to the spot, unable to do anything but suck in shallow breaths.

Behind him, under the glare of the spotlights illuminating this vast arena and crowd, the sky is painted in shades of royal purple, orange, and blushing pink. A riot of color descending into the deepest inky black settled right on the horizon, with a handful of scattered stars starting to make their appearance.

Another long whistle drags his attention, and his gaze falls to mine. Our eyes lock from all that distance away, and it's like the world shrinks down to a narrow tunnel, with Beau Heartford's crooked smile and long-legged stride eating up the space between us.

This man jumps the railing with all the certainty and ease of someone who has done it ten thousand times throughout his life on the pro tour.

He doesn't stop, doesn't pause. One second, his boots are landing on the ground; the next second, the scent and warmth of him stop right there in front of me. I'm blinking rapidly, faintly aware of the wetness running down my hot cheeks.

"What are you doing here?" I hardly get the gasped words out before he tilts his head my way, catching the hat off his head in one hand, using the other to wrap a firm palm around my lower back.

"I'm here to find you, my sunset sky," Beau murmurs, with a hidden smile written in the creases around the corners of his eyes, before he dips me backward and kisses me in front of this packed arena. In front of cameras and media and the multitude of ever so public aspects to his career that he's avoided for such a long time.

My hands fly up to fist the front of his t-shirt, and a torrent of memories come rushing at me the second his mouth seals with mine. The day at the river, when we kissed just like this. His strong arms wrapped around me in the barn. Being in his bed curled into his warm chest. All our stolen moments pulse and flash like a kaleidoscope of rapid-fire scenes that I was convinced I had lost for good. Except this time, that faint hint of leather and the masculine scent of him washes through me and his mouth moves against mine, unhurried and slow.

Beau kisses me like he's got nowhere else to be in this world, and my heart simply explodes.

He makes a gentle, contended rumble of a noise against my lips, before feathering a softer kiss over my tear-stained cheek.

All I can do is cling to him and stare back when he pulls away and looks at me, still unbelieving that this is actually happening. It surely can't be real?

Tucking his hat into the hand pressed against my lower back—the only thing preventing me from crumpling to the ground—he brings his free hand up to nudge the brim of mine, giving me a soft expression as his gaze bounces all over my face. Beau cups my jaw and swipes away the wetness coating my cheeks with a thumb, and I shudder with relief at feeling his warm, calloused touch. It feels just as safe and sure as I remember, even better than any version of his caress that I've been left dreaming of for all this time without him.

"You remember that day you asked me if I had any weaknesses?" His voice is low and relaxed, and I hitch in a breath as he stares down at me. "The truth is, I've climbed onto the back of thousand-pound bulls. I've faced down being stomped and crushed. I never once felt like I had a fear or a soft spot in all those seconds spent in the arena. Right now? I can stand here with my boots in this dirt and tell you I'm terrified of how life might look if you never came back to me, Sage."

I swallow hastily, still without the ability to form words.

"Baby, you are my weakness, my trouble, and this aching heartbeat right here." He lifts my palm to sit squarely over his chest. And that's when I see what he has wrapped around his wrist.

A sob bursts out of me.

Beau's ocean-deep eyes follow mine as he looks down to where he's got my fingers clasped inside his own. He flicks his gaze back to hold me so damn securely when all I feel like doing right now is falling apart. "I never took it off, baby."

The friendship bracelet I made him is sun-worn, the pink beads have faded to a pastel shade, dirt stubbornly sticks to it in a couple of places, and it looks like the entire thing has been threaded back together with something far sturdier than the elastic I originally used. Yet, it's still there, fitted snugly around his wrist bone and tanned skin.

Cock Ring.

He squeezes my fingers. "If all I'll ever have in this lifetime is this thing around my wrist, it'll have to be enough, but it anchors me to you every minute of every goddamn day."

"Beau—I—You don't have to do this—" I sniff and feel the weight of all those long, unending moments without him come crashing through me as more tears fall.

"My heart has been in your hands this entire time, Sage. It doesn't belong to me anymore. It's yours, baby. You deserve a man who is rock steady, who knows himself, and is prepared to take responsibility for his flaws. So here I am, fucking flawed as all hell, but trying to do better every day, begging you to come back to me."

His Adam's apple dips and his face is all I see. All I'll goddamn ever see, I'm certain of that, after how hard it has been to be separated from him.

"I—I don't know how to be a wife." My bottom lip trembles.

Beau shakes his head and laughs, with a brightness about him that seems entirely new compared to all the time I spent with him when there was something unspoken hanging over his head. "Fuck that, Sage. I don't want a wife. I want this spark... our passion... I want someone who will order my ass to go skinny-dipping in the middle of the afternoon, then at night, chase after an ocean of stars in the sky. I want someone I can cook for and take care of, but not because she needs me to. No, in fact, she'll fight me every step of the way because she's stubborn as fuck."

The love of my life tugs me closer and lets his mouth brush over mine before whispering words up close so only I can hear them amidst all the raucous noise and music still going on in the background.

"I'm not looking for an imaginary fairytale... I'm here for my dream girl, who burns hot and bright in my veins, and makes everything come back to life."

A shudder of an exhale gusts out of me, and I bite down on my bottom lip before nodding at him. "I want all of that, too. I love you, Beau Heartford."

"Goddamn, I missed you." He gently tugs my lip out from the pinching hold I've got it in. "Now, can I get you outta here and properly fucking kiss you?"

"That wasn't—"

"Not even close, trouble." The smirk this man gives me is everything I've dreamed of.

That's when a heavy hand drops my camera strap over Beau's shoulder before slapping his back. "Good to see you, bro. I gotta run, or I'm gonna miss my warm-up." Oscar leans in to quickly peck my cheek. "Welcome to the fam, Sage." Then he's making a hasty exit back to the competitor's zone.

"But, wait... I can't just leave?" My eyes wander to the camera and then back to Beau's features, with a tightness starting to creep in because while this is perfect and all, I've got a job to do.

Beau ignores all that and starts to lead me away by the hand. All the while, tiers of crowds in the stand above us start creating a renewed fuss upon seeing us start to walk away. "Let's just say, I might have called in a favor or two. But that means I gotta do a whole signing meet and greet thing tomorrow in return for stealing you tonight." He waves his hat in the air at the crowd, looking every inch the rodeo superstar, and I'm filled with a giddy sort of sensation.

This man loves me enough to do all of this, to turn up for me, to put himself out there for public judgment and scrutiny?

"You don't have to get back? What about the ranch... the horses..."

He threads our fingers together and tugs me to fit right against his side. "Consider this my formal job application. I'm all yours to be your second photographer for the rest of the tour season."

Seeing my confusion, he chuckles. "I got myself a ranch manager to take care of things while I'm gone." He wets his bottom lip and shakes his head a little. "Didn't know how long I'd be needing to convince you for, baby."

"Thank you," I whisper. Not really sure what I'm thanking him for. Maybe just for being the type of man who knows I wouldn't have been able to simply walk away from my work. He's not asking me to give up anything. In fact I'm almost certain this man would be the one to always encourage me to make a plan for my career, the kind that felt good for me first and foremost.

Because that's the type of man Beau Heartford is.

"I missed you so much. I'm sorry for leaving..." I falter a little, but then the way he smiles, gazing down at me with so much love in his eyes, tells me in no uncertain terms that he understands why I did it. He doesn't judge me for doing the hard thing for the both of us.

He dips his head to meet the shell of my ear, sending goose-bumps flying down my arms. "I've spent a lot of lonely nights in hotel rooms. I might know a thing or two about how to make it feel a little less lonesome."

Grinning wide, I beam back at him, contentment flooding through my veins just being near him like this. "Are you offering to keep me up all night, hot stuff?"

"I'm offering to give you everything, trouble. For as long as you'll have me."

EPILOGUE

Sage

Sunset Skies Ranch.

The wood and iron sign hangs proudly overhead as I pull into the long, winding gravel driveway. As usual, I crane my neck to watch through the windshield when I pass beneath those words, with a big ol' grin plastered on my face.

My home. The heartbeat of my business. The place where the love of my life is waiting for me.

Beau Heartford has cemented himself as the king of grand gestures. Not only sweeping me off my feet in front of damn near the entire rodeo community, but naming his ranch after me.

Well, that last part is the little secret we keep to ourselves.

If anyone ever asks what inspired the name, my cowboy gets a mischievous glint in his eye as he shrugs, readjusts his cap, and proceeds to talk at great length about the night skies we get to enjoy here at the ranch. All while silently reminding me within the same breath that it's all for me.

Beau knows exactly how to play it cool in public and then swoops in on the first opportunity to corner me just out of sight and imprint upon my heart and body how the name of this ranch is his commitment to me. His promise that I'll always be his *sunset sky*.

Usually, by the time he's through with me, I'm starry-eyed and panting, and that's the point he readjusts whatever I'm wearing with a wink and a promise of more to come later.

I love him so much I can hardly breathe.

Before Beau, before coming here, it felt like I was always either chasing something, or running from something. A worming, niggling pressure, that I wasn't ever able to comfortably settle without feeling like I needed to seek a new high or thrill, a shiny new goal to act as a distraction from my fears. But here, with him, I feel like I still have the fullness of life, while also trusting that I'm wholly and truly supported by someone who never sees me as *too much.*

As promised, he hasn't clipped my wings or stifled my ambition. Since Beau came to find me—and then stayed by my side for the remainder of the pro rodeo circuit contract I had—the two of us have been able to spend plenty of time together to make up for our year apart. Here we are, a whole year on, a summer season later, and I still can't believe this is our happiest of *happily ever afters.*

In fact, since moving back to the ranch, I've been able to continue to mix travel and clients and also balance that with our life here. Sometimes Beau comes with me, other times, if the ranch needs him, he'll stay behind.

Even with being gone from Crimson Ridge for short bursts of time, those have ended up being some of our more memorable adventures together.

Let's just say my wearable is still controlled by the app on Beau's phone, and I secretly live for the days when he asks me to wear it while I'm working. Our nightly video calls while I'm traveling for work have turned out to be some of the hottest sex I've ever had.

A girl can but endlessly swoon over a cowboy who loves nothing more than to encourage me to indulge in my exhibitionist side.

Just thinking about the last time he had me prop my phone up and show off how well I ride my beloved tentacle playmate makes me squirm.

The surprise I have in store for my cowboy tonight has butterflies bursting to life in my stomach. A wicked smile splits my face as I pull to a stop outside the house—our house.

We had a small, private home built for the two of us, set in a location on the ranch a little way away from the cabins and big house accommodation. The business had become so increasingly busy that it made sense to move out, giving it over to become a facility used for guests and have our own private space.

Over in the distance, I can see the assortment of vehicles and a coach parked up, with the ranch humming. We're currently full with a group of athletes here for a week-long training and conditioning camp. We invested in a new custom-built workout space, which has been a hit with a number of different sporting codes. This particular team is rugby players who have come to base themselves in Crimson Ridge since it's not too far from their regular high-performance base. If it all goes well, they've expressed interest in making this a regular calendar date each season.

We've also had rodeo athletes come to stay for workshops and use the ranch as a base for recovery or training as needed. One of the best things to come from my time working with the tour is the number of competitors who are now clients—many of whom are now close friends. It all started when I took over Oscar's social media and PR, and everything continued to snowball from there.

Tessa and I now work together on an ever-growing client base of athletes, specializing in individuals who prefer to focus on their performance and goals—who understand the importance of a social media brand, but want someone else to handle it for them—rather than being actively present online themselves. Between her experience in managing Beau's pro career and my marketing background... She's the perfect business partner to help with the increased number of requests and roster of clients during the past twelve months.

Which means life is busy, and my days can often end up long if I'm not careful. But I still have time to work with my original clients like The Loaded Hog for one-off events, which is why I'm rushing back to take a quick shower and get changed before this evening.

We've got somewhere to be, and my surprise is one that I've been waiting for the *perfect* moment to gift Beau Heartford.

Tonight is that night.

"You've got that *look* going on." Beau scrubs a hand over his face, sitting back on his heels in the flatbed of his truck.

"What look?" I flutter my eyelashes as I walk around the back and hoist myself onto the tailgate.

My cowboy has done a perfect job of making it comfortable for the two of us, with cushions and comforters to make a soft little nest. A cute outdoor bed set up, where I hope to tempt my cowboy into doing extremely filthy things with me underneath the stars.

"Exactly how much trouble are you planning on causing? This is an outdoor movie..." He trails off, then shakes his head with a chuckle and soft curse. His ocean eyes lock with mine, and I tuck my hair behind one ear, feigning innocence.

He already knows the answer to that question.

"Why don't you open your gift, then you tell me exactly how much *trouble* you're going to enjoy causing right alongside me." I toss him a little box wrapped in ribbon, which he catches and lifts an eyebrow in my direction, glancing between the blue cube and me as I clamber further into the truck bed to cuddle up next to him.

We're in the furthest corner of The Loaded Hog's parking lot, as far back as possible behind other rows of vehicles. I definitely used the excuse of getting here early to help with the event setup as a reason to claim this particular location. While I would love nothing more than to make my cowboy squirm with a whole lot of heavy petting in public, I'm greedy enough to want more than just a little innocent rubbing and making out at an outdoor drive-in movie night.

Hence, our position at the very back of this very *public* event.

The sky overhead has deepened into shades of pearlescent pink and orange, and the opening credits for the movie start to roll. I'm all done with my role for the event, and now I get to lie back, relax... and torment my cowboy. What more could a girl want than to have an opportunity to dress up nicely and smile sweetly while handing out the party favors for everyone who has shown up for this outdoor screening, before being ravaged and treated like his perfect slut?

Beau weighs the tiny package, keeping his eyes on me as I crawl over to the cushions. I toe my boots off, then settle myself under a plush blanket and bat my eyes at him while biting my bottom lip. Putting on a show of angelic proportions, it's the most innocent expression I can muster, all things considered.

Flipping over the edge of the soft throw, I pat the space beside me. "C'mon. I'm ready for our sweet little date night, complete with hand-holding. If you're lucky, I might even allow you to peek at my bra."

His tongue runs a wet line across his bottom lip. Eyes flaring with the hidden taunt behind those words. He knows I mean the exact opposite of everything I just said.

One order for intense, toe-curling orgasms. Coming right up.

Shifting his weight, Beau cuddles up next to me beneath the blanket. On feeling his warmth and masculine scent weave their way into my bloodstream, I let out a contented sigh. This man always smells so damn good; I just want to lick him. It's entirely inconvenient that I can't just give in to that temptation whenever and wherever I feel like it.

Those sexy, veined hands make quick work of untying the ribbon and opening the box. As he lifts the lid, his body starts to shake with silent laughter.

Beau hooks a forefinger through the rubber device and lifts it out to dangle in front of us both.

"No wonder you were so excited about the prospect of watching a *horror* movie." He chuckles, voice dripping with sarcasm.

"Oh, yeah. I couldn't give a shit about the movie." I wave a dismissive hand in the direction of the big screen at the furthest end of the lot. Grinning up at him, I adore the faint flush of redness currently settled high on his cheeks. "There's something else in the box, too."

Upending it reveals a travel-sized bottle of lube, which tumbles out onto the blanket. At the sight of his *additional* present, he makes a rumbling sort of noise. Somewhere between being turned on and internally writhing at the prospect of what this is going to feel like for him. I couldn't have asked for a more perfect combination, really.

"My boy likes to win, doesn't he?" Wriggling around, I turn to face him and stroke over the buttons on the front of his shirt, letting my hand wander to rest on his belt buckle.

"You bet your sweet ass I do." Beau examines the cock ring carefully, brushing a thumb over the thicker part. *The fun part.*

"You can take the bull rider out of the arena, but you can't take away the determination to win a buckle." My fingers walk down to explore his groin, and he lets out a delicious noise when I make contact with his thickening cock behind the fly of his jeans. "Can't erase that competitive edge, huh?"

"What's the prize you've got in mind?" He swallows, watching my hand move beneath the blanket.

I cast a quick look around—checking that we're truly in a position to get up to all sorts of mischief without interruption—then start to work at his belt. As the metal clanks softly, muffled by the blanket covering us both from the waist down, his eyes flicker to mine.

"You get to do your worst, Heartford. I bet you can't make me struggle to keep quiet right out here in public."

"Christ." His voice drops into that deep, sexy tone as his hips shift, lifting up to give me better access to free his cock.

"Would you like a hand with that?" I murmur, letting my gaze drift to the black circle as I pull his rapidly hardening dick out and start stroking his firm, velvety length. God, I'm already squeezing my thighs together, heart fluttering at how wicked it feels to have him wrapped up in my palm. To feel his veins and thickness growing and lengthening steadily with each exploring glide of my touch.

My cowboy's brain has stalled somewhere between the toy clutched in his big paw, the bottle of lube, and the fact I'm fondling him like this in such a public place.

Knowing that he'll play these games with me, that he doesn't judge me for wanting to indulge this side of my desires—especially after everything he's been through—feels like winning the ultimate prize already.

I take the opportunity to move before he forms words. Clicking the cap open, I pluck the cock ring out of his grasp, and keep my eyes firmly connected with his as I lube him and the toy up. Out of the corner of my eye, I'm aware there's enough movement happening, hidden away beneath the blanket, that what I'm doing... well... it's not entirely disguised. If anything, it makes everything insanely hotter, seeing those tiny flutters and ripples of the fabric.

Beau stifles a groan, his eyes growing more and more hooded at the slippery sensation. When I slide the ring over his stiff length, right there under the blanket, he starts squirming at the unfamiliar sensation. His hips roll ever so subtly, like he's not quite sure why he enjoys this as much as he does. "Do I even want to know how you can do this without looking?" His teeth clamp together, trying to be such a good boy and keep quiet.

He shoots a quick look at the way the blanket dips and moves with the shifting of my hands and arms, where they disappear out of sight. He then quickly glances up over the lineup of other vehicles in front of ours.

A pleased hum drifts past my lips. "I can stop if you like?"

That's a lie. There's no way I'm letting him put the brakes on now. I tease gently once I feel it settled around the base of his shaft, my mouth watering at the way his hot, smooth skin keeps swelling the more aroused he becomes. Running my fingertips everywhere, I stroke and squeeze, taking the time to play with his piercing before reaching back down to fondle his balls.

Beau's head drops back with a thud.

"*Fffuuuuck*," he whispers. "That—holy fuck." His mouth forms silent curses.

Seeing this man lose his mind will never cease to be one of my favorite things in the world. And I love the way he eats it up when I give him a taste of his filthy words he blesses me with so often in return.

"*Mmmmm*. I'm no innocent little girl." His cock twitches beneath my hold. "You're not deflowering me in your backseat, Mr. Heartford." I'm rewarded by another wickedly tempting kick of his shaft.

I lean right in close, until my breath fans across his strong throat so I can hit him with the whispered words I hope will drive him to take me up on my challenge. "In fact, I'd like you to rub that piercing over my clit until I see stars, and make a mess of me with that big, fat cock of yours... but I don't know if you're up for the ride."

The rumble comes out of him more as a vibration than a noise, and I have to bite back the squeal of delight that threatens to escape me. Beau flips the switch and hits a new gear, manhandling me in that way I'm entirely addicted to. All raw strength and unmistakable demands. He has me turned around, with my spine tucked against his chest before my heart has time to double-bounce.

With one hand, he pulls the blanket up high—high enough to cover my breasts—which sends a shiver of delight through me. And that's when he lets loose. Those callused palms of his are *everywhere*, grabbing and pawing at me, while his massive fucking erection grinds against my ass with slow, methodical shifts of his hips. It's calculated, purposely shallow, and restricted so that we simply look like we're spooning while watching the movie.

However, if you looked closer, in the fading light, you'd see there's more than one place he's intently palming my curves beneath my dress.

"Make sure to watch the movie, trouble. Wouldn't want you to miss anything important." He pinches my breasts, cupping me to fill his palm while teasing my hardened nipples through the thin fabric of my slip dress.

I press my ass back against him, having to bite down hard on my bottom lip when I feel just how thick and hard he is.

"Too easy." Circling my hips to keep that pressure against him, I'm already a slick mess between my thighs. He just hasn't explored low enough there yet to discover exactly how turned on I am by this game.

He chuckles, and I know that's just added fuel to the fire of his plans to torment me beneath this blanket. Little does he know, I've got my own devious agenda, all I need now is for him to make his move.

Beau slips his hands lower, rucking the fabric of my dress up around the slope of my waist, and hisses when he discovers my bare ass. The weight of his cock settles between my cheeks, and his hold digs in over the swell of my hips as he grabs the side of my thong. Tugging hard on the string, he holds me still and rubs himself against my bare flesh while making a disapproving noise.

"Oops. I think I forgot... was I supposed to wear proper panties?" My quiet hum is chased by a determined thrust of his fingers beneath the skimpy fabric. Beau lets go and dives his touch between my thighs, curling his fingers through my slickness. A flutter of relief washes through my limbs when he doesn't waste any time, plunging inside me with two thick digits.

I feel like I've been on edge, waiting for him to give me this for hours, hanging in anticipation of our moment to finally be connected like this.

"Soaked and needy, *hmm*?" He doesn't plunge in and out like I love it when he does. Instead, it's a steady grind of the heel of his palm over my clit, and curl of his fingertips to stroke inside me. "You're shameless. Out here baring your cunt, while all these people are close enough to hear how sloppy and wet you are for me." That verbal reminder, of just how exposed we are, even if everything we're doing is technically hidden—well, that proves just how much of a perfect slut I am for this cowboy.

As he barely moves but drives me insane with his crude words whispered against my temple, his lubed-up cock presses forward to slip between my thighs. The pierced crown of him nudges against the thin scrap of fabric covering my entrance.

I feed him the softest whimper, and Beau makes a triumphant noise.

"Jesus. You're so fucking soft and desperate, baby." He slips his fingers out, and to my relief, holds the drenched fabric of my thong aside so that he can push the tip of his dick into me. "Need me to fill you and ease that ache?"

Nodding, I carefully readjust my position so that he can push forward. I'm so slick and eager for him, that it's the most intense sensation as he wedges his way in. Giving me inch by tortuous inch, I can *feel* just how thick he is with the cock ring secured in place.

"Holy fuck." He gasps, in a barely audible grunt as his fingers bruise my hips with how tight he's clinging onto me.

"You promised you'd do your worst." I struggle to breathe, the stretch leaving my eyes rolling back in my head.

All this is happening so slowly, so sensually, and with the movie blaring and sounds of other people occupying the trucks and vehicles in the parking lot. I fucking love him so much for giving me this without question.

Beau's hand snakes back around to seek out my clit, and he starts rolling his fingers over the swollen mess evident there. Sparks fly through my blood as he gives me the perfect amount of pressure, the perfect circling motion, evidence of all the tiny details he's taken the time to map out and learn about my body.

This man has the keys to unlock my most intense orgasms, and it's so damn sexy the way he studies every flicker of my muscles and hitch in breathing to hone his talents in that regard.

But he's still playing the game of not giving away any possible hint of what we're doing beneath this blanket, and that's my cue to add in the additional surprise aspect of my *gift.*

Reaching out, with shaking hands, I grab my phone and swipe open the app. Beau keeps strumming my clit to perfection as I hit the setting I know is going to be the killer blow.

Vibrations start up, low and rolling, and the cowboy at my back lets out a choked noise. His hips slam forward into mine, and the waves of pleasure intensify as the cock ring wedges between us.

"Careful, hot stuff. Don't want to start rocking the truck." My words are breathy, a pathetic attempt at stifling the moans I so badly want to allow to float freely.

Beau's heart thuds harder against my back, and the gradually increasing pleasure from the buzzing at the base of his cock feels so unbelievably good. With the way that teases my entrance, I can't even see straight—his cock filling me and deft touch playing my clit to perfection.

My orgasm rises and rises, and I'm panting, biting back all the slutty noises I'm perilously close to making. Beau rubs me harder, and every tremor gives away my secrets. I detonate, clawing at the pillow while turning my face and biting down to disguise any quiet sounds I might forget myself and let out.

Beau keeps going. He's ruthless. Relentless. Giving me exactly what I asked for when his fingers keep playing with my swollen, over-sensitive bundle of nerves.

"Fuck. That's it. You want to use me like one of your toys, baby? You want my dick stuffed inside you driving you insane?" He whispers the filthiest shit as I hardly come down from the first. Another climax crashes through me, the effort not to cry out leaving me a shaking mess in his arms.

"Jesus. Fuck. Baby, I need to come. *Please.*" His hands roam, squeezing my tits and roughly grabbing a handful of my flesh; while the vibrations keep doing their thing, racing through both of us.

I slap my hand around to blindly seek out my phone. With a nod—I don't think I can even speak right now—I turn the ring off and sag back against his chest.

Beau slips out of me, and I whine with the emptiness, forgetting myself for a microsecond.

Who can blame me? My cowboy's cock is a thing of beauty. "*Shhh.*" He reminds me with a ragged exhale, hands moving quickly behind my ass. "Christ, I need to fill you up so bad." Beau shifts, the strain in his voice so sexy it aches, and his breathing intensifies as I feel him work the cock ring free.

His piercing pushes forward as he seals us together once more, and the feeling of him buried inside me triggers another wave of ripples. Maybe it's another orgasm, I don't know, but the way my channel keeps contracting around him unravels Beau.

Behind me, his hips thrust to fill me all the way, in a measured, intense act of owning me. A powerful movement that pushes the boundaries of how much discreet fucking we can actually get away with.

"*Fffuuuck.* Goddamn. Fucking milk me. Take everything—every drop." Beau's raspy croak is so quiet, but I hear the hitch in his voice and feel his cock throb inside me before the air rushes from his lungs. He starts unloading, jerking, pulsing. It's so hot feeling his cum paint my inner walls, coating everything between us, and to know how much he needed this, how much he also enjoys this.

After we lie curled together, with him as deep inside me as possible, my heart finally comes down from being somewhere in the clouds. Beau tilts his head so he can suck on my earlobe and nip the soft skin. "What I need is to get you home so I can spank this perfect ass, fuck you hard all night, and hear you moan my name." His possessive words are right against my ear, leaving me boneless with pleasure, and most definitely wanting all that and more.

He slips out of me, and I follow after the shift in his body weight. Twisting around so I can bury my face into his chest. I'm blissed out of my head, staring up at him as I lift a hand and get lost in the act of stroking his jaw and mustache in a dreamy state.

"Promise?"

He gives me a smile to melt my entire soul into a puddle.

"Always."

"I like the way you look at me, Beau Heartford. Do it every day?" I whisper.

His hold on me tightens, and he ducks his head, allowing gentle lips to brush over mine, speaking quietly as he does so.

"*Forever*, trouble."

THANK YOU FOR READING

I fell head over heels for these two, and I hope you enjoyed Sage and Beau's love story. The extended epilogue from Beau's POV can be found here + settle in for a sneak peek at the first chapter of Book Four in the Crimson Ridge series.

KEEP READING HERE:

https://www.elliottroseauthor.com/bonuses

Loving the Crimson Ridge world and don't want to leave? Me either... Make sure to come and join my reader group - this is where all the announcements and first peeks will be happening on any future bonus content:

https://www.facebook.com/groups/thecauldronelliottrose

—

INSTAGRAM | TIKTOK | FACEBOOK

ACKNOWLEDGEMENTS

Crimson Ridge holds my heart and this series has completely changed my life as an author. I'm incredibly grateful to every single reader who has taken a chance on my cowboys, their leading ladies, and the forbidden love stories set in amongst the mountains.

To my wonderful Mr. Rose, who supports my disappearing off and being lost to the Words—I love you with all my heart.

Lazz, you are my champion, listener, first reader, support Queen extraordinaire... the Elliott Rose - verse would perish and wither away without you and your magic. ILY. ILU.

Brandi, Sam, Colby, Lib, and Lemmy, you ladies have allowed me the breathing room to focus on bringing this book to life. I'm so deeply grateful for everything you do behind the scenes.

Sandra, your talents for creating something PERFECT for our covers never cease to amaze me. I'm forever swooning for our cowboys.

To my editors - a million thank yous for helping to polish this!

To my incredible supporters on Patreon, thank you for taking a chance on an indie author and hanging out in my world month to month! You have no idea how much it all means, and I adore the lot of you! Getting to read your reactions to the goodies (and art!) each month gives me fuel to keep the words flowing.

Of course, bringing a book like this to life takes a village behind the scenes. To my alpha, beta, and early readers, you are absolute magic and thank you for pouring so much love into these two. Thank you for being accomplices in my mischief, the chaos of chapter drops, and my endless questions.

My Street Team, you are EVERYTHING. My ARC team, I send all the gruff dirty talking cowboys your way. To everyone who has shared about this book, hyped, *gently* insisted on a bestie reading it, you are just so damn wonderful.

To every single person who has helped promote one of my books, I am besotted with you, and swoon with heart eyes every time I get to see your creativity and excitement for an Elliott Rose character or story.

From the bottom of my heart, and from Beau and Sage... we send you all our love.

xo

LEAVE A REVIEW

If you enjoyed this book, please consider taking a quick moment to leave a review. Even a couple of words are incredibly helpful and provide the sparkly fuel us Indie Romance Authors thrive on.

(*Well, that and coffee*)

Also by Elliott Rose

Crimson Ridge

Chasing The Wild

Braving The Storm

Taming The Heart

Saving The Rain - Aug 2025

Also from the Crimson Ridge world

Bouquets & Buckles (Novella)

—

Port Macabre Standalones

Why Choose + Dark Romance

Where the Villains get the girl, and each other.

Vengeful Gods

Fox, Ky, Thorne, Ven - HEA Novella

Noire Moon - Prologue Novella

Macabre Gods

—

Nocturnal Hearts

Dark Paranormal-Fantasy Romance

Interconnected Standalones

Sweet Inferno

(Rivals to Lovers x Novella)

In Darkness Waits Desire

(Grumpy x Sunshine)

The Queen's Temptation

(Forbidden x Shadow Daddy Bodyguard)

Vicious Cravings

(MMF x Vampires x Enemies to Lovers)

Brutal Birthright

(Academy Setting, Teacher x Student)

About the Author

Elliott Rose is an author of romance on the forbidden and deliciously dark side. She lives in a teeny tiny beachside community in the south of Aotearoa, New Zealand with her partner and three rescue dogs. Find her with a witchy brew in hand, a notebook overflowing with book ideas, or wandering along the beach.

- Join her reader group *The Cauldron* for exclusive giveaways, BTS details, first looks at character art/inspo, and intimate chats about new and ongoing projects.
- Join her Newsletter for all the goodies and major news direct to your email inbox.

KEEP READING FOR A SNEAK PEEK AT THE NEXT BOOK IN THE CRIMSON RIDGE SERIES

SAVING *the* RAIN

CHAPTER I

Kayce

"Goddamn. That ass was sculpted to wear a pair of wranglers."

Tipping my gaze up, I'm met with the sight of uninhibited, glinting green mischief radiating from the eyes of the cowboy sitting opposite me. One of my closest friends who loves nothing better than to live up to his name—*Chaos* Hayes.

He blows out a low whistle then jerks his chin toward a group of other ranch hands, cowboys, and cowgirls hanging out across the other side of tonight's bonfire. Orange flames dance high into the crisp evening sky, keeping time with the music running low and relaxing through the stereo set up on the porch at our backs.

"Who are you perving at, so I can at least get a chance to warn them," Brad groans as he nears our table. "I really needed to add a warning when I put out the invite. Should've told everyone to bring a squirt bottle, knowing you'd be extra frisky after a win like that." As always, our host for tonight's post-rodeo BBQ at Rhodes Ranch is taking stellar care of us all, in the form of a mounded pile of food fresh off the grill delivered right to the table.

"Fuck yes. Thanks, babe." His boyfriend, Flinn, who is built like a linebacker but kinda looks like a nerd with his glasses, pounces on the food. "It's that new dude. Pretty sure he's just arrived and is working one of the local ranches. He's gonna eat up every guy *and* girl in this place." Reaching forward to help himself, he waves one hand, gesturing vaguely in the direction of whoever this is they're all drooling over.

I shake my head and let out a chuckle. "Trust you, Chaos. Eyeing up the fresh meat before you've even been back in Crimson Ridge for five minutes." We rolled through the main street of this sleepy little place we call home among the mountains at stupid o'clock this morning. After driving what felt like a thousand hours to get back from the latest stop on the rodeo circuit, my eyes were scratchy as fuck and damn near falling out of my head over those final miles.

All I've done since getting home is shower, pass out face down, then roll out my screaming muscles when I finally woke up this afternoon. My last ride was a bastard of a bronc who put me through my paces, thrashing me hard, but the horse scored highly because of it. I walked away with a good enough total to place second overall. Chaos took out the top spot in our bareback division. The smug fuck is still riding the high of his win.

As he should be.

I'm damn proud of him, but even still, it's always the goal to come first. No matter how graciously defeat might be accepted, the motivation to win a buckle pumps hot through your veins as a rough stock rider. *If only I'd scored a few points higher.* All that time driving gave me plenty of opportunity to stew on the tiny details of my ride—my form, the way the horse bucked—anything which might have made all the difference.

Lucky me. Take out second place, and I get to come home to a cold bed and a spine that feels like it's been greeted with a sledgehammer.

Oh, the glamor of pro rodeo behind the scenes.

Brad elbows my ribs, getting me to shuffle sideways and make more room at the outdoor table we're seated around. He huffs at Chaos, before wedging himself onto the bench seat at my side.

"Didn't your dick get enough attention after that win, superstar? Christ. Who are you eyefucking now?"

Chaos flashes a wide, shit-eating grin. Giving off wave after wave of irredeemable asshole energy that acts as both a pussy *and* cock magnet wherever he goes. "What can I say? Us Hayes' have healthy appetites to keep satisfied." He chomps a large bite of steak, before swiping at the sauce running down his chin with a thumb.

Flinn waves his half-eaten burger in the direction of the fire, but all I can see are the climbing flames and shadowy outlines of individuals from where I'm sitting. "Over there in the red flannel. He's got that look about him. You know, the one that says he's bad for your health, and your heart."

As they keep talking about whoever this guy is, that uncomfortable sensation keeps creeping up on me. The one slinking into my awareness far too easily. Weaving around all my organs, it settles somewhere deep inside my stomach. An almost weightless sensation. An awkward feeling as if I'm quietly unspooling. The unsettling knowledge that I'm hiding a massive fucking secret from my closest friends.

I've hidden away the kind of revelation about myself that leaves me feeling as fluttery and nervous as a naive schoolgirl about to go to her first prom. Not at all like I'm in my late twenties, compete on a pro rodeo circuit, and have had more sexual encounters than I can count.

It's when they're talking about *this*—about hot guys—that I turn into a flushed-cheeked, tongue-tied disaster that I gotta do my best to hide.

My friends don't know what I did one night, when I was here for New Year's Eve, while hidden away in the garage. I never told them, not because any of them would treat me any differently... I guess, mainly because I don't understand my goddamn self anymore after that urge hit me outta the blue.

Turns out, getting myself sober in recent years lifted the haze on more things than just pulling my shit together and dragging my ass back in the arena in search of sponsors prepared to back my rodeo career.

"Anyone want another drink?" My knee bounces, and even though I was hungry earlier, now I'm not even interested in finishing my food. Any excuse to walk off this uneasy feeling will do at this stage. "I'm grabbing a soda. Who else wants something?"

"I'll take one." Brad looks my way, then squints thoughtfully. "Pretty sure we're all out of what I had stocked in the kitchen. Everything is in the cooler over there."

Great. I follow his line of sight, my eyes tracking in the direction of this mysterious hot guy. Of course, that's where the drinks are.

"Go chat to what's-her-name while you're there, Wilder," Chaos says through a mouth full of food while giving me a wink. "Pretty sure she was hanging on your every word and move this week."

I know exactly who he's talking about. Jessie is one of the barrel racers who trains with us at Rhodes Ranch. She's cute and sweet, and at one point in time, I for sure would have flashed a smile her way in return. But now? I'm just all sorts of fucking flipped inside out.

Well, one thing I do know for certain is that I'm not worth anyone's time. They might think they're interested in Kayce Wilder, the cowboy package who looks the part to the rest of the world on the outside. Only, once they see the damage beneath the surface, they run a mile.

"C'mon man, you've gotta get back in the saddle. It's been ages since that disaster with the crazy pregnant bimbo. You can't let that overshadow your life."

There's nothing more to be done other than give Chaos my middle finger and let him think I'm taking him up on that challenge. Because, on one hand, he's right, but on the other, he's way off base with what he thinks he knows about me.

Hell, I don't even know about me.

"Game on, fuck face." I click my tongue at him.

If I don't at least *pretend* to be interested and go over there, talk to her for a few minutes... well, that potentially raises too many questions. The kind I have no interest in digging into right now.

If I stroll across to where Jessie's hanging out and put up with a bit of small talk, even if it's with the intention of taking it nowhere, at least it's an easy route to keeping everyone's noses out of my business.

I've spent years running from my own demons, and while it used to be much more convenient to do so while shitfaced, this is just one more night among hundreds of nights when I slap on a mask and be the good-time guy. Only problem is, doing it sober takes a hell of a lot more effort. It's exhausting being a former fuck up who's trying to sort his life out.

One day, and one conversation at a time, I guess.

As I cross to the other side of the fire, weaving my way through the small crowd who have turned up for tonight's gathering, I nod at the familiar faces and say brief hellos as I go past. It's mostly ranchers, rodeo folks, and locals who have horses stabled here.

Shoving my hands in my pockets, I cast a quick glance at Jessie, taking in the sight of her from side-on. I'm trying to figure out why I've never felt more attracted to her when she's literally a cowgirl-doll. Blonde hair. Petite. Cute style. Half the guys in Crimson Ridge have tried to get her number, I'm sure.

What I do realize, all a little too late, is that the group she had been surrounded by before seem to have all disappeared in the time it's taken me to circle the bonfire. Now that I'm a few paces away, I see there's only one guy standing to her side, covered in deeper shadow. Jessie has her head tilted back, smiling up at the spot where he towers over her, and as I get closer, my eyes are drawn to *him* more so than her.

I mean, I'm curious who she's so avidly talking to. I'm intrigued after hearing what was being said about this guy in a *moth-drawn-to-flame-about-to-burn-its-wings-off* kind of way.

Swallowing heavily, my eyes race about, trying to capture a

quick glimpse without making it seem as though I'm outright staring. That would be hella fucking weird. To make matters worse, I'm about two seconds from crashing their intimate little moment for two, surrounded by a cloak of dark and orange firelight licking their skin. Jesus, this is already feeling like a goddamn disaster, and I'm cursing myself silently. Not only for leaping up to avoid my own bullshit, but for snapping at Chaos' bait to come over here, too.

At a stolen glance, I suppose objectively, the guy isn't bad-looking. The lower half of his face is all I catch before my eyes slide lower. Scruffy, worn black jeans, faded along the thighs. Tattoos. Rust red check pattern shirt rolled at the elbows.

His palm is wrapped around a beer bottle, which reveals a map of veins on the back of his hand. They stand out, prominently highlighted by the warm glow of the fire. An inked design of a rose covers the skin there, and my breath catches as I take him in. His hands have got me stumbling, and I don't know what to do with the sensation. I've never even thought twice about what another man's hands look like. Let alone... *appreciated* the sight of them.

What the fuck? I'm feeling all sorts of prickly and clammy beneath my hoodie. Heat crawls up my neck and makes itself at home on my cheeks.

How can it be that I kiss one guy, one time, in a reckless fucking moment on New Year—which was months ago—and now I'm a jangled-up mess at the first sight of some random cowboy arriving in town?

My legs seem to keep moving of their own accord until I'm close enough now to hear them talking. Jessie lets out a breathy, flirtatious laugh before the guy speaks again, and I continue on my path, where I'm about to fumble headlong into disrupting their private fucking conversation. There's a magnetic pull on my body that I can't fight, drawing me closer and closer to encroach on the space where they stand.

"... I might not enjoy a crowd, but I know a lot about pleasing an audience." From the other side of her, the way his focus drags down her body is unmistakable.

"Do you now?" With drink in hand, she holds a straw to her lips and takes a slow sip. Followed by a playful tilt of her head.

I don't hear what he says in reply—with just a low rumble catching on the night air—but my heart is goddamn *pounding* for no good reason.

Another laugh comes from Jessie as she turns, all glossy lips and batting lashes, before her dark eyes flick my way. My presence registers, and an unreadable expression slides across her face for the briefest moment.

"Oh, hey, Kayce." As she takes me in, eyes widening slightly, she smiles. The kind of look that tells me she's more than pleased to show off the attention given by someone else since I haven't been reciprocating any of her hints.

And while I'm figuring out what to even say now that I'm standing here, she ducks her head while reaching up to hook a strand of hair behind her ear. That's the second I get my first proper sighting of the profile of the man at her side—at the same moment he lifts his chin to look toward the bonfire.

I stop dead.

My pulse spasms, heart jumping straight into the back of my throat, before my stomach plunges in the opposite direction and hits my boots.

"What—What the hell?" I croak.

Jessie's brow pinches together. She looks between me and the man at her shoulder, who I'm struggling to wrap my goddamn mind around seeing in the flesh after all this time.

"Do you guys know each other?" she asks. Hesitation evident in her expression.

"What the hell are you doing in Crimson Ridge?" I straight up ignore the girl between us. Jaw locked up tight, ice seeping into my veins.

His dark gaze meets mine and lingers for a drawn-out, weighted pause before speaking. "Got a job. I work here." The words prowl forward, languid, and gritty. No greeting. No acknowledgement. But I wouldn't expect anything less from this asshole.

With an indifferent shrug, his attention tracks up and down my frame. He always was so fucking infuriating with that cold, callus attitude he carries around.

"No. No, you don't. This isn't happening." My teeth grind. "I thought we agreed to stay outta each other's way."

"Gladly. Last I checked, this town ain't yours, snowflake." Lifting his beer, that motion reveals the slight tug of prime intolerable asshole settled on the corner of his lips before he takes a swig from the bottle.

"You can't be serious." *No*. There's no way this is real.

Another lift of his broad shoulder. "Dunno what you expect me to say. I'm working on one of the local ranches. So, run on back to your buddies."

I take a step toward him, bristling.

"You're not coming out here and entering events... you're... you're too old." A protest splutters out of me. My stomach forms a churning mess, thrashing around to the point of seasickness.

"I'll do whatever the fuck I want." He chuckles. "And you know I would still win, too."

Fuck him. Fuck every single goddamn twist of fate that has brought him back into my life.

"This is bullshit. You could literally go anywhere else. Go base yourself on any other ranch." My throat struggles to work down a swallow.

"I could, but this little neck of the woods seems kind of sweet." His gaze slides down to Jessie, while giving her a wink. "I'll bet I can have Crimson Ridge eating out of the palm of my hand. All it'll take is a couple of wins, and that'll be enough."

"Fuck you. Cut the crap."

"Besides, you're almost aged out yourself. Twenty-nine, aren't you?"

My throat works. "I'm twenty-eight. You know that, dick."

"*Mmm.* So basically washed up." One of his tattooed hands rakes through his mess of dark curls.

"Screw you."

"Gonna melt if you stay too close to that fire, snowflake. I'd be careful where you stand." His eyes flicker over me once again, leaving my mouth filled with chalk. "And no, I'm not here to fool around with rodeo. I'm here for a job, but we both know I could still school your ass anytime I like, without even trying."

He leans down to say something in Jessie's ear, then guides her away by the elbow. She offers me an apologetic shrug, before the two of them head off in the direction of the grill, leaving me standing, staring out into the darkness of a fall evening. The kind of night that should be brimming with laughter and celebrating hitting the highs of placing in a competition event.

Instead, I'm numb from head to toe, trying to wrap my brain around what just happened. The gut punch of my past coming back to haunt me in the most unexpected of ways.

The last person I expected to see again.

My goddamn stepbrother.